n0thing

A Sequel to DreamLand

by

Matthew J. Pallamary

Mystic Ink Publishing

Mystic Ink Publishing
San Diego, CA
www.mysticinkpublishing.com

ISBN 10: 0692778055 (sc)
ISBN 13: 978-0692778050 (sc)
Printed in the United States of America
San Bernardino, California

This book is printed on acid-free paper made from 30% post-consumer waste recycled material.

Library of Congress Control Number: 2016914821
Mystic Ink Publishing, San Diego, CA

Book Jacket and Page Design: Matthew J. Pallamary/San Diego CA
Author's Photograph: Matthew J. Pallamary -- Gibbs Photo/Malibu CA

DEDICATION

This book is dedicated to Ken Reeth and Colleen Kennedy.

Acknowledgements

The author would like to thank Rob and Kim Gubala whose support on so many levels made this book possible and to my sister Colleen Pallamary, proof reader extraordinaire, and the only critic I can really trust.

I also want to thank Jim and Cindy Gilbert for bringing n0thing into the world, as well as the rest of the Gilbert clan; Jacob and Amanda, Jarrad and Stephanie, and last but not least, the star of the show, Jordan, along with Truth.

AUTHOR'S NOTE

n0thing pushes through the boundaries of story, genre, and reality itself while redefining literary tradition by putting real life celebrities into a fictional story. This story is titled after my nephew Jordan (**n0thing**) Gilbert, who is one of the main protagonists. The other real life co-star in this unique tale is my dear friend, renowned psychologist Dr. Stanley Krippner.

Jordan **"n0thing"** Gilbert is a professional *Counter-Strike: Global Offensive* player who is one of three players to win nine ESEA Championships.

Dr. Stanley Krippner is a psychologist, parapsychologist, and executive faculty member and Professor of Psychology at Saybrook University in Oakland, California.

He was also the director of the Maimonides Medical Center Dream Research Laboratory.

I would like to express my deepest appreciation and a very special heartfelt THANK YOU to both Stan and Jordan for allowing me to use them as characters in this fevered dream of my imagination.

Did I say dream?

Well maybe, then again…

CHAPTER ONE

A cat-sized rat scurried through the shadows several stories beneath an abandoned dome-shaped complex that sprawled over a space the size of half a dozen football fields a few hundred yards south of a shuttered California/Mexico border crossing. A large mirrored dome occupied the center beneath an overlying framework structure surrounded by eight smaller domes, each several stories high. Heavily armed sentries patrolled the perimeter.

Five stories above the main atrium lobby behind a glass office wall in a private section of the complex known as North tower, a nearly pristine, tastefully decorated office sat empty. A darkened group of eight nineteen inch flat screens surrounded a seventy two inch screen on one wall and two cushioned leather chairs sat on both sides of an expansive console that held a flat screen of its own. A large dark crusted oval stain and a number of similar brown streaks and spatters covered an otherwise immaculate thick snow white carpet.

In every corner and vantage point of the entire complex, dormant video cameras sat motionless, their glazed lenses empty and hollow-eyed.

In another part of the labyrinth red velvet ropes arrayed out from soaring archways, like four points of a five point star from Storybook Kingdom. Images of The Three Bears, Sleeping Beauty, Rumpelstiltskin, and Hansel and Gretel smiled down from darkened pastel colored portals. Black velvet curtains hung beneath the image of a feather capped musician parading in front of a long line of grinning rats at the fifth portal. The sign in front of it said:

PIED PIPER CLOSED UNTIL FURTHER NOTICE

Beneath the Hansel and Gretel portal, a moving walkway, now stilled, passed through a long darkened tunnel lined with artificial trees and kaleidoscopic bunches of fake flowers, leading to a circular room with a domed ceiling. Row after row of man-sized opalescent Easter eggs reminiscent of space capsules faced the walkway from both sides. The front of each egg tilted back at an angle, open to reveal a contoured, padded recliner.

Everything looked immaculate with the exception of one scorched and blackened capsule. Its gaping maw hung open, bloodied with jagged metal like shark's teeth. Extinguished klieg lights surrounded it alongside scattered test equipment, probes, and wires that spilled from an open console as if its innards had been gutted by the ravenous shark.

An elevator from the North tower dropped to the curved subterranean corridor of Z-level several stories below. Behind the mirrored glass of its inner wall, one bed sat by itself in the far corner of a large room with pastel pink walls. Beside it a U-shaped console held a bank of six monitors. A shadowy network of wires and tubes snaked out from receptacles throughout the room, twisting across the ceiling and down walls, dangling from brackets like remnants of an abandoned web. Beside the bed a bundle of wires splayed across the floor alongside an I.V. tube. A congealed mass clumped at the tip of its bloodied needle.

Dried cake frosting smeared a far wall. Below it the smashed remains of the cake and its stained pink box sat in a disintegrating pile. Gobs of a thick dried brown and gray substance splattered the wall behind the bed and across the floor, centered on a wide, hardened black puddle.

Beyond that ran the Hall of Dreams, a long curving corridor lined with hundreds of framed color portraits of men and women of all ages who had been granted PermaDream happiness. The passageway circled the structure's inner circumference and entered the Gallery of Angels where photos of children who dreamed away their final moments playing with friends, picnicking with parents, and riding glittering carousels in fanciful settings covered the walls.

In the last section of corridor, a one way floor-to-ceiling mirror served as the inner wall where an inactive key card reader controlled a door marked:

LIMITED ACCESS AREA

On the other side of the wall banks of lifeless consoles, panels, and work stations faced the glass for non-invasive scrutiny of a massive electronic command center. At the back of the room a roped-off area in front of a blue velvet curtain, a red lettered sign cautioned:

NO ADMITTANCE

Behind that in a silent clean room, every terminal in the complex connected to the control room through a fiber optic network that once kept tabs on such diversified tasks as patient monitoring, intravenous drug and nourishment delivery, facility temperature control, and video feeds from the cameras throughout the structure.

At its very core deep within the recesses of the black velvety darkness a red light throbbed bright, then dimmer in double pulses like the rhythm of a heartbeat.

CHAPTER TWO

Jordan pointed his M4 in front of him and advanced on the last terrorist strong hold flanked by the members of his elite five man counterterrorist strike team. Blond-haired and blue-eyed, his short stature and a voice that sounded ten years younger than his twenty five years made those who didn't know him underestimate him, which often worked to his advantage.

Sprinting toward the battle scarred fortress, he listened to the chatter of his teammates on his headset while assessing the tactical details of their assault.

"We've had one of our best runs yet," he said. "Let's not fuck it up now by being too cocky or too trigger happy. Everybody keep their cool and we'll come out on top."

He approached a looming, pock marked wall at an angle and stayed close when he reached it, easing his way toward the massive splintered wooden doors that hung ajar beneath a central stone arch that marked the entrance. Stopping beside it, he motioned for his team to advance after him, two close on his right, and two close to his left, all pressing themselves flat against the wall.

Once in position, he took a deep breath, then burst through the doors, gun blazing, his teammates coming in after him. Smoke and gun fire erupted from all sides and bullets peppered the wall around him.

"Above you!" someone shouted through his headset.

Jordan rolled to the ground and came up under the cover of some stacked wooden packing crates, firing at a black uniformed assailant scrambling along a walkway above while his teammates fanned out, each finding their own cover. Two of the enemy dropped to the ground and two more ran for an alcove. Jordan fired in their direction and tossed a flash grenade after them.

It exploded in a blinding flash, leaving a thick white cloud drifting from the rubble. Running through the cover of smoke, everyone moved forward to an inner wall with fifty-five gallon drums stacked against it. Jordan clambered up over the barrels and leaped onto the walkway. A black figure came around a corner shooting and Jordan took him out with a head shot, firing from a prone position, then he ran the length of the wall above his teammates to another gateway.

From his vantage point he watched his team approach the gate from outside. Inside he spotted another terrorist diving behind barrels strategically placed around a small courtyard, his gun trained on the gate.

"Stand back from the doorway," he said into his headset. "I'm going to blow it open."

He crouched and fired off a series of bursts, picking off the sniper before dropping a grenade that blasted the gate outward, allowing his teammates to storm the inner yard.

Jordan watched them fan out and clear the area before jumping down off the wall and following them into a dark passage on its far side. He stepped into the shadows of the tunnel amidst bursts of echoing gunfire, listening to the shouts and warnings of his team through his headset.

"Watch out, sniper fire coming in from above!"

"Two more attacking from the corner!"

"Shit! Killjoy is down. Repeat. Killjoy is down."

"Another one coming in from the side. I'm taking heavy…"

An explosion flashed down the tunnel. Jordan hustled to catch up in the silence from the aftermath of the blast, then a voice.

"Not anymore, but we lost Striker and Sureshot," Renegade said, "but I have the defusal kit."

Jordan checked his map and saw that they were closing in on the terrorist's bomb site. "That leaves you and me Renegade, and there isn't much time. I'll be right there."

He sprinted down the tunnel and through the doorway at its end into a smoke-filled room strewn with bodies, collapsed walls, and rubble scattered across the floor. Across it, off to his right, Renegade motioned him forward to where he crouched beside a battered heavy steel door.

"The only way in is to storm it and time is running out, so we need to blitz," Renegade said.

Jordan nodded and Renegade blew the door off its hinges with a grenade and charged into a flurry of gunfire. Jordan counted to three, then dropped and rolled in behind him blasting full auto, coming up behind a command console. Bullets sprayed the wall above him and zinged off the console in front of and around him. Through the smoke he spotted Renegade lying in a prone position behind another console to his right. In front of him he saw a terrorist arming a C4 bomb. A sniper continued firing from above, keeping him and Renegade pinned down.

"Clock's ticking," Renegade said. "Cover me, I got this." He rolled out from behind his cover firing at the bomber while Jordan gave covering fire at the sniper, distracting him. The bomber buckled and dropped to the floor as the words, "Bomb has been planted," came to Jordan through his headset.

"Shit!" Renegade said. "Forty five seconds and it's all over."

Jordan continued exchanging bursts with the sniper, trying to keep his attention away from Renegade, who was pinned down in a new spot a few feet from the bomber.

"Twenty five seconds," Renegade said, "and he's got me covered tighter than a gnat's ass."

"You only need five," Jordan said. "I'm all out of flash grenades, but I have a smoke. Let me see if I can improve your chances."

"Roger that."

Jordan fired a burst and tossed a smoke grenade on the ground between him and Renegade, filling the room with smoke. Renegade dove for the C4 amidst a flurry of gunfire that lit up the smoke like lightning flashes in storm clouds. Jordan fired back at the sniper.

"Fifteen seconds."

Jordan didn't hear anything for a few seconds, then Renegade's voice. "Defusing in five, four, three, two…"

"Renegade! Renegade, do you copy?"

Flashing gunfire continued to light up the smoke filled room. Renegade gave no response.

"Ten seconds."

Jordan sprang into the haze, fumbling for the defuser in a panic while bullets sprayed around him. The countdown continued unabated while he worked the keypad on the defuser.

"Five, four, three, two…"

He punched in the last button of code as the sniper's bullets found him and everything lit up in a blinding flash.

CHAPTER THREE

Looking like a diminutive, dark-haired angel, Rita Cariño fingered the tiny silver winged angel that hung from the delicate chain gracing her neck, silently praying for freedom for her and her friends. Her silver hoop earrings sparkled and her dark eyes glistened with intensity as she looked around the main conference room of the United States Embassy in Mexico City. Her soft-spoken manner was often construed as timidity until her brown eyes flashed and spit fire when she spoke about what she cared about.

Lorenzo Vargas reached under the table from beside her and gave her hand a reassuring squeeze. She glanced over at him, adoring his Spanish-Italian good looks, black hair, and piercing, dark eyes. All hers. She felt a little flutter in her stomach when he smiled at her, showing perfect white teeth and his gentle touch dispersed her fears.

Across from them Jack Scanlon sat balanced on the hind legs of a chair, with sandaled feet on the floor and slender fingers intertwined behind his head. A receding hairline and exaggerated bushy black eyebrows intensified the look of concentration in deep-set brown eyes that seemed to bug out of his head when he launched into a rant about the government's interference with anything, or how it only served the one percent.

Beside him, neuroscientist Cheryl Martin pulled her long strawberry-blonde hair back in a tight bun, offering no hint of warmth to her businesslike demeanor and no hint of what went on in her brilliant and ordered mind. Isolated behind her horn-rimmed glasses, her pale blue eyes rarely welcomed anyone's gaze. She often shut out the world as if drawing an invisible curtain shut in the face of anyone reaching out to befriend her with the exception of Rita, Lorenzo, and Jack. Rita was one of the few people Cheryl could be vulnerable with and Rita could tell a lot from her nuanced expressions.

A large flat screen took up half the wall at the far end of the room. Rita looked from Lorenzo to Jack, then nodded to Cheryl, feeling like she should say something, but they had all spent the last year and a half confined to the embassy under political asylum and could practically read each other's thoughts. The thought they shared at the moment was, "Get me out of here!"

A door opened at the other end of the room and a man in a dark suit came in. Cheryl sat up straight and brightened when he entered while Jack looked down at the floor, shaking his head.

Their visitor stood by the door looking at each of them in turn. Stocky with solid square shoulders and military styled silver brush cut hair, he had icy blue eyes that seemed to look through you, but not at you.

Cop eyes, Rita thought.

His Navy blue suit had an American flag pin on the lapel and he wore a solid red tie with a starched white shirt, pressed pants, and spit-shined shoes; not a hair or a thread out of place.

No wonder Cheryl liked him.

"Hello folks, my name is Crowley, Robert Crowley, US State Department." He gave a curt nod.

Jack looked up, his bushy eyebrows raised. "You ever going to get us out of this shithole?"

Crowley held up a hand. "That depends on you."

"What's that supposed to mean?" Jack shot back.

"We have a complicated international situation that you created." He paused for effect. "You are complicit in the deaths of six people that the Mexican government holds you responsible for, and four more that the United States has linked you to."

"I didn't kill anybody." Jack shook his head and gestured to the others. "Nobody here killed anybody."

"Tell that to the Mexican Government. They have six corpses, shot, poisoned, burned, strangled, and maimed, and an unconfirmed suicide. The gunshot victims are a ruthless drug lord and his son. You say the DreamLand computer is responsible, which nobody believes, and the Mexican government says it's a drug war between cartels."

Lorenzo leaned back in his chair. "What do you think?"

Crowley shrugged. "I don't know what to think, but none of you strike me as murderers or members of any drug cartels."

"Then why have you been sitting on your ass for the last year and a half leaving us to rot in this shithole prison you call an embassy?" Jack's voice rose and he pounded the table. "Why can't you do your fucking job and send us back to the good old US of A where we belong? You..."

"Enough!" Crowley held up his hand, emphasizing his admonition with an icy blue stare.

Jack fell silent, glaring back. His eyes bulged and his face flushed red.

"You think this is a shithole prison?" Crowley said, his words coming even and measured. "You have no idea what a shithole prison is, but if you want to find out, you are free to walk out of the political asylum that the good old US of A has granted you. The Mexican government will be more than happy to grant your wish with a real cell in a very real shithole prison. The door's right there." He jerked his thumb back over his shoulder. "Trust me. They're waiting for you."

"You called us here for a briefing of some sort," Lorenzo said, "so our situation is changing."

Crowley nodded and turned his attention to Lorenzo. "On a far bigger scale than you could have imagined. While you've been protected here, hundreds of hours of negotiations have been taking place between the United States and Mexico and hundreds more between the NSA, the CIA, the FBI, DOD, and DARPA."

"The NSA, CIA, FBI, DOD, and DARPA?" Jack muttered. "We're fucked."

"We're on the threshold of a resolution to this whole sticky mess," Crowley said as if Jack hadn't spoken, "but the solution is up to you." He glared at Jack. "All of you."

Crowley went to the far end of the room and picked up an iPad. "Let's run through the history of this train wreck, so we're all on the same page. You four survivors are the key to this whole mess."

A picture of Lorenzo filled the screen. "Mr. Vargas, you received a full scholarship to the film program at UCLA. After a brief internship, Disney hired you straight out of school, then Edgar Michaels hired you away from them and put you in charge of Dream Development."

He tapped the iPad and head shots of Jack and Cheryl filled the screen. "Cheryl Martin. Your expertise in synaptic modulation and neurotransmitters, coupled with Mr. Scanlon's breakthrough in neural microprocessor design kindled the flame that made computer generated dreams a reality."

Rita held her breath, partially dreading what would come next. Crowley tapped the iPad and her picture flashed onscreen. "Rita Cariño. With Dr. Jackson gone, you are the only remaining expert on the physiological and biological aspects of computer generated dreaming."

He hit the tablet again and an old news story filled the screen. He crossed his arms and waited, giving them time to read.

DIGITAL DREAMS
By Mark Clements (UPI)

The second stage of the controversial PermaDream Euthanasia Center is near completion. Following several months of dormancy, the frenzy of construction that began in August on a huge circular building remains shrouded in secrecy at the center of a heavily guarded area south of the California/Mexico border. Several hundred yards from the soon to be expanded Otay Mesa Crossing, stands a new facility, housing powerful hardware and high-speed memory modules that give Morpheus, the dream computer, what Denise Moore of PermaDream calls, "the magic that makes the miracle".

Since the death of PermaDream founder Edgar Michaels last May, his son Hodge is reported to have been the guest of international businessman and suspected drug kingpin, Oliver Daggett at his Cancun, Mexico compound. Daggett is sought by U.S. authorities for questioning in the Christmas Eve plane crash deaths of Texas Congressman, Roberto Manzur and his family, three years ago.

At the time of his death, Manzur headed a joint task force with an investigative branch of the United States Food and Drug Administration and had initiated extradition proceedings against Daggett with the

Mexican government. Warrants have been filed for Daggett's arrest on several tax-evasion charges in both state and federal courts. To date, the controlling PLC Party in Mexico has rejected any such overtures from the United States. Sources claim that Daggett, a resident of Mexico, is in fact the true owner of PermaDream. Unconfirmed reports state that Hodge Michaels accompanied Daggett to France and the Philippines in an attempt to expand PermaDream.

According to Denise Moore, Project Administrator of the PermaDream research labs in Las Puerta, "Dream technology has grown at a phenomenal pace thanks to a recent breakthrough in synaptic modulation by a team of experts, headed by renowned neuroscientist Cheryl Martin and Jack Scanlon, a leading microprocessor engineer."

When questioned about the future of PermaDream, Moore remained close-mouthed, saying only that, "Hodge Michaels will hold a press conference soon, to announce new plans." While rumors about the further growth of PermaDream and its effect on the burgeoning border employment picture continue to run rampant in Mexico, Moore acknowledged that the PermaDream hospital facility headed by the eminent American physician Morgan Jackson, has recently undergone significant expansion. Jackson is reportedly supervising a series of tests on extended dreams for terminal patients.

When he saw that they had taken in the article, Crowley brought a picture of Congressman Manzur, his wife, and their two children up on the screen. "You folks were all in it from the start and your association with Oliver 'Ollie' Daggett implicates you in the death of Congressman Roberto Manzur and his family." He held up a finger. "But this article and other supporting evidence could also be your saving grace."

"How so?" Cheryl asked, speaking for the first time.

"Careful analysis of the evidence we gathered indicate that Edgar Michaels and his son Hodge were the ones involved with Daggett. The rest of you appeared to be focused on and dedicated to the PermaDream Euthanasia Center."

"That's the truth!" Jack blurted.

"What about Hodge?" Rita asked. "Where is he and how is he? He's also a survivor and you haven't mentioned him."

Crowley looked at the floor, shaking his head. "Hodge Michaels has brain damage and is under twenty four hour guard at a classified government location where he receives round the clock medical care. He has been floating in and out of a coma and in the rare moments that he does become conscious, he's emotional and hysterical, crying and babbling about Denise, Morgan, Eddie, Emily, and rats. On top of that, unless he is heavily medicated, he has frequent bouts of Parkinson's like tremors and sporadic epileptic fits."

"I'd like to examine him," Cheryl said.

"That will be contingent on what happens here," Crowley offered. "It's clear from the news article that you folks had the best intentions with your euthanasia project. You even had a few government grants at its outset. We were very interested in this aspect of your work until Ollie Daggett tightened his stranglehold on the whole project. Fortunately, we were able to obtain this video from the estate of Edgar Michaels. It goes a long way toward clearing you of the murder and conspiracy charges surrounding the death of Congressman Manzur and places the blame on Hodge and Edgar Michaels."

"Edgar would never have anything to do with murder," Rita said, feeling her throat tighten. "He loved people and he loved life. All he ever wanted was to ease the stigma of death."

"He dedicated his life to it," Lorenzo added.

"That may very well be the case, "Crowley said, "but his collusion with Daggett is damning to say the least."

He tapped the iPad and the grim countenance of Edgar Michaels appeared on-screen, gaunt-faced, his eyes buried in dark hollow sockets. An ill-fitting lab coat buttoned to the neck hung from his small shoulders. Snowy hair stuck up in feathery wisps from his balding head. Rita remembered watching the video shortly after Edgar died in PermaDream.

The elder Michaels sat stiffly at his desk, speaking in tortured spurts, pausing often to wheeze for breath. "Forgive the brevity of this good-bye. My speech is painful, not only for me, but also, I'm sure, for you. Still, I have to give this to you straight from the shoulder and tell you why I no longer own PermaDream." He lapsed into a coughing spasm.

Rita looked to Lorenzo, who stared down at his clenched fists.

Edgar continued in a hoarse, cracking voice. "Early on the government endowed us with several modest grants, but they fell far short of what we needed. When they refused more funding, I backed it with everything I owned."

Edgar closed his eyes, took a deep breath, and cleared his throat. "I have always marveled at your unwavering dedication. I vowed we'd never fail, but the time came when I couldn't make payroll and I couldn't cover our bills. Lab supplies, computers, and development costs sapped everything. Collectors hounded me. Accountants and lawyers laughed at our vision and derided the concept of computer generated dreaming. The bank was prepared to shut us down until Ollie Daggett stepped in and saved the project."

"Jesus!" Jack whispered. He put his head in his hand and massaged his temples.

Edgar's breathing came slow and raspy as he persevered. "Everyone knows I never made a snap decision in my life. Before committing to clinical trials, I weighed Daggett's offer to fund our future needs in exchange for full ownership. After much soul searching, I accepted with the stipulation that I maintain administrative control. He paid the bills. I called the shots. Ollie assured me that he'd honor his commitment to keep the team intact. It wouldn't have served any purpose to tell anyone about this until now, but the facts are clear. Without Ollie Daggett, there would be no PermaDream."

He sighed and his eyes took on a faraway look. "I hate to leave you, but I truly relish the thought of embarking on my final dream. I long for the sweet smell of Indiana and the loving arms of my wife." Edgar's voice shook and he scrunched his eyes shut, fighting back tears. One trickled down his cheek. "Dear friends," he said quietly. "The world must reap the benefits of our wonder. Under the leadership of my son, Hodge, PermaDream will succeed. God bless you."

No one spoke. The dazed expressions on their faces said it all. Crowley let them sit in silence for a few moments, then said, "Daggett's true intentions became clear soon after, further implicating Hodge Michaels in the conspiracy and drawing the rest of you in as suspects and accessories in the ensuing murders. This clip from a San Diego news station leaves no doubt about that."

A massive traffic jam filled the screen. A stark headline crawled across the bottom.

DREAMLAND TRAFFIC A BORDER NIGHTMARE

"They're here from all over the world," a reporter's voice over said from a vantage point on a freeway overpass. "Members of virtually every race on the planet are swarming to the Mexican border, southeast of San Diego, hoping to literally fulfill their dreams and fantasies. The magnet drawing them all is the newly opened one-of-a-kind fantasy world where dreams do indeed come true. For a price."

The camera panned back revealing the massive, circular complex looming several hundred yards beyond the international border. "DreamLand literally dominates the horizon here at the border crossing, southeast of San Diego," the reporter said. "In the eyes of some critics, thumbing its nose at the United States Government, rendered virtually powerless by the leaders of the controlling PLC Party in Baja, California, Mexico. While Mexican and U.S. officials bicker over how many new lanes are needed for an enlarged border crossing, the wait at Otay Mesa currently averages three hours. Throngs of vendors on both sides of the border do a brisk business, selling souvenir sleep masks, T-shirts, fish tacos, churros, and cold drinks to a captive throng of would-be dreamers."

The photograph of a fiftyish looking Edgar Michaels appeared on screen.

"In the year and a half since the death of PermaDream founder Edgar Michaels, father of computer generated dreaming, rapid and unprecedented changes have come about in the brain-wave modulation techniques he pioneered at the end of the century. According to his son, Hodge, CEO of DreamLand Enterprises, they are all being utilized at DreamLand."

A tight shot of Hodge's face replaced his father's photograph. His tousled sandy hair and boyish grin made him look childlike and innocent. "If we had stayed on the U.S. side of the border, none of this could have happened," Hodge said, in a take from a press conference held on opening day. "Government agencies and paperwork would have hamstrung us at every step. Here in Mexico, the PLC has the foresight to allow us unfettered research and expansion as long as we continue to make safety our primary concern.

Since our very first series of tests, our medical facilities have exceeded AMA standards and will continue to do so. Everyone is welcome to travel through the wonderful worlds created by Morpheus, our dream computer. The DreamLand experience is both exhilarating and completely safe."

Over a helicopter shot of the huge facility, the reporter said, "Rumored to be the brainchild of alleged drug lord Oliver Daggett, who has never been photographed, DreamLand opened its doors last month to record numbers and the lines have been growing longer every day. When questioned on his association with the reclusive Daggett, Hodge Michaels consistently offers the same statement.

"Mister Daggett was a close friend and adviser to my father," Hodge announced in another clip from the press conference. "I welcome his continued input as a consultant. Without Mr. Daggett's unique vision, DreamLand would never have come into existence."

The reporter added, "Daggett, who lives in Mexico is wanted on tax evasion charges in the United States and is also sought for questioning in the deaths of Congressman Roberto Manzur and his family in a Christmas Eve plane crash four years ago. Prior to the crash, the ruling PLC Party in Baja Mexico had refused to consider Manzur's extradition request. Unnamed sources have accused Daggett of masterminding the sabotage of the private plane in retaliation. He remains unavailable for comment. Meanwhile, at the Mexican border, construction maintains a breakneck pace and the money continues to pour across."

The construction images onscreen froze.

"Speculation runs rampant as to what really happened in DreamLand," Crowley said. "You four survivors are the only ones who know the truth." He tapped his iPad, stepping through pictures. The first was the congressman and his family. "Whatever did happen caused the deaths of Congressman Manzur and his family."

Rita flinched when a picture of Ollie Daggett and his son Chazz came up. The elder Daggett's grim scowl, abetted by a black widow's-peak-hairline and bottle brush eyebrows gave him the look of a mindless brute, yet he had the pale smooth skin and shiny pink cheeks of an elderly female. The grotesque combination reminded Rita of the Frankenstein monster.

A younger version of his father, Chazz was pink-cheeked with a shaved head, and pale blue eyes glaring under lowered brows.

"Also there's Oliver Daggett," Crowley said. "A ruthless murderer and drug lord who pulled strings from behind the scenes, and his son Chazz. And of course your deceased co-workers, Eddie Driscoll, Emily Fulbright, Morgan Jackson, and Denise Moore."

Rita felt a sharp tug at her heart when Morgan's picture came up, followed by feelings of regret when she saw Denise, Eddie, and Emily. She looked to Lorenzo for a reaction, but his expression remained stoic and unreadable.

Crowley tapped his iPad one more time, darkening the screen. "We've been in intense negotiations with the Mexican government for the past eighteen months," he said turning toward the group. "Aside from the charges against you, there are a number of bigger issues regarding eminent domain and international boundaries that come into play to name just a couple, but we are in a position to resolve all of this with your cooperation, including the charges against you."

Jack folded his arms and leaned back in his chair. "Why do I get the feeling that I am about to be asked to sell my soul?"

Crowley ignored him. "Hodge Michaels is not only on life support under twenty four hour medical supervision, but he is in custody. To save him from the terror of his recurring nightmares and delusions, we have sedated him and plan to keep him that way, which unfortunately makes him unresponsive."

"I need to have a look at him," Cheryl said.

"That will be possible if things go as planned."

"And what is the plan?" Lorenzo said.

"The evidence I just showed you is enough to convict Hodge Michaels on all counts of conspiracy, collusion, and murder -- if he were ever to awaken and be coherent enough to stand trial, which he most decidedly will not. Regardless of what really did happen, our cover story, which the Mexican government has indicated that they are ready to accept, is that all of the murders are victims of turf wars between Mexican drug cartels. With Hodge Michaels as the scapegoat, all of the charges against you will be dropped as well as any other illegal activities associated with Daggett, and you will be free."

"Where's the hook?" Jack said.

"And what about DreamLand?" Cheryl added.

Crowley smiled. "That's where you come in."

CHAPTER FOUR

"nOthing wins! My God, nOthing wins!"

Jordan ripped off his headset at the announcement and the lights went up in the packed arena, revealing row after row of cheering fans giving him a standing ovation. Cameras flashed like a Fourth of July finale.

"nOthing clinches the eSports World Cup Finals here in Paris at the Palais Omnisports Paris Bercy Arena!" The announcer continued amidst the cheering.

Renegade, the biggest member of their team, slapped him on the back. "Talk about a photo finish! That sniper took a shot and barely missed, but you pressed the last defuser button a split second before he hit you."

Jordan "nOthing" Gilbert felt both stunned and elated at his down to the wire victory. His top ranked U.S. Seal Team 0 had finally beat Muerte Los Concesionarios, the Spanish three time consecutive ESports World Cup champions.

"I couldn't have done it without you or the rest of the team's amazing play," he said.

Squat, chubby-cheeked Killjoy, wiry Striker, and wild-eyed Sureshot joined them for a group hug while photographers and cameramen surrounded them and the rest of the stage erupted with activity. A slim, attractive, perfectly proportioned woman with long silky black hair pushed through the crowd clutching a microphone, followed by a cameraman.

"Can you guys line up for me?" she asked.

Killjoy and Striker moved to Jordan's left and Sureshot and Renegade lined up on his right and everyone put their arms over each other's shoulders. Todd, their manager, a tall sandy-haired surfer type stood behind them, grinning with a double thumbs up.

"Boy, do we ever have a surprise for you guys!" he said.

The cameraman moved down the line, pausing at each player while the reporter spoke.

"Nicole Starczak, World Network News, coming to you live from the Palais Omnisports Paris Bercy Arena where Sureshot, Renegade, n0thing, Killjoy, and Striker, collectively known as Seal Team 0 from the United States have just unseated the three time Spanish champions Muerte Los Concesionarios."

The cameraman panned back for a group shot, then zoomed in for a closeup of Jordan and Nicole, who held the microphone between them.

"n0thing, you came through with the winning play at the last possible moment, making you the star of the entire tournament with a well-deserved MVP award. How does it feel to shine so bright?" She tilted the microphone toward him.

"This star that is shining so bright has five points and they all have names, Killjoy, Sureshot, Striker, and Renegade."

"That's only four. What about you?"

"I'm n0thing - everybody knows that!"

The crowd burst out laughing.

"Seriously though," Jordan said. "Without my team I literally am nothing. Their combined effort, individual talents, and epic skills made our win happen. Yeah, I was the guy who finished it, but it could have been any one of us and was in fact all of us."

"What did you think going into this? Were you confident?"

"Confident in our game. When you're up against another team, especially one as good as Muerte Los Concesionarios, all bets are off. This game could have gone either way. Everyone saw that."

"Right down to the wire."

"We would have lost it if Renegade hadn't punched his way through and set me up for the final defuse."

"And now it's time to award the trophy and checks," the announcer's voice boomed throughout the arena. "Seal Team 0, please come center stage. Muerte Los Concesionarios, our runner-ups, please line up to the right."

Nicole, her cameraman, and the crowd stepped back. The big screen behind them where the game had played out for the crowd showed them move to center stage. A pair of matching red bikini-clad blonde super models emerged from back stage. One carried the large gold ESports World Cup Trophy and the other carried an oversized five foot long check.

"The new ESports World Champions," the announcer said as the first supermodel strutted up to Jordan and handed him the trophy. "Seal Team 0 from the United States!"

Camera flashes went off everywhere and the crowd erupted in more cheers and applause. The second blonde brought up the giant check and held it out in front of the team.

"And of course the winning check for five hundred thousand dollars!"

The camera flashes continued and the cheers, whistles, and applause intensified. It all felt surreal and dreamlike to Jordan, who enjoyed winning the tournament, but didn't feel like it deserved this much attention.

When the furor died down, the announcer went over and had the supermodels present Muerte Los Concesionarios with their own oversized check for one hundred thousand dollars, then the two teams met at center stage to congratulate each other. When they finished, the crowd swarmed the stage. Guided by Todd carrying the trophy, security stepped in and ushered Seal Team 0 back to their hotel's Presidential Penthouse Suite.

"What's happening here?" Renegade asked, eyes opening wide when the private elevator opened to the palatial suite.

"Holy shit!" Striker said.

Everything seemed to be made of white marble and gold, including the frames on the richly detailed paintings on the walls. Luxurious overstuffed white chairs and couches sat on a large plush white carpet in front of a floor to ceiling circular glass wall that provided a stunning view of Paris sprawling out below them. The city's twinkling lights added to the magic of it all.

Off to the side beneath a large wall mounted flat screen, a long mahogany table held silver ice filled buckets of Red Bull, sodas, beer, shrimp, strawberries, and other fruits. Gold and silver platters of chicken, beef, turkey, ham, and an assortment of the team's favorite snacks filled the rest along with a fully stocked bar.

Todd beamed like a little boy on Christmas morning.

"Tell me this isn't totally over the top," Killjoy said eyeing the spread.

Though he appreciated the effort, seeing their favorite foods and the attention to detail displaying them struck Jordan as overkill. Todd had always done lots for them, but never anything this extravagant and to this extent, then again, this was the ESports World Cup Finals.

"Jeezus," Sureshot finally said. "Thanks Todd. You really went overboard this time. I mean, yeah, we won ESports World Cup, but this is -- is…"

"What you world champions deserve." Todd held up the trophy and shook it, then set it down and picked up a remote control, pointing it at the flat screen. "But I'm not responsible for this. Allow me to introduce your biggest sponsor and strongest supporter."

The screen flickered to life showing a man dressed in a navy blue suit, a solid red tie, and a starched white shirt. He looked stocky with square shoulders, a military styled silver brush cut, and ice blue eyes.

"Hello you amazing world champions," he said with a smile. "My name is Robert Crowley. I hope you enjoy the party I arranged for you. Because of your victory, I have an exciting offer that goes beyond your wildest imaginings, but we'll get into the details of it later. Right now I want you to have fun celebrating your victory."

A knock came on the penthouse door.

"I'll get it," Todd said, smirking.

He went to answer and came back grinning ear to ear, followed by six of the most beautiful women that Jordan had ever seen.

"Party time!" Todd said.

CHAPTER FIVE

Crowley dropped into a chair at the end of the table. "We have a plan that will resolve everything and produce a win - win for everyone involved, including the Mexican government."

A cold, empty feeling gripped Rita's stomach.

"Do tell," Lorenzo said, sounding as skeptical as she felt.

"We want to resurrect and fully fund your original PermaDream Euthanasia project."

Rita gasped, feeling like something exploded inside, triggering a cascade of smaller thought explosions. Lorenzo reached over and put his hand over hers. Its warmth felt reassuring, but her mind reeled.

"Get the fuck out of here!" Jack blurted.

"You can't be serious," Cheryl added. "After all that happened..."

Crowley waved them off. "With the right guidance and proper funding, this has the potential to do far more good than what you might imagine."

"No way we're bringing that fucking monster back to life," Jack said with finality. His face had flushed red.

Lorenzo shook his head. "None of us will ever do that."

Crowley looked at each of them in turn, meeting unwavering stares, then leaned back in his chair. "What about building a new one from scratch?"

Everyone's eyes grew wide, but no one spoke. The room remained quiet for an uncomfortably long time before Lorenzo said, "Are you serious?"

"Technology has been moving ahead in leaps and bounds since you brought the Morpheus Project to fruition. Just think of what you can accomplish now with your combined talents and a solid source of funding."

Jack crossed his arms and leaned back shaking his head. "You need to find somebody else. I for one don't feel comfortable jumping into bed with Uncle Sam."

"I'm going to be honest with you," Crowley said. "We don't know what any of this shit does. We need you. *All* of you. You four are at the center of the whole deal."

"If I understand you correctly," Cheryl said. "You want to fund and support the PermaDream Euthanasia Project all over again from scratch."

"That's correct."

"And this whole mess we are in with the Mexican government," Lorenzo said. "The border issues with the DreamLand complex, the ownership issues, and all the politics and red tape. You can take care of that too?"

"It's all part of the deal."

"Do you plan on making this available to the public?" Rita asked.

Crowley gave a slight shake of his head. "Not at first, but in time it's possible. It depends on how well you succeed. At present we have a humanitarian program that needs your help." Crowley looked directly at Jack. "You would be doing a great service to your country."

"There's a hook in here somewhere," Jack said meeting his stare. "What's the catch?"

Crowley held up both hands. "Listen, this doesn't have to be complicated. Here's the gist of the proposal. The United States government wants to fund your euthanasia project, starting with wounded veterans with the hope of bringing them some peace before they die, with an eye toward extending the treatment for maimed and wounded survivors suffering from PTSD. If we can accomplish that, I don't see why we wouldn't be able to roll it out to the civilian population."

"Back to a medical model instead of an amusement park," Rita said.

"That's a good way to put it."

"I'm familiar with the procedures necessary to administer proper care to those in need," Rita said, "but I am far from a qualified medical doctor. Dr. Jackson was the authority on that. I only assisted."

"We're quite aware of that," Crowley said. "We've been interviewing a number of doctors and specialists."

Lorenzo leaned forward, resting his elbows on the table. "I get the part about funding the project from scratch, but I'm not clear about how the DreamLand facility comes into play and how you plan to unravel that whole mess."

"As I mentioned, we've been negotiating with the Mexican government for the past eighteen months. If you four buy in, we have assurances from them that they'll be on board with our plan."

Jack's eyebrows raised. "How did you manage that?"

"What does on board with our plan mean?" Lorenzo said. "What *is* the plan?"

Crowley nodded. "No one knew what to do with Ollie Daggett's multi-billion dollar complex a few hundred feet from the border, thumbing its nose at the U.S. We know little of the technology and the Mexicans know nothing about it, so it's an albatross for both countries. If you four come on board to help us use this technology in the healing way that you originally intended, the Mexican government has agreed to sell us the entire facility and the surrounding land in a historic international border changing deal that would make it part of the United States." He paused, letting his word sink in. "In return, we've guaranteed long term employment and social programs, including health care for Mexican Nationals. We want to retrofit the entire facility and expand its medical capabilities for trauma treatment and rehabilitation of veterans with physical and mental disabilities."

Jack snorted. "What happens if we don't sign on?"

Crowley gave him a grim smile. "Instead of jumping into bed with Uncle Sam, you'll be jumping into your cot, deep inside a Mexican prison."

CHAPTER SIX

Jordan awoke to the sound of a door closing and a sharp throbbing pain pounding through his head, officially announcing his hangover. His mouth felt dry and sticky. When he opened his eyes, the light pierced his brain in a blinding flash. This was why he wasn't a big drinker. It always hit him hard.

He rolled onto his side, clutching his pillow to his head, smelling her perfume on the pillow beside him where she had slept. Breathing deep, he inhaled her essence and smiled in spite of his headache, remembering the night before.

Brittany had the most perfect body he had ever seen. Firm, exquisite curves, and full lips that he never wanted to stop kissing. Different moments of their night together played through his mind, stirring his feelings below. He missed her already.

"I'll do absolutely anything you want," she said, pressing against him. "I'm here to please you."

Boy did she deliver.

He peeked out from under the pillow with one eye and spotted her frilly red lace panties, seemingly left as a gift and reminder of their special night.

He heard someone puking in another bathroom, causing his own stomach to spasm. "No…"

His mouth flooded with saliva in that all too familiar puke warning and his stomach jerked. He stumbled through the blinding pain of daylight to the bathroom where he dry heaved before vomiting over and over again, squeezing every last burning drop from his battered stomach. His brain screamed in agony from all the heaving. He sat on the floor by the toilet with his head in his hands, then slowly stood and rinsed the nasty puke taste from his mouth at the bathroom sink. He looked up to see his own bloodshot eyes looking back at him from the mirror. "What's up champ?" he muttered.

Even talking hurt. He splashed water on his face and crawled back into bed, lying on his stomach, burying his face in the pillow. He just had the world handed to him, literally on silver platters and now he suffered the consequences of his overindulgence.

Why did getting every pleasure he could ever want leave him feeling so empty? He should be happy, but instead he was uneasy. He thought back to all the great food and drinks they had in this Presidential Penthouse and the way sweet irresistible Brittany approached him. Her perfume, perfect body, and gentle pleasing ways had overwhelmed Jordan like a velvet wave, seducing him.

Everyone on the team was seduced by the girls. Was that a bad thing? Certainly no one complained or resisted. After all they were the winners and deserving of a victory celebration. He should be happy, grateful, and accepting of all the gifts his sponsors gave him, but…

He heard a door close from the main room of the suite and smelled coffee, which drew him out of his cocoon. He threw on his pants and went out barefoot without a shirt to find Todd pouring coffee from a room service cart. Todd looked at Jordan, grinned and shook his head, then handed him two Excedrins and a cup of coffee with half and half.

Jordan popped the Excedrins into his mouth and washed them down with a sip of water, then he found an easy chair to crawl into and nursed his coffee.

Wesley Schulz, known to his fans as Renegade, stumbled out of another room a few minutes later, looking like a little kid pushing his unruly black hair out of his face and rubbing his eyes with balled fists. At six two, with broad shoulders, he was the biggest guy on the team. He smiled with a sheepish grin when he saw Jordan.

Rail thin, Carl Peterson, who went by Sureshot followed, wearing just his boxers, baring his own goofy grin that contrasted his wild eyes. His long red-hair was tied back in its usual pony tail. He stood behind Wesley by the cart where Todd served coffee and Excedrin.

A minute later they heard another door open and the voice of a giggling girl, then one of last night's beauties scampered out, shooting them a furtive look back before leaving. A minute later, short, wiry, fast moving, fast talking John Henry, otherwise known as Striker, came strutting out of his room with his chest puffed out and a dreamy smile on his face. His wild, curly blond hair always looked like he had just crawled out of bed.

Short, squat, chubby cheeked Terry Hinchliffe, who went by Killjoy, the smallest member of their team came last, walking stiff like a zombie, with a dazed, unfocused look in his eyes. Wesley looked at Jordan and the others and smirked.

"Breakfast is on its way up," Todd said, once they all settled in with their coffee. "After that, Mister Crowley wants to Skype with us to tell us about his offer."

"How much do you know about it?" Wesley asked.

"Just as much as you," Todd answered. "Not a thing, but I can tell you this, judging from the party he just gave us, he really likes us!"

Room service delivered a breakfast buffet that rivaled the feast of the night before. Everyone ate around a thick glass table, joking, bragging and teasing each other about their exploits with the girls from the night before. Each person's story tried to top the one that came before it, either in its attention grabbing detail or its absurdity, and all of them ended in wisecracks and laughter with the exception of Killjoy who remained curiously silent.

Finally Carl said, "What's up with you little man? We ain't heard squat from you. You doing okay?"

Terry nodded.

"So what gives?" John asked. "How did you make out with that big-titted blonde beauty? It looked like she was being your Mommy."

Everyone laughed.

Terry shrugged and his chubby cheeks turned red. "I don't know."

"What do you mean you don't know?" Carl said. "You don't know what happened with those big beautiful tits?"

Terry looked down. "I drank too much of the hard stuff and I blacked out. I don't even know if I had sex or anything like that. I don't think I did. The last thing I remember is drinking a rum and coke and putting my head on her boobs like they were pillows."

"Best pillows in the world!" John said.

More laughter.

Todd looked at his watch. "You loverboys ready to Skype with Mr. Crowley?"

They lined their chairs in a semi-circle in front of the big flat screen. Todd tapped his cell phone and the screen flickered to life, then he selected a number and they connected. Square shouldered Crowley came onscreen wearing the same navy blue suit, solid red tie, and starched white shirt.

"Good morning world champions," he said with a smile. "I take it you had a fun filled celebration last night."

"Everyone except Killjoy," Carl said. "He doesn't remember."

"Then he probably had the best time of all," Crowley said, "but if you can't remember, then a repeat performance might be in order." He winked.

Jordan and the others looked at each other with puzzled expressions.

"Nothing but the best for the best," Crowley said.

"Thank you for everything you've done for us," Todd said. "And thank you for believing in us and for being our biggest sponsor."

"And your biggest fan," Crowley added.

Jordan knew all of their sponsors and didn't remember seeing or hearing anything about Crowley, so his question came as if on its own. "Which sponsor are you?"

"Let's just say that I'm an enthusiastic supporter of you and your other sponsors. I've worked closely with them for some time now and I sponsor many of their interests, especially you guys, but I like to keep a low profile. It keeps me from getting flooded with sponsorship requests from other groups."

"I'm dying to know what this exciting offer is," Todd said.

Crowley smiled. "I can only give you a broad overview at this point, then we'll need you to sign non-disclosure agreements before we can give you any details."

Todd looked to each member of the team for acknowledgement, then back to the flat screen, nodding agreement for all of them.

"We have new gaming technology that provides an interactive experience that goes far beyond anything currently on the market," Crowley said.

"A virtual reality game?" Wesley asked.

Crowley brightened. "Everything VR has and more! This technology is interactive on levels you can't even imagine. It's totally immersive."

"Totally immersive?" John said.

"Unlike anything anyone has ever seen." He pointed at them. "And we want you guys to be the first to put the prototype through its paces."

"Totally immersive?" John repeated. "What about our regular practices and competitions? We're at the top of our game and we want to stay there."

"We're developing a special training program," Crowley said. "We plan to keep sponsoring you in the regular competitions and bring you up to speed on this new technology. We're confident that the skill sets that make you world champs in this arena will more than serve you in this new one. In fact, we're confident that playing the two synergistic systems will provide cross training that will make you better players in both worlds."

"What else can you tell us?" Todd asked.

"Not much more than that until we have all the non-disclosure paperwork in place."

Todd looked to the team again, saying, "I think you have us all intrigued. We can sign the agreements, but we'll still have the option of not participating. Correct?"

"That is correct, but I have to tell you, once you see and experience this technology there will be no doubt in your minds about participating."

"What's our next step?" Todd asked.

Crowley sat back in his chair, steepling his fingers. "We'll give you all the details after you return to San Diego and sign the NDAs."

CHAPTER SEVEN

"Jesus Christ, it looks like a fucking prison," Jack said from the backseat of the minibus as they drove past a huge section of the San Ysidro border fence modified to accommodate a heavily guarded entrance, flanked by guard towers. A twenty foot high chain link fence surrounded the entire facility, topped with razor wire. Rita's breath caught at the sight of the main silvered DreamLand dome and she went rigid. Lorenzo put a reassuring hand on her arm, then took her hand, calming her.

"For all intents and purposes it is a prison," Cheryl said in a monotone. "We'll be prisoners here instead of in the embassy."

"Looks more like a military base to me," Lorenzo said.

Rita leaned in closer and put her head on his shoulder. "I think it's a little bit of both, but at least we'll have something to do, and at face value it looks closer to what we originally set out to do."

"We'll see about that," Jack said.

They went through the gate and down a long driveway bordered on both sides by the same chain link fence and razor wire.

"Now it looks like prison," Lorenzo said.

They pulled into a circular driveway leading to the old lobby. Rita squeezed Lorenzo's hand tighter, feeling an odd mixture of curiosity and dread. "I don't know if I'm ready for this," she said quietly.

"According to Crowley, they've been doing a lot of remodeling," Lorenzo said, "but there's a lot they haven't touched because they didn't know what it was or what to do with it. They're leaving those decisions to us. In spite of how it looks on the outside, Crowley promised us a first class medical facility focused on rehabbing wounded vets, and if he's kept his word, Hodge is here under twenty four hour care."

Rita brightened at the thought of seeing Hodge, then remembered his condition and mentally prepared herself for how he might look. She closed her eyes remembering all the times she stood by Chazz Daggett's bed listening to the beeps from the console and the squeaks and whoosh of the air conditioner, and the clinical sounds of Morpheus controlling the release of nutrients and medication into Chazz's veins while he laid motionless, dressed in jeans, a dark tee shirt, leather jacket and boots. He had the waxen look of a hairless corpse awaiting interment. His skeletal fingers fanning across his atrophied thighs matched the talons of the withered tattooed eagles on the back of each hand. She shivered at the memory.

"You okay, honey?" Lorenzo said, putting his arm around her and drawing her closer.

"Sorry. Just remembering Chazz."

"Chazz is the past. Put him out of your mind. We're getting a clean start here."

The minibus rolled to a stop at the front door with the hiss of its air brakes. While Jack and Cheryl grabbed their luggage from the back of the bus, Lorenzo gave Rita a final squeeze and kissed her on the cheek before standing to gather their things.

Rita looked up as they disembarked at the mirrored dome entrance. Metal letters stood out in relief, arranged in an arch over the door.

DEDICATED TO SERVING THOSE
WHO HAVE SERVED US

The front glass doors whooshed open and a beaming Crowley strode out, looking impeccable in his signature Navy blue blazer, red tie, white shirt, and gleaming shoes. "Welcome!" he said. "Welcome to the Pandora Project. You can leave your luggage here. One of the troops will deliver it to your quarters."

"From one jail cell to the next," Jack quipped.

Cheryl swatted him on the shoulder. "I want to see Hodge as soon as possible," she said. "I'm dying to assess the extent of his damage and whether or not anything can be done to help him."

Crowley ushered them through the entrance. "We've restored and upgraded your medical and care facilities beyond Doctor Jackson's original specifications for a more exacting observation and control experience as well as implementing a higher level physiological monitoring system that gathers and analyzes hundreds of critical life support indicators a second."

Rita stifled a chill when she looked up at the glass office wall of the North Tower looming five stories above when they entered the atrium lobby. Everywhere she looked, she saw video cameras.

She took Lorenzo's arm when Crowley led them through the all too familiar part of the labyrinth where red velvet ropes arrayed out from the five soaring archways of Storybook Kingdom that once held images of The Three Bears, Sleeping Beauty, Rumpelstiltskin, Hansel and Gretel, and of course the Pied Piper, the source of her recurring nightmares.

New heavy metal reinforced vault-like electronic security doors with facial recognition scanners had been installed at the entrance to each attraction, closing them off from the outside. An armed guard stood at the center of them all. A backlit sign with bright red letters above each door stated:

RESTRICTED ACCESS

Rita looked at the darkened entryways remembering the moving walkways passing through darkened tunnels lined with banks of artificial trees and kaleidoscopic bunches of fake flowers that led to circular rooms with domed ceilings where rows of man-sized opalescent Easter eggs faced the walkways from both sides, tilted back to reveal contoured, padded recliners.

Crowley led them to the North tower elevator which dropped them to Z-level several stories below. Rita held her breath and closed her eyes while the elevator descended, recalling all the times she thought of ghosts when she peered through the mirrored glass into the huge shadowy PermaDream facility where the comatose form of Chazz Daggett reposed surrounded by red, green, blue, and amber L.E.D.'s pulsing in time to beeps, giving testimony to his pitiful existence.

She opened her eyes when the elevator door hissed open and breathed a sigh of relief when she saw the changes. Behind the mirrored glass of the inner wall, rows of hospital beds filled the large room with pastel pink walls that had previously held Chazz Daggett. Beside each bed a console held banks of monitors. Wires and tubes snaked out from receptacles connecting to each bed. The sign above the doorway said:

Z-LEVEL PERMADREAM PATIENT CARE FACILITY

A short way down the hall brought them to another vault-like door with an armed sentry guarding it. Crowley leaned in to the facial recognition scanner, unlocking the door with a resounding click, and they followed him inside to an observation room.

Behind the thick glass, a smaller octagon shaped intensive care unit packed with digital and video readouts over a keyboard console enclosed a coffin-like Plexiglas bed holding Hodge, who looked feeble and withered. Hundreds of wires came from him.

His eyes jumped and twitched in frenzied REM beneath closed eyelids and his body spasmed in random petit mal seizures. Pulsing waveform displays showed weak, but steady EKG, pulse, respiration, and other vital functions. The window around his head revealed the barely recognizable frail face of Hodge. Fiber optics on the hood and gloves he wore flashed and colored fluids filled the tubing at his wrists.

"When can I examine him?" Cheryl asked.

"I've arranged to have all of his records from the first trauma center report all the way up to the present readings available for you," Crowley said. "Once you've assessed them, you can examine him."

Rita felt like she should contribute to the discussion, but her swirling memories and emotions left her confused. She thought it best to keep her mouth shut and let Cheryl lead on this one. She was more than capable and Rita felt like she had too much nightmarish history babysitting the comatose who floated in the worlds between the living and the dead.

After an uncomfortable silence, Crowley led them out and further down the circular passage to the Hall of Dreams. The long curving corridor lined with framed portraits of the men and women who had been granted PermaDream happiness gave Rita the creeps. The person behind each glowing countenance seemed to look through her.

The passageway ran around the structure's circumference and entered the Gallery of Angels where photos of children covered the walls. In the last section of corridor, a one way floor-to-ceiling mirror served as the inner wall where another sentry and a facial recognition scanner controlled a door marked:

LIMITED ACCESS AREA

On the other side of the wall banks of lifeless consoles, panels, and work stations faced the glass. At the back of the room a roped-off area in front of a blue velvet curtain, a red lettered sign cautioned:

NO ADMITTANCE

Crowley led them through the doors, past the sign to a silent clean room where every terminal in the complex had connected to the control room through a fiber optic network that kept tabs on patient monitoring, intravenous drug and nourishment delivery, facility temperature control, front lobby traffic, and the now deceased Eddie Driscoll's clandestine, after hour games of Toxic Mutant as well as every video feed throughout the entire structure.

At its very core deep within the recesses of the velvety darkness a red light throbbed bright, then dimmer in double pulses to the rhythm of a heartbeat.

CHAPTER EIGHT

Jordan looked out the plane window as they passed over Balboa Park on their right and downtown San Diego on their left before touching down at Lindbergh Field. It felt good to be home after the latest round of travel and tournaments. He and the rest of the team would get a much needed break after winning the championship.

"We're scheduled to meet with Mr. Crowley on Friday," Todd said, leaning forward from the seat behind him.

Jordan leaned back to hear him better. "Have you heard anything more from him about his new super-duper gaming technology?"

"He's very sure about how much we're going to love it, but he won't say anything else until after we sign our NDAs. You can't really blame him with all the hackers and the corporate espionage that goes on, especially in the gaming community where everybody's looking to get an edge."

"Now that we're home I'm even more curious. If it's not virtual reality, then I don't see how it can be more immersive."

"I don't know either, but judging by the party he threw us, not to mention the extra party favors he threw in, he has some serious resources."

Jordan closed his eyes, remembering his night with Brittany like a fast forwarded video, ending with the smell of her perfume on the pillow. The plane touched down with a gentle bump as if putting a dot on the exclamation point of the whole thing.

"I don't know if I can wait until Friday," Jordan said. "I think this is a lot bigger than we realize."

"Friday will be here before you know it."

When they met outside the tall mirrored building in the heart of San Diego where Todd had told them to meet, Jordan looked up, trying to see the top floor where Pandora Partnerships had a group of suites.

"C'mon you guys," Todd said. "Let's find out what this is all about." He led them through a cavernous glass enclosed lobby across pink marble floors to the polished steel doors of an elevator. Todd pushed the UP button, the doors opened, and they piled in. Wesley, the last one in, hit the top floor button.

No one spoke on the way up and remained quiet when the elevator doors opened to a spectacular view of downtown San Diego, the bay, Coronado Island, and beyond. On top of the world, Jordan thought.

An attractive, curvy blonde receptionist smiled at them from behind a large desk. "You must be Seal Team 0!" She stood. "Congratulations on your win. We've been expecting you. Can I get you anything? Soda? Coffee? Red Bull? Water?"

Todd looked at everyone, but no one responded. "No thanks," he said. "Maybe later. Thank you though!"

"Well then come with me." She gestured to a door. "We have a conference room waiting." She pushed through the door and led them down a short hallway to a conference room with another incredible vista. A wall of screens monitoring dozens of online video game competitions took up most of the far wall with the biggest screen at its center.

Six chairs faced the window lining a long conference table. A folder sat in front of each one with a member's team name on the cover along with a pen; **n0thing** for Jordan, **Renegade** for Wesley, **Sureshot** for Carl, **Striker** for John, and **Killjoy** for Terry. One chair faced the other six with the window to its back.

"Please, have a seat by the folder with your name on it," the receptionist said. "Mr. Crowley will be with you in a minute."

Everyone took their seats and opened folders, examining the contents. Terry and Wesley barely looked at theirs before signing them and sliding them across the table. Jordan studied his, scanning each paragraph. This agreement seemed more in-depth and elaborate than any others he had signed and some of the language troubled him.

As if sharing the same thought, Carl spoke out, his slender fingers pointing to a paragraph, his eyes looking a little wilder than usual. The pony tail of his red hair swung behind the baseball cap he wore backwards when he shook his head. "What's all this top secret government background check shit?"

"I was wondering about that myself," John said. "What's the government got to do with this?"

Terry and Wesley pulled their folders back.

Crowley breezed into the room, looking even more imposing in person with his stocky build, square shoulders, and silver brush cut. In person his icy blue eyes felt like they looked through you, but not at you. He had on the same Navy blue suit, solid red power tie, starched white shirt, pressed pants, and spit-shined shoes. "Welcome to Pandora Partnerships, gentlemen and congratulations once again on your win! Don't worry about the government background check stuff," he said. "It's just a formality so we follow federal guidelines."

"For what?" Todd said.

He slid into the chair across from them. "Some of Pandora Partnership's businesses have contracts with the federal government and according to their regulations, we have to add those paragraphs to our standard NDAs. It's only a formality. Your backgrounds have already been checked, so there's no concern there. Once the paperwork is complete we can give you full disclosure, so the sooner we finish here, the sooner we can make that happen."

He gave them an expansive grin and rubbed his hands together. "You guys are going to love it!"

Todd shrugged. "I don't think there's any problem here, guys. This stuff is pretty standard. It's not like we're signing our lives away. There's no commitment here, except to keep our mouths shut about whatever Mr. Crowley shares with us. Isn't that right, Mr. Crowley?"

"That's correct, Todd."

John waved his folder in front of him. "And if we don't sign, you won't show us anything," he said in his fast-talking staccato.

Wesley pushed his folder back toward Crowley. Todd and Killjoy followed suit. After reading through his a bit more, Carl slid his across the table, followed by Jordan. John looked to the others, nodding to each one in turn.

"I guess it's all for one and one for all," he said, making a show of being the last to sign. "I got to back up my homies."

CHAPTER NINE

I t felt like an icy hand gripped her heart when Rita peered into the darkness at the throbbing red light. "What the hell is that?" she blurted.

"That, my dear," Jack said matter-of-factly, "is Edgar Allen Poe's Tell-Tale Heart."

No one laughed.

Jack looked at everyone, frowning. "Okay, okay, I was trying to lighten things up a little. It's a Solar Powered Fail Safe Core Dump Backup."

"It's blinking!" Cheryl said, a little too loud, then her voice sounded shaky. "That's a backup of Morpheus? It shouldn't be blinking. It should be powered off and destroyed."

Rita felt the way Cheryl looked, wide-eyed and pale, even in the subdued light. "I had no idea," she said in a half-whisper, then louder. "Why didn't anyone tell us?"

"It's a standard fail safe on all major networks," Jack said, "especially this one. It's an integral part of the design."

"Solar powered?" Lorenzo said. "Can we disconnect its power and drive the proverbial stake through its damned heart?"

"You told us we were starting from scratch," Rita said, feeling her own voice shaking. "I won't have anything to do with any connection to that!" She pointed at the flashing red light, then held her arms out straight in front of her with her balled fists together. "You might as well put me away in a Mexican prison because I'd rather spend the rest of my life there than have anything to do with that. Tell-Tale Heart indeed!"

Crowley held up his hands. "Hold on a minute. There's no need to get caught up in a bunch of histrionics and useless drama."

"Six dead people and one brain damaged survivor is a far cry from histrionics and useless drama," Lorenzo deadpanned. "You said we're starting from scratch. That means dumping the old and clearing the decks for a fresh start. What do we need to do, Jack?"

Scanlon scratched his head. "Well, for starters…"

"We are starting from scratch," Crowley said. "We're just keeping this thing safe. I'm sorry if it makes you uneasy, but there's too much valuable information trapped in there to simply wipe it all out. It's here for safekeeping. That's why we have a guard over it and the added surveillance." He pointed to cameras around the room.

"I'm telling you right now," Cheryl said. "That monstrosity is infected with a deadly virus."

"A deadly computer virus?" Crowley said. "How can…"

"The body count it racked up is proof of that," Rita added. "You weren't here to witness the nightmare it created, so you have no idea of what you're playing with. Under no circumstances can this malignancy be part of the PermaDream Euthanasia project in any way shape or form, period end of story."

Crowley held up his right hand as if swearing an oath and looked directly at Rita, his ice blue eyes boring into her. "I promise, this will not be connected to Pandora in any way. We didn't know what to do with it, so it was deemed a critical area that we secured to await your determination."

"I want it out of here," Cheryl said. "That's my determination." She looked at the others, who each nodded in turn, then looked back at Crowley with her own penetrating stare.

He looked away. "It won't be connected. You folks are going to be in charge of how everything develops and you can create everything from scratch as promised, besides technology has taken some big jumps since this thing was created. We want you to start new."

Lorenzo crossed his arms. "So you're shutting it down and removing it when?"

Crowley ushered them out of the room, past the sentry. "Let's put that discussion on hold for the time being while I take your comments into consideration."

Rita looked back over her shoulder at the door closing behind them, glimpsing the blinking red light, which seemed to mock her.

"Fucking Tell-Tale Heart," Jack muttered.

"We have a massive, highly sophisticated facility here with a substantial infrastructure," Crowley said. "We've done what we can in your absence to maximize these vast resources with a brand new self-contained network with state of the art servers that have no connections to the outside while utilizing the existing infrastructure. This network has no physical connection to the old CPU which was powered down and removed. The security and surveillance system that used to be controlled by Morpheus has been switched over and hard wired to the new mainframe and is presently in the process of assuming climate control and other functions throughout the whole facility."

"That's great," Jack said as they entered the Gallery of Angels, "But I still don't trust that fucking monster."

Rita kept her eyes on the floor, not wanting to look up at the pictures of the kids lining the walls.

"What if we don't want to use your hardware?" Jack continued.

Crowley led them back down the long curving corridor of the Hall of Dreams. Rita kept her eyes on the floor, glancing over to see Cheryl doing the same. She couldn't get out of there fast enough.

"That is exactly what we anticipated," Crowley said, "so we have a large isolated climate controlled computer room nearing completion for you with room for expansion. You can build your own system from the ground up with your own hardware designs there."

"You can bet your ass on that," Jack said.

"As an added security measure, our surveillance and climate control will operate autonomously from your development network with no links, insuring that you are independent from any external influences."

"Or internal," Cheryl said, eyeing Crowley, who hit the button to the North tower elevator.

"Which brings us to command and control," he said. The door whooshed open and they entered in silence, each lost in their own thoughts as the door shut and the elevator rose, taking them past ground level up to the North Tower.

The door opened to a long hallway that led to the oak office door of Hodge's former glass walled office overlooking the atrium as well as everything else going on around it.

The carpet had been stripped away. A pristine tiled floor remained and a large U-shaped console lined with monitors and chairs took up the spot where Hodge's desk had been, making it look military and utilitarian as opposed to its former expensive trappings.

Crowley tapped an iPad and a paneled wall whispered open revealing eight nineteen inch flat screens surrounding a seventy two inch screen. The image on each monitor sequenced through different parts of the complex, panning buildings, hallways, and other parts of the near empty facility.

"Welcome to ground zero of the Pandora Project," Crowley said. "From here we hope to make your original vision of the PermaDream Euthanasia Project come back to life, reborn and rechristened as the Pandora Project."

CHAPTER TEN

Wesley finger combed his tousled black hair and leaned back in his chair, crossing his arms. His big shoulders filled the wide chair's back. "We signed," he said. "What's the big deal?"

Crowley stood and paced back and forth, speaking like a lecturing professor. The sunlight coming through the window behind him made his silver hair shine like it had a light of its own. "As you know, in the gaming world there's a constant push for more realistic experiences which has driven advances in graphics, audio, video, and interactivity which all combine to make the most immersive gaming experiences possible, especially when you delve into virtual reality, but even then you are still limited to two senses, sight and sound. You might get a hint of touch and vibration if you have a subwoofer with the bass and volume turned up, but you are primarily limited to two senses."

"In terms of the human machine interface concept," Todd said. "How deep can you really go, short of plugging the wires right into our brains?"

Crowley smiled. "Pandora Partnerships has the exclusive rights to a proprietary technology that pushes the boundaries of experience, allowing full immersion of all five senses in an engineered world and we want you to be the first to test it." Crowley tapped his iPad and a curtain slid across the window, darkening the room. All of the screens on the wall went dark except for the biggest center one. "How much of this do any of you remember?"

A video flickered onscreen like a television commercial and an announcer's voice came through the speakers. "They're here from all over the world," he said from a vantage point on a freeway overpass. "Members of virtually every race on the planet are swarming to the U.S. Mexican border, southeast of San Diego, hoping to literally fulfill their dreams and fantasies. The magnet drawing them all is the newly opened one-of-a-kind fantasy world, where dreams do indeed come true."

His voice over continued with shifting camera perspectives. "DreamLand's longest lines form outside Storybook Kingdom."

Giggling children with sparkling eyes queued behind red velvet ropes at the base of four soaring archways. Holographic images of The Three Bears, Sleeping Beauty, Rumpelstiltskin, and Hansel and Gretel smiled down from above each pastel-lit portal. A brief shot of a fifth portal showed black velvet curtains hung beneath the darkened hologram of a feather capped musician, parading in front of a long line of grinning rats with a sign stating:

Our Apologies.
The Pied Piper Dream Is Temporarily Out Of Order.

More happy, festive shots of wide-eyed children played out onscreen.

"Welcome to DreamLand. Please remain in line." A recorded woman's voice, soft and smooth as butter fudge said. "If you wish to awaken from your dream at any time, speak the word Mama or Mommy."

A pause, then, "Hi, folks, I'm your host, Hodge Michaels, reminding you that HistoryLand opens on Labor Day with twelve different events to choose from and dozens more to come. Make reservations now to dream travel to that special time and place in American history. Be in the front row when Lincoln delivers the Gettysburg Address. Visit New York in 1789 to cheer Washington's inauguration. Slap leather in the gunfight at the OK Corral. See the attack on Pearl Harbor from Diamondhead. Don't be disappointed. Plan ahead and enjoy your stay at DreamLand."

At the reservation desk a pretty, blue eyed young blonde smiled answering a reporter's question. "Beginning midnight, New Year's Eve, DreamLand will be open 24 hours a day, instead of closing at eleven." She added, "HistoryLand will be online in two weeks."

"Tell us about the upcoming dream-trip to the moon," a reporter said.

The blonde nodded, her blue eyes sparkling. "Space Adventure opens Thanksgiving week, but it's been sold out through mid-February. We're really proud of it."

The video flickered off and the room remained dark for a moment, then the lights came up. The members of Seal Team 0 all looked at each other with bewildered expressions.

"DreamLand? Are you shitting me?" Jordan said. Flashes of news reports, morbid pictures, and shocking headlines flitted through his mind and a hollow feeling settled in his stomach.

"Jesus!" Terry sat up straight in his chair, eyes wide, their roundness accented by his chubby cheeks. "That's all my parents talked about when it was a big deal. They had me on a three month waiting list. I think they were more excited about it than I was, then they clammed up after everything went wrong."

"No shit!" John's wild, curly blond hair flew about his head when he shook it, then his words came out in machine gun bursts. "If you're thinking about putting us into that spooky shit, there's no way I'm having anything to do it! I saw all the news reports. Some weird shit went down there and nobody knows what really happened. All I know is that it was some weird, scary shit." He looked around at the others, who all nodded.

"Hold your horses." Crowley dropped into his chair. "It's nothing like what you may have heard. The truth is…"

"That half a dozen people died down there," Carl said, finishing Crowley's sentence. The bugged out look in his eyes challenged Crowley, who opened his mouth to speak, but Carl pressed on before he could. "They died under weird circumstances. Shot, poisoned, burned, strangled, maimed, and a suicide, if I remember right."

"It had nothing to do with the dreaming computer or the technology," Crowley said. "It was warring drug cartels. Since that tragedy, hundreds of hours of investigations have taken place between the United States, Mexico, the NSA, the CIA, the FBI, DOD, and DARPA."

"All the more reason to avoid the whole thing," Wesley said.

"Just hear me out," Crowley went on, "and take some time to think about what I have to say. There's no pressure for you to participate.

You are our top choice for the dream team and we've been generous in our support of you and your competitions. If you don't want to work with us, there are plenty of other gamers who will jump at the opportunity, prestige, and financial rewards that this will bring, not to mention the fringe benefits." He winked.

Jordan thought of his night with Brittany. God only knew what else they might have for incentives and bonuses.

"You can't blame us for not wanting to jump into the fire with you," Todd said. "All those dead people? That's some scary shit."

Crowley nodded. "I'd feel the same way if I were you, but I think you might have a change of heart when I tell you what really happened and the precautions we have in place to keep you from any danger."

Todd put his elbows on the table and leaned forward with his chin on his interlaced fingers. "We're all ears."

"Let me give you a little history of how this evolved from something humane into the train wreck it became so you can make your decision with your eyes wide open. We want total transparency here so you have no doubt about our methods and objectives."

He hit the iPad again, the lights dimmed, and a slide show of the DreamLand project showed various stages of its development. He stepped through the pictures, narrating as he went.

"Edgar Michaels started The PermaDream Euthanasia Center with the best intentions built around a supercomputer they called Morpheus after the Greek God of dreams, touting it as, 'the magic that makes the miracle'. They even had government grants at the outset and everything moved along as planned to the point where the PermaDream hospital facility underwent significant expansion that allowed extended dreams for terminal patients. Things could not have gone better until Edgar Michaels passed away and the underbelly of it all was exposed when his son Hodge was reported to be meeting with drug kingpin, Oliver Daggett. Sources claimed that Daggett, a resident of Mexico, was in fact the true owner of PermaDream."

Crowley tapped the iPad and a picture of Edgar Michaels appeared on-screen, gaunt-faced, his eyes buried in dark hollow sockets. Snowy hair stuck up in feathery wisps from his balding head.

A reporter's voice provided the narrative. "In the year and a half since the death of PermaDream founder Edgar Michaels, rapid and unprecedented changes have come about in the use of the brain-wave modulation techniques he pioneered. According to his son, Hodge,

CEO of DreamLand Enterprises, they are all being utilized at DreamLand."

A video of Hodge replaced his father's photograph. His tousled sandy hair and boyish grin made him look childlike. "If we had stayed on the U.S. side of the border, none of this could have happened," Hodge said in a press conference from opening day. "Government agencies and paperwork would have hamstrung us at every step. Here in Mexico, the PLC has the foresight to allow us unfettered research and expansion as long as we continue to make safety our primary concern. Since our very first series of tests, our medical facilities have exceeded AMA standards and will continue to do so. Everyone is welcome to travel through the wonderful worlds created by Morpheus, our dream computer. The DreamLand experience is both exhilarating and completely safe."

The reporter added, "Oliver, 'Ollie' Daggett, who lives in Mexico is wanted on tax evasion charges in the United States and is sought for questioning in the deaths of Congressman Roberto Manzur and his family in a Christmas Eve plane crash four years ago. Prior to the crash, the Mexican government had refused to consider Manzur's extradition request. Unnamed sources accused Daggett of masterminding the sabotage of the private plane in retaliation. He remains unavailable for comment. Meanwhile, construction maintains a breakneck pace at the Mexican border."

Crowley paused the video and faced the team.

"I thought the Mexican government wanted all the inventors jailed for the murders," Wesley said.

"That was true until we uncovered evidence that cleared them of the murder and conspiracy charges surrounding the death of the congressman," Crowley said. "Any involvement on the part of PermaDream or DreamLand was determined to be the result of the actions of Hodge Michaels. Speculation has run rampant as to what really happened in DreamLand, but what they determined for sure is that the murders are victims of turf wars between Mexican drug cartels. Unfortunately, in his desperation, Hodge Michaels implicated himself and paid the price."

"So where does that leave us now?" Jordan asked. "Where do we fit into all this?"

"Yeah, that's what I want to know," Terry said. "I'm not afraid to tell you that the whole idea of hooking myself up to that thing gives me the heebie jeebies."

The important thing to realize," Crowley said looking to each of them, "is that in spite of everything that happened, in the end the dreaming experience is safe. All of the bad things that happened were the result of human actions motivated by greed and had nothing to do with the computer or the people who built it."

CHAPTER ELEVEN

Rita joined the others in front of a row of egg-shaped shells all tilted back at an angle. Multicolored L.E.D.'s flashed down both sides in succession, like blinking runway lights. The front of each egg slid open with a soft whoosh, revealing a contoured, padded recliner. Rita held her breath as a cloaked figure approached, reaching out for her.

The touch of his hand sent her hurtling down through a maelstrom of darkness, plunging into frigid water, swirling like a leaf sucked into a huge drain. She held her breath as brilliant bubbles of emerald phosphorescence boiled around her. Far above on the glittering silver surface, the reflection of the sky grew hazy.

Her lungs felt like balloons stretched to the breaking point. Desperate for air, she kicked and clawed at the seething water.

As if by magic, the churning bubbles changed direction. Stroking against the raging current, she pulled herself up toward the distant hazy light where dusky spots swirled among sparkling bubbles. Every part of her wanted to exhale and take a deep breath, but Rita forced the thought from her mind, thinking only of the blessed air she longed to pull into her lungs. As she neared the surface, the dark spots whirled closer.

She gulped when her head broke the surface. Air. Sweet air, delicious, fresh air.

Something wet and hairy brushed her cheek. Looking up, she saw hordes of rats tumbling off a jagged cliff, screeching and twitching as they hit the water. Hundreds floated on the swells, tiny legs and long tails dangling. Others scratched at her clothing. One clawed at her hair. Another scrambled onto her head.

She screamed, grabbed its cold, slippery tail and threw it as far as she could. A furry head surfaced in front of her, snapping at her face, eyes glinting, yellow teeth clicking, jaws working frantically. Terrified rats clung to her shoulders. Her teeth chattered as she slapped at the fat furry bodies.

The dark chaotic waters whirled in the opposite direction, drawing her away from the cliff and the mass of squealing rats. Again, she swam with all her might, fighting the pull of what she thought of as a giant hand, but the roiling water sucked her under and she plunged downward like a stone spinning into blackness.

She swung her arm out and someone caught it, causing her to panic even more. She screamed, but it came out like a whisper.

"Rita, wake up!" Lorenzo said, drawing her up from the darkness. "You're having one of your nightmares."

She shook her head and Lorenzo's face swam into focus. He put his arm around her, comforting her and she hugged him close, sobbing into his chest.

"It's okay, babe." He stroked her hair and caressed her face. "I'm right here with you and I'm not going to let anyone hurt you."

"I'm sorry," she said between sobs. "Seeing all that stuff today and seeing poor Hodge wired up like Chazz stirred up memories I'd rather not have."

Lorenzo took her face in his hands and looked into her eyes. "You don't have to apologize for anything. Are you kidding me? Today's repeat performance tour stirred up a lot of memories for me too. I've been tossing and turning all night."

He kissed her on the lips and held her for awhile before stretching out onto his back, gently guiding her head to his chest. "We've got to make the best of it," he said. "There's something to be said about starting over again from scratch and it's certainly a better option than a Mexican prison."

"I wish I could wrap my head around it, but none of this feels right. I'll never feel safe knowing there's a backup of Morpheus blinking its evil red eye down there in the darkness. We need to figure out how to shut it down completely."

"I know what you mean." He held her closer. "It feels like some cyclops monster is laughing at us."

"Jack Scanlon's Tell-Tale Heart," she whispered.

CHAPTER TWELVE

Crowley tapped his iPad and the conference room curtains opened, letting in sunlight. "I have to admit," he said pacing with his hands clasped behind his back. "I'm a little envious of you, your talents, and for what's in store for you. Think about it. You will be the pioneers of a grand history making adventure."

"So what you're telling us," Jordan said, "is that you want us to be your guinea pigs and test your new gaming technology for you."

Crowley spun on his heel and turned back to face them. "I wouldn't phrase it quite that way. We plan on custom modeling our first gaming scenarios to play to your unique championship talents." He held his arms wide. "From there we hope to branch out and create an expansive new world of gaming that no one could have ever imagined possible -- and you will be its ambassadors!"

"In what you call a new technology that pushes the boundaries of experience, allowing full immersion of all five senses in an engineered world," John said.

"And you want us to be the first to test it," Carl added.

Crowley nodded.

"Our 'unique championship talents', as you call them," Terry said, "are shooting people and blowing things up. That's okay in a game, because we don't feel anything in a regular game, but what happens if we get shot or blown up in this full immersion game? If it's so real, will it hurt?"

John shook his head. "I ain't ready for that shit."

Crowley held his hands up in surrender. "Believe me, there's nothing at all to fear. You'll have the ability to come out of the experience whenever you want by saying a word."

"I'm not so sure I like the idea of being connected to this dreaming thing after all the bad shit that happened with the old DreamLand," Wesley said. "It still scares me. I hate the idea of getting any kind of mutated virus or cooties or something like that. I heard some weird stories from one of my sister's friends about what really happened there..."

"Stories, that's all they are," Crowley said. "You've seen the real story here." He gestured toward the big screen.

Todd nodded, affirming his belief. "You said you had precautions in place to keep anyone from getting exposed to anything dangerous. What are they?"

Crowley gestured as he talked, becoming more animated with each word. "We're developing an entirely new platform based on some of the original technology, but we're doing it with brand new code on updated hardware that will be totally independent from the old system." He looked at Wesley, pinning him with his penetrating blue eyes. "So there's no chance that anyone will get any kind of virus or cooties or anything like that."

Everyone laughed and the mood in the room lightened.

Crowley grinned from ear to ear. "The prototype we'll be testing will be closely monitored in a tightly controlled environment to guarantee you absolute safety."

Todd looked around at the others, who each gave a single nod. The room remained quiet for a moment before Crowley broke the silence with a smile, saying, "And you'll be well compensated for your time and effort." He pointed at Wesley. "That's a guarantee!"

A goofy smile spread across Wesley's face.

"So we're in agreement." Crowley held out his fist.

Wesley nodded and Crowley leaned across the table to fist bump him, then he went down the line fist bumping each team member in turn, ending with Jordan.

"So when do we get started?" Todd asked. "What do we need to do to get ready?"

"Now that you are all on board, we'll need you to sign more paperwork and contracts to cover the last of the details so we can put you on the payroll."

"Where do I sign?" Wesley said. "I'm all about getting on the payroll."

Crowley chuckled. "It includes a full benefits package and a small signing bonus."

"Small signing bonus?" Terry's eyes grew round, their expression exaggerated by his plump face.

Crowley tapped his lapel. "I just happen to have it right here. Let's get the formality over with and move on to the fun stuff." He tapped his iPad and his receptionist came in with a handful of folders.

She went down the line, opening each folder in front of its owner, pointing to the places where colored Post-it stickers marked signature spots. The sheaf of papers were thicker than the NDAs they had signed and had more fine print. Jordan thought he should take the time to read them in more detail, but it looked like boilerplate and everybody else signed without as much as a second glance.

He felt a little lost when the secretary leaned in with his folder and instructions. The combination of her long blonde hair, perfume, and cleavage distracted him. He signed everywhere she pointed, then watched her firm ass ease out the door, leaving him with a vague sense of longing.

Crowley clapped his hands together. "Now it's official." He reached into his inner Jacket pocket and pulled out a handful of envelopes, plopping one down in front of each of them.

Jordan picked his up and looked inside, smiling when he saw a cashier's check for five thousand dollars.

CHAPTER THIRTEEN

Rita and Lorenzo followed Jack, Cheryl, and Crowley into the old ProtoLab. "We didn't touch anything in here," Crowley said, flicking on the lights. "We wanted you to be able to pick up where you left off."

Rita paused in the doorway scanning the room full of workbenches littered with electronics, tools, tangles of wires, and displays of all types. Cabinets lined the walls. Nothing had changed, which gave her an unsettling sense of deja-vu. Two half-finished pods lay open, with mazes of wires, sensors, and electronics spilling from them. A third fully functional pod sat upright, its front hatch gaping like an open mouth.

"I want those abominations out of here," Cheryl said, giving voice to what Rita felt. "I can't stand to look at them."

"We thought you might like to keep them for R&D and testing purposes," Crowley said.

Cheryl waved at the pods dismissively. "You said we're starting from scratch. Scratch means scratch."

"But…"

She dropped into a chair and crossed her arms. "There is no but. I want them out!" She stared straight at Crowley, giving her own formidable version of a penetrating stare.

He looked down and nodded. "Consider it done."

Jack leaned against a table beside Cheryl. "That technology is crude and out of date anyway. Cheryl and I were working on a much more elegant design that we're ready to take to the next level." He went to a cabinet at the back of the lab and retrieved a light-weight silk hood with a Velcro strap and a USB port on its side. He held it up for everyone to see, showing off a geometrical pattern of miniature circuitry stitched across its surface.

Cheryl drew back at the sight of it. Rita sensed by the way she acted that something else had happened to her in the chaos of DreamLand's collapse, but Cheryl was close-mouthed about everything and gave no hints about what it might have been.

"Nothing we had designed so far matched the field strength of this configuration." Jack held it up higher. "Since then I've been doing some research and thinking about how we can achieve better, more remote functioning."

"And I've been working on an improved algorithm," Cheryl chimed in. "while Jack has been fine-tuning his magnetoresonators to improve the field strength and match the equations."

Jack pursed his lips and nodded. "There are some new super conductive materials on the market that have the potential to radically improve our data transfer rates." He laid the hood down on a table so everyone could see it and pointed to different parts of it as he spoke. "There have been some new breakthroughs in sensor technology since we were detained in Mexico. We plan to incorporate these so we can closely monitor a host of bodily functions, including respiration, heart rate, sweat, brain waves, PET and FMRI Imaging,."

"And the output," Lorenzo said, leaning in to examine the hood. "Same protocol and power requirements as before?"

Jack nodded.

Cheryl looked at everyone over her glasses. "We want to focus our attention on the medical aspects of this device, especially the monitoring functions. Our subjects will be on the verge of death, so we need to observe everything closely."

"Aside from the passive monitoring functions," Rita asked, "what about drug and nutrient delivery?"

Jack held up a finger and his bushy eyebrows brightened. "Good question, Rita! That's where we can make some real inroads. We have plans for a new chip that will be part of the hood's actual hardware."

Cheryl adjusted her glasses and picked up the hood, pointing to different parts of it as she spoke. "With two primary modes of customizable parameters, a non-invasive mode, for non-medical dreaming situations, and an invasive mode when medical intervention becomes necessary, such as when patients have head injuries. Researchers have developed fibers that can deliver simultaneous stimuli. Implanted into the brain or spinal column, they can transmit drugs, light, and electrical signals. Conventional neural probes are designed to record a single type of signaling, limiting the information that can be derived from the brain in real time. We can overcome that with this new technology."

Jack nodded emphatically. "I'm confident that we can pack everything into one chip that will be part of the hood, which will make it more portable and versatile. For brain damaged patients we're using multi-modal fibers less than the width of a hair in a system that delivers optical signals and drugs directly into the brain along with an electrical grid that monitors the effects of the inputs."

Cheryl set the hood down again. "The new fibers are made of polymers that resemble normal tissues, allowing them to stay in the body much longer without harming the delicate tissue around them."

Crowley rubbed his hands together, eyes bright with excitement. "This is just what we need to help our wounded vets, a combined physiological and a psychological approach. I have a good feeling about this."

"Our new interface will interact with tissues in a more organic way," Cheryl said, looking over her glasses again. "These polymer fibers are soft, flexible, and look like natural nerves. Most neural recording and stimulation devices are made of metals, semiconductors, or glass, and can damage surrounding tissue. Neural prosthetics are typically stiff and sharp, so when you take a step and the brain moves with respect to the device, you end up scrambling tissue."

Lorenzo frowned. "How do they make something so complicated, so small?"

Jack put his hand on the hood, tapping it as he talked. "They start with a larger scale version of the network that has the desired arrangement of channels within the fiber, including optical waveguides to carry light, hollow tubes to carry drugs, and conductive electrodes to carry electrical signals. These polymer templates with dimensions on the scale of inches are heated until they become soft, and drawn into thinner fiber while retaining the exact arrangement of features." He held up a finger, shaking it. "A single reduction of this fiber reduces the cross-section of the material two hundred fold and the process can be repeated, making the fibers thinner each time, approaching nanometer-scale."

Lorenzo whistled.

"Features that started out being inches across become microns," Cheryl added. "Combining the different channels in a single fiber can enable precision mapping of neural activity and treatment of neurological disorders that aren't possible with single function neural probes. Light can be transmitted through the optical channels to enable optogenetic neural stimulation which can be monitored with embedded electrodes. Additionally, precise dosages of drugs can be injected into the brain through the hollow channels, while electrical signals in the neurons are recorded in real time indicating what affect the drugs or any other stimuli are having. They call it a customizable toolkit for neural engineering."

"Our long term goal is to calibrate this technology with our electromagnetic cranial stimulation arrays," Jack said, "and perform as many external functions as possible."

Cheryl pushed her glasses up on her nose. "It offers a versatile collection of multi-functional fibers tailored for insertion into the brain where they can stimulate and record neural behavior through electrical, optical, and fluidic means for specific applications by creating the exact combination of needed channels. The fibers can also be used for precision mapping of the responses of different regions of the brain or spinal cord to treat conditions like epilepsy and Parkinson's disease."

Rita flashed on an image of Hodge, feeble and withered, his eyes jumping in frenzied REM and his body twitching in petit mal seizures.

"Wow," Crowley said. "Everything packed into one chip. A customized electronic biomedical human machine command and control interface.

"Command and control sounds a little too military for me," Jack said.

"Then what else would you call it?" Crowley shook his head. "We're designating it the command and control chip. It describes it perfectly. And it's customizable! We're going to have to choose our first subject carefully, especially when we consider the medical implications."

"We already have our first subject," Cheryl said.

Crowley looked puzzled. "Who?"

"That's a no-brainer," Rita said, studying Cheryl, who looked stoic and resolute.

Cheryl's eyes met hers, registering acknowledgement, then she gave a tiny nod. "Hodge," she said.

CHAPTER FOURTEEN

"What's all this shit about Morpheus and Pandora?" Terry asked from the end of the table at Dick's Last Resort, a roadhouse themed bar in San Diego's Gaslamp Quarter. Stevie Ray Vaughan's 'Crossfire' blasted from a jukebox and the smell of lunch filled the air undercut by the lingering odor of stale beer. A group of cute girls chattered around a table by the window and clusters of people ate burgers, crab legs, fish and chips, and other appetizers.

Todd sipped his beer. "The inventors of DreamLand were on target when they named their computer after the Greek god of dreams."

"I remember Morpheus from that Matrix movie," Wesley said.

Jordan took out his cell phone and tapped "Morpheus" into the Google search bar. Wikipedia came up. "He's much more than that," Jordan said. "Listen to this! The Greek Morpheus had the ability to mimic any human form and appear in dreams. His true semblance was a winged demon. Classical depictions of him say he wore a white and black coat, with a horn and ivory box full of dreams of the same colors to signify good and bad."

John downed the last of his beer. "I wouldn't want to be on his bad side." He looked around for a waitress, got her attention and waved his finger in a circle indicating a round for the table.

Jordan continued. "His name comes from the Greek word morphe which means form. According to the Greeks, he was the one who shaped and formed dreams."

Jordan looked up from his phone and saw everyone listening.

"Keep reading," Todd said. "This shit is interesting."

"According to this, Morpheus was responsible for the dreams of people and when in his arms they enjoyed sound sleep, but they could also dream about their future. Morpheus was the dream messenger of the Gods communicating divine messages through images and stories created as dreams. He had the ability to send and shape images to the visions of people and give form to the creatures that lived in dreams. He also had a talent for mimicking humans in the dreams."

"Like a beautiful babe with big tits," John said, pointing the tip of his bottle at Terry. "Then you'd be able to make up for your lost time."

"Fuck you!" Terry said.

Everybody laughed before Jordan went on.

"According to Ovid the Poet, 'King Sleep was father of a thousand sons, and out of them all he chose Morpheus who had great skill miming human forms. None could match his artistry in counterfeiting men, their voice, gait, face, and moods. He imitated how they dressed and the words they used the most, but he only mimed men…"

"Looks like you're shit out of luck, Terry," John said. "No big tits for you."

"That's just the ancient Greek politically incorrect figure of speech," Carl said. "Didn't you hear Jordan say he can take any form he wants?" Lifting his head to Terry, he said. "No worries, bro. You still have a chance to regain your lost glory."

"And manhood!" John added.

Killjoy flipped him off amidst more laughter.

Todd shook his head. "Is there more Jordan?"

Jordan nodded and continued reading. "In his real form Morpheus had wings given to him and his brothers by their uncle Thanatos, the deity of death. Morpheus used his wings to reach those who needed help in their dreams and to carry his father, the wingless Hypnos, to the dream world in the caves when he needed to be saved from Zeus. Hypnos was the personification of sleep, seen as god and the devil. His mother Pasithea, was the deity of Hallucinations and his grandmother Nyx was the deity of Night."

"I remember Eros and Thanatos from a mythology class," Todd said. "Sex and death were two sides of the same coin representing the energies of birth and death."

"Here's the last part," Jordan said. "Morpheus's brother Icelus was responsible for the reality parts of the dreams, Phobetor was the creator of phobic or fearful dreams, while Phantasus created unreal dreams full of phantasms. What made Morpheus the biggest among his brothers was his ability to oversee the dreams of heroes and kings and influence the dreams of Gods."

Jordan looked up, eyeing each of them, finally letting his gaze come to rest on Wesley. "You're going to love this part."

Wesley sat up straight.

"Morpheus slept in a cave full of poppy seeds. That mythical fact is probably why morphine borrowed its name from Morpheus."

"I'll try some of that," Carl said.

Jordan smiled in spite of himself. "The dream world of Morpheus was the place where his family lived and The River of Forgetfulness and the River of Oblivion were found there, protected by gates under the supervision of two monsters that materialized the fears of uninvited visitors. Only the gods from Olympus were allowed in this family nest."

"A real family man, huh?" Carl said.

"Morpheus was one of the busiest deities so he didn't have a wife," Jordan said, "but some interpretations saw him with Iris, the personification of the rainbow and messenger of the gods."

"What about Pandora?" John said. His wild eyes had a mischievous glint. "She was Greek. You think maybe she and Morpheus…" He shrugged. "You know…" He circled the thumb and index finger of his left hand and moved his right index finger in and out of it eliciting a giggle from Terry.

"According to the myth," Todd said, "Pandora opened a jar, but it was mistranslated as "Pandora's box", and released all the evils of humanity, leaving only hope inside once she closed it again."

"Sounds like Terry's night of sex." John's eyes brightened. "Only his girl closed up her box before he even got started and instead of leaving him with hope, she left him hopeless."

They erupted in laughter, fueled even harder when Wesley laughed mid-sip sending beer shooting out his nose and mouth. Terry's pudgy face turned red, but he couldn't contain himself and became swept up in the hilarity of the others.

"Jesus, you guys never quit," Jordan said, catching his breath.

"No rest for the wicked!" Carl said, holding up a finger.

"If Terry missed out, then he was lucky." Todd held up his cell phone. "Dig this. Pandora means gift, the all-endowed, the all-gifted or the all-giving."

"That big-titted blonde was definitely all endowed, ay Terry?" John said.

"But he'll never know if she was all giving," Carl said, setting off another round of snickers.

"You wouldn't want what she had," Todd said, reading once more from his phone. "After humans received the stolen gift of fire from Prometheus, Zeus decided to give them a punishing gift to compensate for the boon they got and commanded Hephaestus to mold from earth the first woman, a "beautiful evil" whose descendants would torment the human race. Athena dressed her in a silvery gown, an embroidered veil, garlands, and a silver crown. When she first appeared before gods and mortals, wonder seized them when they looked at her, but she was sheer guile, not to be withstood by men."

"Sounds like a lot of women I've met," Wesley said.

"But none as gifted," Todd continued. "Athena taught her needlework and weaving; Aphrodite shed grace on her head and cruel longing that wearied her. Hermes gave her a shameful mind and deceitful nature. He also gave her the power of speech, putting in her lies and crafty words. After Athena clothed her, Persuasion and the Charites adorned her with necklaces and other finery and the Horae adorned her with a garland crown. Finally, Hermes named her Pandora. All-gifted, because all the Olympians gave her gifts."

"Shit John," Carl said. "I wouldn't fuck her with your dick!"

Terry burst out with a too loud guffaw until John quieted him with a stare. A smirk turned up the corner of his mouth.

"In the end," Todd said, "Pandora's deceitful nature became the least of humanity's worries. The biggest problem was the box containing the toil and sickness that brings death to men, diseases, and other pains. Prometheus warned his brother not to accept any gifts from Zeus, but Epimetheus didn't listen and accepted Pandora, who scattered what was in her box until the earth and sea were full of evils".

"Wouldn't want that box," Wesley said.

"Well you're going to get it." Jordan looked at him, then at the others. "We all just signed up to fully immerse ourselves in it."

"And the only thing that stayed in the box was hope," Todd said, looking up from his cell phone.

CHAPTER FIFTEEN

Rita and Cheryl hovered over Hodge dressed in scrubs and masks, examining him in his Plexiglas coffin-like bed on the inside of the thick glass that closed off the ICU. The unusual angled shape of the eight glass observation walls of the small octagon shaped room made her claustrophobic in the strangest way. She felt like a bee caught in the queen's chambers of some giant hive.

Her heart raced and her throat tightened at the sight of feeble and withered Hodge. How young and handsome he had once looked. She didn't think she'd ever get over seeing him this way with his perpetually furrowed brow changing expressions as he moaned and mumbled as if struggling with some overwhelming problem. His eyes twitched in a frenzy beneath closed eyelids and his body shuddered in random tremors.

The window around his bald head had been removed along with the hood that covered his damaged skull, revealing the pinkish gray fatty mass of his brain surrounded by sterile paper. Fiber optics from the carefully set aside hood and gloves he still wore flashed, and colored fluids filled the tubing at his wrists. An additional set of probes and wires went straight from his brain through a bundled cable to an added panel of readouts over a keyboard console. Pulsing waveforms showed weak, but steady EKG, pulse, respiration, fMRI and PET imaging as well as other vital functions.

Cheryl, looking every bit the scientist with her long strawberry-blonde hair pulled back in a bun and her pale blue eyes focused behind her horn-rimmed glasses, kept her attention on a bank of multicolored images measuring brain activity. Using a micromanipulator combined with other specialized instruments, she carefully slid a series of hair-thin wires and tubes deeper into and out of Hodge's brain, causing colored shifts and changes to the displays as well as alterations in other waveforms that Rita diligently recorded on an iPad under Cheryl's guidance.

"You can see when I hit a sweet spot." Cheryl nodded toward the monitors after adjusting a wire and starting a new one. "The resulting brain activation is presented graphically by color-coding the strength of activation across the specific regions we're studying so I can localize brain activity. The data we gather here along with the proper probe placement will help us custom design Hodge's dream hood and control chip function to both monitor and administer a combination of electronic and drug delivered neurochemical controls, which will hopefully allow him to rest easier."

"It would be nice to see him without all the added REM and seizures."

"I'd love to alleviate those symptoms. A large number of Parkinson patients have already reduced their tremors considerably with this technology. There is still a bit of hit and miss with this approach, but with the state that he's in and the technology we have at our disposal, this is our best shot."

"What about his mental state? Do you think it will calm him?"

She nodded toward a thin tube she was adjusting. "The present drug delivery system barely keeps that under control. If we overmedicate him, we risk sending him into a coma. Fortunately, the command and control chip drug delivery function gives us more precise dosage control and a greater margin of safety. I'm hoping that a reduction in his physical symptoms will calm his overall mental activity, but if it doesn't, I have another non-invasive approach that I'd like to try based on technology we've already developed."

Cheryl made some last minute adjustments, fine-tuning the wires and tubes in different parts of Hodge's brain and rechecking the monitors before carefully arranging everything around Hodge's head, replacing the hood and sealing off the window over his head, once more fully enclosing him.

"That just about does it." She backed away from Hodge and wiped her brow on her sleeve. "I sure miss Morgan and his rock solid bedside manner."

"You're doing great," Rita said, "but I do feel lost without him, even though part of me feels like he's always with me. I don't feel confident with all the medical details."

"And I can only do so much," Cheryl added. "I'm a neuroscientist, but I am no expert on life support functions and I'm swamped with my own work with Jack."

Rita set the iPad down and stretched. "We need a full time doctor, but not just any doctor. Morgan was a specialist. I don't think we can ever find anyone with his qualifications."

"I've been bending Crowley's ear about it and he's hinted that he has someone in mind if he can convince them to come on board."

"From what I've seen, money shouldn't be a problem."

"He's assured me that it's not the money. It's more to do with ethics and practices."

"You mean he has no prison terms to hold over the good doctor's head?"

Cheryl gave Rita a rare smile and looked over her glasses. "Something like that." She gestured toward the door with her head and led Rita out of the ICU. "Come on." She pulled off her mask. "Let's go have a talk with Lorenzo."

Rita walked through the curving hallways alongside Cheryl in silence, wondering about the mystery doctor while Cheryl studied the data they had collected on the iPad. No one could ever replace Morgan, but she hoped for someone who could help.

They found Lorenzo at work at one of the three video editing bays that lined the walls of his lab. Each station had a large screen and a floor to ceiling rack of blinking electronics. A large desk took up part of the fourth wall. Chairs, tables, and a couch sat at the room's center, making a comfortable break area to talk in.

"Hey ladies." He pointed to the couch with his thumb. "I'll be with you in a minute. I need to wrap up this sequence. Make yourself at home."

Cheryl found an overstuffed chair and dropped into it, still focused on her iPad. Rita took a spot on the couch, keeping quiet, listening to the clicks of Lorenzo's mouse and keyboard while Cheryl tapped away on her iPad.

"Stick a fork in it," Lorenzo said after a final mouse click. He stood, stretched, and came around the end of the couch, dropping into the spot beside Rita. "Hey babe." He hugged her and gave her a quick kiss on the cheek, then he put his arm around her and they sat back on the couch. "Hi Cheryl. How are my two beautiful brainiac brain surgeons?"

Cheryl looked up from her iPad and gave Lorenzo a faint smile. Her pale blue eyes looked big behind her glasses. Rita was happy to see that the smile touched her eyes.

"What's the scoop on poor Hodge, Chief Surgeon Martin?"

"I'm far from Chief Surgeon material," Cheryl said, shaking her head. "But with the help of your little Florence Nightingale there, we've collected some preliminary data and all the tubing, wires, sensors, and probes are in place and ready to be attached to Jack's new command and control chip. We're both excited about its capabilities and are working on designing new lightweight dreaming hoods around it. Our next generation will not have any of the invasive functions that this one has, but they will have enhanced magnetoresonators with their own version of input and feedback loops. We custom designed this first prototype specifically for Hodge."

Lorenzo inclined his head toward the console where he had been working. "Instead of The Pied Piper and Hansel and Gretel, Crowley has me working on a battle scenario based on a video game. He wants to put PTSD vets into dreaming situations similar to the ones they were in when they were wounded, and have them change their perspective by changing the outcome. He thinks we can heal them of their psychological traumas by helping them to face their fears in a very real, but safe environment."

"That may help them psychologically," Rita said, "but so many of them are missing limbs, are brain damaged, or maimed in other ways, including internal organ damage."

Cheryl's eyes narrowed. "That's why Crowley is so gung ho on this chip design and why he's approved our approach with Hodge. He wants us to have the capability of customizing our C and C chip to each individual for their specific needs. We expect many of them to be brain damaged in the same way Hodge is, so we can have the capability to treat them all accordingly. Many of the vets are only traumatized mentally. We hope the non-invasive dreaming protocol will heal them of their psychological wounds, while the invasive protocols assist those with severe brain damage."

"Each person using a dream hood whether invasive or non-invasive will have a digital profile that will be updated and modified with each use," Lorenzo said, "improving their performance the same way voice recognition software learns and updates itself, similar to the way video games save player levels and scores."

Cheryl shook a finger. "That raises another question."

Lorenzo leaned forward. "Do tell."

"Sometimes the line between real and imagined trauma can be blurred, making it hard to locate the source."

"Can you give me an example?" Rita said.

Cheryl set her iPad down on the table. "Let's take Hodge as an example. He's experiencing Parkinson's like seizures. We have signal wires in place to stimulate the parts of his brain related to those seizures with miniscule electric pulses controlled by Jack's C and C chip. I'm confident that it will quell his tremors, but who knows where he is mentally? We may be treating symptoms, but we don't know anything about his subjective experience. He could be in a twenty four hour hell."

Rita flashed on her own nightmares and felt a chill. She leaned in closer to Lorenzo.

"Wherever he is," Cheryl continued, "he's not in his happy place. He mumbles, moans, and shakes, and frequently has bewildered frowns or wide-eyed terror, yet he's oblivious to the world around him. He'll have all the functionality of a standard dream hood, along with Jack's chip hard wired into his brain." Her eyes took on a faraway look, then came back into focus. "Lorenzo, I was wondering if you could come up with a simple dream sequence that might calm his mind. Something soothing - perhaps even meditative."

"Crowley's been pushing me to finish this battle scenario, but fuck him. Hodge is more important than Crowley. Besides, we're not going to let him test the dream hood on anybody until we test it on Hodge. What were you thinking? Nature scenes? Waves crashing on the shore? Birds and other calming nature sounds?"

Cheryl pursed her lips and nodded slowly. "I trust your judgment on the audio and visual components, but I have an idea about the audio that I want to work out between us."

"Different sounds?"

"And imagery. A different approach to delivering sights and sounds that could bring a whole new level to the depth and resonance of the entire dreaming experience."

Lorenzo crossed his arms. "Enlighten me."

"Have you ever heard of binaural frequencies?"

"I remember reading about them."

Cheryl picked up her iPad and tapped away, then looked over her glasses at Rita and Lorenzo. "Binaural beats, or binaural tones, are auditory processing artifacts that help induce relaxation, meditation, creativity, and other desirable mental states. The effect on brainwaves depends on the difference in frequencies of each tone: for example, if three hundred hertz was played in one ear and three hundred ten in the other, then the binaural beat would have a frequency of ten hertz."

"This sounds similar to holography," Lorenzo said. "Interference patterns between two or more beams of coherent light are captured. One beam shines on the recording medium and acts as a reference to the light scattered from the illuminated scene. The resulting recorded image is a three-dimensional hologram."

"That's a great analogy," Cheryl said. "The brain produces a phenomenon resulting in low-frequency pulsations in the amplitude and sound localization of a perceived sound when two tones at slightly different frequencies are presented separately to each ear. A beating tone is perceived as if the two tones mixed naturally, out of the brain. The frequencies must be below one thousand hertz for the beating to be noticeable. The difference between the two frequencies must be less than or equal to thirty hertz for the effect to occur, otherwise the two tones are heard separately and no beat is perceived." She looked up from her tablet. "Binaural beats influence the brain in more subtle ways through the entrainment of brainwaves and provide other health benefits like control over pain."

"Pain control?" Rita said. "Using sound instead of drugs?"

Cheryl read again from her tablet like a professor delivering a lecture. "The sensation of binaural beats is believed to originate in the superior olivary nucleus part of the brain stem and appear to be related to the brain's ability to locate the sources of sounds in three dimensions and track moving sounds, which involves inferior colliculus neurons. Auditory rhythms rapidly entrain motor responses into stable steady synchronization states below and above conscious perception thresholds. Activated regions include primary sensorimotor and cingulate areas, bilateral opercular premotor areas, bilateral SII, ventral prefrontal cortex, and, subcortically, anterior insula, putamen, and thalamus. Within the cerebellum, vermal regions and anterior hemispheres ipsilateral to the movement become activated. Tracking

78

temporal modulations also activate right prefrontal, anterior cingulate, and intraparietal regions as well as posterior cerebellar hemispheres."

"So all of that mumbo jumbo says that those brain regions can be activated by controlling the delivery of audio information in a non-invasive manner," Lorenzo said.

Cheryl nodded. "Binaural beats can influence brain functions in other ways in what is called frequency following response. If someone receives a stimulus with a frequency in the range of brain waves, the predominant brainwave frequency is likely to move toward the frequency of the stimulus, which is referred to as entrainment. It relates to spatial perception, stereo auditory recognition, and activation of various sites in the brain."

"Can you describe the physiological effects a little more?" Rita asked.

"When the perceived beat frequency corresponds to the delta, theta, alpha, beta, or gamma range of brainwave frequencies, the waves entrain to it. For example, if a three hundred fifteen hertz sine wave is played into the right ear and a three hundred twenty five hertz is played into the left ear, the brain is entrained towards the beat frequency ten hertz, in the alpha range which is associated with relaxation, or if in the beta range, more alertness. An experiment using beat frequencies in the beta range on some participants and the delta-theta range on others found better vigilance, performance and mood in those on the alert state of beta-range stimulation."

"So it can have a sedating and a relaxing effect," Rita added.

"Not only that. Binaural beat stimulation has been used to induce a variety of states of consciousness and work has been done regarding the effects of these stimuli on relaxation, focus, attention, and states of consciousness. With repeated training that distinguishes close frequency sounds, a plastic reorganization of the brain occurs for the trained frequencies that are capable of asymmetric hemispheric balancing. Now get this!" She jabbed her index finger for emphasis. "The stimulus can be visual or a combination of aural and visual." She stopped as if she'd been hit and her eyes widened behind her horn rimmed glasses, making her look owl-like. "My God," she whispered. "I didn't think of this before."

Rita and Lorenzo leaned forward together.

"The visual has already been done with what they called..." She clutched her hands to her chest as if worried. "The Dreamachine," she said in a half-whisper.

Rita couldn't believe what she heard. "Are you serious?"

"It's a stroboscopic flicker device that produces visual stimuli. In its original form it was made from a cylinder with slits cut in the sides that rotated at seventy eight or forty five revolutions per minute. A light bulb was suspended in the center of the cylinder and the rotation speed allowed the light to come out from the holes at a constant frequency between eight and thirteen pulses per second, which corresponded to alpha waves normally present in the human brain while relaxing. The dreamachine was 'viewed' with the eyes closed. The pulsating light stimulated the optical nerve and altered the brain's electrical oscillations. Users experienced increasingly bright, complex patterns of color behind their closed eyelids and the patterns became swirling shapes and symbols until the user felt surrounded by colors. Using a dreamachine allowed anyone to enter into the hypnagogic state between sleep and wakefulness. The experience can be intense, but to escape it, the subject only needed to open their eyes."

"We have to work out a method of modulating the signals," Rita said. "Our subjects will be dreaming and unable to open their eyes."

Cheryl nodded emphatically. "The dreamachine was considered dangerous for people with photosensitive epilepsy or other nervous disorders and one out of ten thousand adults experienced seizures while viewing it. Twice as many children had similar ill effects."

"All the more reason to start with minimal signal strengths," Rita said. "Hodge is suffering from seizures already. We don't want to trigger more."

"Between Lorenzo, Jack, and I," Cheryl said. "I think we can dial in an optimum signal strength. Some people find pure sine waves unpleasant, so pink noise or other backgrounds like natural river sounds can be mixed with them. As long as the beat is audible, increasing the volume doesn't improve its effectiveness, so low volume is recommended, reduced to the point that the beating is not audible."

Lorenzo took his arm from around Rita and leaned forward. "This dovetails with the work we've already done."

Cheryl set her iPad down. "I've saved the best part for last. It fits right in with Crowley's PTSD program."

Rita leaned forward beside Lorenzo, touching knees with him.

"In addition to lowering the brain frequency to relax the listener," Cheryl said, "by using specific frequencies, an individual can stimulate certain glands to produce desired hormones. Beta-endorphin has been modulated in studies using alpha-theta brain wave training and dopamine with binaural beats. Some have even succeeded in inducing lucid dreams. Alpha-theta brainwave training has also been used successfully for the treatment of addictions and recovery of repressed memories, but it can lead to false memories."

"Which might be useful for traumatized vets," Lorenzo said.

"Kind of like brainwashing, isn't it?" Rita asked.

Cheryl frowned. "Brain washing?"

"You know - implanting false memories and all."

Cheryl took off her glasses and rubbed her temples. "I don't know. It's a subjective experience. Some would argue that a pleasant false memory is better than a traumatic one."

CHAPTER SIXTEEN

In the months following their meeting with Robert Crowley, Jordan and the rest of Seal Team 0 continued racking up first and second place wins at lesser tournaments. One night after a particularly intense game, Jordan stretched out on his bed replaying scenarios in his mind. Seal Team 0 was playing in top form, and though it often went fast and down to the wire, part of him felt bored with all of it, which made him wonder what was happening with Crowley.

He opened his eyes and looked up at what he called his "wall of shame", shelves of trophies, posters, swag from sponsors, and other awards and felt a strong urge to stretch outside of his boundaries.

He hoped that Crowley's promises would make that happen, but since their meeting at his fancy offices, nothing more had happened and all the buzz about Morpheus and Pandora that the guys jabbered about had died down. He thought about calling Todd to ask if he heard anything new when his cell rang, displaying the name Wesley Schulz. Jordan hit the phone icon and put it on speaker. "Wuddup Wesley?"

"Hey Jordy, good job with the headshots in that last series we just did."

"Thanks! We got a good roll going. I hope it lasts. Everyone's been playing their A game."

Jordan heard the sound of gurgling water from Wesley's bong. "It does help kill the time," Wesley said after a delay followed by his exhale, "but I'm getting pretty antsy. This waiting around shit is killing me. You heard anything else about Crowley?"

"I was just thinking about that when you called."

"What the fuck is taking so long? He was so pumped up about it and even gave us a bad ass bonus. Now a lot of time has passed and nothing's happened. I'm starting to wonder if anything is ever going to happen."

"The last time I talked to Todd," Jordan said. "He told me that Crowley's lab monkeys were working on some newer features that would make us have a better experience and asked that we stay patient and keep kicking ass in the tournaments the way we have been. He's still fully sponsoring us there."

"Good point."

"He also hinted that they're working on what he called recreational dreams."

"Maybe a taste of Pandora's box like we had in Paris after winning ESports World Cup Finals?"

They both broke out laughing.

"He hinted at something like that," Jordan said, "but he wasn't clear. Something about added incentives and rewards. He also said that they wanted to thoroughly test it before they let us play with it."

"That makes sense. I've been thinking about what a fully immersive gaming experience might be like, and I can't help thinking that it's too good to be true, and if it's too good to be true -- if you want to know the truth, it scares me."

"What's there to be scared about? It will only be a dream. Nothing real. You can wake up out of it."

"What does it mean to be fully immersive?" Wesley said. "If I get shot, blown up, or hurt, will it really hurt? What if I die in a dream? No matter what Crowley told us, I heard some scary stories about DreamLand."

"The way I understand it, if something like that happens, you wake up from the dream and come out of battle the same way you come out of it in a game. Besides, they're not using the same computer. It's newer technology. What he calls sleek and sexy second generation hardware, software, and firmware."

"As long as we don't get lost in Pandora's box, huh?"

They chuckled, then Jordan said. "If we ever did get lost in it, don't forget -- we'll always have hope."

"What did you say, Jordan? We'll always have dope?"

Wesley's bong water gurgled again.

CHAPTER SEVENTEEN

R ita and Cheryl hovered over Hodge inside the thick glass walls of the octagon shaped ICU that Rita thought of as the queen's chamber in a giant hive. With Hodge at the center of it all, she found it ironic in more ways than one. The phrase "the inmates are running the asylum" ran through her head.

A large observation theater encircled the eight walls, providing a view of the proceedings from multiple angles, enhanced by strategically placed cameras, providing added detail and zoom capability. Larger monitors covered the outer walls of the observation area, providing multiple perspectives and three fully loaded workstations sat in the largest front observation platform.

Robert Crowley hovered close to the glass to the left of the front, his eyes darting from Cheryl and Rita to monitor after monitor, assessing every detail. Jack Scanlon sat at the console to the left, nearest Crowley, his slender fingers intertwined behind his head, the concentration in his deep-set brown eyes on his monitor and keyboard exaggerated by his bushy black eyebrows. Lorenzo sat at the console to the right, his contrasting full head of black hair bent down, his dark eyes focused on his screen. Both men wore headsets.

Rita looked down at Hodge's perpetually changing expressions as he moaned and mumbled as though sensing their presence, but he was somewhere else judging by the way his eyes twitched and his body shuddered.

She held the prototype dream hood close to the fatty mass of Hodge's brain surrounded by sterile paper as Cheryl, blue eyes focused behind her horn-rimmed glasses, deftly manipulated wires and probes, periodically checking a schematic display before snapping each tiny connector in place on the dream hood with the micromanipulator while observing her actions on a large magnified display. Each time she made a connection, Jack's voice came through speakers in the ICU, stating, "Circuit closed," followed by a bright colored red dot that lit up the relevant point on the schematic.

After rechecking her connections, Cheryl fine-tuned the wires and tubes in Hodge's brain and rechecked the monitors. With Rita's help, she gently placed the new hood over Hodge's skull and secured the window over his face, once more sealing him in his enclosure.

"Okay." Cheryl stepped back. "We're done here. I'm going out to the console to observe the process. Even though it's monitored in every way possible, I'd like you to stay here by his side as an added precaution against the rare possibility that something goes wrong."

"Sure."

"Thank you. Let's keep our fingers crossed." She held up both hands showing crossed fingers, then took off her mask and gloves and started for the door. "I'll walk us through it over the intercom and headsets so we're all on the same page." She stopped and turned back, her eyes meeting Rita's. "I hope and pray that some healing comes from this. You and I have seen the dark side of what can happen. I'm hoping this time that it takes us to the light."

"That makes two of us," Rita said. "I'm still having nightmares from the dark."

"You're not alone there." Cheryl studied her a moment. "I have my own nightmares. Let's see if we can do something to make poor Hodge's a little brighter. Who knows? It might help us get over our own."

Cheryl went out and talked with Crowley before taking her place at the center console between Jack and Lorenzo where she tapped at the keyboard and clicked the mouse until Hodge's vital signs, fMRI, PET and other relevant images filled the main screens of the observation deck, then she put on a headset and adjusted the mouthpiece. A moment later her voice came over the ICU speakers.

"For the audio and video records, this is the first trial of the hybrid command and control chip in a direct human machine interface. Our subject is Hodge Michaels, forty two years of age, with extensive brain damage. Our intervention will proceed in two phases. Phase one, overseen by Jack Scanlon will implement the hard wired neural stimulations for tremor control followed by multi-functional fiber testing, with stimulated and recorded neural behaviors through electrical, optical, and fluidic means to precisely map the responses of different brain regions."

"All systems are locked and loaded here," Jack said. "I'll activate each circuit and communication pathway with miniscule signal levels and gradually raise them to our pre-calculated optimal levels."

"If we find stability with phase one," Cheryl continued, "we'll move to phase two which will be implemented by Lorenzo Vargas. Though still under the control of the command and control chip, this dreaming content will be delivered through non-invasive magnetoresonators based on the original design created by PermDream Labs. This new advanced network has been fine tuned to deliver focused signals to specifically targeted parts of the brain, which we hope will produce a more vivid experience."

Cheryl looked over at Crowley, then to Lorenzo before nodding to Jack who clicked his mouse. One by one the red dots lighting the schematic dimmed and turned gray, then slowly lit up to bright green.

Rita continued looking back and forth from the displays to Hodge. With each green light, he grew calmer in subtle ways, then she saw his tremors diminish until his body dropped into motionless repose. Fearing he may have died, she looked up at the screens. All of his vital signs looked subdued except his brainwave activity which looked erratic, but with fewer spikes and less amplitude. The large display of multicolored fMRI and PET images shifted, showing heightened brain activity and blood flows.

"Everything is under C and C control." Jack leaned back and rubbed his hands together. "And all of our telemetry is successfully being transmitted wirelessly through the chip and the dreaming hood."

"Let's give him a few minutes to make sure he's stabilized before moving forward with phase two," Cheryl said. "If this settles out the way I hope, we can look into tapering off his medications and maybe bringing him more awareness of his surroundings."

Hodge remained immobile, but his face appeared lost in its own private struggle, as if all his tension, uneasiness, and bodily discomfort had gone into his face.

Lorenzo tapped a few keys. "I'll bring up the audio and video imagery that we'll be transmitting through Jack's chip and the hood's magnetoresonators. Whenever you give the signal, Cheryl, I'll start the sequence with the lowest detectable signal strengths like we discussed, and gradually increase them to optimum."

Rita glanced at the monitors, mentally checking off critical functions, troubled only by the erratic brainwaves and heightened activity of the fMRI. Hodge remained motionless, but a multitude of unpleasant emotions appeared to pass over his features at high speed like rapidly gathering storm clouds. She hoped Cheryl's theory about the dreaming content calming things turned out to be true. She wasn't prepared for a thunderstorm.

Her apprehension rose until Cheryl's voice broke the rising tension.

"Okay Lorenzo, let's see if your magic mojo can help bring things into some kind of stasis."

"Coming up on monitor six," he said.

At first came barely audible white noise, then the sound of waves crashing on the beach, followed by a dim image of waves that brightened along with rising music and other sounds that intermingled into an audio and video collage that felt like an otherworldly lullaby.

She gasped when Hodge's eyes shot open and he looked at her without seeing. His blank stare showed no sign of intelligence. The meditative music and imagery rose into a gentle crescendo full of running water and waves along with tribal chants, digeridoos, flutes and stringed instruments, then Hodge's eyes snapped shut, signaling his exit to some other realm. He dropped into a steady state of rhythmic REM.

His face became calm like a still pond with a flat, mirror-like expressionless surface. His brainwaves and heightened fMRI and PET activity followed suit, reflecting tranquility not only in his physical form, but in every indicator that was displayed.

Bliss seemed to pervade everything.

Lights are on, but nobody's home, Rita thought as chills cascaded over her. It was the only time she had seen Hodge with his eyes open since the wild-eyed panic of his injury. Seeing into his emptiness struck at the core of her soul. She looked to the others who no doubt had seen the same thing on the monitors. Everyone looked back at her wide-eyed, except Crowley, whose eyes narrowed.

CHAPTER EIGHTEEN

Jordan couldn't stop himself from smiling when the elevator doors opened to the panorama of San Diego, Coronado Island, and beyond.

"I just love this view," Todd said, voicing Jordan's feelings.

Crowley's beautiful blonde receptionist graced them with her one hundred watt smile from behind her desk. "Seal Team 0!" She stood. "My favorite warriors! Welcome back to Pandora Partnerships. Can I get you anything? Soda? Coffee? Red Bull? Water?"

"I'll take a water," Jordan said.

Todd looked around at the others who all nodded. "Waters all around," he said.

She pushed open the door leading through the short hallway to the conference room where the wall of screens showed ongoing video game competitions. "Have a seat," she said. "Mr. Crowley will be with you in a minute."

They took the same chairs as before, lining the conference table facing the window. The secretary came back depositing a cold bottle of water in front of each of them and left the room saying, "He's on his way."

Crowley breezed in a few minutes later looking impeccable in his Navy blue suit, red tie, and spit-shined shoes. The attention he paid to his appearance made Jordan wonder if he owned any other clothes, but his dress always looked fresh, crisp, and new. He probably had a closetful of the same outfit. The uniformity of his attire made Jordan think military. Maybe retired.

"Welcome back to Pandora Partnerships," Crowley said, taking a seat across from them. "I'm sorry this is taking so long."

"We were beginning to wonder if it's real." Carl's long red-hair was tied back in a ponytail, covered by a San Diego Padres baseball cap worn backward. His wild eyes held a challenge.

"It's been close to six months," John's eyes narrowed beneath his mop of wild, curly blond hair.

Crowley nodded. "Don't worry. It's happening. Be patient." He lowered his voice. "This project is much bigger than you realize and the government, because of its history and all of the politics around the DreamLand fiasco is more involved than we'd like them to be, which puts a damper on how fast we can move forward, but they're taking all the extra measures and time to insure your safety." He lowered his voice, speaking conspiratorially. "And if you want to know the truth, I'd rather see the delays than have any hint of problems for you guys."

"We appreciate that," Todd said.

Wesley leaned in, putting his elbows on the table. "Why do I get the feeling that there's more to what you are telling us?"

Terry squirmed in his chair. "Does it have anything to do with the government crawling up our asses?"

"Don't worry about the government background check stuff," Crowley said. "Like I told you before, it's just a formality to keep us inside federal guidelines."

"Why can't they mind their own business?" Wesley said.

"It is kind of their business," Crowley answered. "They pushed their way into this more than we'd like, but they're the ones who licensed the technology to us, so when you get down to brass tacks, we're wrapped up in a partnership deal with them."

"So who are we working for?" Jordan asked. "Pandora Partnerships, or Uncle Sam?"

"Technically, you work for Pandora Partnerships, but you can think of yourselves as government contractors because Pandora is a government contractor and you are representatives of Pandora..."

"We're working for the feds?" John blurted.

"Don't think of it like that. What's at issue here is the research and development lab on government property, so it's more a matter of security."

Terry's round face lit up like a jack o'lantern. "We're working for the government? Like spies?"

"Kind of like that, but you'll never be in danger. In the end, this is all being done for your safety. We intend to keep things under wraps until our technology is more developed. The government wants to make sure that it is not misused by the wrong people the way it was with DreamLand."

Jordan nodded in agreement, though he didn't feel like he was. He understood secrecy when it came to proprietary technologies and corporate spies, and he understood the government's concern for safety, especially after what happened with DreamLand. What didn't sit right with him was the way Crowley referred to the project being "much bigger than they realized". Something about his words and demeanor didn't match, and though he had answers for everything, Jordan couldn't help but feel like there might be some kind of double talk.

He looked around at the others. With the exception of Terry, who still looked excited at the prospect of being a secret government spy, none of the rest of his team seemed convinced by Crowley's story.

CHAPTER NINETEEN

Rita fingered the tiny silver angel that hung from her neck and looked around the Pandora Project conference room. Lorenzo sat beside her. Across from them sat Jack Scanlon and beside him Cheryl, looking more animated than Rita had seen her in some time as she adjusted her glasses and fingered her iPad. A large flat screen at the end of the conference table showed videos, graphs, and readouts from the ICU. Crowley sat at the far end of the table away from the others, hands folded in his lap, listening.

"As you can see," Cheryl said, cycling through images, "Jack's C and C chip has done a superb job monitoring and administering to Hodge's needs." She patted Jack on the shoulder and clicked on one of the smaller displays filling the big screen. Hodge's vital signs, brainwaves, and other monitored functions filled it and all showed him resting peacefully. "In the past few weeks we disconnected all of the external support equipment and I am happy to report that between Jack's chip and our new computer, the entire support system is self-contained."

Crowley listened closely, giving Cheryl his full attention. "I have to say that I'm impressed with what I witnessed. Good job Doctor Martin." He looked to each of them. "Good job to all of you." He levelled his gaze at Cheryl again and bowed his head. "You have my respect."

Jack and Lorenzo gave barely perceptible nods and the usually stoic Cheryl fumbled with her iPad. Her cheeks had flushed. Rita thought it was cute and stifled a grin. No doubt about it. Cheryl had the hots for Crowley.

"As I understand it," Crowley continued, "all of the information from the C and C chip's monitoring and drug delivery systems are not only recorded and analyzed, but they're input into Mr. Vargas's digital profile in a continuous update."

"Hundreds of times a second." Jack said.

"You described these profiles as similar to voice recognition software that learns and updates with each use and video game profiles that keep player levels and scores."

"That's correct," Lorenzo said. "It creates a feedback loop between the profile and telemetry from the subject through Jack's C and C chip with the profile feedback altering the chip's input and output to strengthen positive behaviors as a learning tool with an eye toward performance enhancement."

Crowley's eyebrows raised. "Directed by the profile?"

"Yes, but dependent on the way the profile is programmed," Lorenzo said. "In our case it's directed toward faster and more efficient decision making under high stress conditions. We're breaking new ground here. Actually Cheryl's been breaking new ground with some of her own performance enhancing voodoo. It has tremendous potential for learning."

Crowley leaned forward, eyes brightening. "Fascinating Doctor Martin. Voodoo?"

Cheryl's eyelashes fluttered behind her big glasses, exaggerating her expression. "Lorenzo is too modest. He's been working closely with me, as has Jack and Rita. Everyone deserves credit."

"Don't listen to her," Jack said, waving his hand. "She's the brainiac leading the charge here."

Cheryl flushed more and sighed, then tapped her iPad, replacing Hodge's vitals with a new set of waveforms. "We're working on implementing sound-induced and visually based brain synchronization into Lorenzo's scenarios to enhance learning ability. Induced alpha brain waves have the ability to enable subjects to assimilate more information with greater long-term retention. Additionally the presence of theta patterns is associated with increased receptivity for learning and decreased filtering by the left hemisphere. Biofeedback facilitates healthy individuals in learning to increase specific components of their EEG activity and facilitate a working memory task, and to a lesser extent focused attention."

She tapped her iPad and brought up a diagram showing a cross-section of the brain. Pointing with a small laser, she showed different parts as she talked.

"The two brain regions that are key to learning are the hippocampus and the prefrontal cortex. They use two different frequencies to communicate as the brain learns to associate unrelated objects." She pointed from the brain to a graph of waveforms. "Whenever the brain correctly identifies the objects, the waves oscillate at a higher frequency called beta, around nine to sixteen hertz. When incorrect, they oscillate in the theta range, around two to six hertz."

Crowley rubbed his chin thoughtfully. "Enhanced learning." He paused, then, "So we're building a profile for Hodge Michaels, but he's only getting your repeating dream that is passive and requires no interaction. Can we use this technology to train Hodge into getting better?"

"No!" Rita blurted. "Let him have his peace."

"Besides," Lorenzo said. "We need someone who is fully functional to effectively utilize all of the device's capabilities."

"I'm working on that," Crowley said.

CHAPTER TWENTY

J ordan felt like a rock star when the stretch limo pulled up in front of his parent's house and a little embarrassed when his mom came out snapping pictures of him getting in, but her happiness, excitement, and pride made him happy for her. He looked around seeing the neighbors watching and couldn't stop himself from smiling when he tossed his luggage into the trunk and climbed in to the luxury interior with its stocked bar, fancy lighting, tinted windows, and flat screen. He had packed as instructed for an extended stay in what Crowley called an "off season dream team boot camp".

Wesley, Carl, Terry, and John greeted him with raised bottles from their spots on the wrap around bench seat. Wesley took up the back, his big shoulders filling up the entire back seat. John and Carl sat beside him across from Terry.

"Jesus, are you knuckleheads drinking already?" Jordan said, sliding into the spot beside cherub faced Terry.

"Relax," John said, his blue eyes widening in exaggerated shock under his mop of curly blond hair. He turned his bottle face out so Jordan could see the label. "It's Perrier. We're just living large."

Carl handed him a bottle as the limo pulled away.

Jordan nodded and took it. "Where's Todd?"

As if in answer to his question, Wesley's cell phone announced the arrival of a text with the sound of gun fire. He tapped the screen and read, then looked up from under his tousled black hair with dark narrowed eyes. "He's not coming."

Everyone else's cell phones sounded off, their alerts ranging from the Star Wars theme to riffs from Tool.

Jordan looked at his phone and saw the text from Todd. "Why not?"

"Crowley said there was some kind of a hitch with his security clearance," Wesley said.

"Sounds like bullshit to me," Terry said beside Jordan.

"I wonder why Todd didn't tell us?"

"He just did," Carl said.

The others held up their phones.

"It was some kind of last minute cluster fuck." Wesley held up his cell phone. "His text says that he wishes he was here, but can't come, and for everyone not to worry. Aside from the security clearance issue, Crowley said he was, get this, 'non-essential personnel', meaning he's not an actual team player, so he will not be doing any of the testing and there is no need for him to be there."

Terry took a long sip from his bottle and belched.

Carl took off his Padres cap and ran his fingers through his red hair all the way through to his ponytail, then his wild eyes zeroed in on Terry. "That's the most intelligent thing I've heard you say all day, my pudgy little friend."

"That's what I think about Todd not being here," Terry shot back.

"I agree," Jordan said. "It doesn't feel right without him. I'll be curious to see what Crowley says."

"That makes two of us," Wesley said.

"That makes all of us," John added.

The group grew quiet when the limo pulled onto the freeway and headed South on I-805, heading for the Mexican border. While everyone busied themselves with their cell phones, Jordan looked out the window, feeling an odd mixture of excitement tinged with fear.

Two thoughts spun around in his head. Crowley's cryptic comments about this being a lot bigger than they realized and Todd's last minute absence at this initial test. Though Crowley always had answers, Jordan had the nagging feeling that he wasn't telling them everything. Sure, Crowley gave them whatever they wanted and more, but even that bothered him.

He closed his eyes and tried to lose himself in images, thoughts, and moments from his magical night with Brittany, then he opened them thinking that it was all too good to be true which bothered him more than anything.

CHAPTER TWENTY ONE

R ita strained to listen, first hearing white noise growing into the sound of waves crashing on the beach, followed by a dim image of waves that brightened with rising music that intermingled into an audio and video collage that felt like a distorted lullaby.

Cheryl stood beside her, once more examining Hodge in the claustrophobic ICU. Rita's her heart raced at the sight of Hodge, who moaned and mumbled. His eyes darted in frenzied REM and he shuddered with seizures. Every display showed erratic EKG, pulse, and respiration. She glanced at Cheryl whose brow was knitted in perplexity.

What could have went wrong?

Hodge's eyes shot open, his blank stare showing no intelligence, then the music and imagery rose to a cacophony that made Rita nauseous. Hodge's eyes grew larger and his mouth opened wider. She thought it was his tongue flopping around until the wet snout of a rat popped out from between his lips and wriggled free. She stumbled back, breathless. Hodge's stomach undulated with moving lumps before splitting open, releasing a wave of rats that filled his enclosure until they overflowed onto the floor, scurrying straight for Cheryl and Rita.

Rita screamed without sound and hurtled down through a maelstrom of darkness, plunging into frigid water as if sucked into a huge drain. She flailed, kicking and clawing while something wet and hairy brushed her cheek.

Looking up, she saw hordes of rats tumbling off a jagged cliff, screeching as they hit the water, floating on swells, tiny legs and long tails dangling, scratching at her. One clawed at her hair and another scrambled onto her head. She grabbed its cold, slippery tail and threw it, then another furry head surfaced in front of her, eyes glinting, yellow teeth clicking, jaws working. The roiling water sucked her under again until she plunged deeper, screaming until something shook her.

"Rita! Wake up!"

Lorenzo.

Her eyes flew open and she looked up into his dark concerned eyes. She felt cold and clammy and struggled for air.

Lorenzo.

"It's okay, honey," he said softly. "I'm here." He smiled, showing his perfect teeth, then he pulled her into his arms. His warmth, gentle touch and familiar smell dispersed her fears. She pushed herself into his muscular chest and held on tight, anchoring herself in his grounding presence.

"I don't know what I'd do without you," she whispered. "You are my rock."

He stroked her hair making her feel like a little girl, safe in his arms. "I'll always be here for you as long as I'm alive and breathing and if it's possible, I'll be with you even after that."

She found herself smiling into his chest at his words which calmed her breathing and brought her racing heart back. "Will these nightmares ever end?"

"They've haunted you ever since DreamLand imploded. We should look into getting you some help."

"They've gotten a lot worse since coming back. I can't go on like this. It's too much."

She snuggled closer, resting her head on his shoulder and chest and they stayed quiet for awhile until Lorenzo broke the silence.

"In the short term, the best thing I can think of is aversion therapy to keep your mind off of your troubles," he said.

"Aversion therapy? What do you mean by that?"

He leaned into her and planted his lips on hers, his tongue finding hers in a dance that led to passionate lovemaking. She lost herself in the throes of his ministrations until she forgot about her nightmares -- for the moment.

CHAPTER TWENTY TWO

Jordan looked out the limo window in silence as they drove along a section of the San Ysidro border fence the length of a few football fields that enclosed a heavily guarded entrance. Two guard towers stood at each end and a high chain link fence topped with razor wire surrounded everything, partially obscuring a massive silvered dome surrounded by smaller ones.

"Holy shit!" Wesley said under his breath. "Dream team boot camp? You gotta be shitting me."

"Fucking dream team prison," Carl said.

John pointed. "Look at the size of that thing!"

They turned in and went through the gate, down a long driveway bordered by fence and razor wire until they pulled into a circular driveway. Jordan looked up at the mirrored dome entrance as he climbed out of the limo. The metal letters arranged in an arch over the door caught his attention.

DEDICATED TO SERVING THOSE WHO HAVE SERVED US

John climbed out behind him and pointed to it. "What the fuck is that?"

Jordan shook his head, "I don't know what to make of it, but I'll tell you this, this is an awful lot of security for a frigging computer game."

"It must have something to do with all the Dreamland bullshit," Wesley said from behind them. "It was a total clusterfuck with all the people that died here when things went wrong."

"And it created a lot of problems with the Mexican government," Carl added.

"Kinda scary." Terry looked around. "It's so fucking big!"

John slapped him on the back. "Don't be a little pussy, butterball. You're the scariest looking thing here."

The front glass doors whooshed open and Crowley strode out, looking immaculate in his standard blazer, tie, and gleaming shoes. "Welcome!" He said. "Welcome to the Pandora Project."

Jordan couldn't help but notice the addition of an American flag pin on Crowley's lapel. Its appearance along with the size and scope of everything made him uneasy. He's been bullshitting us, Jordan thought. He's not some happy go lucky game loving sponsor. He's a fed. That's what the flag on his lapel is for. Now he knew what Crowley meant by *This whole thing is a lot bigger than you realize.*

Crowley shook everyone's hand vigorously. "I can't tell you how excited I am that you're here."

"How come Todd isn't here?" Carl said.

"There was a problem with his security clearance," Crowley said, waving off the question. "I wouldn't worry about it. I'm sure it's just a technicality. They'll figure it out. Besides, he's not an active member of Seal Team 0, so his presence isn't needed."

"But he's our manager," Terry said. "It doesn't feel right without him. If you ask me, he'd want to see all of this"

"And he will when the time is right." Crowley put his arm around Terry and ushered them through the entrance into an atrium lobby. Jordan looked up at the glass wall of a tower looming five stories above, then around the rest of the atrium. Video cameras were everywhere.

Crowley led them through an expanding labyrinth into an area where red velvet ropes arrayed out from five soaring archways. Metal reinforced security doors had facial recognition scanners at the entrance to each and an armed guard stood at the center. A backlit sign with bright red letters above each door stated:

RESTRICTED ACCESS

Crowley led them to an elevator that dropped them several stories below to a curved subterranean corridor.

Wesley let out a long whistle when the elevator doors whispered open. "Talk about the fucking belly of the beast."

A short way down the hall brought them to another vault-like door with an armed sentry guarding it. Crowley leaned in to the facial recognition scanner, unlocking the door with a resounding click.

CHAPTER TWENTY THREE

Rita sat at one of four consoles beside Lorenzo, Jack, and Cheryl, facing a large window that allowed them to observe the Dream Lab where a row of five open human-sized, enclosures that looked like space capsules faced the mirrored one-way glass. Each capsule tilted back at an angle, displaying a contoured, padded recliner, reminding her of DreamLand. Though open at the front, she felt butterflies in her stomach at the sight of them.

She studied the segmented grid on the screen in front of her, cycling through each one, bringing it to the forefront, first checking the zoom and panning functions of five high resolution cameras that recorded the minute nuances of their test subject's facial expressions. Flat-lined heart rates, respiration, perspiration, body temperature, brain wave and blood pressure readouts flickered below each display.

Rita felt an added sense of uneasiness and lack of confidence in her medical abilities. God forbid, if something happened that required her intervention. She closed her eyes and fingered the angel at her neck, silently praying that nothing would go wrong and that someone like Morgan would come to relieve her of her burden. Crowley said he was working on it, but she had her doubts. Morgan's expertise had been highly specialized.

As if reading her mind, Lorenzo's hand covered hers. She opened her eyes to his compassionate look, the one he only gave to her. His gentle touch and loving gaze brought her comfort. He graced her with his perfect smile. "Don't worry yourself, love," he said in a low voice. "I'm right here." He gave her hand a tender squeeze and kissed her cheek.

She looked down the line at Jack, who busied himself at his keyboard, nodding and mumbling to himself, then at Cheryl, who looked a little haggard and distracted. She clicked and moved her mouse a few times, then stopped and looked over her monitor, appearing to stare off into space.

"You okay, Cheryl?" Rita asked.

She shook her head and looked over at Rita, blinking behind her glasses like an owl. "Just a little preoccupied, that's all. I didn't sleep very well last night."

"Nightmares?"

Cheryl's eyes grew wide. "How did..." She caught herself. "You too?"

Rita nodded.

Jack looked sideways at Cheryl. "You want to talk about it?"

"No!" She snapped.

Rita and Lorenzo looked at each other, sharing thoughts with their expressions.

"You don't have to bite my head off!" Jack retorted. "I'm only trying to help."

Cheryl sighed. "I'm sorry Jack, I didn't mean to snap at you. I'm a little edgy."

He waved his hand. "Don't worry about it. I understand." He patted her on the shoulder.

"If you're open to it later," Rita said, "Maybe we can compare notes."

Cheryl pursed her lips and gave a slow nod. "That might be a good idea. I'll let you know."

The door to the pod-lined Dream Lab clicked open and Crowley entered, followed by five young men who looked around, taking it all in, wide-eyed and curious.

"Here comes our guinea pigs," Jack said.

Cheryl looked up and shook her head. "They're kids."

Crowley directed each one to a pod and had them stand in front of it, then turned toward the window. "Allow me to introduce the world class, world champion, Seal Team Zero."

Starting at the first pod, he moved down the line, resting a hand on each team member's shoulder as he introduced them.

"In the first spot we have Jordan Gilbert, better known as n0thing. He's Seal Team Zero's In Game Leader."

A short, slight of build, blue-eyed young man with blond hair, nodded.

"In the number two spot we have Wesley Schulz, who goes by Renegade."

The tallest of the bunch stood straight and saluted. He had unruly black hair, broad shoulders, and a mischievous glint in his eye, accented by a sheepish grin.

"At three we have Carl Peterson, whose handle is Sureshot."

The rail thin young man nodded with a goofy grin that contrasted his wild eyes. His long red hair was tied back in a ponytail and he wore a Padres ball cap backwards on his head.

"At number four we have John Henry, who goes by Striker."

Slightly taller than Jordan, this one seemed like an electric current moved through him. You could see it in his eyes when he snapped a short, jerky salute. His unkempt curly blond hair looked like it had never been combed.

"And last but not least, we have Terry Hinchliffe, known as Killjoy."

Short, squat, and chubby cheeked, this one really did look like a kid. The shortest member of the team gave them a small wave of the hand.

"Who are you talking to?" Sureshot said. "It looks like we're talking to ourselves in the mirror."

"That's the most intelligent conversation you're ever going to get," Renegade quipped.

Striker guffawed and the rest of the team broke into chuckles and grins.

Crowley smiled and shook his head, then looked to the window and waved Rita and the others in.

CHAPTER TWENTY FOUR

Jordan felt like his heart skipped a beat when the first woman came through the door. Dark-haired and petite, her soft, brown eyes drew him in. He could tell from her demeanor that she had been through a lot. A tiny silver winged angel hung from a delicate silver chain on her neck, accented by silver hoop earrings. Beautiful, he thought. She reminds me of Penélope Cruz, the Spanish actress. He felt himself falling in love until he spotted the ring on her finger.

Close behind her came a guy that looked like a younger Antonio Banderas. Tall, he had a solid build, classic Spanish-Italian good looks, black hair, and piercing, dark eyes. Not someone to mess with. They had to be together. Lucky guy! He mentally nicknamed them Antonio and Penélope.

An older guy with a little pot belly followed Antonio. Slender, he had a receding hairline and bushy black eyebrows that seemed to intensify his deep-set brown eyes. I must be watching too many movies, Jordan thought. He looks like Jack Nicholson.

The last one through the door was a middle-aged woman with long strawberry-blonde hair pulled back in a bun. Her pale blue eyes looked distant behind horn-rimmed glasses. She seemed no nonsense. Jordan thought that if she lightened up and literally let her hair down, she could be pretty good looking for an older woman. He puzzled over what actress she reminded him of, and thought of the older lady from Terms of Endearment, one of his mom's favorite movies. Shirley Maclaine. Come to think of it, Jack Nicholson had been in that movie too.

"Gentleman," Crowley said, ushering them in. "Allow me to introduce the talented and amazing brains behind Pandora. First, I'd like to introduce Rita Cariño, our chief medical specialist."

She smiled. When she shook hands with Jordan, her eyes met his, making him feel giddy and tongue-tied. He could barely get out, "Pleased to meet you."

Her gaze lingered on him for a moment, then she moved down the line shaking each team member's hand in turn.

"Our top video programmer and master dreamweaver, Lorenzo Vargas," Crowley continued.

Lorenzo's handshake felt firm, and his eyes sincere.

"Jack Scanlon, our genius hardware and microprocessor guru."

"Pleased to meet ya, kid," Jack shook Jordan's hand vigorously.

"And doctor Cheryl Martin, our resident top notch neuroscientist."

Cheryl took Jordan's hand in both of hers and squeezed gently. "It's great to have you on board. We look forward to working with you."

"Why don't you guys take a seat in the dream cradles," Crowley said, "and get a feel for them while we brief you on what to expect, then we'll answer questions."

Jordan settled into the cradle along with the others. The chair's padding formed to his body, relaxing everything. Jeez, he thought, I could almost go to sleep right now. This won't be hard to take.

Crowley nodded, crossing his arms with a satisfied expression. "Cheryl, can you fill everyone in with a little show and tell?"

"Sure." Doctor Martin grabbed something from behind Terry's dream cradle and stood in front of the team where everyone could see her like a stewardess giving a safety lecture. She held up a light-weight silk hood with a Velcro strap and a USB port on its side, showing off the circuitry stitched across its surface, then she pointed to Jack Scanlon. "This is mostly the brainchild of Mr. Scanlon."

"Cheryl had a lot of input on the design," Jack said. "She deserves half the credit."

Cheryl smiled, nodded, and continued. "Aside from the dreaming telemetry, this unit has a high speed transceiver that allows us to monitor your respiration, heart rate, sweat, brain wave patterns, with room for other physiological functions that might come into play. Rita will be watching these closely."

"So you have nothing to worry about," Crowley added. "We'll be keeping a very close eye on you."

"Has it been tested on anyone before?" Wesley asked.

"We have one subject who has extended dream time with this unit and everything has gone smoothly."

John sat up in his cradle. "What happens when we put it on and you turn on the juice?"

"At the onset, you'll find yourself fading," Cheryl said. "Though it happens in a very short period of time, it will feel longer, like you are drifting off to sleep, then literally in a few blinks of the eye, you will find yourself immersed in the dreaming scenario."

"Are you sure this is safe?" Wesley said. "I heard some pretty weird stories about DreamLand."

Rita and Cheryl looked at each other, exchanging an uncomfortable glance.

"What happens if I get killed in the dream?" Terry said before Cheryl could respond. "I heard that if you get killed in a dream you really die."

"Yeah, what if we get hurt in the dream?" Carl added. "Will we feel it?"

Crowley stepped in, holding up a hand. "Though this is based on the same technology that DreamLand was based on, this is a brand new, isolated system that has no connection to the old one and no connection to the outside world. In fact it's top secret. That's why you had to go through all that you did. You can't get hurt. These are only dreams. They are not real."

Jordan sat up in his cradle, leaned out and looked down the line at his teammates. The rest of them were also sitting up. They didn't look convinced.

"Should you feel threatened or uncomfortable in any way," Lorenzo said, "the escape words are mama, or mommy. Speak either one and you'll pop awake feeling rested and refreshed."

John leaned further out of his cradle and looked at Terry. "Who's going to pussy out first and call for Momma?"

"Hey, show a little respect to the ladies here John!" Jordan said.

Cheryl and Jack looked at each other and Jack grinned.

John's eyes widened. "I was only…"

"Jordan's right," Wesley said. "Show a little class will ya. Put a cork in it and watch your mouth."

John hung his head. "Sorry, I got a little carried away."

Rita shook her head. "No offense taken. Forget about it." She looked over at Jordan. "But thank you for being a gentleman."

Jordan felt his face grow hot and looked away.

"So what's this dream going to be like?" Carl said. "What can we expect? Are we each going to have our own dream?"

"You're all going to have the same dream based on your winning scenario," Lorenzo said. "Mister Crowley supplied us with the video and we added our own enhancements."

Carl's brow furrowed. "We'll be in each other's dreams?"

"That's what we're hoping for," Lorenzo answered, "but we're not sure. It's never been done this way before. That's part of our test. Needless to say, if we're successful, you'll be making history."

Terry's eyes grew wide like a little kid who just opened his longed for Christmas present. "Wow, how fu - I mean how cool is that?"

"If you don't mind," Carl said. "Can you show us the rest of the starship bridge on the other side of that mirrored window? We're all geeks here and really want to see the whole operation."

Lorenzo's face lit up with a wide smile, showing off perfect teeth. "My pleasure." He held out a hand and led them all out a door.

Carl pushed ahead of the others and leaned in close, watching everything Lorenzo did with rapt attention.

"Hey Carl," Wesley said. "Can you get any closer? What are you trying to do, kiss him?"

Carl flipped him off and leaned in even closer.

Smiling, Lorenzo dropped into his seat at the console where he punched in his password and ran the team through a demonstration of how everything worked.

CHAPTER TWENTY FIVE

The group stayed quiet, letting everything sink in. Rita smiled again at Jordan and he smiled back, nodding, this time not looking away so quickly. He's shy, she thought, but he's assertive when he needs to be.

"If everyone's comfortable," Crowley said, "we can start dialing in the equipment. Any more questions?"

Crowley's "dream team" looked to each other silently questioning, but no one said anything. Rita felt the tension in the air and saw fear, excitement, and anticipation passing over their faces.

After being led back into the dream lab, Jordan leaned back in his chair and pointed his finger straight ahead. "Engage warp drive Number One. Let's see what's out there."

The others chuckled nervously and leaned back, following his lead. Rita couldn't help smiling herself.

Starting with Terry, Jack and Cheryl worked their way down the line putting hoods on everyone one by one, finishing with Jordan.

"We'll let you know when we're about to begin," Crowley said. "It'll take a few minutes to calibrate."

Rita went to her station at the observation console beside Lorenzo and put on her headset while Jack and Cheryl made last minute checks to the dreaming hoods. When they finished, Crowley put on a headset, pulled up a chair and sat off to the side, holding an iPad in his lap.

Cheryl and Jack joined Rita and Lorenzo at the console and put on their headsets while the members of Seal Team 0 settled back in their dream cradles.

"Let me do a sensor array check," Jack said, "then Cheryl can run through her telemetry. Once we're satisfied, Rita can follow through

108

with the team's vital sign readings. If they are all copacetic, we'll turn it over to you Lorenzo."

"We're locked and loaded here," Lorenzo said.

Jack cycled through a series of screens before nodding. "Looking good here. Cheryl?"

Cheryl did the same before looking over at Rita. "Good here."

Rita went through each team member's vitals checking heart rates, respiration, perspiration, body temperature, blood pressure and brain wave readouts, then she zoomed in on Terry's face, which looked flushed.

"Your vitals are a little on the high side, Terry," she said into her microphone. "You're a little excited, which is understandable. Take a few deep breaths and try to calm yourself."

Terry scrunched his eyes shut and started breathing in slow and deep.

"Remember, it's only a dream," Crowley added. "You can't get hurt."

Terry nodded.

"As a matter of fact," Rita said. "It's a good idea for all of you to do some slow, deep breathing. It will put your brainwaves into a relaxed, receptive state. Let's all breathe together. It will help everyone get in sync with each other."

She breathed in and out at a steady rate, setting the pace for the others. As the team fell into rhythm with her, she watched their brain waves stabilize, followed by their other vital signs. Terry's still ran a little higher than the others, but they had lowered considerably.

"Much better," she said in her best soothing voice. "Lorenzo, you can initiate the sequence at your discretion."

"Okay," Lorenzo said, keying his microphone. "The sequence is queued and we are initiating in five, four, three…"

CHAPTER TWENTY SIX

"Two, one..."

Jordan felt his body grow heavy at the sound of Lorenzo's final count of one, then he nodded off, feeling the sensation of falling into a void that shifted from utter darkness to white as though someone flicked a light switch on and off over and over again.

The heaviness left him and he came into awareness blinking, while pointing an M4 in front of him, advancing on the terrorist stronghold from their game winning scenario. His teammates flanked him.

Holy shit, he thought. This is working!

Everything was the way he remembered it, yet everything was different. The immediacy of it scared him. He felt the weight of the gun in his hands, the breeze against his skin, and the bitter smell of smoke in the air. Remembering the adage of pinching yourself in a dream, he did just that and it hurt, scaring him even more.

It's still only a dream, he reminded himself.

Sprinting toward the battle scarred fortress, he listened to the excited chatter of his teammates on his headset while reassessing the tactical details of their assault.

"Holy shit!" Wesley said.

"Un-fucking believable," John added.

"We're definitely not in Kansas anymore, Toto," Carl said, his voice tinged with fear.

"I'm scared shit," Terry whined. "I don't know if I can handle this. It's a little bit too real."

"Listen, you guys," Jordan said. "I'm a little spooked myself, but we've been here before and we know what we need to do. Let's show them what Seal Team Zero is made of."

"Fuckin ay right," John said a little too loud. "Let's kick ass and take names."

Feeling an odd sense of déjà vu, Jordan approached the looming wall at an angle and stayed close when he reached it, rubbing his hands and body against the stone, marveling at how real they felt, then he eased his way toward the splintered wooden doors that hung ajar beneath the stone arch over the entrance.

Stopping beside it, he motioned for his team to advance after him, Wesley and Carl on his right, and John and Terry close to his left, pressing themselves flat against the wall.

"You guys all agree that we're sharing the same dream?"

He looked to his left and right, seeing the others nodding agreement. Terry's eyes were wide with fear.

He looked each one of them in the eye as he spoke to drive his message home. "Once again, we've all been through this before, so we know what to do to come out on top."

"Let's do it!" Wesley said.

Jordan took a deep breath, then burst through the doors, gun blazing, his teammates coming in after him, firing away. Smoke and gun fire erupted from all sides and bullets peppered the wall around him. Smoke burned his eyes and he felt the sting from kicked up debris hitting him.

"Above you!" someone shouted through his headset.

Jordan rolled to the ground and came up under the cover of some stacked wooden packing crates firing at a black uniformed assailant scrambling along the walkways above. His teammates fanned out, each finding their own cover. Two of the enemy dropped to the ground and two more ran for an alcove. Jordan fired in their direction and tossed a flash grenade after them.

It exploded in a blinding flash, making his ears ring and leaving a thick white cloud drifting through the rubble. Squinting, he ran through the cover of the smoke while the others moved forward to an inner wall with fifty-five gallon drums stacked against it. Jordan clambered up over the barrels and leaped onto the wall.

A black figure came around a corner shooting at him and Jordan took him out with a head shot, firing from a prone position, feeling a little nausea when the man's head exploded in a realistic crimson shower of blood and guts, then he ran the length of the wall above his teammates to another gateway.

From his vantage point he saw his team approaching from outside and like before he spotted a terrorist diving behind barrels around the courtyard inside.

"Stand back from the doorway," he said into his headset. "I'm going to blow it open."

He crouched and fired off a series of bursts, picking off the hidden sniper before dropping a grenade that blasted the gate outward, allowing his teammates to storm the inner yard.

Jordan watched them fan out and clear the area before jumping down off the wall and following them into a dark passage. He stepped into the shadows of the tunnel amidst bursts of echoing gunfire, eyes watering and sneezing while listening to the shouts and warnings of his team through his headset.

"Watch out, sniper fire coming from above!"

"Two more attacking from the corner!"

"Shit! Killjoy is down. Repeat. Killjoy is down."

"Another one coming in from the side, I'm taking heavy…"

An explosion flashed down the tunnel, blasting Jordan in the face, making him stagger backward. Smoke burned his throat, causing him to cough and he could barely see. He hustled to catch up in the ringing aftermath of the blast.

"We lost Striker and Sureshot like before," Wesley said. "I have the defusal kit."

Jordan didn't bother to check his map. "That leaves you and me Wesley. We know how this is going to go. I'll be right there."

He sprinted down the tunnel and through the doorway at its end into a smoke-filled room strewn with bodies, collapsed walls, and rubble scattered across the floor. Across it, off to his right, Wesley motioned him forward to where he crouched beside a battered heavy steel door.

"The clock's ticking, so it's time to blitz," Wesley said.

Jordan nodded and they both stepped back. Wesley blew the door off its hinges with a grenade and charged into a flurry of gunfire, leaving Jordan's ears and body feeling battered all over. He counted to three, then dropped and rolled in through the door behind him blasting full auto, coming up behind a command console.

Bullets sprayed the wall above him, showering him with rubble and zinging off the console in front of and around him. Through the smoke he spotted Wesley lying prone behind another console to his right. In front of him, he saw a terrorist arming a C4 bomb. A sniper continued firing from above, keeping them pinned down.

"Cover me, I got this!" Wesley rolled out from behind his cover firing at the bomber while Jordan gave covering fire at the sniper, distracting him. The bomber buckled and dropped to the floor as the words, "Bomb has been planted," came to Jordan through his headset.

"Shit!" Wesley said. "Forty five seconds."

Jordan continued exchanging bursts with the sniper, keeping his attention away from Wesley, who was pinned down a few feet from the bomber.

"Twenty five seconds," Wesley said."

"You only need five," Jordan said. "I'm all out of flash grenades, but I have a smoke, just like before."

"Roger that."

Jordan fired a burst and tossed a smoke grenade at the sniper, following it up with another on the ground between him and Wesley, filling the room with smoke from both ends. Wesley dove for the C4 amidst a flurry of gunfire that lit up the smoke like lightning flashes in storm clouds. Jordan fired back at the sniper.

"Fifteen seconds."

Jordan couldn't hear anything for a few seconds, then he barely heard Wesley's voice. "Defusing in five, four, three, two..."

Flashing gunfire lit up the smoke filled room.

Jordan sprang forward into the haze, fumbling for the defuser while bullets sprayed around him. The countdown continued while he worked the keypad on the defuser.

"Five, four, three, two..."

He punched in the last button as everything lit up in a blinding flash and felt brief stinging as the sniper's bullets found him.

CHAPTER TWENTY SEVEN

Jordan popped up straight in his chair, eyes wide, while Jack and Cheryl hovered over poor little apple-cheeked Terry, who sobbed and blubbered in his cradle.

"There, there," Cheryl said with a tenderness Rita had never heard before. She slipped the dreaming hood off of his head and pulled the trembling Terry to her breast, gently stroking his head. "It's only a dream, honey. You're okay."

"Shake it off, kid," Jack said. "You're back in the real world. Nothing can hurt you here."

The rest of the team sat up, blinking and bewildered. Rita glanced at her console. Their vital signs had skyrocketed and their brain waves readings were all over the place.

The sight of it and the emotional energy pervading the room tore at her heart and made her stomach flip-flop. She had all she could do to keep from vomiting.

"Breathe in deep," she found herself saying into her microphone, drawing in deep breaths as much for herself as for the team.

Everyone literally looked shell-shocked except Crowley, who had a glint in his eye and a barely suppressed smile. Wesley looked shaken, Jordan had a blank expression, probably from shock, and Carl's eyes bugged out of his head, like he had just witnessed an accident.

Though he looked disconnected, John's maniacal look worried her more than the others. This one was an adrenaline junkie for sure. "What a rush that was," he half-whispered as his excitement came down a notch. He glanced sidelong at Jordan. "Bad ass!"

Jordan stared at him wide-eyed.

"Keep breathing in deep," Rita said, keeping up the rhythm. "It will help calm you."

Terry's breaths came in stuttering sobs that tore at her. She struggled to keep from crying herself. When Lorenzo put his arm around her and pulled her close, she relaxed into him.

Inside the Dream Lab, Cheryl and Jack helped Terry out of his dream cradle, reminding Rita of a similar scene with another chubby kid named Albert Moffitt, only the Moffitt kid was a little shit. There was a heartbreaking sweetness to this kid Terry. Cheryl put a mothering arm around him and guided him out of the room.

"I'm going to take him someplace to lie down for awhile," she said. "This was a little too much for him."

Crowley stood in front of the rest of the team with his arms crossed and his legs in a wide stance. "What about the rest of you warriors?"

The rest of the team exchanged glances, but no one said anything.

"You guys were amazing!" Crowley said, filling in the silence. "I've seen the best of them in action, and you guys are a cut above."

John brightened at this, but the expressions on Jordan, Carl, and Wesley's faces said they weren't buying into Crowley's bullshit so easily.

"I think you need to give them a little space," Lorenzo said. "They've just been through a battle and they need a little time to assimilate their experience."

Crowley looked back, frowning.

"He's right," Rita said. "We've had a lot of experience with this kind of thing."

Crowley turned back to his dream team, nodding. "I understand. We'll give it some time, then when you feel ready, we'll have a full debriefing so we can analyze every aspect of the mission from the inside out."

Mission? Rita thought, not liking the sound of it.

After Jack helped remove their dreaming hoods, Crowley ushered the rest of Seal Team Zero out of the Dream Lab, then popped his head back in the door, saying, "Assimilate all your data and we'll meet in the Z Level conference room in an hour. After we go through your reports, we'll call the boys in."

Rita let go of Lorenzo and concentrated on her console. Jack came in shaking his head. "I'm not so sure about this," he said in a low voice. "Seeing that little shit freak out and pulling him from that dream cradle reminded me too much of what we went through with that Moffitt brat. Kinda gave me the creepy crawlies."

"That's what I thought," Rita said. "I don't care what Crowley says. This whole thing feels wrong."

Jack shrugged and let out a sigh. "What else can we do? The son-of-a-bitch has us by the short and curlys. It's either work with him, or three hots and a cot in a Mexican slammer." He shook his head.

"I don't know what he has in mind," Lorenzo said, "but this is a fully functional medical facility which is supposed to help wounded vets. At this point all we can do is follow through on his program and hope that we can influence him in a positive way. The important thing is for us to stick together."

"Amen to that, brother." Jack dropped into his seat.

Rita busied herself, sorting through her data. "I can't wait to hear what the boys have to say."

"That makes three of us," Lorenzo said.

Jack, Lorenzo, and Rita walked into the Z level conference room an hour later joined by Cheryl. Every one carried iPads. They found Crowley watching a video of the boys in the test area on a big high resolution flat screen that covered the wall.

He smiled, pausing the playback with a tap. "You can really see the depth of their experience by their facial expressions."

"You should try it," Lorenzo said.

Crowley's eyes widened. "Try it? Me? I'm not..."

"Sure you are," Jack said. "You don't have any problem putting these kids through it. Why don't you give it a shot? Then you can have an idea of what you're putting them through."

Crowley opened his mouth to speak, but didn't. Rita struggled to keep from laughing at his discomfort.

"W-well," he stammered. "Why don't *you* try it?"

"Already did," Lorenzo quipped.

"What about..."

"We all did," Rita said.

"You're the only one who hasn't," Cheryl added.

Crowley looked at each of them in turn and gestured to the empty chairs around the table. "Please, take a seat. Let's take a look at the data you have and see where it's leading us."

While they took their seats, Crowley tapped his iPad until close ups of the five team members filled the screen. A freeze frame of the dream sequence filled the spot at the bottom right, making three screens at the top and three on the bottom.

Tapping their tablets, Rita and Lorenzo changed the big screen's arrangement so Lorenzo's dream sequence took up the top third. Video close-ups of the five team members lined the middle section. Below that Rita matched up the vital signs and brain wave readings of each to their face on the screen.

"They're all calibrated to the timing track," Lorenzo said after a few more taps.

"Good!" Crowley dimmed the room lights. "Let's give it a run through and take a look at how it all comes together."

Lorenzo tapped his iPad and the dream sequence began. Everyone watched in rapt silence as the battle unfolded. Rita felt a combination of amazement and discomfort watching the rapid eye movements, facial expressions, vital signs, and brain wave activity precisely track the unfolding action of the team's assault on the fortress.

Everyone's readings spiked at the onset of the dream, then each went into their individual levels of fear and excitement, depending on where they were in the scenario and their part in the action.

Jordan had facial expressions that showed flashes of fear reflected at certain points by highly elevated brain wave activity and racing vital signs until it shifted into a pinched grimace of hardened determination that carried him through to the end of the mission.

Beside him, Wesley had chaotic brain waves and a mixed expression of fear and determination that remained steady throughout the assault, ending in a look of surprise when his part ended.

Carl had an alternating expression and brain waves that showed fear at each point of confrontation, shifting into a hard mask of determination each time he overcame it.

The last two disturbed Rita for different reasons.

John went into frenetic brain wave patterns the moment the dream began and his vital signs spiked in the beginning and rose steadily with the action. His facial expressions could only be described as maniacal.

She could barely watch Terry and felt his fear in the pit of her stomach. His brain waves spiked way out of proportion to the others and his mouth opened and closed. His lower lip trembled and tears rolled from beneath his eyelids, but to his credit, he followed through on his part all the way to the end when he awoke sobbing and blubbering.

Everyone sat in silence when the playback ended and Crowley raised the lights. Rita stole glances at the others, seeing each of them adrift in their own thoughts. She could almost see the gears turning in Jack's brain behind his furrowed brow. He spoke up first.

"I'm not so sure I'm in agreement with our approach, but I have to say, I'm very pleased with the hood's performance and the efficiency of the bilateral data transfer."

"I agree," Cheryl said. "The technology appears to be performing flawlessly." She looked at Rita. "It's the subjects that I'm worried about."

"I couldn't agree more," Rita said.

Crowley clapped his hands and rubbed them together. "I can't tell you how impressed I am with what you've accomplished. We made history here. From everything I've seen and all the data we've collected, you my friends, have orchestrated a shared dream experience between five subjects, who not only had their own personal experiences, but interacted and directly influenced each other in those experiences."

Lorenzo shook his head. "I have to admit, I'm not only amazed that they dreamed in sequence, but the dream scenario, the timing of events, their interactions with it, and their physiological responses all happened together, like they were having a real experience. It felt like we were watching a live action movie."

"We co-created a new shared reality," Crowley said.

"More like controlled chaos," Jack said.

"Controlled being the key word here," Crowley said. "They had the option of aborting at any point by simply saying 'Mama'. The fact that they didn't shows their dedication to each other and the high level of teamwork they're capable of."

Cheryl set her iPad down. "It will be interesting to see what the boys have to say about what they went through and if their accounts confirm our findings."

Crowley leaned back in his chair, steepling his fingers. "I don't want to wait too long to talk to them. It's important that we get their impressions while they're still fresh."

He looked around at the others. When no one spoke up, he tapped his iPad, blanking out the big screen. "They don't need to see any of that. It could be disturbing."

For once Rita agreed with him.

CHAPTER TWENTY EIGHT

Jordan followed his teammates into the conference room, feeling out of sorts. His stomach didn't feel right and a dull headache threatened to grow into a full bore head banger. They found Crowley waiting at the end of a long table with a big flat screen on the wall behind him, an expectant look on his face. He stood when they filed in, snapping off a crisp salute.

"Welcome warriors."

Jordan pushed his discomfort to the back of his mind. This needed his full attention.

Doctor Martin, who had mothered Terry, sat to Crowley's right followed by the quirky Jack Scanlon, the cool Lorenzo, and Jordan's favorite, the beautiful Rita.

Terry sat across from Cheryl and John sat across from Scanlon, which seemed appropriate as they both had an edge to them. He imagined John growing into an old man who resembled Scanlon.

Wesley sat across from Lorenzo and Carl faced Rita. Jordan sat at the end with no one across from him.

"We've collected a lot of data," Crowley said, "but we're really looking forward to what you guys have to report about your experience."

"I don't think this will ever work in a competition," Jordan said. "It's too intense for the average gamer." He looked down at the rest of the team, who all nodded in agreement

"You know how you wake up from a dream and don't always remember it?" Wesley said, "Or maybe just parts of it? Well that's not the case here. Every detail of it is tattooed into my brain like it really happened."

"Like a vivid nightmare," Carl added. "I never thought things could hurt in the dream, but they did!"

Crowley leaned forward. "But you're okay now. No real damage was done."

Carl jerked his thumb toward Terry. "Tell Killjoy that. He doesn't want to go back - ever."

"What about you, Striker?" Crowley said, focusing on John.

"I thought it was bad ass! I can't wait to try it again. Best rush I ever had!"

"What about the rest of you?"

Carl shrugged and held his hands out. "I don't know."

"I'm not so sure either," Wesley said.

Terry gave no response.

"We need more time to think about it," Jordan said. "We're still assimilating the whole thing."

"Fair enough."

Lorenzo leaned forward with his elbows on the table, resting his chin on his hands. "What did you think about the whole scenario? It's clear that you all felt like it was real and any one of you could have gotten out at any time, but you all kept in the game and toughed it out, even when it felt like it hurt. That takes a special level of commitment."

"In a way this was easy because it was based on what we already knew and already won at," Jordan said, "What we don't know is what would happen in a situation that we haven't been in."

"Isn't that how it is when you go up against different teams in competitions?" Crowley said. "Surely, no two teams are the same."

"That's true, but we know the landscapes and practice in them, even though the strategies of different teams are never the same."

"That's where I would expect your tactical training to come in," Crowley said, nodding. "In a case like that you could have the option of exiting the scenario at any time, simply by saying 'Momma'."

The team members looked at each other.

John hit the table with his fist. "We're not quitters. That goes against everything we've been trained to do!"

"Which is exactly why we chose you!" Crowley jabbed his finger, emphasizing his point.

"Aside from Terry," Rita said in a softer voice. "How did the rest of you feel afterward? Not mentally or emotionally, but physically."

"I feel pretty tapped out," Wesley offered. "Like I just did a long day of hard physical work."

"It reminds me of the time I went sky diving," Carl said. "Though my jump only lasted a few minutes, I felt totally drained the rest of the day."

Cheryl looked to Rita, then addressed the team. "The kind of let down you get after a big adrenaline rush."

"I feel pumped," John said, clenching his fists.

"I feel drained and my stomach's a little upset," Jordan said. "Not queasy like I'm about to puke or anything, more like heartburn, and I have a little headache."

Wesley rubbed his stomach. "Now that you mention it, mine feels that way too!"

"Mine too!" Carl said. "Just a little."

Jordan looked down the line at Terry who hung his head, not saying anything. No doubt about how he felt. I've never seen him rattled like this, Jordan thought. Not something I would have predicted, but who would have ever thought that a game could be as real and intense as this one was?

"So at the risk of sounding redundant," Rita said looking directly at Crowley. "Is it fair to say that you all feel like you went through a real experience? Kind of like an aftershock?"

"That's a good way of putting it," Carl said. "It felt *that* real."

With the exception of Terry, who continued to hang his head, the rest of the team nodded. Rita glanced at Cheryl, affirming something that Jordan sensed, but couldn't define.

"Well if it's any consolation," Crowley said. "You guys just made history by co-creating and participating in the world's first fully interactive, shared dream. Together you created a new reality that transcends the rules of time and space as we know them, with endless possibilities."

"How soon can we do it again?" John asked, clasping his hands together like a little kid begging for a cookie.

"You need time to recharge," Cheryl said before anyone could answer.

Rita looked at Jordan. "Besides, the rest of the team is pretty beat and they haven't had any time to make up their minds about whether they want to continue."

"We have a group area set up like a team house for you," Crowley said. "You'll find your luggage in your own private rooms off the main room and all you can eat and drink. Think of it as a celebration. You certainly earned it!"

"Sounds good to me," Jordan said. "I can use a break and it will give us time to talk things over."

Crowley tapped his iPad and looked up. "An escort will meet you outside the door and take you to your quarters. If you need anything, just ask and we'll see that you get it."

"Thank you," Jordan said, standing. "C'mon guys, let's hit the door."

John shot up from his chair. "Let's make like an Australian sheep herder and get the flock out of here. It's party time!"

Jack Scanlon shook his head, chuckling, then Jordan led them out, glancing back to see Terry walking with his head down, shuffling like a zombie. He noticed Rita watching him too, then she looked back and her eyes met Jordan's, reflecting his concern.

CHAPTER TWENTY NINE

"I'm concerned about Terry," Cheryl said after the team left. "He'll be all right," Crowley said with a dismissive wave. "It was only a dream. Nothing a good night's rest and some R and R won't cure."

You son-of-a-bitch, Rita thought, bristling at his attitude.

Cheryl stood red-faced, her clenched fists shaking, eyes blazing behind her glasses which exaggerated her rage. Mama bear was in the house. "Don't brush it off so lightly, you pompous ass!"

Crowley's head snapped back and his eyes widened. He opened his mouth to respond, but Cheryl unloaded before he could get a word out. Go get him girl, Rita thought.

"If you had any brains in that thick skull of yours or any shred of compassion in that black heart of yours, you'd see that they're all suffering from PTSD, especially poor little Terry!"

Crowley held up both hands as of warding off a physical attack. "Whoa, whoa, just hold on a minute here. Let's not get emotional…"

Rita's words erupted in a torrent. "No, you hold on a minute," she blurted. Now she was shaking. "Shut up and listen to what your top notch neuroscientist is telling you!"

Crowley kept his hands up. His eyes darted from Rita to Cheryl and back again. Like a trapped rat, Rita thought. Cheryl looked at her with an expression of gratitude. Jack and Lorenzo smirked, obviously enjoying the show.

"Okay, okay," Crowley said, regaining his composure. "Calm down. You got my attention. I'm all ears."

Cheryl took a deep breath and let out a long sigh. "That was more than a dream to him. In his mind it was no different than if it really happened. As a matter of fact, for him it really did happen. It *was* real for him."

Crowley nodded as she spoke, and to his credit he didn't interrupt.

"Terry's showing classic PTSD symptoms," she continued. "You brought us in here to help cure it and we're creating more. I spent some time talking to him, but psychiatry is not my forte. I'm more about the physical aspects of neuroscience like neurons, dendrites, and synapses. That poor little guy is traumatized by what he went through. You saw him. He didn't say a word in the meeting. He's emotionally cut off from the others. He told me he doesn't care about anything and his mind jumps around. He can't seem to focus on anything. He needs help. More than I can give him."

Crowley leaned forward, speaking low. "Sorry, I didn't realize the extent of it. I'm not a psychiatrist either. What do you propose we do?"

"If you don't mind, I'd like to address that Cheryl," Rita said.

Cheryl sat back and crossed her arms. "By all means."

"I mentioned this before," Rita said, "but now it warrants greater urgency. We need a qualified medical and psychiatric expert who can take the place of Doctor Jackson, rest his soul. I don't think there's anyone who can fill his shoes, but we need somebody. I'm not ashamed to say that I feel inadequate when it comes to dealing with the deeper aspects of this program. Sure, I can treat the physical signs of trauma, but we're in uncharted territory here, especially with the wild swings in brain waves and vital signs that we observed. We're pushing the limits of what we know here and I don't feel qualified to handle what could happen. Today has proven that."

"She's right," Cheryl added. "We've had a huge hole in our research since we lost Doctor Jackson and after what I've witnessed today, I don't want to continue until we find someone."

"We all feel the same way," Lorenzo said, nodding toward Jack.

"We have been looking," Crowley said. "It's hard trying to find someone with the right qualifications and we'll never get a perfect match, but we're narrowing it down."

"I'm more concerned with the psychological side of things," Cheryl said, "especially the PTSD part of it." She looked at Rita. "I do have surgical experience and I'm confident in Rita's medical abilities, even if she may not be herself. She has more experience than anyone else when it comes to this kind of situation."

Crowley rubbed his chin. "I have one candidate that I think would be a great fit, but he hasn't shown much enthusiasm."

"Have you offered him enough?" Cheryl asked.

"It's not a matter of money. He's kind of a maverick with different priorities. A guy who literally marches to the beat of his own drum."

Jack leaned forward resting his chin on his hand, his exaggerated brow wrinkled in concentration. "Would you characterize him as a rebel? Maybe a non-conformist?"

"He *is* a bit of an enigma. Yes, you could say that."

Jack slapped the table, smiled, and looked around at the others. "That's our man!"

Lorenzo shook with suppressed laughter.

"We need someone to shake things up around here," Jack continued. "An independent thinker who's not afraid to think outside the box. That's where we're working, right?"

"True dat," Lorenzo said.

"I could give a shit about his politics and philosophy," Cheryl said more to Jack than the others. "My main concern is his experience and qualifications."

"I'm with Cheryl," Rita said.

"Get him in here," Jack said. "Do whatever it takes. I'm telling you. I can feel it in my gut. He's our man!"

"I'll see what I can do," Crowley said. "In the meantime, I'd like to ask you all to keep moving the project forward. There are other more extensive aspects of it that I haven't discussed with you yet."

"Why not?" Lorenzo asked.

"For a number of reasons, the primary one being that the information regarding them has been on a need to know basis, but on a more practical note, I didn't want to distract you from the work you've been doing so far."

A sour look stole over Jack's face. "How many more secrets are you keeping from us?"

Crowley waved him off. "You'll find out when the time is right. In the interim, until I get someone to fill this slot, I need you to push forward."

"As long as you are actively pursuing someone," Cheryl said. "I'm willing to keep working, but I will not - I repeat, I will not participate in any more forays into the dream world until we have that position filled."

Jack held up a finger. "I second that!"

Lorenzo nodded. "Ditto."

Crowley stood. "Fair enough."

CHAPTER THIRTY

Jordan leaned back in an easy chair, sipping on a bottle of Newcastle Brown Ale in their carpeted lounge. A picked over buffet lined one wall alongside a stocked bar. Though windowless, large flat screens covered each wall displaying pleasant shifting nature scenes, giving the room a sense of expansiveness.

After popping an Excedrin and filling his stomach, the cold beer made Jordan more relaxed, but he still felt jittery.

"Shit!" John said, banging on his smart phone's screen.

"What's up?" Carl said.

"I can't get any bars on my cell. No service!"

Jordan checked his phone. Sure enough, no service.

Wesley sat in a recliner beside him while John and Carl sprawled on two ends of a long couch, checking their phones. No one had service.

John had his feet up on a coffee table. "Just as well," he said. "I think we can all use a little break from technology about now."

Everyone drank beer except Terry, who sat by himself in a far corner working on a vodka and tonic.

Wesley raised a hand to the side of his mouth and leaned toward Jordan whispering, "I'm worried about Terry. He got spooked pretty bad and he's been acting weird ever since. That's his third drink and they're more vodka than tonic."

John and Carl looked over at Terry, then leaned in closer to listen to Jordan.

"It's like he snapped in some way," Jordan said, sotto voce. "I tried to talk to him, but he won't say anything and if I push, he gets hostile, so I've been leaving him alone."

"Maybe we should all have a talk with him?" Carl whispered. "Show him a little love from the whole team."

Jordan sipped his beer and shook his head. "Let him be for now. The way he's acting, he might feel like we're ganging up on him or something. Maybe the booze and a good night's sleep will help settle him down."

John shook his head and continued in a half-whisper. "I don't get it. Sure, it was an intense experience, but it was still only a dream."

"It seemed real while it was happening," Carl said, "didn't it?"

Wesley nodded. "More hyper-real. Intense like one of those lucid dreams…"

"Shush," Jordan said, inclining his head toward Terry.

Terry rose unsteadily from his chair and shuffled over to the bar where he filled his glass with more vodka, topped by a splash of tonic, then he turned from the table and glared at the group.

"I know you mutha fuckas are talking about me," he slurred. "You think I'm fuckin' deaf and dumb, but I got news for ya!" He held up a waving finger, slopping vodka over the top of his glass. "I can hear just fine and I ain't no fuckin' pussy!"

"Nobody said you were, Bro," John said.

Terry took a gulp from his glass and staggered back to his corner. "Fuck you!" He dropped into his chair. "Fuck all uh ya! I'm done with you assholes!"

"It's okay," Jordan said. "We get it. Give it a rest."

Terry took another gulp and leaned back, eyes bulging out of his swaying head as if they were going in two different directions. "Fuck you. You ain't nuthin'! No wait, you *arrre* nuthin'! No wait, you ain't nuthin. You ain't shit!" He erupted in an eerie high-pitched giggle that sent shivers rippling over Jordan.

This wasn't Terry. It was like someone or something else spoke through him. Jordan looked to Wesley, John, and Carl, who all stared back, puzzled.

"Maybe we should put him to bed," Wesley said.

"Leave him alone," Jordan whispered. "Don't give him any energy. He'll pass out soon, then we'll put him to bed."

They lapsed into silence and sure enough, a few minutes later they heard a gurgling snore coming from the corner.

"Give him a few more minutes, then we'll tuck him in," Jordan said.

"Geez, that was some spooky shit," Carl said.

"It reminded me of that movie, The Exorcist," John added.

"No shit, huh?" Wesley said. "That scared the shit out of me when I was a kid. I hope we don't see any pea soup coming out of him."

"He's our Bro and we need to take care of him," Jordan said.

John rolled his eyes. "I wouldn't want to be in his head. He's going to be one hurting unit in the morning."

Carl sipped his beer and belched. "I think we ought to say something to Crowley."

"Fuck Crowley," Wesley said. "He doesn't give a shit."

"I'll talk to Rita, that cute medical babe," Jordan said. "She'll listen."

John held up his beer as if toasting. "And what a babe she is!"

Jordan found himself smiling. "She reminds me of that hot Spanish actress Penélope Cruz."

Wesley nodded. "You're right. I was trying to think of who she reminded me of. That's the one!"

Carl and John nodded, then John held up his bottle again. "To Penélope!"

"To Penélope," the others said, swigging from their bottles.

Another loud snore came from the corner.

"I think that's our cue," Jordan said. "C'mon you guys, I'm going to need a hand."

John set his beer down and stood. "That you will. He's a little porker."

They went over to the corner where Jordan eased the drink out of Terry's hand and pulled him by one arm, while Wesley pulled the other until he was vertical. His head lolled to the side.

"What the fu…" Terry slurred, his whole body sagging.

"Don't worry about it, buddy," Jordan said. "We're putting you to bed."

Wesley and Jordan put his arms over their shoulders and dragged him the rest of the way.

"Jesus Christ, he's heavy." Wesley looked to Carl and John. "Grab his feet."

They each took a leg and the four of them carried Terry to his room. He started thrashing when they struggled through the door with him. "What the fuck are you doin'?" He muttered. "I told you to leave me the fuck alone."

"Almost there," Jordan said.

"You fuckin' assho…"

Terry started heaving and his body jerked.

"Hurry up!" Wesley said. "He's going to launch!"

They hustled Terry into his bed where he plopped down on his back.

"Turn him onto his side so he doesn't choke on his puke," Jordan said. "Carl, quick, grab that waste basket!"

Carl grabbed the waste basket and slid it over by Terry's head when Jordan and Wesley rolled him onto his side. It all came together in one orchestrated moment when Terry erupted in gut wrenching heaves, spewing the foul smelling contents of his stomach into the basket.

"Now that's team work," Carl said backing away.

"Direct hit!" John said.

"Good thing he puked," Jordan said. "He drank way too much, too fast. I was worried about alcohol poisoning. John, do me a favor and grab a wet facecloth and a dry towel so I can clean the puke off of his face."

John and Jordan cleaned Terry up while the others stood by watching. When he finished, Wesley put pillows under Terry's head and Carl and John pulled his shoes off.

"Thanks guys," Jordan said. "He can sleep it off now. We'll leave the waste basket there in case he decides to puke again."

They went back to the lounge and took up their former positions.

"I'm curious," John said, kicking his feet up on the coffee table. "What do you guys think?"

Carl looked over at him. "About what?"

John smiled and his eyes brightened. "You ready to go back into the dream game?"

"I'm not so sure," Wesley said. "I've been on the fence about it."

John held up a finger. "Remember, it *is* only a dream,"

"Maybe so," Wesley countered, "But it's so fucking real! Look at how poor Terry's reacting to it. I'm not ashamed to tell you that he's freaking me out." He paused, then said in a low voice. "I wish I had some weed. That would chill me out."

Carl chuckled. "That makes two of us!"

"You haven't said much, Jordan," Wesley said. "What do you think?"

"I've been flip-flopping. I think it's a little early for anyone to make any decisions. I'm still taking it all in. I'm going to sleep on it and see how I feel in the morning."

"Sounds good to me." Carl drained the last of his beer, plopped it down on the table and stood. "I don't know about you guys, but I'm tapped out after all we went through today. I'm ready to call it."

Wesley stifled a yawn and finished his beer. "Right behind you, buddy."

"Me too!" Jordan pushed the lever on the side of his recliner, stood, and went to his room, leaving John alone on the couch.

Jordan drifted off into a deep sleep soon after his head hit the pillow, coming to sometime later in the middle of the dream battle they had fought. Though vivid, it didn't have the immediacy of his earlier experience. It felt more like a kind of shadow world, yet his emotions ran high as he moved through the stages of their assault, knowing what would come, reacting to it without thinking.

His excitement shot to a new peak when he heard a far off voice crying, "Momma! Mommy! Mommy!"

In his dreaming state he couldn't understand where the cries came from. Their urgency grew until he abandoned the mission objective and set off in search of them. They came louder and seemed to come from everywhere. Panicking, he searched frantically, trying to locate their source until he shot up straight in bed wide awake, covered with sweat.

"Momma!" It cried in a heartbreaking wail. Momma! Mommy!"

Shit, Terry, he thought. I'm not dreaming.

He stumbled out of bed and raced to Terry's room where he flicked on the lights to see Terry sitting straight up in bed crying and sobbing, his eyes wide and unseeing. Tears streamed down his cheeks.

Jordan rushed to his side, shaking him. "Wake up! You're having a nightmare."

Terry screamed at that and flailed, barely missing Jordan's head, then the rest of Seal Team Zero rushed into the room.

Jordan shook him harder. "Wake up, it's a nightmare."

Terry dropped his arms and his eyes swam into focus. "Jesus Christ," he said between sobs. "They were going to torture me."

"Shhh, shhh," Jordan said, fighting back his own emotion. Part of him felt like crying for Terry out of sympathy. He felt for him like a parent would with a little boy. "It's okay. It was just a bad dream, that's all." He patted Terry on the back. "Take some deep breaths.

Terry looked at him with a pained expression and drew in deep sobbing breaths while looking to the rest of the team who gathered in close. "This whole thing is a bad dream," he whispered. "I wish I never got involved with it."

CHAPTER THIRTY ONE

Rita struggled to push her way up through a heavy, gauze-like web from the chaotic remnants of another nightmare. This one centered around the battle scenario from the day before and in this one Jordan abandoned the mission to go off in search of Terry, who cried for his mother in some far off place.

A gentle shake brought her out of it until she sat up with a sharp intake of breath, peering into the loving warmth of Lorenzo's eyes. She shook, realizing she was covered with sweat.

Lorenzo caressed her face and pushed her hair back, whispering, "Another nightmare, love. You're okay now."

He put his arm around her and laid back with her head on his chest. "Once Crowley gets his whiz-bang psychologist in here, I'm going to make sure you talk to him."

"After little Terry."

"Of course."

"I mean what I said about not moving forward until he comes on board, and even then I won't do anything unless I'm satisfied with his approach."

"Crowley gets that. Between you, me, Cheryl, and Jack, we've showed a unified front. Today he's going to give us a tour and show us the rest of his master plan for Pandora. We need to play it cool and see what he has up his sleeve. We have plenty of work to do without staging any more dreams."

"You're right." Rita hugged him. "We'll stick to our guns until he gets the help we need."

Lorenzo stroked her hair, relaxing her. "Oddly enough he wants to start his tour with Hodge, which I find strange, but I have a sneaking suspicion of what he's up to."

"Using Hodge's sedation dream on Terry?"

She felt Lorenzo chuckling though his chest. "Nothing gets past you, babe." He took her face in his free hand and planted a kiss on her lips.

A few hours later, Rita and Cheryl hovered over Hodge. The Fiber optics from his hood flashed and colored fluids ran through the tubing at his wrists.

As usual, Cheryl's strawberry-blonde hair was pulled back in a bun. Her pale blue eyes had bags under them exaggerated by her glasses. Rita sensed that she too had been the victim of a nightmare, especially after the emotional scene with Terry, but she didn't want to say anything in front of the others, especially Crowley.

Jack Scanlon sat at a console to the left, near Crowley, focused on the screen in front of him. Lorenzo sat to his right. Rita followed Cheryl out of the ICU and watched her take her place between Jack and Lorenzo where she clicked a mouse. Hodge's vital signs, fMRI, PET, and other relevant images filled the main screens of the observation deck. She looked over at Crowley, then to Lorenzo before nodding to Jack who tapped at his keyboard until the monitoring points on the schematic screen glowed bright green.

Rita looked from the displays to Hodge, who remained motionless. The large display of multicolored fMRI and PET images shifted and changed showing relaxed brain activity and blood flows.

"Okay, Lorenzo," Cheryl said. "Bring up the audio and video imagery we're transmitting through Jack's chip and the magnetoresonators on the dreaming hood so we can see the whole thing."

Lorenzo clicked his mouse until soft white noise filled the room, turning into waves crashing on the beach. An image of waves on the main display coupled with rising and falling music and other sounds intermingled into an audio and video collage that sounded like an exotic lullaby of running water, waves, chants, digeridoos, flutes, and stringed instruments. Hodge's eye movements shifted back and forth in a steady beat like a metronome and his face remained expressionless.

"This is working great." Crowley rubbed his hands together. "You guys have done an amazing job! I wanted to start the tour here for a reason."

Rita and Lorenzo's eyes met and he graced her with a smirk and a wink.

"And that is?" Jack asked.

"Let's go up to the command and control center where I can show you what has been evolving alongside your work."

"Okay Kemosabe," Jack said.

After returning Hodge's monitoring systems to its previous state, they took the elevator up to the Command and Control Center in the glass walled office in the North Tower. Rita struggled to shut out the unpleasant memories of everything that happened there.

The pristine tiled floor and U-shaped console lined with monitors helped dispel the memories, but the view overlooking the atrium and everything around it wouldn't let her forget them completely.

A large couch and overstuffed chairs sat in front of the console centered around a circular table. Crowley took a seat strategically placed at the head of the circle and motioned for the others to sit. Rita sat beside Lorenzo on the couch and Jack and Cheryl took the chairs on each side of her, flanking Crowley.

He pulled an iPad from a pocket on the side of his chair and tapped it. A paneled wall whispered open revealing the eight screens surrounding the larger seventy two inch display. Images sequenced through different areas of the complex on each screen, panning open areas, hallways, and other parts of the facility.

"Before we proceed, I want to reiterate how happy I am with your progress. In spite of the glitches we've run into with Lorenzo's masterful scenario, it's been an overwhelming success." He paused and made eye contact with each person before continuing. "Together we have created a shared interactive reality and perfected dream sleep, which has a sedating effect. I wanted to drive that point home with our visit with Hodge to reinforce its effectiveness."

Here it comes, Rita thought.

"While we're waiting for our psychologist, I thought Terry would be the perfect subject to…"

"Forget it," Cheryl said. "It's not happening."

"But…"

"No more dreaming scenarios until we get help," Rita said.

Cheryl crossed her arms. "And we mean what we say."

The enthusiasm drained from Crowley's face.

"I spent a lot of time with Terry yesterday," Cheryl continued, "and I doubt he will have anything to do with Pandora."

"Okay, I can see that's not going anywhere." Crowley tapped at his iPad and inclined his head toward the wall screens, cycling through a series of images that showed a large dome outfitted as a fully equipped hospital complex complete with patient rooms, a huge cafeteria, operating rooms, X-Ray facilities, laboratories, laundry, lounges, and everything else that a modern hospital contained, then he switched to a different set of views.

Rita flinched when she recognized the former Storybook Kingdom and the entryways. The arch over the Three Bears attraction remained shrouded in darkness with no signage on it except:

UNDER CONSTRUCTION

Backlit metal letters similar to the ones on the front of the building stood out in relief on the arches over the remaining three doorways. The one over Hansel and Gretel, now said:

IMMERSIVE COMBAT

"This is where the combat dream scenarios will be refined and tested before they go out to the wards. We hope to program general scenarios, like ambushes, land mines, and loss of limb damage from IEDs which we hope to customize to the unique circumstances of each victim." He tapped at his iPad bringing up a screen showing a domed room lined with rows of dreaming cradles. The sight of so many of them made Rita uncomfortable.

Crowley tapped again, displaying the arch over Pied Piper. The backlit letters on it said:

DREAMSLEEP

The view cycled into another domed room lined with rows of hospital beds. Groups of workers moved throughout guiding equipment in and installing consoles beside each bed.

"Here those who have been traumatized and brain damaged will be put into Dream Sleep using the same protocols that we developed for Hodge to give them relief from their terrors with an eye toward curing them if there is any possibility of doing so."

Crowley tapped again, displaying the arch over the old Rumplestiltskin. The backlit letters on it said:

CYBERNETIC LIMB FACILITY

Crowley gave a wide grin. "What we have in the works here has been developing in parallel with your work, but to date has had no connection." He switched the view to show crates and forklifts carrying heavy machinery to what looked like the beginning of several assembly lines.

"This is where we will be fabricating the latest cybernetic limbs for those wounded warriors who have lost appendages with the goal of restoring total functionality and mobility wherever possible. This facility will be run by state of the art robotics which will be self-maintaining and one hundred percent self-sufficient."

Jack sat up in his chair and whistled low. "You got my attention there, chief. Now *that's* impressive!"

"Then you're really going to love this," Crowley said, brightening like a little boy sharing a new toy.

The camera view showed the former Sleeping Beauty arch now titled:

CYBERNETIC ORGAN FACILITY

The big screen changed views displaying a domed room that resembled the previous one.

"Using the same technologies that we make cybernetic limbs combined with stem cell therapy and soft tissue growth, we'll be manufacturing damaged organs to replace and augment those whose functionality have been compromised from injuries."

Cheryl's eyes grew owl wide at this. "My God," she whispered. "I had no idea."

Rita studied Lorenzo, who watched with rapt attention. She felt overwhelmed by everything she saw and could find no words to express her feelings, then a question popped into her mind. "What about the last one? The Three Bears. What will that be?"

Crowley set his tablet down. "We haven't come up with the proper designation for that one and we may not give it a name because we want to be discreet about it, but we're building it partly out of necessity, and partly out of our promise to you."

"Promise?"

"For those who have no hope of survival and are too far gone and in too much pain to have any chance of staying alive, they will meet their end there in what we are secretly calling the Euthanasia Room."

CHAPTER THIRTY TWO

Jordan sat on the edge of his chair in an office across from Rita feeling giddy being alone with her, but more than that he felt uneasy about the topic of their meeting. "I appreciate you taking the time to see me without Mister Crowley, your co-workers, or my teammates."

She studied him, her big doe-like brown eyes questioning. "How can I help you?"

"It's about Terry," he said. "That's why I didn't want anybody else here. I don't want to freak anybody out, but I'm worried about him."

Her eyes softened and a boundary seemed to disappear, like she was letting him in. Aside from his infatuation, in that moment he felt a different kind of connection with her on a deeper level. She lowered her voice when she spoke next.

"I'm not afraid to tell you that I'm worried about him too."

Her admission both worried and comforted him.

"You saw how he freaked out after the game," Jordan continued.

"And he was sullen and withdrawn in the meeting."

"After that he wouldn't talk to anybody and he got really plastered. When we tried to put him to bed, he was calling us names and acting like he wanted to fight us. It was spooky, like it wasn't Terry, but somebody else. I've known him for four or five years now and I've *never* seen him act like that."

"How are the other guys holding out?"

"They're doing okay, but I can tell you that even though they're not showing it, it's wigging them out a little. Between the realistic battle we fought and Terry's reaction to it, I'm not so sure they're going to want to continue, except John." Jordan smirked. "He's got a whole different screw loose."

Rita leaned forward and put her chin in her hand. "I'm curious. How did Terry sleep?"

"He woke us all up this morning at o-dark-thirty screaming for his mother like he was stuck in yesterday's dream."

Her eyes widened and she bit her lower lip. A faraway look stole over her. Jordan stayed quiet, curious to hear what she might say. After a long silence her gaze came back into focus. "Did you have any dreams yourself?"

"I dreamed that I was in the same battle with him trying to save him. He must have been screaming for awhile. I think I picked up on it and made it part of my dream. I'm sure you've had the experience of hearing something outside yourself that becomes part of your dream, haven't you?"

"Well - yes I have, but..." She waved the thought off. "It's probably just a coincidence. We all had a powerful experience yesterday and it affected us pretty deeply."

"What's a coincidence?"

She studied him, seeming to come to a decision. "Promise me you won't repeat this to anybody. Not even your teammates."

Jordan nodded. "Promise."

"I woke up from the same dream."

Her words sent chills dancing all over Jordan's arms, back, and head. "Excuse me?"

"I'm sure it wasn't as clear as yours, in fact it was kind of fuzzy, but I woke up from the same dream."

"Holy shit," Jordan whispered.

She waved her hands. "Let's not get carried away. It still may only be a coincidence. In the same way that you said we incorporate what we hear into our dreams, we can incorporate a day's events, especially ones as emotionally charged as ours were."

Jordan wanted to believe that, but his chills told him different. "That's just too weird," he said. "I'm not sure what to think."

"Let's keep it to ourselves for the time being. We don't want to cause any panic. I won't say a word to anybody, but I will discreetly ask Doctor Martin if she had the same dream, because I suspect she may have."

Jordan made a zipping gesture across his lips. "I'll keep my mouth shut."

Rita smiled. "Pay close attention to your dreams and anything else weird that goes on in your head and I'll do the same. When the opportunity presents itself we'll compare notes."

"I'm in. In the meantime, what are we going to do about Terry? He's the one I'm really worried about."

"We've been after Crowley to get a psychologist on staff. He says he's working on it, but it'll take someone with specialized qualifications. I don't know if we can wait any longer."

"What are you going to do?"

"After Terry's reaction to yesterday's session, our team told Crowley that we won't perform any more dream journeys without a psychologist who is among other things, an expert on PTSD. I will share what you told me about Terry's drinking and his nightmare with Crowley to motivate him more."

Jordan sighed, feeling lighter. "That's great! We still haven't decided if we're going to continue. What's been happening with Terry has made us lean toward not doing it again. This will buy us more time to think things over -- especially with all this other weird stuff."

CHAPTER THIRTY THREE

Cheryl looked up frowning from the video screens that filled the wall beside her desk when Rita knocked on the door frame of her office. Her expression softened when she recognized Rita. "Am I interrupting anything?" Rita asked.

"Nothing that can't wait." Cheryl gestured to the chair on the other side of her desk. "What can I do for you?"

Rita glanced up and down the hall behind her before closing the office door and taking a seat across from Cheryl. "Yesterday sure was an emotionally charged day, wasn't it?"

"My heart was breaking for poor little Terry. He was blubbering like a baby."

"I had a heart to heart with their leader Jordan," Rita said, leaning in and speaking confidentially. "Terry had a rough night."

Cheryl leaned forward, eyebrows raised.

"As soon as he got back to their rooms Terry got drunk and when they tried to put him to bed he was hostile. Jordan said that they had never seen him act like that before."

"Did he finally settle down?"

"Until the middle of the night when he woke up screaming in a nightmare where he was reliving the battle."

Cheryl's head jerked like she'd been jolted by an electric shock. Her mouth dropped.

"You had a similar dream at the same time, didn't you?" Rita blurted.

Cheryl's eyes widened. "Don't tell me you…"

Rita nodded.

"Nightmares are a classic symptom of PTSD," Cheryl said, speaking rapid-fire. "This kid clearly has it and..."

"So do we," Rita finished.

"But the same dream?"

"I know I've had nightmares since I spent so much time immersed in the literal nightmare that DreamLand became with Albert Moffitt, the rats, Chazz and the rest of that whole horror show."

Cheryl pursed her lips. "I've had nightmares too. Just as many as you, no doubt, but the same dream?"

"You didn't spend as much time in the DreamLand scenarios as I did, so I wouldn't think you would be affected so deeply."

Cheryl studied her, but didn't reply.

The moment went on for a little too long, so Rita continued, "After all the hell we all went through, anyone who had any part in it would have nightmares, whether they were subject to Morpheus or not."

Cheryl nodded slowly. "Having the same dream is unsettling, and if I didn't know better, I'd think it was connected to Morpheus, but Jack periodically checks and rechecks the entire system and there are no connections to Morpheus, so that's impossible."

Rita sighed. "I wish they would destroy that back up, even if it isn't connected. I'd feel so much better if they did." She wanted to tell Cheryl that Jordan had the same dream, but she was upset enough. Rita wanted to run it by Lorenzo too, but she wanted to honor her promise to Jordan for the time being, so she kept her mouth shut.

"Things are moving a little too fast," Cheryl said. "I'm not afraid to say that I'm intimidated by the extent of the expansion that Crowley is pushing in other parts of the complex. Did you see the size of that hospital and its facilities? Then there are the specialties -- cybernetic limbs and organs, Dreamsleep, Immersive Combat, and a secret Euthanasia room. It feels like too much too soon."

"I agree. It's an added pressure that I would rather not have."

"We have too many unanswered questions to be going this fast."

"But we do have some say in things. We're not totally helpless. Excuse the pun, but together we stuck to our guns and made it clear that we aren't running any more dream scenarios until we get our psychologist in here to help us sort out this mess. That ought to put a fire under Crowley's ass."

Cheryl waved her finger. "Good point. I don't give a shit about any of his other projects until I'm satisfied that this one is safe."

"If that's possible. I sure do miss Morgan."

Cheryl sighed. "I do too. He was one in a million with big shoes to fill."

"What if Terry acts out and hurts someone," Rita said, "or what if these problems go deeper - beyond psychology to some kind of neurochemical imbalance like schizophrenia or something?"

"According to Crowley, we'll not only have our psychologist, we'll have an entire team of top drawer doctors and specialists to draw on if the need for serious medical intervention arises. No matter what we do or what kind of progress or lack of progress we make, you can rest assured that he's moving ahead with his plans to make this complex the largest fully functional rehabilitation center in the world."

"He doesn't need us for any of that."

"Though this whole wounded warrior project is built around our work," Cheryl said, "we're only a small part of the big picture. Crowley is hell bent on tackling rehabilitation at the roots on all fronts; physical, mental, and emotional."

CHAPTER THIRTY FOUR

Jordan went back to the team lounge to find Wesley in one of the easy chairs finishing off his breakfast. John and Carl sprawled on the ends of the couch across from him, their empty plates littering the coffee table.

"How did your meeting with Penélope go?" John asked. "Did you get lucky?"

Jordan smiled. "Funny John. I wanted to make sure they knew about our fun night." He filled his plate at the buffet, then took a seat in the recliner beside Wesley. "Terry still sleeping?"

"Thankfully yes." Wesley stuffed a last bite of toast into his mouth and set his plate down. "We've been keeping it down. Hopefully he slept off all that weird drinking, paranoia, and nightmare shit."

"I wouldn't bet on it," John said. "I don't think I've ever seen anybody as wigged out as that. We all know how real it seemed, but I never forgot that it was a dream. That's what kept me going."

"What about the rest of you guys?" Jordan asked.

"I'll admit, I got the shit scared out of me a few times,' Carl said, "but I never forgot that it was a dream."

"I got so into it that I forgot a few times," Wesley said. "I had to keep reminding myself."

"Same for me," Jordan added. "I was in and out of it, but no matter what I thought or felt, my drive to complete the mission overruled everything."

Wesley rubbed his chin. "I'm wondering if Terry got so blown away by the realism of it all that he totally forgot he was in a dream."

"It's possible," Jordan said. "Listen, give him a break when he wakes up. We need to give him some space and let him talk when he wants. Who knows where his head is at after the game, the drinking, and the nightmare? Maybe he slept some of it off."

"That's exactly what happened," Terry mumbled, shuffling out of his room, holding his head. "It was so real, I forgot I was dreaming and thought the whole thing was real. My head's killing me. I need some aspirin."

Jordan set his plate on the coffee table and went to the bathroom. "I'll get you some. You need to eat. Get something in your stomach."

He hurried back with a glass of water and handed it to Terry along with two aspirin.

"Thanks." Terry washed the aspirin down with water and filled a plate.

Jordan went back to his chair and his breakfast while Terry pulled up another chair by the far end of the coffee table to sit down and eat. Jordan set his plate down and looked to the others who all had questioning looks.

"It must have kept going in your head," Jordan said. "That was quite the nightmare you had."

Terry looked up. "What nightmare?"

Wesley frowned. "Last night, don't you…"

"You don't remember anything from last night?" Jordan cut in.

Terry shook his head. "The last thing I remember is coming here and getting a drink. The rest is a blank. I remember getting lost in our battle which kind of seems more real than being here now with you guys."

"Missing in action," John quipped.

Jordan gave him a look that shut him up.

"The whole thing together," Terry added, staring down at the floor, "ever since we got here feels like one big blurred nightmare. If you want to know the truth, I'm confused about what's real and what isn't."

Carl leaned forward and patted Terry on the arm. "Don't beat yourself up over it. It was intense for all of us."

"And it did seem more than real," Wesley added.

"But in the end it was only a dream," John said.

"I had a talk with our angel nurse this morning," Jordan said. "They're not going to put us into any more dreams until they get a shrink to help us make sense of it all."

"I don't care what they tell me," Terry said in a barely audible voice. "I don't think I want to do that again."

"I can't wait to get back into it," John said.

Jordan looked to Wesley and Carl. "What about you guys?"

"I'm still on the fence about it," Carl said. "Part of me is scared shit, but that was our first time. It might feel more comfortable going back into it with the experience we now have under our belts."

"Return to the scene of the crime," John said. "That's the way to do it!"

Jordan looked over at Wesley, who nodded. "I'm a little freaked out too, but I'm thinking that the secret lies in remembering that it is a dream even though it seems real when it's happening. I'm not ready to go back yet, but maybe if I give it some time." He rubbed his chin. "What about you, Jordy?"

"There might be something to remembering that it is a dream when we're in it, but I don't think I'm ready to try again for awhile."

"No matter which way you look at it," Carl said, "It was a mind fuck of major proportions. Bring on the shrinks. Let's figure out what the fuck is going on with this shit."

John nodded. "Yeah, let's get it on and see how far we can take it."

Jordan exchanged glances with Wesley and Carl, seeing the same look in their eyes, reflecting his own concerns about John's gung ho attitude.

They heard a knock on the door and after a short pause, Crowley strode in beaming. Terry looked up when he entered.

"How's my history making dream team doing today?" Crowley circled around and stood by the end of the couch.

"We were just trying to figure that out ourselves," Wesley said.

Crowley moved closer to Terry and rested a hand on his shoulder in a fatherly gesture. "How about you, Killjoy?" Crowley lowered his voice. "Feeling any better after a good night's sleep and a solid breakfast?"

"I don't know. I guess I'm okay, but I'm not going back into that dream, I can tell you that."

Crowley patted his shoulder. "Don't worry, son. Nobody's going to make you do anything you don't want to." He looked around at Carl, John, and Wesley, then to Jordan. "What about the rest of you?"

"I'm ready to rock and roll!" John said, pumping his fist.

"The rest of us haven't made up our minds," Jordan said, speaking for the team.

"I hate to sound like a doomsayer," Wesley said, "but I don't think this computer dreaming stuff is going to work as a game." He pointed at Terry. "Killjoy here is a top notch pro."

Terry looked up and brightened at the mention of his professional status.

Wesley nodded. "Even he got a little freaked out playing this thing because it was so real. What do you think will happen with the thousands of other less experienced wannabes and younger kids?"

Crowley stood. "Let me remind you that what we are doing here is not only groundbreaking, but it's in the early prototype stages." He shook his finger like a lecturing professor. "Were in this for the long run and anticipate issues that need to be dealt with. Aside from your direct involvement, we have been collecting extensive information on every aspect of your play and performance, including your psychological and physiological responses in a master profile that we hope to manipulate in ways that can enhance your performance. There are hundreds of variables we can alter to change multiple aspects of the experience. Make no mistake about it, gentlemen, this goes far beyond simple gaming."

He made a sweeping gesture. "The gaming possibilities are only a small portion of this multibillion dollar program. We also have plans for medical applications of this technology."

Carl sat up frowning. "Medical applications? For dreaming games? How can you do medical things in a dream?"

John leaned in, finger in the air. "That's what the 'Dedicated to Serving Those Who Have Served Us' sign we saw on the way in means!"

Crowley smiled. "That's right!"

"Does this have anything to do with that euthanasia stuff that they started this project with?" Carl said.

Terry looked up, eyes wide. "They're going to use this to kill people?"

Crowley held up both hands. "Not like that. It's part of a much bigger project to help war veterans."

"That's why everything here is so big and secret," Wesley said.

"And why we had to go through all that security clearance crap," Jordan added.

Crowley sighed and spoke in a low intimate tone. "We've kept most of our bigger plans under a code of silence, but with the success of yesterday's test, we want you to know that what you are doing here goes way beyond simple gaming. In fact, the groundbreaking work that you're doing here is a great service to your country."

The room fell silent while everyone digested Crowley's words.

Finally, Wesley said, "It sounds like we enlisted in the military."

"Kind of," Crowley said, "but your status is more that of a government contractor."

Jordan looked at his teammates, seeing the same confused frowns.

Crowley reached into an inner pocket of his jacket, pulled out five envelopes, and handed one to each member of the team. "I'm not asking you for a further commitment at this point. I understand that you all need time to think everything through, but there is a five thousand dollar check for each of you as a bonus for this first success. You have already done a great service for us."

In the silence that followed everyone's expressions went from frowns to wide eyed amazement. No one said anything. They didn't have to. Their stunned expressions said it all.

"Regardless of whether you choose to continue or not, we need you to stay here for awhile for observation, especially with Terry's reaction to the scenario. We have a psychiatrist coming on board in the next couple of days who we hope can help you make sense out of everything and give you a healthy perspective."

"How long do we have to stay?" Jordan asked.

"Indefinitely."

CHAPTER THIRTY FIVE

Rita followed Jack and Cheryl into a conference room with Lorenzo coming in behind her to find Crowley sitting at the end of the table with an older gentleman dressed in a gray suit and a red striped tie. They both rose when everyone filed in.

Wizened, Rita thought, an impression that deepened when his blue eyes met hers, followed by a mischievous glint. Wiry and slender, his lined face conveyed the wisdom of his years, but his vitality was apparent in the way he moved.

Crowley grinned and held out his hand to the older man. "I'm pleased to introduce you to the newest member of our team, Doctor Stanley Krippner, psychologist. Doctor Krippner has written and done extensive research on altered states of consciousness, dream telepathy, hypnosis, shamanism, dissociation, and parapsychology."

Cheryl looked at Rita with raised eyebrows, then Jack Scanlon, with the widest grin Rita had seen in quite some time stuck his hand out to Krippner. "Jack Scanlon," he said. "I'm a big fan of yours. I'm a Deadhead! You were best buddies with Mickey Hart and the shaman Rolling Thunder."

Krippner smiled and took Jack's hand in both of his. "Thank you." He looked a little embarrassed by Jack's enthusiasm.

Cheryl shook hands with him next. "Cheryl Martin. I'm also a bit of a fan of your work, Doctor Krippner, but not in the same way Jack is. I look forward to working closely with you." She made a little curtsy.

Krippner gave a lopsided smile. "Please everyone, enough with the formality. Call me Stan." He took Rita's hand and gave it a warm squeeze.

"Rita Cariño," she said. "I can't tell you how pleased we are to have you."

"Same here," Lorenzo said, shaking Stan's hand. "Good to have you on board. We needed a dream doctor, which is almost impossible to find, but if anyone can do the job, my money's on you."

"Please, everyone have a seat," Crowley said, dropping back into his chair. "I've briefed Stan on the situation with Terry. He'll be talking to him this afternoon and hopefully get a sense of what's going on in his head."

Stan nodded. "After I spend some time with him and assess the level of his trauma, I'll visit with the rest of the team one at a time so I can do individual assessments."

He looked from Cheryl to Jack to Rita, then to Lorenzo. "Once we get a handle on Terry and his teammates, I will be assessing each one of you. I've been briefed on everything you went through in the demise of DreamLand, not to mention the stresses of political asylum and the threat of Mexican prison. From the fascinating accounts I read, whether real or imagined, you have all been through plenty of your own traumas."

Cheryl looked over at Rita and gave her a slight nod.

"We plan to integrate Stan's assessments into our psychological profiles," Crowley said, "as part of an enhanced profile of every gamer including the information on their play and performance, and their psychological and physiological responses. We hope to manipulate this master profile in ways that can improve performance."

"That's part of the deal," Stan said. "I don't really care about improving play and performance. In fact, I have nothing to do with that part of the project. I'm interested in helping people come to terms with their traumas."

"We also plan to use these same profiles for vets with PTSD and other psychological issues," Crowley said, as if in defense of the profiles. "As a possible adjunct in their therapy."

"That could be promising," Stan said. "I look forward to seeing how all this whiz-bang technology works. I'm used to more what might be called 'primitive' methods."

Rita imagined him being perfectly at home sitting cross-legged in some large open air hut in the middle of the jungle with a feathered shaman dancing around chanting and blowing smoke.

"Our primary goal here above all else, including enhanced

performance," Crowley said, "is what the sign over the door says. Dedicated to serving those who have served us." He made a sweeping gesture. "This whole facility will be teeming with personnel in the coming weeks and months, all dedicated to that goal. We expect to be fully operational in under a year."

"If you don't mind," Stan said putting his hands on the table and rising. "I'd like to get settled and have that talk with Terry. I'll meet with each of you later -- informally of course, so we can get to know each other better and discover what kind of healing we can do."

He smiled and bowed his head.

CHAPTER THIRTY SIX

"I'm not so sure about this shit." Wesley put his recliner in the upright position and rested his head in his hand.

"What are you talking about?" John said. "We just got five grand each for playing that game!"

"That's great," Wesley answered, "but what's up with this staying here indefinitely shit and where the fuck is Todd?"

"I've been wondering about that myself," Jordan said. "I'm also wondering about what they expect us to do to help war veterans, not to mention all the security clearance crap, and the fact that we're stuck in what could be either a prison or a military base, depending on the way you look at it."

Terry shook his head. "I'm more mixed up than ever. There's no fucking way I want to go back into that dreaming game." He waved his envelope in the air. "But I have to admit, this five G's is giving me second thoughts."

"Crowley promised us a shrink," Carl said. "Maybe he'll help us decide."

"I don't know about you guys," Wesley said, "but I'm getting a little stir crazy. Sure the money, the food, and anything else we want is great, and Crowley has been more than nice to us, but I wouldn't mind getting out and doing a little clubbing. Find me a honey."

John nodded and grabbed his crotch. "That's a good point. I haven't been laid in awhile." He nodded toward Terry. "It's been even longer for Terry."

Terry flipped his middle finger up at John and they all laughed.

Things seem to be getting a little back to normal, Jordan thought.

"Why don't we all demand another talk with Crowley?" Carl said. "Maybe he can give us a day pass or something."

One of the big screens on the far wall flickered to life and Crowley's face filled it. "Our psychologist Doctor Krippner is on the premises," he said, "and I think you guys are going to like him. He's going to talk to Terry first, then he'll have a chat with the rest of you, but I'd like to talk to all of you first and address your concerns."

Address our concerns? Jordan thought. Was he listening to us?

"I'm sending someone to come get you," Crowley said. "I want you to see just how big the entire Pandora Project really is and I want to air out any concerns you have so you can talk freely with Doctor Krippner about your dreaming experience without any distractions or confusion about your role here."

A knock came on the door.

"That's your escort," Crowley said.

A lanky red-headed army sergeant poked his head in the door. "I'm ready whenever you guys are."

"I'll see you in a few minutes," Crowley said, then the monitor went dark.

The sergeant led them through the creepy Gallery of Angels. Jordan wondered how they became angels, but didn't want to ask. Next they went down a long curving corridor called the Hall of Dreams. Its pictures of adults looked creepy in their own right.

The guard hit the button on an elevator at the far end of the hall and the door whooshed open. No one said anything when the door shut and the elevator rose, taking them past ground level up to the North Tower. The door opened to a long hallway that led to an oak office door that opened into a glass walled office overlooking an atrium.

"Welcome to ground zero of the Pandora Project," Crowley said from behind a large U-shaped console at the center of a tiled floor. "Have a seat." He gestured to five chairs across from him and tapped an iPad. A wall of eight screens surrounding a bigger screen sequenced through different areas of the complex. "I wanted to give you guys a little visual of what's coming up the pike."

He cycled through a series of camera pans that showed a large dome outfitted as a hospital with patient rooms, a large cafeteria, operating rooms, X-Ray facilities, laboratories, laundry, and lounges, then he switched to different views of a tunnel leading to another large circular room with a domed ceiling lined with rows of dreaming cradles, then another lined with hospital beds. Groups of workers moved equipment in and worked on consoles beside each bed.

"Like I mentioned before, our primary goal is to heal the wounded with this technology," Crowley said. "With your help, we hope to market the gaming side of it to make money to fund everything else." He looked directly at Wesley. "That's where Todd will come in. He's going to be our primary liaison with the gaming community."

Either he's reading our minds or he can hear what we talk about, Jordan thought. Maybe even see us. I'm not comfortable with that. He took a deep mental breath. Let's see how this plays out.

"I understand how challenging it must be for you to stay here," Crowley went on. "You all have personal lives, friends, and girlfriends." He winked at John, who smiled. "But we're at a critical point in the project and we need your full cooperation. We've made special arrangements for all your needs to be taken care of, that means bills, expenses, and any other ongoing obligations you might have in the outside world. We also have a generous incentive program that you got a taste of earlier today."

"But you have no idea how long we have to stay?" Wesley asked.

Crowley shook his head. "Sorry, it's too early to tell."

"If it drags on too long," John said. "Do you think you can hook us up with some ladies like you did after the Paris tournament?"

Crowley broke out in a wide grin. "We could probably arrange something."

"Maybe a little field trip?" Carl asked.

"That's a possibility," Crowley answered, "but let's not get ahead of ourselves. Give it a little time." He looked to Terry, who sat up, leaning forward, listening closely. "We don't want any of you to do anything you don't want to. It's important to have your full cooperation. We have other teams lined up who are more than willing to take part in our history making tests, but you guys are the best and we would rather work with you."

He looked to each of them ending at Jordan. "Once Doctor Krippner talks to Terry and evaluates the rest of you, we'll meet again. If you decide to move forward and re-immerse yourselves in the experience, then I can promise you this. Each time you go into a battle scenario your bonus will increase and there will be added incentives for exceptional performance."

"I'm in!" John said. "I love this shit!"

The others all looked at each other.

Crowley smiled and shook his head. "Give yourself a little time, hotshot. Think it over. You don't have to kamikaze everything."

"Oh yes, he does!" Carl said. "That boy's a cruise missile."

"He's right," Wesley said, nodding. "He can't help himself."

John brightened until Terry said, "Even when he's being an asshole!"

John's anger flashed across his face and the rest of the team burst out laughing, which made Jordan relax more. Carl slapped Terry on the back and they both shook with laughter, then Crowley guffawed followed by Jordan and John, completing the circle.

Jordan felt lighter after they settled down, but he still felt uneasy.

Crowley clapped his hands together and rubbed them. "I think that covers things for the moment unless any of you dream team warriors have any more burning questions."

When no one said anything he stood and came around his desk to stand beside Terry. "I'll have the escort bring you back to your quarters. Thank you for understanding our need to keep you here. Take some time to think about what we discussed." He put his hand on Terry's shoulder. "I'm going to take Terry down to meet Doctor Krippner."

CHAPTER THIRTY SEVEN

Crowley led Rita, Lorenzo, Jack, and Cheryl through a doorway to one of the massive outer domes of the sprawling complex that opened into the hospital. Doctors, nurses, and orderlies moved about, getting everything in readiness. Crowley led them past a nurse's station and down a long hallway lined with immaculate rooms.

"We're getting our first wave of patients tomorrow from the San Diego Naval Medical Center near Balboa Park," he said. "Most of them will be amputees, but we're expecting some who are intact with severe PTSD."

"I take it Doctor Krippner will be looking after them," Cheryl said, passing through a doorway to another hall, close behind Crowley.

Crowley stopped. "Not directly, no. We have a staff of psychiatrists and therapists to help them. Doctor Krippner's focus will be on our dream team and our staff." He nodded toward Rita and the others. "His contribution to the enhanced profiles we're developing is vital to the project."

Crowley pushed through the door into a cafeteria where pots and pans clinked and staff members worked, then he led them through pristine operating rooms and X-Ray facilities where technicians made last minute adjustments to equipment. After passing through a number of fully staffed laboratories, they ended the hospital tour in a tastefully furnished lounge where Crowley stood in a wide stance, arms crossed, speaking with passion and authority. "We're giving them the best care possible and hope to do something beyond that."

"It's impressive," Lorenzo said.

"None of this would be here if it wasn't for the groundbreaking work you folks did in your initial euthanasia project, which we intend to expand and honor as an integral part of our overall objective."

Lorenzo rubbed his chin. "These enhanced profiles you keep referring to," he said. "I see how that works with gamers, their performance, and their scenarios. That kind of thing has been done since the inception of gaming, but never in any way with information as dense as what we're developing. What about these vets? Their profiles will be quite different from a gamer's. How do you plan to implement them?"

"I think Jack is the best one to answer that," Crowley said.

Jack's eyebrows wiggled and his voice came matter of fact. "We're making design changes to the dream hood and control chip function that will allow the profiles to be downloaded to individual hoods, which will personalize them. I'm calling it DreamWare for DreamWear." He finished with a Cheshire Cat grin.

Cheryl smirked and shook her head, then Crowley led them back through circular hallways to the main building until they stood underneath the arch with the backlit metal letters that said:

IMMERSIVE COMBAT

"I have to admit, that title doesn't bring up pictures of healing for me," Rita said.

"It does sounds a little hawkish," Cheryl added.

"We need to return to the scene of the crime," Crowley said, ushering them into the former Hansel and Gretel attraction. "Doc Krippner will tell you that the only way to effectively deal with trauma is to confront and face the terror head on, which is never fun or pleasant."

"Get back on the horse that threw you," Jack said.

"If you can do that in a safe, supervised environment," Crowley continued, "where you relive the event in the most realistic way possible, without any real danger of physically getting harmed, you can release the trauma and gain a new perspective that will diminish if not completely eliminate PTSD symptoms."

Rita went in last with Lorenzo following into the inner dome lined with dreaming cradles. The sight of so many of them in what had been Hansel and Gretel made Rita uneasy, but part of her felt accepting in spite of her discomfort. She never felt comfortable with Crowley and questioned his methods, but what he said here and his logic behind it echoed what she had learned in more than one psych class. What he proposed had the potential to bring about drastic changes in the behavior of those who had been psychologically traumatized. She wasn't sure how that would play in to those with physical traumas, but it had to be a step in the right direction.

She glanced over at Cheryl who appeared lost in thought and wondered if she might be thinking the same thing. The thought of going into another dream made her shiver, but the prospect of escaping her nightmares tugged another way. Her experience went beyond war. It was a surreal, demented fairy tale that stretched the bounds of sanity and reality. Could any of this take her back to that? She thought of rats and shivered again.

She didn't want to know.

"This is where enhanced profiles and combat dream scenarios like ambushes, mines, and loss of limb from IED's will be customized to the unique circumstances of each victim."

Crowley led them out and over to what had been the Pied Piper. The backlit letters on this arch said:

DREAMSLEEP

They filed into another dome, only this one was lined with rows of hospital beds. Workers moved equipment and made adjustments to consoles stationed beside each bed.

"This one looks a little more serious," Lorenzo said.

Crowley nodded. "Those who have been brain damaged like Hodge will be put into Dream Sleep using the same protocols we developed for him with the hope of curing them one day if there is any possibility of doing so."

"Kind of like deep freezing them," Jack said.

Lorenzo nodded slowly, adding, "In an electronic purgatory somewhere between dreaming and dying."

Cheryl spoke up. "More like a dream coma, but without pain, with all their vital signs monitored, and all their needs met. In the same way that we stabilized Hodge, we can monitor each patient with a hybrid combination of drugs and dreaming that suits their specific condition."

"Which brings us to the final step in this managed care model, the Euthanasia Room," Crowley said. "It's virtually identical to this one, so I won't show you it, but it's a place for those too far gone and in too much pain to stay alive. They will meet their end there in the most peaceful and loving environments that you can create."

"What about the cybernetic limb and organ labs?" Jack said. "I've been reading up on those. They're incorporating more and more microprocessors into the designs."

"We're taking that to the next level," Crowley said. "You of all people are going to love this, Jack. Come on!" He motioned with his head and led everyone to the doorway under the arch that said:

CYBERNETIC LIMB FACILITY

This room held several partially constructed assembly lines dotted with robotic arms and associated machinery. Numerous crates remained unopened and scores of technicians tinkered with equipment and drove forklifts carrying heavy machinery, tools, and parts while drones buzzed back and forth like worker bees, seemingly of their own accord, picking up and dropping off smaller items.

"We have been developing this project in parallel with your work, but to date have had no connection. Eventually, we want to tie in the command and control functions of the cybernetic limbs developed here directly into the command and control functions of the microprocessor in Jack and Cheryl's dreaming hood."

Jack pursed his lips. "One stop shopping and centralized control, especially for those tasks requiring mobility and dexterity." He held up a finger. "I like the concept of having everything in one place. It simplifies things!"

"And it will be alongside the physiological and life support monitoring," Cheryl said, "with an option for drug, nutrient, and hormone delivery."

Crowley nodded toward the room. "Which could become more critical when you factor in the variables involved with cybernetic organs and what might be needed to keep the body from rejecting them, but I'm getting ahead of myself. This facility will be automated by state of the art robotics which will be self maintaining and self sufficient."

"It will fix itself?" Rita asked.

"With a combination of the latest in 3D printing technologies that produce production parts using a variety of metals and alloys from 3D CAD data without the need for tooling.

It will also use a fusion technique that melts metal powder with an electron beam in a high vacuum and selective laser melting using 3D CAD data as a digital information source, and a high power laser to sinter powdered metal by aiming the laser at points in space defined by a 3D model."

"No human intervention, ever?" Rita said, finding it hard to imagine.

Crowley nodded emphatically. "That's our goal. Self sufficiency and maximum efficiency. Having every manufacturing process automated means we'll need no lights, require less overall environmental control, and there will be no need for breaks or loss of production, except for rare maintenance cycles."

"I don't know why," Rita said, "but it makes me think of a runaway train."

"You can rest assured that everything will be precisely monitored," Crowley said in a reassuring tone, "to exacting specifications and zero error tolerance."

He gestured toward the door. "The same will hold true for our last stop on the tour, only this will be controlled in a different way as we'll be introducing biological elements that require a higher level of precision and monitoring."

He led them into the dome entrance under the arch titled:

CYBERNETIC ORGAN FACILITY

The assembly line work stations lined up under this dome looked like the previous one, but its stations had additional Plexiglas holding tanks fed by colored tubes that came down from ceiling pipes and conduits.

"Using similar manufacturing principles that we applied to making cybernetic limbs, we've combined stem cell therapy and soft tissue growth to manufacture organs to replace and augment those whose functionality have been compromised from injuries."

"And I take it, this will be automated too," Rita said, stating the obvious.

"Yes, but due to the delicacy of the processes, we'll keep a closer human eye on this part of the operation."

Lorenzo shook his head. "I don't know what to think. Part of me is amazed at all this cybernetics, robotics, and self-sufficiency, but another part can't stop thinking about how much this reminds me of Skynet and the Terminator."

"Or the Borg," Rita added.

"I ain't wearing no red shirt!" Jack quipped, laughing at his own joke.

CHAPTER THIRTY EIGHT

"What the fuck is going on with all this guard and escort shit?" Carl said, after the guard brought them back to their lounge. "It's starting to bug me. I don't know about you guys, but I'm starting to feel like I'm in prison or something."

"They need the security," John said. "This is next level shit we're working on here and they're paying us big bucks to do it."

Wesley stretched out on one end of the couch. "I'm loving the money and it hasn't been boring, but I have to admit, something doesn't feel right."

John sat on the other end of the couch and Carl took a recliner, while Jordan sat in the big chair by the end of the couch where Terry usually sat.

"What do you mean?" John said. "We're making bank and blazing a trail into a whole new world of gaming and we're getting rock star treatment. You can't let Terry's freak out…"

"It's got nothing to do with Terry," Wesley cut in. "It's my gut, but I can't put my finger on it." He looked around at the others until his gaze came to rest on Jordan. "You're pretty quiet, Jordan. Something bugging you too?"

"Just thinking," Jordan said. After their meeting with Crowley, he had no doubt that Crowley was watching, listening, and recording everything they said and did. It didn't surprise him, but it made him feel exposed and violated.

Wesley stared at him, puzzled.

Jordan glanced around at the screens on the walls, acting like he was stretching. Every red power indicator glowed active and in that moment it dawned on him that all the monitors had cameras and two way communication that acted like one way mirrors. The realization that they lived in a fishbowl made him queasy.

"I've been thinking about our strategies." He pushed himself up from his chair. "There's an article in Game Developer magazine that I want you guys to take a look at."

"That's pretty random," John said. "We're talking about making history and helping wounded vets with the most realistic gaming platform anyone has ever seen and you're thinking about an article in Game Developer? Hello? Earth to Jordan."

Jordan went to his room, found the magazine, a note pad, and a pen. With his back to the screen on his wall he hunched over the magazine and scribbled a note.

> Don't react when you read this. Be cool. They're watching everything we say and do through the cameras on all the screens. I'll bet that's what's bugging Wesley. I know it's been bothering me.
>
> Think about what we just talked about with Crowley. How did he know so much about our concerns, especially about Todd?

Jordan tore the note from the pad and tucked it between the pages of the magazine, then went back to the others. He looked Carl in the eye when he handed him the magazine and pointed to the note. "This is a great strategy."

Carl frowned as he read it, then looked up at Jordan with mild surprise. "I see what you mean." He nodded and handed the magazine to John, pointing to the note.

John grabbed it and read, then looked up, his mouth moving as if trying to find the right words. "Can't argue with that. Good strategy," he said, sounding awkward. He handed the magazine to Wesley, taking care to keep his finger on the note.

Wesley's eyes narrowed as he read, then he looked up, straight at Jordan. "That makes sense." He lowered his head and nodded. "It explains a lot. We'll have to incorporate that into our next game." He

closed the magazine and handed it back to Jordan. "We'll have to share it with Terry when he gets back."

An uneasy silence fell over them. Jordan didn't want it to go on too long, so he thought up things to say to make the conversation sound natural. "Speaking of Terry, I wonder how he's making out with that shrink?"

"I hope it helps," Carl said. "I'd hate to lose him."

"Agreed." Wesley sighed. "The team wouldn't be the same without Killjoy."

"I can't help but wonder how our game playing is going to help those wounded vets?" Jordan said, finding something he felt safe talking about.

"That's a no-brainer," John answered. "Crowley told us they plan to make bank on the game version of these dreams to continue funding the project with Pandora Partnerships as the official sponsor."

Wesley put his hands behind his head and stretched backward. "They're putting a lot of time and energy into us and this program based on our winning game to help veterans with PTSD." He sat up straight. "And the first time we play it, it's so real one of our own freaks out. Doesn't that seem a little weird?"

"Maybe a little too close to home," Carl said.

"Think about it," Jordan said. "We all shared the same winning battle scenario in the middle of a huge hospital built for wounded veterans who have their own PTSD nightmares." He crossed his arms and looked around at his teammates. "Where do you think this is going?"

The door to their room opened and Terry walked in, head down, shoulders slouched, with his hands in his pockets.

"Terry!" John said. "We were just talking about you. How did you make out with the shrink?"

Terry shrugged and sat down in the recliner next to Carl. "I don't know. I have to see him again tomorrow."

"What did he tell you?" Carl asked.

"He thinks I should go back into the dream and face what scares me."

"What do you think?" Wesley asked.

Terry shrugged. "Don't know."

"Did he give you any good drugs?" John asked, wiggling his eyebrows. "Something to chill you out a little more instead of booze?"

"He's not a fan of prescription drugs," Terry said, "or booze. He thinks we can talk things out and work through my issues in the dreams, but only if I'm willing. He made it clear that he's not telling me what to do or forcing me to do anything I don't want to. It's up to me and I have to make up my own mind. He promised to guide me if I want to move ahead with the project."

"But you're still up in the air," Jordan said.

Terry nodded.

Jordan winked and handed him the magazine, marking the page with his finger. "I'm not trying to influence you in any way, but we've been thinking about a new strategy that I found in Game Developer."

"Really? In Game Developer?" Terry looked at the others, his brow knitted in perplexity, then he opened the magazine. His face showed a gamut of emotions as he read, ending with an expression that hovered between fear and confusion.

CHAPTER THIRTY NINE

R ita walked through the curving hallway to Lorenzo's lab with her arm around his waist and his arm draped over her shoulder. Cheryl and Jack followed. The three big screen video editing bays lining the walls of his lab had different parts of Seal Team 0's battle scenario frozen in pause mode. Cheryl and Jack sat in two overstuffed chairs at the room's lounge area at its center and Rita sat next to Lorenzo on the couch.

"I never would have imagined things getting this big," Lorenzo said, "then again, I never would have imagined what happened to DreamLand either."

"A little too big, if you ask me," Jack said. "It's moving too fast and in too many directions." He held up a finger and spun it in a circle. "I have to admit, I'm a little conflicted."

Cheryl looked up from her iPad, eyebrows raised. "Do tell."

"I'm beside myself with the possibilities of integrating my C and C chip in the dreaming hood and into the command and control functions of the cybernetic limbs, especially when you consider the possibilities that downloadable profiles bring to the equation."

Cheryl shook her head. "It's one thing to integrate it into the dreaming hood and its downloadable profiles, but it's a whole 'nother ball of wax when we get into implanting microprocessors into the brain the way we have with Hodge. It's painstaking work that will have to be fine-tuned to each individual. Not a lot of room for error."

"It has pluses and minuses," Jack said thoughtfully. "The whole concept of centralized control makes sense from an engineering standpoint for the amputees, especially those tasks requiring mobility and dexterity."

Cheryl's brow furrowed. "It gets infinitely more complicated when you factor in the physiological and life support aspects, not to mention the possibilities that drug and hormone delivery bring. I wish we could slow everything down. Crowley's pushing it all too fast."

"And it's so big," Rita said, holding her hands out. "And there are so many details, none of which can be ignored."

"It feels like it could go off the rails at any time," Lorenzo added.

"Crowley told us it was big," Rita said, "but I had no idea how extensive it is. It makes me nervous." She leaned in closer to Lorenzo, feeling comfort in his closeness.

Cheryl looked into her eyes. "At least we have Doctor Krippner on board now. He's no Morgan, but it's something. I have a good feeling about him."

"I do too," Rita said, feeling her loss well up inside. "He'll never replace Morgan, but I couldn't think of a better replacement. I like his attitude and what he had to say about what kind of healing we can do."

Cheryl nodded. "I'm hoping he can be the voice of reason that can reel Crowley in."

Lorenzo shook with laughter. "Like that's going to happen."

Jack leaned forward, speaking in a low conspiratorial tone. "The thing of it is, this has a life of its own that's bigger than us, but we're at the core of it and have a lot of control over how it develops."

"I hope Doctor Krippner sees things our way and doesn't become another tool for Crowley," Rita said. "It would be great to have him on our side."

"The jury is still out on him as far as I'm concerned," Lorenzo said. "He's a wild card, but I'm encouraged by what I've seen. Obviously Crowley hires people who will push his agenda, but he's also caught in a bit of a Catch 22, because he needs people with specific skill sets, so we can hope that Doctor Krippner is an independent thinker who shares our concerns more than he shares Crowley's."

"I couldn't have said it any better," Cheryl said.

"I wouldn't worry about Doc Krippner," Jack said with his trademark Cheshire Cat grin. He held up a finger. "Remember, Crowley said that he 'literally marches to the beat of his own drum'." Jack held up his hand as if taking a pledge. "Trust me. I'm here to tell you, that's probably the only thing Crowley and I agree on."

Lorenzo chuckled and gave Rita's hand a gentle squeeze. "We'll see how the mystery unfolds."

CHAPTER FORTY

"How about you, Jordan?" Doctor Krippner asked. "Have you been having nightmares since your dream game?" His blue eyes questioned Jordan the way his mother looked at him when he got into trouble as a kid. He could never lie to her when she looked at him that way.

Wiry, slender, and dapper, Krippner's lined face conveyed insight and intelligence. In spite of his years he crackled with energy. His tailored gray suit and red striped tie seemed to amplify his authority. Jordan thought of him as a skinny Yoda.

Feeling uncomfortable, Jordan looked around the office. The ever present screen on one wall made him feel like he was being spied on. Shelves lined with books covered two other walls, along with feathered tribal art, rattles, a shaman's drum, and native embroidery, making this office feel warmer and more natural than any of the others he had been in.

"Terry's nightmare is no secret," Stan said, getting Jordan's attention.

"Wesley and Carl had them too," Jordan said, "but not as bad as Terry. The only one who hasn't is John. He has battle dreams, but he doesn't react to them like nightmares."

Stan's wry smile helped Jordan relax a notch.

"I wanted to talk to you last," Stan continued. "You're what they call the in game leader and you seem to be the most level headed. Your teammates agree, especially Wesley. I'm willing to bet that you've had extracurricular dreams? Whether they're nightmares or not depends on you."

"Yeah," Jordan offered, gauging how much to share. Though the monitor on the wall made him feel exposed, he felt safe talking to Stan. "Well doc, one of the things I can honestly say is that the boundaries between sleeping, dreaming, and what is real all feel blurred."

"Can you give me an example of what you mean?"

Jordan sighed. "It's the weirdest thing, but around here everything feels weird."

Stan chuckled. "I'm afraid I'm inclined to agree."

"That night that Terry had his nightmare, I was dreaming that I was back in the dream battle we had gone into that day too -- at the same time. Though it seemed real, it wasn't that big of a deal to me, partly because it was a repeat of our winning game, but my dream didn't have the intensity of the computer dream. It felt more like a kind of shadow world and I knew how to act until I heard Terry crying. He sounded so freaked out that my dream turned into a nightmare until I woke up and heard him crying for real, which really spooked me."

"So you think you were sharing his dream?"

Jordan nodded. "Yeah. It could have freaked me out even more, except that we had all just shared the same dream when we were in the computer dream, so this -- I don't know -- dream hangover?"

"Maybe a kind of reflection," Stan offered. "You know, like an echo or the ripples from a rock dropped into a pond."

"That sounds about right," Jordan said.

Stan smiled. "It's the image that came to mind after talking to the rest of the team."

Jordan contemplated the echo effect and started to tell Stan that Rita had shared the same dream, then he caught himself, remembering his promise.

"What is it?" Stan asked.

"Nothing." Jordan waved his hand. "I'm just thinking about your ripple example. The more I think about it the more it makes sense."

"There's no pressure from me with this next question. I'm just curious. Do you think you'll go back into the Pandora dreams?"

"You told the other guys that you thought they should, especially the ones with the nightmares."

Stan held up a hand. "I didn't push them. They have to make their own choices, but yes, I did suggest it."

"I would think that you'd push the more comfortable ones like John a little harder, and ease up on the more sensitive ones like Terry."

"If you want to know the truth," Stan said, lowering his voice and leaning conspiratorially across his desk. "I'm not comfortable with the process here and I am admittedly not up to speed on how it works. I have some concerns after all the stories I heard about DreamLand, but I have yet to talk to anyone first hand about it. That's next on my list, but I wanted to talk to you and your teammates first, especially with Terry's reaction."

"Do you think he has PTSD?"

"Textbook," Stan said.

"But you suggested that he go back into the dream."

"The only way to overcome fear is to face it. Though I have my reservations about what happened in DreamLand, the battles you guys went through are only dreams and as far as I can tell, can only cause psychological trauma, which is what I want to heal."

"So you're worried about the DreamLand stories too?"

Stan shrugged. "The DreamLand computer is shut down and off line, so I've tempered my concerns about it, although we're still dealing with a host of unknowns here. I don't know that I would have thrown you guys into this so soon. I might have taken a different approach, but I got dragged into this after everything was set in motion, so I'm doing a bit of triage while trying to play catch up."

Jordan found Stan's honesty and apparent transparency appealing. He didn't push the way Crowley did and seemed to have the team's interest more at heart as opposed to Crowley who had the project as his number one priority and the concerns of the team secondary.

"You never did answer my question," Stan said. "Do you think you'll go back into the computer dreams?"

Jordan crossed his arms and sat back. "I might be persuaded, but that depends on what the rest of the team wants to do. We stick together."

"That's a big part of what makes you guys so good at what you do. I admire and respect that."

"I admit, I was a little freaked out in the dream because it seemed so real, but part of me liked the thrill. Reminding myself that it was a dream helped, but sometimes when the action got intense I forgot."

Stan's eyes brightened. "You just summed up the two ends of the spectrum. John never forgot it was a dream, which empowered him while the realism overwhelmed Terry, convincing him that it was real. From what I've heard, you, Wesley, and Carl bounced back and forth between the poles, but kept things in perspective while Terry and John gravitated to the extremes."

"So you think the key is to stay aggressive and never forget that it's a dream?"

"Easier said than done and not necessarily the answer. The realism is so strong that at times a participant can become so engaged that they forget they're dreaming. I think the secret lies in a newer, dare I say higher state of awareness between the two extremes. I'm thinking that it's a question of navigating a separate reality that follows a more flexible set of rules."

"That opens up a whole 'nother way of looking at it, doesn't it? A separate reality? Saying it that way literally adds a whole new dimension."

Stan leaned back, a thoughtful expression filling his face. His eyes had a faraway look. "Dimensions might be more accurate. Like the mind, the possibilities are infinite, but I'm only speculating at this point based on what I've heard from you and the rest of the team. Once I examine the hard data in your enhanced profiles that Mister Crowley is so gung ho about, and I get some time to talk to the survivors of DreamLand, I may think differently, but based on what I've heard so far, that's my hypothesis going forward."

"That's some pretty far out stuff," Jordan said. "I'm curious. As I understand it, Crowley recruited us because we're a winning team and he's been pushing us because he wants to market this as a fully immersive point and shoot game that will fund everything else."

"That's how I understand it," Stan said.

"I can't help noticing that we're in a hospital and a big part of the work here is to heal PTSD."

"On all levels; physical, emotional, and psychological."

"And the dream game that we're working in is giving people PTSD instead of curing it."

"So it seems, but it's too early to tell, and too early to make any blanket statements. We only have one person out of five showing symptoms at this point."

"All the pieces seem to be here," Jordan said. The rest of his words poured out as if of their own accord. "With all this talk about profiles and everything else I've seen, Crowley plans to train us in this game, but it goes way beyond simple gaming and tournaments, doesn't it?"

Stan nodded.

"He wants us to get so good at this that he wants us to go into battle dreams with PTSD vets, doesn't he?"

Stan nodded faster.

Jordan felt a flash of rage accompanying his feeling of betrayal for Crowley not telling them more and leading everyone on like it was all about the game. "Why didn't he just come out and tell us instead of dancing around it and playing all those word games?"

"He probably didn't want you preoccupied with the thought of it so you would stay focused on the immediate test at hand," Stan said, "and he probably downplayed it even more after Terry's reaction so he didn't scare you guys off."

"More of his need to know bullshit, huh?"

"Something like that. I didn't realize that he hadn't discussed it with you."

"It seems kind of sneaky that he didn't just come out and say it."

"I can see where you would think that. I don't agree with his approach, but I understand why he might have held back after Terry's episode. I'll talk to him about it."

"Better you than me. You can let him know it pissed me off."

"I get it," Stan said. "He didn't bring it up, but from what I've seen and heard, he wasn't hiding it either."

"True," Jordan said, "but he wasn't exactly forthcoming about it."

CHAPTER FORTY ONE

Rita felt comforted in Stan Krippner's office. The bookshelves lining two walls kept it from looking sterile like the other technology enhanced rooms. Feathered tribal art, rattles, shaman's drum, and embroidery on the walls added to her feeling of safety, like an invisible protective container was watched over by ancient *curanderos* and *curanderas*.

"When I interviewed Cheryl Martin," Stan said from behind his desk. "She told me that she has PTSD from the tragedy you both experienced when DreamLand was shut down, and that you might have it worse. She said you both have been plagued by nightmares since DreamLand."

Rita let out a long sigh. "My dreams have never been the same since that whole senseless tragedy, and neither have I. I didn't realize that Cheryl was having nightmares too, until recently. Maybe seeing Hodge, or just being here has made our nightmare flashbacks stronger. They certainly presented strong triggers. I can't speak for Cheryl, but in all honesty, after what happened to me in DreamLand, I'm not so sure of what is real and what is not any more."

Stan leaned forward, listening closely. "That's what Terry said, and he was only dreaming. There is a difference between being traumatized in a dream where you think and believe you are damaged, and real world waking experiences where you actually get physically damaged."

"That's what was so bizarre about DreamLand. All those lines were fuzzy."

"In all the reports I read, you, Jack Scanlon, Cheryl Martin, and Lorenzo all claimed that the dreams became real."

Rita nodded, feeling her heart constrict at the memory.

"But it could have been a shared hallucination," Stan said. "You four are the only survivors. How many died?"

"First Edgar Michaels, who was like a father."

"Hodge's father."

She nodded, feeling her tears welling. "Then Morgan Jackson, who was like a second father." Her voice started to tremble. She cleared her throat, pushing through the rest. "Eddie Driscoll, Denise Moore, the two Daggett's and that poor Emily Fulbright. Seven people." Her tears flowed freely now. "Sorry."

Stan handed her a tissue. "No need to apologize. Seven dead, possibly victims of a mass hallucination. That last one. Emily Fulbright. She allegedly turned into a rat."

"She - she..." Rita sobbed with the words.

Stan leaned across the desk and put his hand on hers. "Take your time. Take a few deep breaths."

Rita took three deep, shuddering breaths and blurted, "She really did. That's why Morgan killed himself! Don't you believe me?"

"I believe that you're convinced, but there was no physical proof of any of this in any of the forensics. You have to admit, it's hard to believe that something like that could actually happen."

Rita felt an emotional dam burst inside her, pouring forth a torrent of grief, anger, and frustration. Stan leaned back and let her cry without comment.

"I'm sorry," she whispered.

"No need to apologize," Stan said softly. "Have a good cry. The release will do you good."

She let it all go until her emotions subsided. Her next words came out as an emotion laced cry. "All we ever wanted to do was relieve the pain and suffering around death and all we got for all our hard work was pain, suffering, and death."

Stan nodded slow, without judgment, which calmed Rita. She wiped her tears with a tissue. "And now we're left with poor brain damaged Hodge, trapped in a drug and dream induced purgatory somewhere between living and dying."

"Your traumas are more immediate than Terry's. You've suffered real loss. One of your mentors died from natural causes and the other took his own life - that's a double abandonment wound."

She nodded and breathed slower, regaining her composure. "I don't know what I would do without my Lorenzo," she said. "I'd be lost without him. He's been my one guiding light in the darkness. My rock."

Stan smiled. "He's a good man. I found him remarkably stable, especially after everything all of you have been through. The hallucinations and murders at DreamLand, the threat of prosecution for murder and life in a Mexican prison. He and Jack Scanlon have been through almost as much as you and Cheryl, but neither of them are suffering from recurring nightmares. Do you think it's because they are stoic males and you and Cheryl are more sensitive to the tragedy?"

She shook her head. "It's not that at all. It's because I spent more time in the dreams. Cheryl must have spent more time in them than I realized. Jack and Lorenzo hardly spent any time in them."

Stan held up both hands. "Hold on a minute. You think your PTSD nightmares are from your dreaming experiences at DreamLand like Terry's is here and not from the actual real world deaths?"

"I don't think. I know. Don't get me wrong, I'm not insensitive to my losses. I was devastated by my grief which I thought would never end, but the nightmares..." She thought about telling Stan about the shared dream she had with Jordan and Terry, but caught herself, remembering her promise. Another time. It still might have been a coincidence. No sense in muddying the waters with that.

"Hmmm..." Stan rubbed his chin thoughtfully. "I told Terry that the only way to overcome his fear is to face it head on. I suggested going back into the dream to confront it. You might want to consider..."

"No way in hell." Rita pushed back in her chair. "There's no way I'm letting any electronics anywhere near my head. That's what started all the problems in the first place. I wouldn't even be here working on it right now if it wasn't for the threat of Mexican prison."

Stan made a calming gesture with both hands. "Nobody's going to make you do anything. It's just a thought, that's all. You have nothing to worry about. The DreamLand computer is shut down. In the mean time, I'm going to consider other ways to overcome your nightmares. I'd like to see you in private once a week. If it's any comfort, I have a similar arrangement with Cheryl."

Rita drew in a long, shaky breath and wiped at her eyes with the tissue. Stan's offer and the possibility of freeing herself from the nightmares made her feel lighter and for the first time in a long time, she had hope.

"Thank you," she whispered.

CHAPTER FORTY TWO

"We're ready to enter the next phase of the program," Crowley said, "but before we talk about that, I thought you'd appreciate how fully active the Pandora Project has become, because you guys are a *big* part of it." He stood from behind the console and tapped his iPad.

Jordan, Wesley, Carl, John, and Terry sat across from him in his glass walled command and control center watching the big central screen cycle through images showing the dome containing the hospital bustling with doctors, patients, and orderlies, the cafeteria full of people, operating rooms with ongoing surgeries, laboratories, laundry, and lounges -- all active and full of people.

Crowley turned from the screen, smiling. "All of you have had a chance to talk to Doctor Krippner and he and I have discussed your concerns. Based on his suggestions, we have come up with an approach that might make getting acclimated in the dream world a little easier."

Crowley leaned against the console with his arms crossed. "If you are having second thoughts, now is the time for you to speak up. We have other players targeted to take your place, but that would be a setback. We really want you. Your superior team work and diverse personalities have established a solid benchmark to work from."

"What about the veteran's dreams you want us to go into?" Jordan said. "It's one thing to go into a realistic battle based on a game that we're good at, and another to go into someone else's nightmare."

"Let's not get ahead of ourselves," Crowley said. "Those are some long term goals, but we're not even close to doing anything like that and never will be unless you or anyone else is willing to attempt it. What you are willing to do will dictate where we go and how far we push. Don't forget, this is a collaboration. You have a lot of say in how things go. We're listening."

And watching too, Jordan thought.

"So what's the plan," John said. "I'm ready to go. Game dreams. Veteran's dreams. Bring it!"

Crowley chuckled. "And then there's Geronimo here who wants to charge in and take on everything."

Terry giggled, which brought more snickers from the others. Jordan felt everyone relax a little.

"We have to go with what we know," Crowley said, pointing a finger. "Starting with our strong points. We want to run you through your winning scenario over and over again to allow you to get acclimated and gain familiarity while we gather data that expands your profiles. Think of it as a refining process to help us work out the bugs. We hope to develop this winning scenario into the first release of our immersive gaming platform into world wide markets."

"Practice drills," Carl said. "Like getting ready for a tournament."

"Just like that," Crowley said, "only we want you to think of it more like a test drive. Once you're more familiar with its parameters, we want you to do things different, take chances, and push the envelope."

"That's what I'm talking about," John said.

"At this stage of the process," Crowley said, "it's not so much about winning as it is about gathering data about you, the game, the equipment, the environment, and all the variables that can be manipulated to bring about improved performance."

"Like the Mythbuster guy used to say," Wesley said, speaking up. "In the spirit of science, there really is no such thing as a 'failed experiment.' Any test that yields valid data is a valid test."

Crowley grinned. "That's our philosophy. Our biggest goal is to make things better so you can do more in the dream world. Flex your muscles more there if you will."

"We're trying to get what Doctor Krippner called a specialized state of awareness that lets you navigate a separate reality with a more flexible set of rules," Jordan said.

Crowley's eyebrows raised. "Impressive Jordan. Impressive."

His praise made Jordan feel self-conscious, but he had been mulling over his talk with Stan Krippner. A lot of what he said made sense and had the ring of truth.

"Through manipulation of key elements in a player's profile, we hope to customize it to enhance their strengths and diminish their weaknesses," Crowley said.

"Like when you get super powers or invisibility in a video game," Terry said, speaking for the first time.

"That's a great analogy." Crowley pushed himself up from the console and stood with his hands on his hips. "So what's it going to be, team? Who's in and who's out?"

John's hand shot up before Crowley finished speaking. Jordan looked at the others, who all looked to him, but nobody moved, then on impulse, his hand shot up. What was the big deal? They were only dreams and the same one over and over again at that -- and he had already been through it, so he didn't expect any surprises, and he could quit at any time.

Wesley gave a little nod, then his hand went up. John stared at Carl for a moment until Carl's hand went up. After a pause, Terry's hand tentatively rose to join the others.

"Seal Team Zero is in the house!" Crowley said, clapping his hands together.

CHAPTER FORTY THREE

Rita sat at the end of a conference room table beside Lorenzo, Cheryl, and Jack, with Crowley at the far end. Detailed schematics, three dimensional renderings of their dreaming hood, dream cradles, and graphs of information filled the screen behind him.

Crowley tapped his iPad until a psychological assessment table came on screen. "These profiles will be the basis for an expanding program that will include online gamers, with the goal of integrating everything into comprehensive psychological profiles for a virtually unlimited market. We plan to use the same model for our vets to individualize what we program for them into the command and control chips."

"DreamWare downloaded into DreamWear," Jack said, when a large three dimensional model of the dreaming hood filled the screen. "It brings new meaning to the expression, 'It's all good in the hood.'"

He laughed at his own joke and Rita couldn't help laughing along with the others. Crowley scrolled through more displays until a series of microprocessor chip designs came on screen.

"Based on the protocol you developed with Hodge Michaels," he said, turning and addressing Rita directly. "Which incidentally we're naming the Michaels protocol in honor of Hodge and his father Edgar," then to the others. "We plan to branch out -- actually branching in might be more accurate."

"It's not going to be easy," Cheryl said. "It's not something that can be mass produced. Each case is unique with specific challenges that require painstaking detail."

Crowley lowered his head and nodded. "We plan on expanding your staff with specialists that you will oversee to handle the anticipated work load."

"Work load?" Lorenzo said. "That doesn't sound like fun."

"We're expecting a steady stream of brain damaged casualties who will need chip implants like Hodge," Crowley said. "We want to put them on the same protocol, combining electronic stimulation with precisely controlled drug and hormone delivery to keep them in the most stable and comfortable environment we can provide."

"I apologize for sounding negative," Lorenzo said, "but it sounds like an army of zombies."

"That's one way of looking at it," Crowley said, "but a better way to look at it is that they will be resting comfortably, and each of them will supply us with a steady stream of data that will benefit those who follow, and they may not all be 'zombies' as you call them either. Unlike Hodge, many of our subjects will be functional, but impaired."

He scrolled through more screens, displaying detailed engineering drawings for cybernetic arms, legs, fingers, eyeballs and other organs. "We hope to remedy many of the damaged organs with implants that can restore memory, vision, and in some cases, mobility. We have a program mapped out that integrates drugs and dreaming as well as cybernetic limbs and organs all under the control of microprocessor implants which can be wirelessly monitored and manipulated. We're also adding other features like integrated GPS and RFID so we can easily locate, monitor and in some cases treat patients with complications or other medical emergencies."

"Since you first mentioned it, Cheryl and I have been reading up a lot," Jack said. "With the extent of head injuries we'll be encountering, we anticipate this technology bringing us to the point of replacing certain areas of the brain with microchips, but that approach opens up an entirely new set of issues."

Crowley's eyebrows raised. "And they are?"

"Will these implants be hackable? Will we be opening the human body to cyber attack? What if somebody performed the equivalent of identity theft and took over someone who was dependent on their C and C chip and flooded them with hormones or some other drug and manipulated their behavior?"

Crowley held up both hands. "We'll have advanced encryption protocols in place that would prevent anything like that from happening."

"Isn't that what the banks say they are doing now?" Lorenzo said. "I had my identity stolen and my accounts cleaned out a few years ago. It's a huge problem."

Jack leaned in. "Not to mention Wikileaks, Anonymous, and God knows what other hackers who would love to jump in and raise hell."

Crowley gave a tight smile. "The banks and commercial sector have their own approaches to security and encryption, but we are the government and we have far more experience than they do. Numerous wars and conflicts have helped us refine our approach."

Rita looked at Lorenzo whose expression said he wasn't buying Crowley's reassurances. Cheryl and Jack had similar looks.

"I'm not holding anything back when it comes to helping our veterans," Crowley added. "They have made too many sacrifices to keep us safe and free and I for one intend to do anything within my power to give back whatever I can. We have the brain power and technology to overcome any obstacles that might present themselves and I intend to use them to their full extent."

CHAPTER FORTY FOUR

Jordan felt like he was falling into a void that shifted back and forth from black to white like someone flicked a light switch on and off, then he was pointing his M4 in front of him, advancing on the terrorist strong hold.

He felt the weight of the gun, the breeze on his skin, and the smell of smoke, then he sprinted toward the battle scarred fortress, listening to the chatter of his teammates on his headset.

"I don't know if I can handle this," Killjoy whined. "It's too real."

His words and panicked tone struck at Jordan's heart, making it nearly impossible to move. He willed himself to run, but his whole being felt weighted. He tried to talk to his teammates, but no words came, then he screamed without sound, which amplified his paralyzing terror.

A horde of black uniformed enemy spilled out of the fortress and charged him, guns blazing. Multiple points of white hot pain pierced him, then his voice came, screaming.

He awoke thrashing at his covers, slick with sweat, then the lights to his room came on and Wesley and Carl stood over him with shocked expressions.

"What the fuck?" Wesley said.

Jordan took a deep breath and put his hand on his chest. "Sorry guys. Bad dream. Scared the shit out of me!"

"Me too," Carl said with quick nods.

"Well that doesn't exactly give me the warm fuzzies," Wesley said. "We're going back into our game today on Pandora and you're having nightmares before we even get started? What's up with that?"

Jordan kept breathing, calming himself. "Sorry guys, it was a bad dream, not a freak out like Terry had and it wasn't from Pandora either. It was just a dream, probably from thinking too much about going back in and all the stuff Crowley talked about, you know, going into veteran's nightmares and the rest of it. Sorry I woke you."

Carl waved him off. "Quit apologizing. This shit's crazy enough as it is. Any of us can have a bad dream at any time."

"And we all had the same Pandora dream," Wesley said, "so as far as I am concerned if any one of us has a nightmare, we all had a nightmare." He fist bumped Carl, who smiled.

"So go back to sleep," Wesley said, then in a baby voice, "Unless you want us to get you some milk and cookies?"

"Or you want us to stay here, hold your hand, and leave the light on so the boogey man doesn't get you," Carl said.

They both chuckled and Jordan gave them each a middle finger which made all of them laugh, then the lights went out.

"See you in the morning," Wesley said. "Get your beauty rest."

"Yeah, even though you're beyond hope," Carl said. "You need as much of that as you can get."

Their departing laughter left Jordan smiling.

No one mentioned it the following morning and to Jordan, it was no big deal, only a bad dream, now only a wisp of memory. The big dream that he would soon be immersed in was what occupied his mind as he and the rest of the team walked down the curving hallway toward the Dream Lab.

He went over what Stan Krippner said about becoming so engaged in the action that you forget you're dreaming. He liked the idea of a higher, specialized state of awareness that followed a more flexible set of rules with infinite possibilities. How cool was that? Could he do it? His desire to find out outstripped any fear he had. At this point there was no question. This was something he *had* to do.

They found Crowley, Jack Scanlon, Cheryl, Lorenzo, and Rita waiting in the Dream Lab. Jordan nodded when he spotted Rita and she gave a nod back, followed with a little smile.

"Have a seat," Crowley said. "Get comfortable. Remember," he said as everyone reclined in their dream cradles, "it's not so much about winning as it is about gathering data about you, the game, the equipment, and the environment. What was that the Mythbuster guy said Renegade?"

"In the spirit of science, there really is no such thing as a failed experiment. Any test that yields valid data is a valid test."

Crowley fist bumped him and stepped back. "What about the rest of you guys? Ready?"

Carl gave him a thumbs up, John gave him a fist pump and Terry gave a half-hearted wave. Jordan nodded, settling in to the soft comfort of the cradle. His body relaxed, but he felt his heart beating a little too fast, so he made himself breathe deeper.

Stan Krippner popped his head in through the door at the far end of the room. "I wanted you to know that I'm here and I'll be watching you from the control room. I've never seen anything like this before, so this will be a first for me."

Seeing him and hearing his voice had a calming effect on Jordan. He continued breathing slow and deep while Jack Scanlon and Doctor Martin moved down the line helping everyone get their hoods on and checking the signals. When they finished, Rita followed, checking on everyone, finishing with Jordan. She took his hand in hers for a moment and gave a light squeeze. "Like Doctor Krippner said, we'll be watching from the control room."

Jordan nodded and returned the squeeze. "Thanks!"

Rita smiled and followed the others out.

"Okay," Lorenzo's voice said. "The sequence is queued and we are initiating in five, four, three…"

Like before, Jordan felt his body grow heavy at the count of one, then he fell into the void, shifting between dark and light, reminding himself, this is only a dream and in it I'm trying to find a higher awareness to navigate a reality that follows a more flexible set of rules.

He came into awareness pointing his M4. The realism of the weight of the gun in his hands, the breeze against his skin, and the smell of smoke still spooked him. It's still only a dream, he reminded himself. He recognized the terrorist stronghold and saw his teammates flanking him. Terry looked ashen with terror.

"Calm down," Jordan said, "Remember it's only a drea…"

"Momma!" Terry cried. "Mommy!"

He disappeared in a flash of white.

John shook his head. "That little pussy. At least we know that the escape code works."

Wesley and Carl looked to Jordan in mild surprise.

"We're down one," Jordan said. "We're probably going to get screwed, but remember, like I was trying to tell Terry, this is only a dream." He pointed to the fortress. "Let's get it on!"

Wesley took off saying, "We can still win."

Together they sprinted toward the battered doors under the stone arch of the entrance. Jordan burst through, gun blazing, his teammates coming in after him. Gun fire erupted from all sides and bullets peppered the wall around him. Smoke burned his eyes and he felt the sting of debris.

"We're fucked," Carl said.

Jordan rolled to the ground and came up under the cover of the stacked packing crates, firing at his assailant scrambling along the walkway above while his teammates fanned out. Two of the enemy dropped to the ground and two more ran for an alcove, then a blinding flash rocked Jordan, sending him spinning into the place between the dark and light until he opened his eyes to the Dream Lab.

He saw Doctor Martin helping Terry out of his dream cradle while Wesley, John, and Carl, pressed back in theirs, deep in REM.

CHAPTER FORTY FIVE

Rita watched Jordan sit up and stare at his teammates while Cheryl led Terry out of the room. Wesley's eyes popped open a minute later followed by Carl, then John, who sat up in his cradle yelling, "Yeehah!"

Jordan rolled his eyes and shook his head. Rita suppressed a smile at his reaction.

"How's everyone doing?" Lorenzo asked.

The remaining four nodded. They all looked a little dazed.

"Let's do it again," John said, "I think I'm getting the hang of it."

"No!" Stan said. "Once a day is enough. I'm concerned about overstimulation and the possibility of neurochemical overload or depletion. There are too many unknowns here. We need to pace ourselves and give you time to recharge."

Crowley looked disappointed, but he sighed, saying "You're right Stan. We don't want to rush things."

"Besides, we need time to analyze the data," Rita said.

Cheryl came back into the observation room.

"How's Terry?" Stan asked. "He okay? He was only under for a few seconds."

"He's okay," Cheryl said, "just a little embarrassed that he chickened out. I told him it's no big deal."

"I'll talk it out with him later," Stan said.

"What about the rest of you?" Crowley said, addressing Jack and Lorenzo. "Everything go okay on your end."

"The DreamWear circuitry is working flawlessly," Jack said.

"As is the video sequencing," Lorenzo added.

Crowley clasped his hands together. "Beautiful!"

"Let's talk to the team," Stan said. "See what they have to say."

Rita followed them out of the observation room into the Dream Lab where Jack and Cheryl removed dreaming hoods and Lorenzo helped the team members out of their cradles.

"It's a little crowded in here," Crowley said. "Let's go to the conference room so we can compare notes. Cheryl, can you go get Terry and have him join us? I'm sure he has valuable input to share, even if he was only under for a few seconds. It will be interesting to see how his physiological responses match up with his dreaming experience."

"Will do." Cheryl bowed out and joined everyone a few minutes later in the conference room with Terry in tow.

"Come on in," Crowley said from the head of the table. Stan sat to his left followed by Jack, Lorenzo, and Rita. John sat across from Stan, Carl across from Jack, Wesley across from Lorenzo, and Jordan faced Rita, which felt right. Cheryl took the seat beside her and Terry slid into the seat next to Jordan, keeping his head low. Rita felt a wave of compassion when Jordan nudged Terry with his elbow and winked when Terry looked up.

"You guys did a great job," Crowley said, once everyone was seated, then to Terry, "Thank you for having the foresight to test the escape code, Terry. That's probably the most important function that needed verification."

Terry looked up and gave a little smile.

"Jordan, you got blown up shortly after that. What was that like?"

Jordan shook his head. "It must've been a direct hit, because I was feeling everything before that. All that shit flying up around me stung, but when the grenade hit, all I felt was a super bright hot flash that sent me spinning out of there."

"Are you ready to go back and do it again?"

"I'll do it again, but not right away. I need a little time to assimilate, you know what I mean?"

Crowley looked over at Stan and smiled. Stan nodded back.

"What about the rest of you?" Crowley said to Wesley, John, and Carl.

"I'm ready to go back in and kick ass right now," John said. "I'm loving this shit!"

"I'm with Jordan," Wesley said. "A little break and I'm ready to try again."

"Me too," Carl said.

"I think we should give it a couple of days at least," Stan said.

"I don't need any time off," John said. "I want to strike while the iron's hot."

Crowley frowned. "Do you really think that's necessary, Stan?"

"I'm curious to see if anyone else has nightmares," Stan said. "I'm concerned about that side effect. The last thing we want to do is hurry. There's no need for that."

"We could use the time to study the new data," Rita offered.

"I agree with Rita," Cheryl said, looking to the others.

Jack and Lorenzo nodded their agreement.

"Okay," Crowley said. "You guys are the brains behind this operation, so our next test will be in two days."

Later that night, Rita lay in Lorenzo's arms, her mind spinning with questions. She turned and looked at him. "What do you think about Doctor Krippner?"

"I think he's doing a good job of putting the brakes on gung ho Crowley."

"I agree. How did your meeting go with him?"

"He had a lot of questions about DreamLand that I answered as straightforward as possible. I could tell that he was skeptical, but I didn't feel like he was judging me."

"I felt the same way. He mentioned a shared hallucination, which is what anyone would think."

"Unless they witnessed it first hand. Did you discuss your nightmares with him?"

"Cheryl's too." Rita flashed on her shared nightmare with Jordan, but resolved to keep her promise until she had a chance to talk to him again. "She and I will be meeting him privately once a week. He thinks he can help."

Lorenzo gave her a gentle squeeze. "That's great. I've been a little leery of him, mostly because Crowley hired him, but I think he has a good heart."

"Actions speak louder than words," Rita said, "and so far his actions show that."

Lorenzo nodded. "I think we have a solid ally."

"Jack sure thinks so. Me too!"

He kissed her on the forehead. "I'm starting to drift here honey. I've got a ton of work ahead of me, so I'm going to zonk out."

She kissed him and he rolled over. A couple of minutes later, his deep breathing told her he was sound asleep. She concentrated on her own breathing, trying to still her overactive brain, which kept replaying Lorenzo's scenario they had watched on their displays while monitoring the vitals of Seal Team 0. It felt like she did that for a long time until she drifted into grayness that turned into smoke.

She smelled and recognized the terrorist stronghold from the scenario, then she looked around and saw Jordan's teammates flanking her. She had the strangest sensation that she was both Jordan and floating outside watching him at the same time.

"Momma!" Terry cried. "Mommy!"

He disappeared in a flash of white.

John shook his head. "That little pussy. At least we know that the escape code works."

Wesley and Carl looked to her, surprised, then Wesley took off saying, "We can still win."

Together they sprinted toward the big splintered doors under the stone arch. Smoke and gun fire erupted and bullets peppered the wall around her. Smoke burned her eyes and she felt the sting of flying debris.

"We're fucked," Carl said.

Rita rolled to the ground and came up under the cover of some stacked crates firing at a black uniformed assailant scrambling along a walkway. Two of the enemy dropped to the ground and two more ran for an alcove, then a blinding flash rocked her, sending her spinning between dark and light until she shot up straight in bed, heart racing.

Lorenzo slept soundly beside her.

CHAPTER FORTY SIX

J ordan felt the weight of his M4, the breeze on his skin, and the smell of smoke. His arms and legs felt heavy and it took every ounce of willpower he had to move. It's only a dream, he reminded himself. Terry looked ashen with terror.

"Calm down," Jordan said, "Remember it's only a drea…"

"Momma!" Terry cried. "Mommy!"

He disappeared in a flash of white.

John shook his head. "That little pussy. At least we know that the escape code works."

Wesley and Carl looked to Jordan, surprised.

"We're down one," Jordan said, feeling like he had already said and done this.

Wesley took off saying, "We can still win."

They sprinted toward the fortress and Jordan burst through the doors, gun blazing. The sensation of added weight in his arms and legs made him feel like everything unfolded in slow motion. Gun fire erupted and smoke burned his eyes, then he felt the sting from flying debris.

"We're fucked," Carl said.

Jordan rolled to the ground and came up under the cover of the stacked crates, firing at his assailant on the walkway above. Two of the enemy dropped to the ground and two more ran for an alcove, then a hot blinding flash sent Jordan spinning into the dark and light until he sat up in bed, heart pounding.

Shit, he thought, breathing deep. At least I didn't wake up screaming and waking everybody. He thought about Rita and wondered if anyone else was having nightmares.

No one said anything the next morning, not even Terry, so he figured it was his nightmare, nothing more.

When they went to the Dream Lab the following morning Terry stayed behind, saying he was sick and maybe coming down with the flu. Wesley shut John up before he said anything, and they went into their winning battle dream the same way they had before, only this time, the moment they went in, John gave Jordan a crazed look and charged ahead of everyone else yelling, "Geronimo!"

A flurry of explosions followed and Jordan and the rest of the team were blown up at the gate the moment they entered.

"Jesus that happened fast," Carl said when they woke up together.

"What's wrong with you, you fucking idiot?" Wesley shook his head. "We never had a chance to do anything!"

John sat up grinning and stuck his middle finger up at Wesley. "I wanted to see what it was like to go kamikaze and I want to let Terry know that he's puss -- chickening out and that this shit can't hurt him."

Wesley took off his dream hood and stood from his dream cradle. "I ought to kick your punk ass!"

Crowley came in waving his hands and shaking his head. "It's no big deal Wesley, remember..."

"Yeah, yeah, yeah, I remember." Wesley dropped back into his cradle. "There's no such thing as a failed experiment. Any test that yields valid data is a valid test, but that doesn't mean that dipshit John can go in and ruin everything for the rest of us. We're trying to get the hang of this thing and he's off on his own suicide mission without thinking about the rest of us."

"I'm sure he needed to do that," Crowley said, turning his attention to John, "and we did get some data, but he won't be doing that again, right Striker?"

John shrugged. "I wanted to see what would happen."

"Let it go," Jordan said. "We're a team. We need to keep our shit together." He thought about his nightmare. "I don't know about you guys, but in a way, I can't blame John. I'm feeling a little nuts myself. It's starting to feel like Groundhog Day around here."

"Yeah," Carl said. "I think we're all getting a little uptight from being cooped up for so long."

Crowley's eyebrows raised and he nodded slowly. "You're right,

Sureshot. We've been pushing you guys pretty hard. You need a little R and R. Let me see what I can do."

Wesley nodded. "That would be great. Sorry about jumping in your shit, John. I've been feeling jittery and I haven't been sleeping much."

"Me neither," said Carl.

John waved it off. "No worries, mate. Sorry I got a wild hair up my ass. Jordan's right. We need to stick together."

"Well I'm glad you two kissed and made up," Carl said.

Wesley and John both gave him the finger, which brought chuckles and lightened the mood.

"Let's call it a day," Crowley said. "I want you guys to go back to your quarters and relax. I'm going to call in some top notch masseuses to relieve some of the tension."

"I hope they're as good as the ones in Paris," Carl wisecracked.

Jordan peeked into Terry's room when they returned to their quarters and saw him sitting up in bed. "Feeling any better?"

"Not really."

"Well their sending in masseuses for us. You up for a massage?"

He shrugged. "I guess so."

Five attractive young Mexican women showed up a short time later, and worked on everyone in their rooms, but to the disappointment of most of the team, all they got were massages. When they complained, Jordan discreetly shared a note that said:

> You guys should be happy.
> With all the cameras around here, you're lucky the whole world won't see you fucking Mexican hookers on YouTube.

Crowley gave them an extra day so Terry could recover, but when it was time to go back, he said he still felt sick, so they did the next game without him and the one after that.

They spent most of the next week repeating it over and over again without Terry, sometimes winning, but more often than not, losing. Jordan's nightmares of reliving their battles followed every session and had the quality of heavy limbs and impaired movement which helped him determine the difference between the two, but his sleep became more disturbed, making him edgy.

In real time, he spent most of his time awake, but between Pandora and his regular dreams, he felt trapped by their repetitiveness.

He saw exhaustion in Carl and Wesley's faces and bags under their eyes, while John's eyes seemed to be doing the opposite, bugging out of his head. He thrived on the pressure. Jordan started thinking of him as having crazy Charlie Manson eyes.

While John's enthusiasm bordered on obnoxiousness, Terry grew more withdrawn. Other than daily visits with Stan Krippner, he spent most of his time alone in his room until one day when they came back from a winning game and found him gone.

Jordan felt like something inside of him had been ripped out.

CHAPTER FORTY SEVEN

"I know how crazy this sounds," Rita said, "but my nightmares are getting worse the more the team goes into Pandora's scenarios. Maybe it's from watching it so much on the monitors, but I can't shake the feeling that there's more to it than that."

She looked up at the art, rattles, and shaman's drum on Doctor Krippner's wall and found strange comfort there.

Stan leaned forward in his chair. "What do you mean by more?"

"They're just as terrifying, but before now all I dreamed about was Hansel and Gretel, Chazz and Ollie Daggett, rats, witches, and all the other horrible memories of DreamLand."

Krippner rubbed his chin. "Cheryl's also been having nightmares from DreamLand which appear to be escalating."

"I wonder if she's dreaming about war games too?"

"It's hard to tell. She's more closed off about what's in her dreams than you are, but from what I can gather, they have a different quality from yours. It's a paradox because on one level they seem to be more deep seated, but they don't strike me as being more vivid and at the forefront of her consciousness the way yours are."

"Now I find myself in the battle dreams, sometimes as one of the team, and sometimes like I'm outside watching the action. You know that feeling you get in dreams when you're in both places at the same time?"

Stan nodded. "It's a common sensation. One of those strange things that happen in dreams that would normally seem bizarre, but that you totally accept in that state of consciousness."

"Aside from feeling like I'm one of them in the battle and watching from outside, sometimes I feel fully conscious of being in two places at the exact same time, both trapped with the rats and fighting in the battles."

"When you say you feel like you are one of the team members in the dream, you're referring to Jordan, right?"

Rita couldn't hide her amazement. "How did you know?"

"I've been talking to him too, but what's interesting," Stan said, making his point with his finger, "is what he didn't say. It told me more than what he did say. I've been analyzing everyone in the project, but the parallels between the two of you are uncanny. As a matter of fact, I'd like to talk to the two of you together."

Rita felt embarrassed as if she'd been caught doing something she shouldn't. "Sure, okay, as long as he's all right with it."

Krippner smiled and tapped a few keys on his keyboard, then he leaned into his monitor. "Come on up, Jordan. I'm in here with Rita and I want to talk to the two of you together."

"On my way," Rita heard from the speaker.

"I know you won't go back to the scene of the crime to confront your fears in Pandora again, and from what you've told me, real or imagined, I can't say that I blame you. Cheryl nearly became hysterical when I suggested it to her, so that's not an option either, but I'm hoping to give you and Jordan a deeper understanding of how you might cope."

"Don't you think we should include Cheryl in this discussion?"

He shook his head no. "Aside from the fact that you and Jordan appear to have some kind of telepathic connection, Cheryl has been so tight-lipped about her nightmares, that I'm not comfortable pushing her at this point."

"A telepathic connection? Really?"

"Normally, I'd be more skeptical, but we're covering new ground here and we have first hand testimony backed up by synchronized brain wave patterns and precisely matched physiological responses that support my observations. If those boys shared some kind of telepathic connection through the agency of the dreaming computer, perhaps through your own empathy and intuition, you tuned in to them -- at least to one of them in particular."

Rita shook her head. "I wouldn't believe it either if I hadn't been through the whole bizarre crossover that I experienced in DreamLand."

"Other than Cheryl, none of the other survivors have been as troubled as you have been with their nightmares. Maybe it's because you're empathic?"

"None of them spent as much time in the twisted dream worlds of Morpheus as I did and to be honest I'm surprised that Cheryl had nightmares like me because I don't remember her spending any more time in those dreams than the others. It's very puzzling."

"Do you think it might have anything to do with the fact that you're both women who are more empathetic than the men?"

She shook her head. "Something tells me no. If she was more empathetic as you say, like me, wouldn't she be sharing this telepathic connection?"

Stan nodded. "Good point! It's quite the mystery isn't it?"

A tentative knock came on the door.

"Come on in," Stan said.

Jordan stuck his head in, smiling when he saw Rita. She couldn't help smiling herself.

Still smiling he looked to Stan. "What's up doc?"

Stan joined the smile fest, adding a chuckle. The whole exchange made Rita feel relaxed, warm, and connected. She glanced up at the shamanic décor on Stan's wall, which completed her sense of safety.

Stan pointed to a chair beside Rita. "Have a seat, Jordan. I'm sorry Terry had to go, but it was of his own volition and ultimately what was best for the project. He refused to go back into another dream and we weren't about to force him. How are you and the rest of the crew holding up?"

Jordan pulled up the chair, speaking as he slid into it. "I think we're all going a little nuts. None of us are sleeping much and every time I go into a Pandora dream battle I get rewarded with a repeat performance nightmare that night. I think it's happening to the other guys too, except John. He's always in that dream battle space whether he really is, or if he's awake or sleeping. I've never seen him this spun up."

"I told Crowley that daily sessions were too much. I'll tell him to give you guys a break."

"I think we need a real break," Jordan said, glancing at Rita and back to Stan. "Like a get out of Dodge break to give us a change of scenery. A little fresh air, you know? We're all getting stir crazy."

Stan made a calming gesture. "I'll make sure Crowley understands that."

"Thanks!"

"Listen," Stan said, lowering his voice, "neither one of you said anything to me about your dreams and their connection. I figured it out on my own."

Jordan and Rita looked at each other.

Right now nobody else needs to know until we investigate further," Stan said, nodding to them. "I want to help you figure this out and above all I want to help free you from the nightmares. Nobody should live like that."

"I'll do anything to get free of them," Rita said, "except go back into a computer dream."

"Terry was a very sensitive young man who got traumatized easily," Stan said. "You two have had far more exposure, but your psychological make ups are tougher and more flexible than Terry's. I think we can work together to bring about some resolution."

"What do you suggest?" Rita said.

"Yeah," Jordan said. "I've been doing nothing but going into Pandora dreams, which only makes things worse."

"Rita's experience was quite different from yours," Stan said, "but the common factor to both of your experiences is that they have been violent. I've brought this up to Crowley and I think it needs some kind of offset."

Jordan frowned. "An offset?"

"It would be interesting to see what kind of reactions people had if their experiences were pleasant."

Jordan's frown deepened and he said more to himself, "Something like that might bring John's enthusiasm down a notch, which wouldn't be a bad thing."

"I don't know how you do it Jordan," Rita said. "I've had more than my share of night terrors and I haven't been under the influence of a computer for some time now, while you keep getting a double whammy, day and night."

"Aside from sharing the same dream with my teammates when I'm under Pandora's influence, I've noticed a difference between what happens there and my night dreams."

Stan leaned forward, resting his elbows on the desk. "How would you characterize that?"

Jordan rubbed his chin and his eyes looked distant as he pondered the question. "They both seem more than real in many ways, but I've noticed that when I relive our Pandora battles in my own dreams, a lot of the time it's almost impossible to move my arms and legs, which puts me on the verge of panic. That never happens in Pandora's dreams."

"That happens to me all the time in my nightmares," Rita said.

CHAPTER FORTY EIGHT

Stan held up a finger. "That's a fascinating distinction between the generated Pandora dreams and the inner personal ones. Something I'll look into more. Let's address the sleep paralysis first, since it provides a good stepping off point to some navigational suggestions I have."

Jordan and Rita leaned in together.

"It's also known as the Hag Effect, the Incubus Effect and Witch Riding."

Rita flinched when she heard the word witch.

"Ordinarily in REM sleep our muscles are paralyzed. It's a biological feature that keeps us from hurting ourselves or our sleeping partners if we're thrashing around in a particularly active dream. Sometimes we wake up," Stan said, making quotation marks with his fingers to emphasize his point, "while still in REM paralysis into a confusing mixture of waking perception and dreaming imagination."

"I think John is stuck somewhere in there all the time," Jordan said.

Stan grinned. "It's the original nightmare where no one can hear you scream." He looked directly at Rita. "People see apparitions, often nightmarish figures that they sometimes feel are touching them, yet they have full mental awareness, swearing that 'It was real'."

Rita shook her head and Stan smiled again. "Muscle paralysis occurs when our brain is flooded with acetylcholine, which suppresses muscle tone in all the major muscle groups that aren't autonomic like the heart, intestines, and lungs, but when someone loses sleep over it, it contributes to insomnia and increases the odds of another attack."

He put his attention on Rita again. "It's associated with powerful hypnagogic hallucinations where you can feel your body, but you can't move it while your vision and senses are filled with dream-like imagery, known as REM intrusion. If you can overcome the fear that goes with it, it can become a magical, hybrid state of consciousness. That's where I think I can help you two."

Jordan sat up straight, sensing something important coming. "This is that higher, specialized state of awareness between the two extremes you talked about, isn't it?"

Stan gave him a slow, emphatic nod.

Jordan glanced sideways at Rita. "Navigating a separate reality that follows a more flexible set of rules with infinite possibilities." He smiled.

"You're a quick study," Stan said, pointing at Jordan.

Rita looked confused. "Higher, specialized hybrid states of consciousness? Navigating separate realities? It sounds like something out of Carlos Castaneda's Don Juan stories. You get stuck between waking and sleeping, right?"

Stan became animated, his passion evident in his words and gestures. "Most indigenous cultures make no distinction between sleeping, waking, and dreaming. For them it is all one continuum. In that stuck between state, the mind awakens while the body sleeps, essentially dreaming with your eyes open. For most it's terrifying because you assume you're awake. Fear increases, driving more dream-based imagery, and what results is the worst thing imaginable." He did the quote thing with his fingers again. "The Stranger. The feeling that someone is in the room. A presence that sometimes can't be seen. Other times it makes itself clear." More finger quotes. "The Other. The man with no face. This is where sleep paralysis and hypnagogic hallucinations merge into lucid nightmares."

Rita nodded. "It explains how people think they see ghosts."

"There's a long history and lots of superstition behind it," Stan continued. "In Medieval times the Incubus was the demon known to sit on women's chests to molest them. In Hawaiian society, the spirits are known as Night Walkers. In Teutonic lore Doppelgangers." He held up a wagging finger. "And we can't overlook the fact that many alien abduction tales start with being paralyzed in bed. People have said, 'I felt choked, hit and held down. My throat and vocal cords were paralyzed when I tried to scream. Someone was lying on top of me.

Demons tried to possess me, trying to break my neck, scream in my face, and engulf me in a thick, damp, humid, God-awful feeling of sinister corruption."

"I wonder if Terry was feeling anything like that?" Jordan said.

Stan leaned forward, emphasizing his words with his finger like a concert conductor. "In that moment of fear and hopelessness lies the opportunity to launch into a lucid dream by learning how to banish your fear, and become more comfortable with the ambiguity in the dreaming world. It can be an initiation into the dreaming arts for those who have thin boundaries, or what researcher Ernest Hartmann called 'vulnerability.'"

"And Terry was a little too vulnerable," Jordan said.

"That's right! What all sleep paralysis sufferers have in common is a greater ability to be touched by the world and experience life and all of its pain as well as its beauty."

"It all sounds so simple," Rita said, and yet..."

"Once you get past the fear, it is! There are simple ways to lessen sleep paralysis if you want the attacks to go away. Transforming them into lucid dreams or out-of-body experiences is another way to spin this unique state of consciousness into a new realm of perception."

"I like the idea of realm," Rita said. "It sounds so expansive!"

"It's the polar opposite of fear, which is contraction." Stan clenched his fists and brought them together.

"Fear is contraction?" Jordan said.

"And love is expansion," Stan said, holding his hands out. "That's what lies on the other side of fear. It's the essence of shamanic transformation. When you confront and overcome the 'other' in that fear paralyzed moment, who shows up? It can be a deceased relative, an angel, or a goddess who has something to tell you."

At the mention of a goddess, Jordan thought about Pandora. A goddess?

"If you're fortuitous enough for that to happen," Stan continued, "then you have to listen carefully because sometimes they whisper. Sometimes the stranger can tell the dreamer something that turns out to be "uncanny" information that the dreamer could not have known. In that case lucidity is not used to control the dream, or even to escape it in an out of body adventure, but rather to gather courage to face the encounter that is naturally unfolding."

"Like riding a wave," Jordan said.

"Sometimes just knowing that the experience doesn't have to be a nightmare is enough for people to break out of paralysis and explore the amazing dream worlds that are just around the bend. The best way to approach these unique experiences is to make room for the uncanny intelligence of this state of mind. What it brings for you is personal." He paused, letting his words sink in, then, "but I assure you that gaining the courage to meet the unknown will lead to self-knowledge, a greater passion for living, and perhaps even wisdom. Instead of running away, you run to your fear if you want to continue exploring the mystery and promise."

"There's so much we don't know and so many new things being discovered," Rita said.

"Shamans have known this for millennia. They're masters at navigating altered states of consciousness and expert at cultivating that specialized state of awareness that allows them to navigate separate realities that follow more flexible rules that have the potential to expand into infinite possibilities."

"What we think of as altered states," Rita said, "shamans see as other worlds and other dimensions, don't they?"

"No matter which world you are in," Stan continued, "whether sleeping, waking, dreaming, or in a visionary state, it's all about navigation which comes from understanding what is called radical subjectivity. The key to a shaman's navigational freedom is paying equal attention to the inner and outer states that they experience. It's what I like to think of as the dreaming threshold between being externally controlled and inwardly focused with the ability to control dream elements to the point of becoming lucid. This appears to be especially true in the hyper-real dream worlds generated by Pandora. It makes all the difference between manipulated 'external' environments and the control over all the filters we have by understanding our own radical subjectivity."

"And this crosses all the worlds that we separate and the shamans see as one and the same," Jordan said.

"From a radically subjective point of view, a sign that a person has mastered this navigation is when they realize and observe that their inner world reflects their outer, first in dreams, then in the 'real world'."

Jordan thought about what he and his teammates had been experiencing and wasn't so sure he was comfortable with the idea.

CHAPTER FORTY NINE

C rowley stood in the foreground with his arms crossed, studying Hodge in his coffin-like bed inside the glass walls of the ICU. Behind him Jack Scanlon sat at the left console, his slender fingers tapping his keyboard and Lorenzo sat to the right, focused on his screen. Both men wore headsets.

Rita stood behind Cheryl, who sat at the center console clicking her mouse until Hodge's vital signs filled the main screens of the observation deck with pulsing waveforms that showed weak EKG, pulse, and respiration. The large display of fMRI and PET images shifted and changed colors, showing heightened brain activity, as if Hodge somehow knew they were there.

"Coming up on monitor six," Lorenzo said.

The white noise came like waves crashing on the beach, followed by a dim image of brightening waves and rising music that intermingled into an audio and video collage that felt and sounded like an exotic otherworldly lullaby.

Rita felt her heart rise and expand with the meditative music and imagery as it rose to a gentle crescendo of running water and waves along with chants, digeridoos, flutes, and strings.

Hodge's face remained serene like a pond with a flat mirror-like surface and a feeling of bliss pervaded everything.

Crowley turned from the window to face everyone, grinning beatifically. He spoke with a hint of awe in his voice. "You guys have done an amazing job of stabilizing Hodge with your technology. Aside from the hard-wired neural stimulation and drug delivery system, his dreaming content is delivered separately by transcranial magnetic stimulation." He ran his hand over his head. "And your magnetoresonators deliver focused signals to specifically targeted parts of the brain."

Cheryl nodded. "Everything works in concert."

Crowley continued. "Hodge is the prototype for what we want to implement in brain damaged veterans to give them relief from their terrors with an eye toward curing them one day." He made a sweeping gesture toward the biggest monitors. "Aside from the drug delivery that addresses physiological issues, would it be safe to say that Hodge's peace of mind primarily comes from Lorenzo's masterful programming?"

"That's actually been proven," Jack said. "Lorenzo, Cheryl and I tested that by manipulating signal strengths and effective drug delivery thresholds."

"Direct medication can provide sedation and pacification," Cheryl added, "but it's less active mentally and more sedating, although we have strong indicators that transcranial magnetic stimulation can trigger neurochemicals through its own non-drug stimulation."

Crowley rocked back and forth on his heels, smiling. "Exactly! Doctor Krippner has made me very aware of the impact of repeated immersion into battle scenarios with the team. As a matter of fact, he believes that what is supposed to be working toward a cure for PTSD is actually creating more of it. Terry provided us ample proof of that and we're seeing its effects on the rest of the team."

"And it's escalating," Rita said. "They need a break."

"I'm well aware of that," Crowley said, "That's why I gathered you here today. I want to use this Dream Sleep model we established with Hodge as a baseline, without the implanted drug delivery sedation. I want you to manipulate the transcranial magnetic stimulation outputs to deliver focused signals to trigger the release of neurochemicals in the brain's pleasure centers."

"Electronic dope," Lorenzo joked.

"Like you've done here with Hodge, only to a lesser degree. I'm hoping you can incorporate pleasant subliminal messages that will motivate the players to want to play more."

Lorenzo leaned back in his chair and studied Crowley. "You're talking about a reward system."

"That's one way of characterizing it. I was thinking more along the lines of balancing out the unpleasant with the pleasant."

"That sounds like an addiction cycle," Cheryl said.

Crowley held up his hands and shook his head. "I wouldn't go that far, but to give them an incentive to play more? Yes. Studies suggest that when gamers are engrossed in Internet games, certain pathways in their brains are triggered in the same way that a drug addict's brain is affected by a particular substance. The gaming prompts a neurological response that influences feelings of pleasure and reward, and the result, in the extreme, is manifested as addictive behavior. Obviously we don't want to go to the extreme and create addicts, but a little bit of pleasure and reward does have the potential to relieve trauma."

"I get it!" Jack said, slapping the table. "We train 'em like dogs. They do the tricks, they get the treats."

"I wouldn't put it that way."

"Lab rats hitting the right switch to get their cocaine," Lorenzo said, voicing what Rita thought. "Is that more accurate?"

Crowley's face reddened. "I'm not here to argue or get sidetracked with a bunch of verbal sparring and personal opinions. I'm -- we're here to alleviate the suffering that comes with PTSD. We're here to help our wounded vets in any way possible, whether physical or mental. If we can provide realistic battle scenarios, then we can spend as much energy if not more to ease their suffering by providing a pleasant escape. It's the least we can do. This directive is not up for discussion. It's one of our primary objectives."

CHAPTER FIFTY

J ordan, Wesley, John, and Carl sat at workstations set up on one side of a table and Lorenzo sat across from them at another workstation flanked by Crowley on his right and Stan Krippner on his left.

"Based on research into virtual reality therapies," Crowley said, "and an analysis of a wide range of psychoanalytic work with traumatized veterans, including what we analyzed from your developing profiles, Lorenzo, our video guru has come up with our first battle scenario based on the actual experiences of war veterans."

Lorenzo stood, put his hands together, and gave a slight bow. "I've combined many of the dynamics from your winning game into this one so that it plays out like a game in much the same way the original did. Like before, the idea is to get you used to it in this format, like a dress rehearsal, so when you go into the fully immersive Pandora version, you'll have a greater sense of what might happen."

"I don't need this shit." John swiped his hand in front of himself like he was swatting a bug, then he bounced in his chair like he had to go to the bathroom. "Let's just dive into the dreams."

"One step at a time," Crowley said. "We want to follow a protocol that gives us the best chances of success."

John looked around at the others, head bobbing, eyes blinking. He's looking and acting more like a frigging tweaker every day, Jordan thought.

"For the record," John said, "I don't need this shit. I'm ready to go, but I'll slow down and wait for the rest of you." His head bobbing turned into a nod.

Jordan looked over at Wesley and Carl who both shook their heads.

"Though this comes from the experiences of war veterans, we want you to keep it light," Lorenzo said. "In other words approach it like a game."

"We want to help vets with this," Crowley added, "but we also want to expand it into commercial gaming markets where we believe it can do even more good." He gestured to Doctor Krippner. "Stan can explain the philosophy behind what we hope to achieve by venturing into classic veteran nightmares."

Classic veteran nightmares, Jordan thought. I'm not so sure I like the sound of that. We're all burned out on this shit as it is. None of us are sleeping very good and John's about to go off the rails any minute. At least this is a game and not more dreams.

Stan cleared his throat and Lorenzo sat back down.

"Our approach is to simulate traumatic events with high realism in virtual scenarios that can evoke the different stressful events that represent the trauma." He wagged his finger. "The focus is not on realism, but on customized aspects that evoke an emotional reaction in the participant that helps achieve the emotional processing of the trauma in a safe environment that helps them recover."

"We want to bring them back to the scene of the crime such as it is," Crowley said, "so they can re-experience their trauma in a way that allows them to process it differently and emerge with a healthier perspective."

Stan continued. "Working with individual veteran profiles created in the same way yours are, we plan to develop immersive environments for each situation, once again, not so much to recreate the reality, but to achieve environments relevant to the person. The important point is to develop therapeutic contexts that help them confront their problems and open up the possibility of living their lives in a more satisfactory way."

"So what I am hearing," Wesley said, "is that you want us to go into these no win situations with these guys and share their trauma."

Stan shook his head. "Not share their trauma, but save them from it in a 'timeless space' where the traumas are activated and people can relive their experiences safely. In this timeless space the vets will be supported by you guys and therapists. The global space they share will reflect their emotions and alternative possibilities. The goal is to work with negative emotions related to their problems as well as the positive ones. We want to help veterans experience these emotions and experiences so they can touch them, feel them, and accept them, and like Bob said, to live with them from another perspective."

Carl leaned back and crossed his arms. "And be their companions and guides into their own personal hells."

"That's right," Crowley said, "only instead of defusing make believe bombs you'll be saving people."

Wesley looked around at his teammates. "Unlike John, I'm feeling fried from all this war shit. What about that R and R you promised us?"

Crowley's eyebrows raised, followed by a smile. "We have a special surprise for you, but it's taking a little longer than we thought. If you can bear with us through this initial testing phase of vet's dreams, I think you'll find that it's worth the wait."

Carl shrugged. "Playing a videogame with a keyboard and a mouse again will be a nice break to get us outside the game instead of being in the middle of what feels real."

"Amen to that," Jordan said.

"Gentlemen," Lorenzo said. "Log in on your keyboards, fire up your mice, and let's rock and roll!"

Lorenzo led them into the game, guiding them through each battlefield encounter, telling them what to expect to help them learn it as fast as they could. Jordan was amazed at how much it was like their original winning game. They could choose all the same weapons when they started and the interface looked identical. What did change was the landscape, the type of battle they fought, and the tactics of their enemies. The unpredictability of events in this scenario would have taken them out of the game in its early stages without Lorenzo's guidance and because it was not a matter of defusing a bomb, there were no time constraints, making it feel open ended. The expansiveness of the battlefield contributed to its sense of endlessness. It would be easy to get lost here as opposed to the warehouses, fortresses, factories, and other enclosed strongholds Seal Team 0 was used to storming.

In the last part of the game they rode in a Humvee caravan until the one in front of them blew up in a series of explosive flashes. Before anybody could say or do anything to react, the Humvee they rode in also blew up, taking them with it.

"Holy shit!" John said. "Why didn't you tell us that was coming? How do you defend against that?"

"You don't," Lorenzo said.

"What do you mean?" Carl said.

"Though it played like a game," Lorenzo said, "it was a scenario based on war time experiences, and in war some situations have no defense."

CHAPTER FIFTY ONE

Rita sat in Stan Krippner's office looking for comfort from him and the sense of calm she felt from the art on his wall. Stan leaned back in his chair with steepled fingers, listening.

"I have to admit," Rita said. "I'm uncomfortable using the Dream Sleep model we've established with Hodge to release neurochemicals to the brain's pleasure centers. Lorenzo called it electronic dope, and Cheryl said it was an addiction cycle. I agree. I understand relieving suffering like we did with Hodge, but the idea of a reward system of subliminal physiological messages that motivate players to play more? Is that Crowley's idea of rest and recuperation?"

Stan nodded. "It's his Assassin's Paradise."

"Assassin's Paradise?"

"A long time ago, a man named Al-Hassan used hashish to enlist young men into his private army known as assassins, from the term aschishin, which meant followers of Hassan, the head of an obscure party of fanatics who seized a castle in the mountains. He kept boys around twelve years old who seemed destined to become courageous men at his court and sent them into the garden, giving them hashish to drink."

"The same thing Crowley wants to do with the boys now, except with technology," Rita said.

Stan rewarded her with a grim smile. "They slept for three days and were carried to a beautiful secret garden which was impenetrable and unseen by any but those intended to be his haschishin. When they awoke in the garden surrounded by beautiful naked women and boys, they were told they were in Paradise. After a few hours of bliss, they were made unconscious again with the drink, awakening back in the presence of Hassan who told them he had given them this glimpse of Paradise and that they would go there if they entered his service and followed his instructions or died in his service. Modern day jihadists still believe in this myth started by al-Hassan and his hashish."

"That's exactly what Crowley is doing!" Rita said, waving her finger. "It's one thing if you are incapacitated and in untreatable chronic pain like Hodge. In that case an opiate addiction like Morphine, Oxycodone, or any of the others is secondary in comparison to the urgency for pain relief, but I can't condone rewarding war games, especially if it can lead to addiction. I hate to say it, but it strikes me as sinister."

Stan nodded emphatically. "Even something used as a subconscious marketing ploy to make more people want to play the game comes too close to the border of what is ethical as far as I'm concerned."

"What can we do about it?"

"We're still in the early phase of our research and we haven't done anything definitive yet, so the best we can do is keep vigilant and put the brakes on anything that has potential for abuse."

Rita shook her head. "These video games are addictive enough without any help from a pusher or some kind of cyber assassin master, and they don't serve any good except to teach kids how to shoot, kill, and be assassins themselves, even if it is only a game. They glorify war!"

Stan held up a finger. "They're not a total waste. Studies have shown that action video games that include fast-moving targets moving in and out of view amid lots of clutter that require players to make rapid, accurate decisions are beneficial to cognitive function and have been linked to improving attention skills, brain processing, and cognitive functions including low-level vision and high-level cognition."

"I didn't realize that. I have to admit, these kids are pretty sharp."

"It goes back to their inherited genetic heritage of hunting to survive. A study using MRI imaging compared the brains of 78 adolescent gamers with the brains of 73 adolescents who didn't play. The teens who played showed increased connectivity between 7 paired regions of the brain that can lead to enhanced cognitive ability, like the connections between the frontal eye field and auditory complex where the brain processes audio and visual signals. These parts of the brain that make up the salience network of our brains are responsible for processing what is important and what isn't. Hyperconnectivity between these networks can lead to a more robust ability to direct attention toward targets and recognize novel information in the environment. For better or worse, the members of Seal Team 0 are literally at the top of their game. My job is to help cultivate what brings out the best in them while protecting them from the worst."

"What do you think the worst is?"

Stan gave a wry smile. "Like the cliché goes, sometimes we're our own worst enemies."

CHAPTER FIFTY TWO

"Fight or fuck, I'm ready for all of it," John said, his words coming rapid-fire as he paced back and forth behind the easy chairs in their team lounge. Jordan reclined in the big chair beside the couch watching him move back and forth like an animated parrot on its perch.

"Fuck this baby ass video game shit," John continued. "I want to get into the real war games. We need to move things along faster."

"Dude, you need to bring it down a notch," Carl said from the couch. "It's one thing to have an edge and another to go over it."

Wesley sat at the other end of the couch, nodding. "Yeah, why don't you sit down, chill out, and take a few deep breaths. I'm getting worn out just watching you."

John's eyes looked like they were going to jump out of his head. "Fuck you guys! I'm climbing the fucking walls here. I can't keep sitting around on my ass waiting for you."

Carl flipped him off and John's face reddened. Jordan took a deep breath. Both Carl and Wesley had bags under their eyes and looked like they had aged. Weariness tinged their voices. Jordan's nerves felt stretched to their limits. "We're a team," he said. "We need to stick together. It's bad enough that we lost Terry."

"Fuck that little pussy!" John spat. "He doesn't have the balls to go into a fucking dream. What does that tell you?"

Wesley and Carl both stood.

"Listen Rambo," Carl said. "I've had enough of your shit and I'm tired of listening to it."

John stopped pacing. His eyes narrowed and he stuck his jaw out. "You're tired of listening to my shit? Well, fuck you! You think you can shut me up?"

Wesley moved around the end of the couch and stepped toward John. "Listen," he said in a measured tone. "We're your teammates. There's no need to talk to us like that."

"He's right," Carl said coming around the other side to face John. "There's no need…"

Everything happened fast, but to Jordan it unfolded in slow motion. John lunged at Carl with his fist cocked, but Wesley's long leg slid out, sending John sprawling across the floor.

Carl stepped back with his fists raised, a mixture of shock and disbelief on his face. John scrambled to his feet, red faced and raging, then he went after Carl again, but Wesley, moving deceptively fast for his big frame caught him in a bear hug from behind, lifting him flailing up off the ground.

"Let me go, you big dumb fuck!" John screamed. "I'll kick both your asses!"

"Enough!" Crowley said, coming through the door. "I'll bounce all of you right out of here without another dollar and suspend you from the project."

Perfect timing, Jordan thought. He was watching the whole thing.

John went limp in Wesley's arms.

"I'm going to let you go," Wesley said under his breath, but if you try any shit, I promise, you'll get an ass whooping like you've never had." He pushed John away and stepped back.

John stood alone, face crimson, fists clenching and unclenching. His lower lip quivered, but he kept his mouth shut.

"Now what the hell is going on here?" Crowley demanded.

"I'll tell you what's going on," Jordan said. "This shit's driving us nuts. None of us can sleep. Every time I do, another nightmare comes. It's getting to the point where I can't tell if I'm in a computer dream or a real one. It was too much for Terry. Now John thinks that he's too much for it."

"We need to get out of here," Wesley said. "This whole thing feels like a big pressure cooker and it's starting to blow."

"Yeah," Carl added. "What's up with this R and R and the surprise you promised? We've been holding up our end of the bargain and doing everything you've asked."

"And some of us are still willing," John muttered.

Crowley held up his hands. "All right. All right. John take a seat. You too Wesley and Carl. I apologize for pushing you guys so hard. I couldn't say anything to you before, but the pressure we've been putting on you has been part of the process of creating your profiles. We needed to find out where your stress thresholds were and we've clearly reached them. Unfortunately, Terry had a much lower threshold than we anticipated which made him drop out and John keeps pushing in the opposite direction. The harder we push, the more he wants!"

John smiled in spite of himself and dropped back into his chair with his hands behind his head. Wesley and Carl looked at each other and Carl rolled his eyes.

"The rest of you have fallen somewhere in between," Crowley said. "Between all of you we've assimilated an ideal range of responses which will help us fine tune our scenarios going forth."

"Great." Wesley sat back and crossed his arms. "Now that you've gotten your precious data from your lab rats, how about that break you promised?"

Crowley gave him a lopsided grin. "We have one more critical test we need you to do to give us a complete data set."

"Don't tell me you want us to go into another dream," Carl said.

"This will be the last one for awhile. I promise."

John stood again. "What are we waiting for? Let's get it on!"

"One more?" Carl groaned.

"I'm not afraid to say that the unpredictability of that veteran's scenario you had us go through on the computers doesn't give me the warm fuzzies," Jordan said. "Just thinking about it puts me even more on edge. It's one thing to play it as a game and another to go into it like it's real."

"This isn't just any old video game," Wesley said. "It's based on the war experiences of wounded vets. Anything can happen. Normally I wouldn't care, but I feel like I'm ready to break."

"The unpredictability is exactly what draws me to it," John said. "I'm not ready to break, that's for sure."

"You just did, you fucking pinhead!" Carl said.

John opened his mouth, then closed it, glaring at Carl. He bit his lower lip while rage and a flurry of other negative emotions passed over his face, but he remained quiet.

"I'm not going to push you guys to do it," Crowley said, "but I promise we will reward you with an extra bonus for this one -- and this will complete this phase of the project that we have all worked so hard toward."

"When can we get it over with," Jordan said. "I'm ready to get past it and move on to our break."

"How about tomorrow morning?" Crowley asked. He looked from Carl, to Wesley, and finally to John. "Can I trust you guys to keep from killing each other until then?"

"Sure." John threw up his hands. "As long as we keep moving forward."

Carl and Wesley nodded.

"What time should we show up?" Jordan asked.

Crowley clapped his hands together and smiled. "We'll see you at ten." He spun on his heels and went back out the door, leaving the four remaining members of Seal Team 0 in an awkward silence.

They went to the Dream Lab the following morning and found Jack Scanlon waiting. His deep-set brown eyes seemed to have an extra sparkle beneath his bushy eyebrows.

"Here come the troops," he said when they went in.

As if in counterpoint to Scanlon's sparkle, poker faced Cheryl Martin came in, her pale blue eyes unreadable behind her horn-rimmed glasses. As always, she wore her long strawberry-blonde hair in a bun. All business. She had softened after interacting with Terry, but since he had gone, she seemed even more distant than ever.

"Go ahead and get comfortable in your seats," she said, nodding toward the dream cradles.

When everyone settled in, she went down the line helping each one on with their hoods, followed by Scanlon who did a final check. Satisfied, they went back to their control room on the other side of the mirrored window.

"Okay," Crowley's voice said through Jordan's headset. "This thing's ready to go. Remember, this will be a different experience from what you've come to expect."

His words made Jordan stiffen and his heart pump faster. He started breathing deeper to calm himself and his thoughts spun in a flurry of guns, bombs, bullets, and war. Feeling more vulnerable than any of his past experiences, he braced himself for what was coming.

"Okay guys," Lorenzo said through his headset. "Here we go. Five, four, three, two…"

Like before, Jordan grew heavy at the count of one, then he fell into the void, shifting between dark and light, reminding himself, it's only a dream. I'm trying to find a higher awareness to navigate a reality that follows a more flexible set of rules.

The falling sensation lasted longer than before and then he heard before he saw anything. A barely audible white noise that rose to the sound of waves crashing on a beach, followed by a dim image of waves that brightened along with rising music and other sounds that intermingled into a strange complicated alien sounding lullaby. His breathing came lighter and the tension he felt washed away with every crash of the waves.

His heart lightened and his emotions expanded as they rose with the music and imagery. His whole body shook with an exquisite depth of feeling that peaked in a crescendo of running water and waves that blended with chants, digeridoos, flutes, and stringed instruments of what he imagined to be a divine cosmic symphony.

I'm having a full on body orgasm, he thought as wave after wave of pure ecstasy overwhelmed him, sending him sailing out into an exquisite tapestry of thought, feeling, and emotion that he could never in a million years put into words.

CHAPTER FIFTY THREE

Rita's heart raced when she saw the closeup of every team member's eyes twitching beneath closed eyelids in unison, as if everyone danced to the same tune. At first the readouts showed differing EKG, pulse, and respiration, then they too synced up, matching each other perfectly. Their erratic brainwaves and heightened fMRI and PET activity followed suit, reflecting tranquility.

She gasped when all of their eyes shot open as one and looked without seeing, the same way Hodge's had, and their expressionless faces looked identical.

Bliss pervaded everything which had the opposite effect of driving her panic higher. She drew in long stuttering breaths that felt like sobs and her hands shook. Lights are on, but nobody's home, she thought as chills cascaded over her. She glanced over at Cheryl, Jack, and Lorenzo who all looked back at her with their own stunned expressions, except Crowley, who smiled and Stan Krippner, who looked troubled.

Lorenzo's warm hand came down on hers, which helped to ground her, but she still didn't stop the shaking. She looked deep into his dark eyes for strength and felt his empathy, then he slid closer and put his arm around her in a protective hug. She continued sobbing while hot tears rolled down her cheeks.

"Are you okay?" Stan asked.

She nodded, but couldn't find words.

He studied her, his expression telling her he was unconvinced. "Maybe we ought to shut it down."

"Are you kidding me?" Crowley pointed. "Look at those readouts!

Those are some happy campers. How much time in this scenario, Lorenzo?"

"It's been in a loop for just under five minutes." Lorenzo tapped his mouse and the readouts became erratic, once again going out of synch and returning to normal. Rita felt a weight lifted from her heart and she could breathe again, but she still shook.

The four members of Seal Team 0 sat forward blinking with dazed expressions. Jordan and Wesley shook their heads and Carl looked around with a quizzical expression. John had a wide sinister looking grin that gave Rita the creeps.

"What did you stop it for?" Crowley demanded.

"Because it was the right thing to do," Stan said before Lorenzo could answer. "We have more than enough data and I'm concerned about overstimulation. It's imperative that we proceed with caution."

Crowley frowned. "But they were happy and blissed out."

"That's not necessarily all good," Cheryl said. "Listen to your psychologist and the rest of your team." She glanced at Rita and winked. "You're always charging ahead when you should be giving more thought to safety."

Crowley looked taken aback, but everyone's expression said the same thing, so he shrugged. "Let's see what the boys have to say."

Lorenzo kissed Rita on the forehead. "You going to be all right, honey?"

"I'll be okay." She waved him on. "Go ahead. I'll be along in a minute." She breathed in long and deep to compose herself while Jack and Cheryl helped the dazed looking team members out of their dream hoods and cradles, then she followed everyone to a conference room. Crowley sat at the head of the table flanked on his left by Stan, Cheryl, Jack, and Lorenzo. Wesley, Carl, John, and Jordan sat to the right.

"Un-fucking-believable!" John said as she entered. "I've never experienced anything like that in my life and never on so many levels. It was like doing ecstasy on steroids and then some. I can't even put into words how good it made me feel. "

"I think you just did," Crowley said, beaming.

John turned to Wesley and Carl. "I'm sorry for being such an asshole, guys. I don't know what got into me. I was so spun up, but now…" He rubbed his chin and had a distant look, then seemed to come back. "I see things differently now," he said. "Better still, I feel differently about them."

Carl waved him off. "Don't worry about it, John. We were all getting overspun. I feel better about things now too. Like the slate was wiped clean."

"Yeah," Wesley said. "Forget it. I feel better too. Like I had a deep relaxing sleep that caught me up on the hours of sleep that I really needed. We must have been under for quite awhile."

"Just under five minutes," Lorenzo said.

John's eyes went wide in disbelief, Carl's jaw dropped, and Wesley's mouth opened and closed, like he was speaking, but he said nothing. Jordan's expression went blank, like something big and invisible hit him.

"What about you, Jordan?"

Stan Krippner's voice seemed to pull him out of his stupor.

"I can't put it into words," Jordan said. "It's a big complicated mixture of thoughts, feelings, attitudes, and images, but not in any normal way, maybe more like, I don't know. Concepts? They seem more complex and abstract, like the very act of defining them makes limits that they are too big to fit into." He stopped himself and looked at the others. "Does anything I'm saying make any sense?"

"Try not to struggle too much with it," Stan said. "The same for the rest of you." He nodded to the others. "You've had an overwhelming non-rational experience and your linear minds are struggling to make sense out of something that doesn't follow logic. I suggest trying to observe it without making any judgements to give your rational mind time to assimilate the experience."

"To be honest with you," Jordan said. "It freaked me out. Like there's something wrong with feeling *that* good."

Wesley nodded, adding, "It gave me a good scare."

"Me too," Carl said. "I think the proper word is awe."

"The proper word is awe*some*," John said. "When can we do it again?"

"Not so fast," Stan said. "It appears to have affected your attitudes and emotions in a positive way, but we need to give it time to see if it has any effect on your overall stress levels, sleep patterns, or any other physiological indicators, and to see if the shifts you've experienced are permanent."

CHAPTER FIFTY FOUR

Jordan and the rest of the team slept for twelve hours straight without nightmares and woke up feeling refreshed and ready to go, as if every stressful experience had been wiped from their minds. Wesley sprawled on one end of the couch in their lounge and Jordan sat at the other end with his feet up on the coffee table. Carl sat in the big chair beside him and John stretched out on a recliner.

"That whole thing was amazing," Wesley said, sipping coffee. "I've never felt better."

"That was quite the surprise," John said. "I wasn't expecting anything like that."

"It's like beating your head against the wall," Jordan said.

The others looked at him baffled.

"It feels so good when you stop."

Carl chuckled and Wesley shook his head.

John frowned. "What do you mean by that?"

"I admit, it felt awesome," Jordan said. "It's one of the most amazing things I've ever experienced, but I can't help thinking about how shitty we felt before. I can really notice it now. It's like getting pushed deep down into a dark, hellish kind of a place, then getting launched like a slingshot into a heavenly stratosphere."

John continued frowning. "I still don't get it."

Carl smiled. "What Jordan is saying is that one of the reasons it felt so good and intense has a lot to do with how bad we felt going in. One extreme makes the other stronger. In other words the darker it is on one end of the spectrum, the brighter it is on the other."

Jordan sipped his coffee and held his cup up, toasting Carl. "I couldn't have said it better!"

Wesley looked to the others and slowly inclined his head and eyes toward the big wall monitor. When he spoke, his voice sounded a little louder. "I'm thankful for the break and really appreciated the experience, but I still feel cabin fever. Crowley promised us some R and R. I hope that wasn't it."

Carl picked up on Wesley's lead and winked. "I don't know about you guys, but I need to get the fuck out of here." He grabbed his crotch. "I need to get laid."

Wesley laughed, spraying coffee all over himself, setting off a round of laughter. "Tell us how you really feel Carl," he said, getting up to clean himself and his coffee spill. "We know what brain you're thinking with this morning."

"He said all along that we're free to do what we want," Carl said. "The only thing that has kept us cooped up here is more money, but I have to be honest, right now I'm giving a shit about it less and less."

John held up his coffee cup. "I'm feeling the same way. I need some nooky to balance things out."

"You know what's funny?" Wesley said. "It just dawned on me that I haven't thought about pussy at all since we've been here."

"None of us have except for Jordan," John said. "He's hot for Penélope."

Jordan stuck up his middle finger. "She's a babe all right, but she's with Lorenzo, Mr. Cool."

John wiggled his eyebrows up and down. "I think we need a load of strange, like we had in Paris. That would set me right!"

Jordan closed his eyes, remembering his night with Brittany. Different moments of it played through his mind, stirring his feelings below. Wesley was right. He did feel a strong attraction to Rita. There was something different about it, but he couldn't put his finger on it. Brittany in all her beauty brought out more of what he thought of as his animal side. His feelings for Rita also bordered on erotic, but there was something deeper with her that went beyond physical cravings.

A quick knock came on the door and Crowley waltzed in, all smiles, followed by two guys in suits. "You guys have done an amazing job and I want to thank you for sticking it out when it got tough," he said. "Yesterday was a surprise, but I realize that you've been stuck in here for awhile, so I've arranged a little field trip."

John nodded toward the two suits. "Are those our baby sitters?"

Crowley continued smiling. "Your groundbreaking work here has made you high value government assets, so we want to make sure that you have all the fun that we can give you while making sure you stay safe. Don't think of these guys as babysitters. Think of them as tour guides."

"And where is the tour taking us?" Carl asked.

Crowley rubbed his hands together. "Someplace to let off a little steam."

Like a Jack in the box, Jordan thought, glancing over at a wall monitor. We say what we're missing and he pops up with something to keep us happy. I know where this is going.

Jordan blinked in the sunlight and felt less like a rock star when the stretch limo pulled up in front of the compound, but it felt good to be outside breathing fresh air.

"No matter what you guys might think," he said under his breath. "Be careful what you say. I'm willing to bet that our ride is a lot less private than it seems. They're watching everything we say and do."

"Yeah, that's obvious," Wesley said sotto voce. "It's a weird feeling."

Jordan patted him on the back and followed him, John, and Carl into the limo. Its bar, fancy lighting, tinted windows, and flat screen didn't impress him the way it had the first time. What once felt new and exciting now seemed predictable.

Their escorts sat up front, separated from the team by soundproof glass. They drove for about an hour until they came to a remote sprawling ranch house that Jordan thought was South of the border.

"Have a good time boys," the driver said when he opened the door for them, "and take as much time as you want. We'll be here waiting for you."

Everyone looked at each other questioning, then John hopped out followed by Wesley and Carl. Jordan followed them into the house where they were greeted by a beautiful big breasted Hispanic looking blonde who led them into a large comfortably furnished room with a stocked bar and half a dozen scantily clad, drop dead gorgeous women who could all rate as Victoria's Secret models.

"Your pleasure is ours," she said. "Anything you want. All any of us want is to please you."

CHAPTER FIFTY FIVE

Rita sat with Lorenzo across from Jack and Cheryl in a conference room waiting for Crowley. Stan Krippner sat beside her checking notes on his tablet.

"I know he's going to want to charge ahead," Stan said, "but we need to proceed carefully. We can't rush this. We need time to observe any possible negative indicators or longer term consequences."

"I couldn't agree more," Cheryl said.

Jack and Lorenzo nodded in agreement.

Crowley strode into the room clapping his hands. "You folks did an incredible job!" He slid into his chair. "I can't begin to tell you how impressed I am with what you achieved. It's a miracle. You may very well have come up with a cure for PTSD!"

"I don't know if I'd go that far yet," Stan said. "It could be temporary. We'll know more in a few days."

"I'll tell you this," Crowley said, "No matter how you cut it that last scenario was absolutely brilliant in so many ways."

He stood and put his hands behind his back, pacing back and forth as he spoke. "We've been focused on using this technology to cure our wounded veterans, but we also plan to use it in the commercial gaming community as another mode of outreach." He nodded to Lorenzo. "Lorenzo has taken the first PTSD veteran scenario and modeled it into a point and shoot game interface that our dream team has tested on gaming computers. We plan to market that to create a revenue stream that supports this hospital and research complex."

"The next test of that scenario will be in the immersive dreaming state," Lorenzo said. "Do you plan on commercializing that too?"

Crowley smiled and grabbed an iPad, tapping it. Graphs, spreadsheets, and pie charts filled the big screen. He pointed to some graphs that showed red and green lines on a sharp incline. "I hired a top notch public relations guru to help us develop an approach to bring this technology to the public."

"I'm sure that projection is pretty far into the future," Stan said. "We have a ton of issues that need resolution before we do anything on that scale."

"I'm not talking about time frame here," Crowley said. "I'm talking about long term goals, one if which is to make this place self sufficient. Using Lorenzo's point and shoot model, we plan to put our veteran battle scenarios into multi-level computer games at a discounted price, or for free."

"Using the computer games as a marketing tool," Jack said. "As an incentive to get them to the immersive dreaming where you'll rake in the dinero."

Crowley smiled. "We'll have an incentive based system. At first the players will have to beat the video game to become eligible for the immersive dreaming experience, which will in effect train them for it."

"Clever," Stan said.

Crowley held up a finger. "It gets better once they're in the dreaming games because when they advance a level they will get rewarded with a little taste of what the boys got in their last outing."

Stan sat up. "I'm not so sure…"

Crowley held up a hand. "I'm sure we can cultivate the ability to modulate signal strengths to give milder experiences at the lower levels with increasing intensities at the higher ones."

Stan shook his head.

"Don't forget," Crowley said. "The primary intention of these games is to provide a healing modality that is accessible to as many people as possible for the greater good and healing of those that need it."

Jack's bushy eyebrows arched. "Easily accessible to people's wallets."

"Every bit of which will go into healing those that need it here, not into some corporation's pocket."

"You're putting a lot of emphasis on the potentially addictive aspects of this technology," Stan said. "Your methods may not be as pure as you think. I suggest giving that some serious thought."

Crowley sat back down. "We don't really know that it's addictive.

Coffee, food, sex, alcohol, lots of things have the potential of being addicting. Is it so bad to be mildly addicted to coffee, chocolate, or some other pleasure? As I've made clear, the gaming mind set prompts a neurological response that influences feelings of pleasure and reward already, we're just building on that with a little added incentive. Think of it as a bonus for better performers."

Rita listened, unconvinced. She couldn't stop thinking about Lorenzo's comment about lab rats hitting the right switch to get their cocaine and Stan Krippner's Assassin's Paradise.

"Don't forget," Crowley said. "As we have proven with Hodge Michaels, our primary motivator in this whole pleasure and reward model is to relieve suffering and contribute to the comfort of those too wounded or damaged to function. In cases where Dream Sleep is the only option, any concerns about addiction have no relevance."

"True," Rita said. "But what about the gamers? They're not suffering in any way."

"Unless we overdo it and overstimulate them," Cheryl added. "Especially any as sensitive as Terry."

"Is it right to motivate them by dangling pleasure and rewards as motivators?" Lorenzo said. "Do they really need the carrot and stick? It seems to me that they're motivated enough on their own."

"Without the crack," Jack said.

Crowley frowned. "Crack?"

Jack's eyebrows went into a deep V of a frown and he shook his head. "I'm sorry, but it sounds to me like you want to make them crackheads and junkies. That's how they do it on the street you know. A little snort here, a little bump there." He tapped the inside of his elbow with his thumb, index and middle finger, pantomiming the act of shooting up. "The next thing you know they're mainlining it!"

Crowley waved him off, speaking a little more forcefully. "Not everything has to go to extremes!" He lowered his voice. "I'm confident that we have the ability to attenuate the signal strength to low levels so our subjects have milder experiences at lower levels. Think of it like a subtle hint of spice that gives just the right flavor without overdoing it."

"Just one little snort," Jack quipped. "It won't hurt you."

Rita had all she could do to keep from smiling. Jack wasn't letting up and she secretly enjoyed Crowley's frustration.

"But once you get a taste for it..." Lorenzo said.

CHAPTER FIFTY SIX

After their field trip, Seal Team 0 did nothing but eat, sleep and watch movies for a few days with no gaming and no dreaming. Everyone slept through the night with no nightmares. By the end of the third day, John started getting antsy until Crowley called them in for a meeting in his Command and Control Center. Jordan wasn't in a hurry to do anything. He was relieved to be free of the nightmares and happy to see his teammates getting along.

"You guys look great!" Crowley said when they went in. "Do you feel as refreshed as you look?"

Jordan, Wesley, John, and Carl all nodded and took seats around Crowley's console. His wall of observation screens cycled through images showing the bustling hospital complex, cafeteria, operating rooms, labs, and lounges full of doctors, nurses, patients, and orderlies.

"Looks like you have a full house," Jordan said.

Crowley turned from the display, smiling. "There's a lot of good healing work going on all over this place," he said with a sweep of his hand, "and I want you to know that you guys are the force behind keeping it alive."

Carl, John, and Wesley looked puzzled.

"I don't get it," John said. "How are we the force behind keeping it alive?" He shook his finger at Crowley. "*You're* the one doing that."

Crowley shook his head and pointed to each of them. "You guys are going to be the face of Pandora by being our ambassadors to the gaming world." He made a bigger expansive sweeping gesture toward the wall of screens."

"We plan to make this place self sufficient by putting our veteran battle scenarios into multi-level games."

"What about the immersive dreaming games we're testing?" Carl said. "How will that fit in with the video games?"

Crowley clapped his hands together and rubbed them. "Using an incentive based system, players will have to beat the video game to become eligible for the full blown immersive dreaming experience, which will also provide the platform to train them."

"Not only will it make them earn it," John said. "It will filter out the losers and bring in the cream of the crop!"

Jordan had to admit, it was an impressive plan that would change the gaming world forever.

"Only the best of those will be able to follow in your trail blazing footsteps," Crowley said. "You guys are the first official dream team who are making it possible for the others who follow to have the same powerful experiences. Not only that," Crowley said holding up a finger, "but your hard work and dedication will continue to pay off. The way we have the program mapped out, there are additional incentives for you at critical milestones as well as programmed pay raises. You're all about to become very wealthy men at the center of an entirely new concept in gaming."

"What about Todd and Terry?" Carl said. "They've been a part of our team for a long time. We wouldn't be here if it weren't for their part in making it happen."

"No one's going to be left out," Crowley said. "Todd and Terry will be our primary liaisons between you guys and the gaming community at large. Don't worry. Seal Team 0 will be intact. In fact we plan to brand you as The Seal Team 0 Dream Team."

"That's great!" Carl said.

"I'm definitely down with that," Wesley added.

"Me too," John chimed in.

Jordan nodded to all of it, but said nothing.

Crowley smiled like a little kid. "We have plans for a wide release, a gaming league, T-shirts, key chains, coffee cups, thumb drives, and any other swag they come up with. We plan to roll out each new version with different situations and environments, including mountains, jungles, deserts, hot, cold, and every other situation imaginable."

John rocked back and forth in his chair. "We're going to get to play in both versions of the game, which will give us a better edge all around." He nodded toward Crowley, wiggling his eyebrows. "Are we going to get our minds blown more with Lorenzo's bad ass electronic crack?"

Crowley flinched when John said 'crack'. "It seems to have done wonders for you guys," he said in a measured tone, "so it has an important place, but we need to give it the respect it deserves and utilize it in the most beneficial way. It's already being implemented with those who have been wounded to the point of necessitating a coma."

He clicked the remote, bringing up an image on the big central screen of a sterile looking domed room lined with rows of hospital beds inside Plexiglas coffin like enclosures with consoles beside each one. Some held normal looking men in deep restful sleep, but most were occupied by men with missing arms, legs, and heavily bandaged head wounds.

He zoomed the camera in on a bald, emaciated young man with a furrowed brow whose eyes twitched in REM inside a Plexiglas enclosure set off from the others. His body shuddered in tremors. Jordan recognized a modified Dream Wear hood partially covering his damaged skull, revealing the pinkish gray fatty mass of his brain. The sight made his stomach flip-flop.

Fiber optics from the hood flashed and colored fluids flowed through tubing at his elbow. An additional set of wires and probes went straight from his brain through a bundled cable to the panel of video readouts on the console beside him showing waveforms and other vital functions.

"Staff Sergeant Mickey Palmer, Special Forces, victim of a road side I.E.D.," Crowley said. "Based on our first test subject and all of the data we've gathered from your experiences, we are in the process of utilizing this technology to bring peace to Sergeant Palmer's tortured mind by making him the first United States veteran to benefit from our fledgling Dream Sleep program. We fully expect all of his physiological indicators to settle in to a deep resting state when we put him fully under the control of our Dream Sleep protocols."

Carl pointed. "And the rest of those guys?"

"We're in the process of analyzing and prioritizing their injuries," Crowley said, "then every one of them will be fitted with a Dream Wear hood customized to their specialized needs."

CHAPTER FIFTY SEVEN

Rita and Cheryl hovered over Hodge, dressed in scrubs and masks, examining him inside the glass walls of the octagon shaped ICU. His furrowed brow changed expressions as he moaned and mumbled and his eyes jumped beneath closed lids while his body remained immobile. A multitude of unpleasant emotions passed over his face before Hodge's eyes shot open. "Rats!" He yelled.

Rita stumbled back flailing for balance until a wall stopped her. Hodge stared at her without seeing. Peering into his emptiness struck at her core, making it hard to breathe.

He sat up, eyes wide, his mouth opening and closing like a beached fish, then the words came in a torrent, accented by waving arms and wild eyes that looked ready to jump out of their sockets.

"Rats!" he yelled again. "They're coming!" He put his hands to his mouth and his eyes grew wider. "With Emily! Oh my God, please help us!" He screamed, sounding like a little girl. "Chazz and Ollie too! Run as far away from here as you can. You think you stopped them by shutting down Morpheus, but they've been waiting to get out and now they're coming." His breath came in spurts. "Denise. Eddie. Morgan. Emily and the rats are brig-ig-ig…" He gagged and grabbed at his throat, making deep guttural dry heaves, then a rat popped its head out from between his lips, its black beady eyes darting back and forth before it scrambled out of his mouth, followed by another.

Rita screamed soundlessly. More rats scurried up around Hodge, overflowing his enclosure, falling to the floor with muted wet thumps, scurrying toward her. She turned and ran straight into the pale blue eyes of Chazz Daggett glaring at her from under lowered brows. Tall and emaciated with a shaved head, he wore his trademark black tee-shirt, leather jacket and hobnailed boots.

Rita tried to scream again and he forced his hand over her mouth, jamming a walnut-sized, ruby eyed, silver skull ring between her teeth. Ollie Daggett came up behind her and savagely ripped her jeans off with a knife, pulling her backward, exposing her, then Chazz was on top of her, jamming his cold slimy tongue into her mouth and forcing her legs apart with brutal thrusts of his hips.

It felt as if he violated every opening in her body until something wet and hairy brushed her cheek and she saw hordes of rats tumbling off a jagged cliff. Hundreds floated on the swells, tiny legs and long tails dangling. One clawed at her hair and a furry head snapped at her face. Her teeth chattered as she slapped at the furry bodies and the dark chaotic waters whirled in the opposite direction, drawing her away from the cliff and squealing rats until the roiling water sucked her under.

She finally found her voice and screamed with everything she had as she plunged downward spinning into blackness, then her whole body shook.

She opened her eyes to Lorenzo shaking her awake.

"It's okay, babe." He pulled her close. "You're safe now."

She continued shaking as hot tears and heavy sobs overwhelmed her. Lorenzo cradled her in his arms, stroked her hair, and wiped her tears away, calming her. She buried her head in his chest.

"It was horrible," she whispered. "I hoped that when the team's nightmares went away that mine might too, but they're worse than ever."

"I think a sit down with Doctor Krippner is in order. If anyone can help you get over this, he can." Lorenzo kissed her cheek. "Now come on, settle down, lover. No one's going to hurt you on my watch." She kissed his chest and pressed her cheek to it, feeling safety in his arms.

She went straight to Stan Krippner's office the following morning, surprised to find Cheryl waiting there ahead of her. Her pale blue eyes widened behind her horn-rimmed glasses when she saw Rita, like a surprised owl. Her face looked haggard.

"You're not going to believe the nightmare I had last night," she blurted when Rita sat down in the chair beside her. "It was horrible."

Her words hit Rita like an invisible fist. She knew what Cheryl was about to say before she said it and stiffened, resisting what was coming.

"You and I were working on Hodge when he came to life yelling, 'Rats!'"

Rita jumped when she said 'Rats!', but Cheryl didn't seem to notice.

"He went crazy yelling 'They're coming! With Emily!', then he screamed like a little girl telling us to run and that we didn't stop them by shutting down Morpheus, but that they were coming. He kept going on about Chazz, Ollie, Denise, Eddie, and Morgan while rats came from everywhere, then Chazz and Ollie tried to rape me until I woke up screaming!"

"What's all this about Chazz, Ollie, Denise, Eddie, and Morgan?" Stan asked, coming in the door. He walked around the edge of his desk and took his place beneath his wall of artifacts.

"My nightmare," Cheryl said. "I thought they were gone, but they've gotten worse since coming here."

"And what about you?" Stan said to Rita.

"I had the same nightmare as Cheryl," Rita said, struggling to sound calm.

Cheryl's owl eyes returned. "My God," she whispered, putting her hand to her chest.

"I don't understand it," Rita said through trembling breaths. "I was having the same nightmares as Jordan until Lorenzo's, what did you call it, Assassin's Paradise?"

Stan nodded.

"Until that stopped Jordan's nightmares." She looked over at Cheryl who looked frozen with her hand to her mouth listening. "I foolishly thought that mine might stop too, but they're worse than ever. This last one was more vivid and it wasn't about war games, it was a DreamLand nightmare."

Cheryl nodded quickly in agreement.

"Is it possible that coming back here has triggered repressed memories?" Stan asked.

Rita thought for a moment. "If you want to know the truth, the nightmares from DreamLand have never stopped."

"Same for you, Cheryl?" Stan said.

She gave another quick nod.

"So you both have ongoing nightmares from the DreamLand computer. Cheryl, in your professional opinion would you characterize this as PTSD?"

She pursed her lips and her eyes went out of focus for a moment, then she was back. "Yes, I would."

"Rita has told me in depth details about how she spent a lot of time in the distorted dreams that Morpheus generated, but I haven't heard much from you about your time under the computer's control. Is there anything you want to share that might be helpful?"

Cheryl blinked and her mouth moved, but she had trouble getting the words out. Her face flushed crimson. "I - well - er - they were - ah - personal. I'm not comfortable discussing them."

Stan held up his hands making calming gestures. "Don't worry about it. If you're not comfortable discussing it, there's no sense in forcing anything. Is it fair to say they were the same as Rita's?"

"Yes!" Cheryl said almost too fast.

She doesn't know what mine are like, Rita thought. I never told her any details. I can't begin to imagine what hers were like. I never saw her spending much time in any DreamLand dreams, so it's an even bigger mystery.

"The only way I know of that can put a stop to recurring traumas like this is to find a way to face this fear head on to confront your demons."

"There's no way I'm going back into any computer dreams!" Cheryl said. "I don't care if it's feel good computer generated crack. That alone scares me even more. This whole thing makes me jumpy. I don't trust it." She crossed her arms and sat back in her chair. "I wish I had nothing to do with any of it. The only reason I'm here is because I was forced into it."

"I can't say that I blame you," Stan said. "I'm not comfortable with it myself. My main reason for being here is to be as much of a watch dog as possible and do my best to mitigate any damage that might come of it. My greatest fear is that little Terry was just the tip of the iceberg."

"I'm in the same boat as Cheryl," Rita said. "I'm here against my will, and there's no way in hell I'm going to be subjected to another computer generated dream. No one believes that the nightmares from Morpheus crossed over into the real world, but look what's happening here? I've had the same nightmares as Jordan, and now even though

Cheryl and I have been having recurring nightmares since Morpheus was shut down we've never had the same one at the same time -- with Hodge nonetheless! Sure it's not a physical cross-over, but it's still a cross-over. Who knows what can come of it?"

Cheryl nodded in agreement. "I hope that Morpheus not only stays disconnected, but that they destroy that damned backup before all hell breaks loose."

"Amen," Rita said fingering the angel that hung from her neck and glancing up at Stan's shamanic artifacts.

Stan steepled his fingers and leaned back in his chair. "The only way to get past your nightmares is to face your fear head on. It can be done in the dreams themselves, but that takes a higher level of awareness that isn't obvious when you're overwhelmed by terror."

"That wouldn't have done any good in DreamLand," Cheryl said.

Stan held up his hands. "For starters, this isn't DreamLand, this is an entirely different set of circumstances. One slower and gentler method of resolving issues like this is to delve into specifics in in-depth psychotherapy sessions, possibly involving hypnosis, and there have been some positive results using MDMA, which goes by the street name of ecstasy, but even then there could be issues if you're uncomfortable sharing details of your trauma or exposing yourself in any way that makes you feel vulnerable."

Rita looked over at Cheryl, who sat up rigid, keeping her arms crossed.

"Regardless of the approach, the concept is the same," Stan continued. "The idea is to return to the traumatic event with a higher awareness that I call witness consciousness. When you are first confronted with a trauma, you have no precedent for what happens, so the mind compartmentalizes the event to keep your conscious mind safe in what is essentially an act of denial that serves as a survival technique. The problem is that it never goes away."

"The gift that keeps on giving," Cheryl said under her breath.

"It's stuck negative energy," Stan continued. "And it takes energy to keep it there, in what is termed an energy leak."

"An energy leak?" Rita asked.

"Your nightmares are proof of it and they won't go away unless you deal with them. In dreaming states you have some level of awareness because your mind is active in a state of semi-consciousness, so the boundary between your conscious and subconscious is thinner, which lets the leak out. If you return to the scene of the crime with the higher awareness of your witness consciousness, it plays the role of parent to your creation, and allows you to re-experience the trauma and rescue the lost child in the safety of its 'parent', which is you, its actual creator, and what many think of as a higher self."

"It's the equivalent of mommy or daddy coming in to your room and turning the lights on to chase away the monsters," Cheryl said.

"That's a great analogy!" Stan said. "In this case you have to be your own mommy and daddy, but if you work through personal issues like this the results can be empowering."

"Are there any faster approaches?" Rita said.

Stan nodded. "There is a more fast acting natural approach which can bring dramatic results by putting you in what is called a waking dream. In your normal waking state, your left 'male' brain is more active, which helps you function in waking reality, while the right side 'female' brain is repressed. This is generally more true with males, while women are more in touch with their right brains, which explains female empathy and intuition. The left brain is logical and serialized, while the right brain speaks an entirely different language of symbolism, concepts, and emotions. When we go to sleep at night, the left brain gets a rest and the right brain comes out to play, which is what dreaming is, the language of the right brain. That's why we're so accepting of the bizarre images and feelings of the dreaming state."

"That sounds like the way to go," Cheryl said, brightening. "And this natural method brings about witness consciousness?"

"In this case they consider the witness to be the mother, but it doesn't come easy and it often brings a lot of physical discomfort."

Cheryl leaned forward. "What kind of physical discomfort?"

"Primarily nausea, vomiting, and shitting."

She sat back again, seeming deflated. "For how long?"

"Typically four to six hours, but it's an individual thing. Some people don't have those reactions and some rare individuals are not affected at all."

Rita glanced over at Cheryl, who sat rigid, gazing back at Rita, her eyes full of questions.

"Do we have to talk to anybody or expose our secrets through sharing or psychotherapy?"

She's hiding something that must be really horrifying, Rita thought, but no matter how embarrassing, I trust Stan and feel like I can tell him anything.

"The only one you will have to talk to is 'the Mother'," Stan said, "and the dialogue will be strictly inside of you, unless you start vocalizing it."

"The Mother?" Rita said.

Stan's expression approached reverence when he spoke next. "La Madre. Madre Ayahuasca."

Cheryl frowned. "Madre Ayawhatsca?"

"Ayahuasca has been used throughout the jungles of South America since prehistoric times. It's primarily a mixture of two plants, although other plants are sometimes added. The Ayahuasca vine used in the brew that carries its name is classified as Banisteriopsis Caapi, also known as The Vine of Death, The Vine of the Soul, Caapi, Yajé, and many other names. Though it contains trace amounts of Dimethyltryptamine, the Ayahuasca vine is not the primary psychoactive component of the brew. Another plant the natives call Chacruna, classified as Psychotria Viridis, contains the psychoactive DMT component. Taken orally by itself, the stomach's MAO enzymes digest the DMT in the Chacruna before it can cross the blood brain barrier. Adding the Ayahuasca vine to the DMT loaded Chacruna leaves provides an MAO inhibitor, making the DMT in the Chacruna orally active, producing profound and startling experiences."

He leaned back studying them, giving them time to let it all sink in. "Anthropologists, psychiatrists, and other metal health professionals have been drawn to it for numerous reasons. Ayahuasca gained a reputation for providing telepathic powers. In fact, a psychoactive alkaloid found in it was named telepathine, which is now known to be harmine. Amazonian shamans call it the Mother of all the plants."

Cheryl's face pinched into a frown. "I find it hard to understand how anybody would want to drink something that makes them sick."

"It is often referred to as 'la purga', and is credited with purging toxins and sickness on physical, psychological, and spiritual levels. Many think it is well worth a few hours of discomfort to alleviate deep seated traumas."

"It sounds pretty extreme," Rita said.

"Like some of the nightmares you've described," Stan said. "If you ask me a night of puking and shitting is a small price to pay for healing yourselves of your nightmares, but it isn't for everybody. You might be better off taking the slower route of psychotherapy, but in order to do that, you're going to have to open up about exactly what goes on in your nightmares, otherwise…"

"I need to think this through," Cheryl said.

Stan looked from her to Rita.

"I need to do the same," Rita said.

"I understand," Stan said. "The dynamics of what needs to happen are the same in every case, but the speed and method of how you deal with it varies. How you proceed, if you do in fact decide to pursue relieving your PTSD is up to you. My job is to facilitate your healing and provide you with options, regardless of how you want to approach it."

CHAPTER FIFTY EIGHT

"**O**kay," Lorenzo's voice said. "The sequence is queued and we are initiating in five, four, three..."
Like all the times before, Jordan grew heavy at the count of one and fell into the shifting void between dark and light, reminding himself, this is only a dream and in it I'm trying to find a higher awareness to navigate a reality that follows a more flexible set of rules.

He had a moment of battlefield clarity before the hot flash of a mortar explosion knocked him to the ground. His ears rang and everything went fuzzy. The smell of explosives, smoke, and debris burned his nose and eyes causing him to sneeze repeatedly. Jesus, Lorenzo wasn't kidding when he said these scenarios were unpredictable like a real battle.

He regained his bearings and found his M4, then scrambled to his feet, looking for the rest of his team.

"Over here!" John called out.

Through the haze, Jordan saw his arm up, waving him over to a foxhole. Another explosion behind him added an extra push that sent Jordan sprinting toward the ditch where he found John crouched below the berm. His eyes looked wild and his mouth turned up in a half-crazed grin. He winked at Jordan.

Wesley and Carl hunkered down beside John along with a young, skinny, red haired corporal who white knuckled his rifle. His nametag said FRIEDMAN.

"It's going to happen any second now," Friedman said. "I can feel it!"

"You're okay, pal," John said. "You're with Seal Team 0 now and we're going to get you past this thing."

Friedman grabbed his arm. "Don't you get it? We're going to get blown up!"

Carl patted him on the shoulder. "Listen, you're reliving this thing over and over again. You don't have to keep doing that."

"But the rest of my squad. They all…"

"Let them go. We're here to show you that you survived."

Friedman jumped when a bomb exploded in front of them, showering them with dirt. Everyone ducked, then bullets pinged the ground above them. Friedman's eyes darted back and forth from man to man, questioning.

"We're with you to the end," Jordan reassured him, "because this does end. In fact it's over. You're the only one keeping it alive."

Jordan looked up over the foxhole. Like the game they had played, the expansiveness of the battlefield looked endless.

"We're going to get blown up right here in this foxhole," Friedman said. "I just know it!"

"Then let's get moving!" John yanked him up and ran along the length of the foxhole, half dragging him.

"That crazy fuck!" Wesley said.

He and Carl looked at Jordan, literally looking shell shocked. Jordan threw up his hands and jerked his head in the direction John went. "We're all in this together," he said. "Yeah, it's scary as shit, but remember it's only a dream. Let's get moving!"

He bolted after John and Friedman with Carl and Wesley following close behind. Together they scrambled up out of the foxhole and ran staying low, zig-zagging through explosions toward a cratered road. They caught up to John struggling to pull Friedman, but Friedman stayed rooted to his spot, pointing at a partially exposed mine. "That's it!" He blubbered. "That's the mine that got us!"

He flinched when a mortar exploded close by that nearly knocked them off their feet.

"What do you mean, that's the mine?" Carl shouted above the din. "How the fuck would you know that that's the mine?"

"I d-don't know," Friedman stammered, "but I know. That's it!"

"Proof that this is all in your head," Jordan said. "Think about it. How else would you know?"

"I'm not going to stand here arguing about it," Wesley said, "but if it is, let's go around it."

Friedman's mouth moved and his head shook 'No'. The rest of him remained frozen.

"Fuck it!" John grabbed his hand and pulled hard. "Like Jordan said, this is all in your head and I'm going to prove it. Come on."

"Nooo!" Friedman shrieked.

John slammed into him, wrapping him in a bear hug and the two tumbled forward onto the mine, exploding in a bright thunderous flash that sent them spinning into darkness.

Jordan came to stunned amidst a cloud of acrid smoke, feeling the ground shaking beneath him, not knowing where he was or what he was doing. In the next moment he found himself in a Humvee with Wesley and Carl, totally disoriented.

"What the fuck's going on?" Carl said.

Wesley's eyes bugged out. "Where are we? What happened?"

"I'm lost and scared shit," Carl said in a trembling half-whisper.

Jordan went to answer, finding only a mental abyss that gave no explanation as to how he got into a war zone. The terror of his mortality held him in an icy grip.

The Humvee in front of them blew up in a series of spectacular explosions and before anybody could react, the Humvee they rode in blew up, taking them with it.

CHAPTER FIFTY NINE

Rita watched John through the observation window and on the monitors feeling mild shock when he sat up and a gamut of confused expressions passed over his face like wind clearing away storm clouds, then his smile broke through, blazing sunlight. His raging vital signs diminished from the console in time with his dawning recognition of where he was.

In contrast, the video from Corporal Friedman, who wore a dream hood in a separate room, showed an open-mouthed silent scream highlighting a frozen expression of wide-eyed terror. His vital signs all spiked into the red danger zone. Zooming the observation camera back, her breath hitched when she saw the dark spread of urine at his crotch.

"Breathe deep," she heard herself say into the headset. "Breathe in slow and deep. Everything is okay. You're safe."

His face remained frozen in an eerie grimace and he showed no reaction to her words. She tapped her mouse, silencing the alarms that gave him electronic screams that his mouth would not. Her own internal alarms prompted her to medicate him until his sharp intake of breath preceded a heart rending scream that pegged his vital signs, followed by more shrieks.

Each outburst brought his vitals down by degrees, like a whistling tea kettle venting steam until he shook with sobs that broke down into soft, anguished cries. Two nurses hovered over him, calming him.

Rita focused on her own breath, consciously diminishing her own terror. She glanced sideways at Cheryl, Jack, and Lorenzo at the consoles beside her. They all seemed equally startled. Lorenzo put a calming hand on her arm and the rest of Seal Team 0 opened their eyes together, looking equally as terror stricken and confused as Corporal Friedman.

If the situation hadn't been so emotionally charged, it would have been comical watching Jordan, Wesley, and Carl wrestling with their individual fear and disorientation expressing the exact same reactions in a precisely choreographed sequence.

"Breathe deep," Rita commanded. "You're safe!"

"What the fuck?" Wesley blurted, catching his breath.

"Where the fuck are we?" Carl said. "Dead?"

Jordan shook his head. His eyes looked wild and unfocused. He gripped the edge of his dream cradle and sat up, looking over at his teammates. "Jesus, I thought we were, but were not. We're in the dream lab!"

With those words, everybody's vital signs diminished with the exception of John, whose vitals stayed raised, but steady. He shook with suppressed laughter.

Carl sat up, pulled off his dream hood and glared at John. "Asshole!"

John laughed harder.

"What kind of stupid shit was that?" Wesley said, following Carl's lead.

John's eyes opened wide in mock terror and he giggled.

Wesley pulled himself up out of his dream cradle into a standing position, clenched his fists, and started toward John. "I'm going to kick your ass, you fucking moron…"

Crowley stepped into the room and put himself between them. "That was absolutely amazing!" He said, first to Wesley, then to the rest of the team. "You guys just made history. Again. Do you have any idea of what you just accomplished?"

"Yeah," Carl said, standing from his dream cradle, glowering at John. "I thought I was dead. What the fuck is wrong with you, John?"

Crowley stayed in front of John, holding up his hands in surrender. "Slow down, boys. There's a lot of complicated stuff going on here that none of us have ever seen before. We need to keep cool and put our heads together so we can figure out what happened."

"We lost it, that's what happened," Jordan said.

"Come on!" Crowley helped John from his cradle and guided him out the door ahead of the others. "We need to do a full debriefing while everything is still fresh."

Lorenzo rubbed Rita's shoulder. "C'mon babe."

She stood and he put his arm around her, following the others to a conference room where Crowley sat at the head of the table with the members of Seal Team 0 lining one side, and Stan, Cheryl, and Jack lining the other. Seeing Cheryl sitting bolt upright looking pale and strained added to Rita's uneasiness. She slid her chair closer to Lorenzo. The boys looked unsettled too, except for John, who looked smug. Wesley and Carl still looked startled and Jordan looked contemplative.

Crowley leaned in, putting his attention on Jordan. "You're the in game leader," he said. "What happened from your point of view?" He looked to the other team members. "I want to hear from everybody, but I want to start with Jordan."

Jordan sighed and looked to Wesley. "To put it in a nut shell, we lost it and it got real."

"Not all of us lost it," John said, sounding self-satisfied.

"No!" Wesley shot back. "The rest of us lost it because of you, you selfish prick."

"Put a lid on it!" Crowley said, leaning in closer. "I said I want to hear from Jordan first, so if you can show a little respect and wait your turn like I asked, everybody will get a chance to speak."

Wesley glared at John with narrowed eyes and sat back, nodding to Jordan.

"It's made me more aware of something that I've been worried about," Jordan said, "and I'm starting to think that it might be dangerous." He looked over at Wesley again, who nodded.

"Go on," Crowley said.

"When I first went into the sequence, I had a sense of clarity on the battlefield which I credit to Lorenzo taking us through the scenario in his game before we did the actual dream sequence, then I felt the hot flash of a mortar explosion that knocked me on my ass and it hurt!"

Carl and Wesley both nodded. John shook his head.

"My ears rang and everything went fuzzy," Jordan went on, "then the smell of smoke and gunpowder burned my nose and eyes. I've felt pain in these gaming dreams before, but this time it was more intense. I think because it was an unpredictable situation that Lorenzo did his best to prepare us for as opposed to something that we were familiar with."

He paused, searching for the right words. "But I can't help feeling -- and I can't give any logical explanation for this. It's more of a gut feeling that because this was based on Corporal Friedman's emotional memories, it somehow made the whole experience more real and more intense."

Stan leaned in listening closely, his face a study of concentration. Beside him Cheryl blinked and her hands white-knuckled the arms of her chair. Watching her made Rita's insides tighten.

Jordan glanced around, gauging everyone's reactions before continuing. "I saw John waving me over to a foxhole, so I went to it and found him, Wesley, and Carl with Corporal Friedman. An explosion showered us with dirt and bullets pinged the ground above us. By this time I was worried and poor Corporal Friedman was scared shitless." He shook his head. "Man, could I ever see it in his eyes! That scared me more. I looked up over the edge of the foxhole. Like the game we played with Lorenzo, the battlefield looked endless, then Friedman started really freaking out, so John grabbed him and dragged him along the foxhole."

John smiled at this.

"So we followed them," Jordan said. "We were there to rescue Friedman and I couldn't wait to get the hell out of there! We caught up to John and Friedman pointed at a mine, swearing it was the one that killed his squad, then John grabbed him in a bear hug and jumped onto the mine causing it to explode in a bright flash that sent me into blackness. I don't know how long I was out for, but when I came to I forgot where I was and what I was supposed to be doing. I was in a Humvee with Wesley and Carl. We were all scared shit and we all forgot we were dreaming." His voice rose. "At that point it was real to us, then just like the game we went through with Lorenzo, the Humvee in front of us blew up and the one we rode in blew up right after it."

The room fell silent.

Cheryl looked paper white and Jack and Lorenzo seemed lost in thought. Stan rubbed his chin and Crowley broke the silence.

"You guys did a hell of a job!"

Jordan frowned.

"Just so I'm clear," Stan said. "You can feel everything in the dreams, pain and all, as if it's really happening."

"That's right!" Jordan said.

"But it doesn't hurt anything," Crowley said. "You wake up from it and you're not hurt in any way."

"I don't think so," Cheryl said in a half-whisper.

Stan put his hand on her arm, calming her.

Wesley shook his head. "Just because it doesn't happen in the real world doesn't mean you're not feeling pain when it's happening to you in the dream."

"Come on, it can't be that bad," Crowley said. "It's only a dream…"

"If it's not so bad," Wesley retorted, "Why don't you come with us and find out for yourself?"

Crowley flushed and seemed at a loss for words, but it didn't last. "You guys changed Corporal Friedman's memory of his trauma. I'm willing to bet that seeing you guys in the flesh and talking about the experience you shared will reinforce the shift in his perspective and possibly free him of his PTSD."

"That remains to be seen," Stan said. "These new developments worry me. I'm not comfortable with anybody suffering pain, real or imagined. Aside from that I'm concerned about this Dreamnesia the boys are describing."

"Dream whatcha?" Carl said.

"Dreamnesia. Dream Amnesia. When you can't remember your dreams, or when you forget you're dreaming. It makes your experience become both real and fluid."

"You get lost," Carl said.

"That's another way of putting it," Stan said. "You're literally lost in a dream."

"That's how we woke up in the Humvee," Wesley said.

"Exactly!"

"Well that sure puts another spin on things, doesn't it?" Crowley said. "But it's still only a dream."

"That's a matter of perspective," Stan cut in. "Anyone who shows signs of PTSD from a dream experience is traumatized."

Crowley stared at him.

"Maybe you should go into a dream with the boys like Wesley suggested," Stan said, "then you can see for yourself first hand."

"I'll think it over," Crowley said.

"I'm not comfortable with any of this," Cheryl said, looking back and forth from one end of the table to the other.

Crowley stood and held up his hands. "Hang on a minute."

"No, you hang on a minute!" Cheryl rose, her hands clutching the table's edge, her voice raised to a wavering childlike treble. "You have no idea what you're dealing with here." She gestured to Jack, Lorenzo, and Rita, her words coming faster. "We've been through this shit before and know what can happen. You don't have a clue. I'll be damned if I'm going to go through anything like that again. Did you hear any of what Doctor Krippner said? Pain is pain and trauma is trauma no matter what, when, where and how it happens."

"Jesus," Lorenzo whispered to Rita. "Cheryl's bang on. Can you imagine how much this shit would get out of hand if Morpheus was back online?"

Cheryl sighed and addressed the team. "I'm sorry boys. I apologize for losing my temper in front of you, but I worry about you."

"You can stick up for us any day," Jordan said. "You kidding me? You're awesome. Don't ever stop!"

She smiled and looked flustered as she sank back into her chair. Her hands shook.

"Damn skippy!" Wesley stood and clapped. The rest of Seal Team 0 stood with him and followed suit. Rita felt her heart swell and found herself on her feet clapping with them, followed by Lorenzo, Jack Scanlon, and Stan Krippner. Cheryl blushed and her eyes teared up. Jack put a comforting hand on her back.

When it became obvious that he was the only one sitting, Crowley stood and clapped half-heartedly with the others.

CHAPTER SIXTY

J ordan had a moment of clarity before the hot flash of a mortar explosion knocked him to the ground, causing his ears to ring, then everything went fuzzy.

"Over here!" John called out.

Through the haze, Jordan saw John waving him over to a foxhole. Another explosion behind him sent Jordan sprinting toward it.

Carl and Wesley hunkered down beside John with Corporal Friedman. John yanked Friedman up and ran along the length of the foxhole, half dragging him.

"That crazy fuck!" Wesley said.

Everything that followed came in stroboscopic flashes.

John slammed into Friedman and the two tumbled forward onto the mine, exploding in a bright thunderous flash.

Jordan found himself in a Humvee with Wesley and Carl.

"What the fuck's going on?" Carl said.

A Humvee in front of them blew up, followed by the one they rode in.

Jordan's eyes flew open. He bit back a scream when he recognized the ceiling of his room and sat up wiping sweat from his face with his sheet. Jesus, he thought. Third night in a row since Friedman's nightmare. I half-expected this, but three nights in a row? I better have a talk with Doc Krippner. Wesley and Carl are having nightmares too, but John hasn't said shit. He's a loose cannon and he's getting more nuts all the time. He's the one who sent us off into never-never land by jumping on that mine. He has no idea what it's like to get lost like its real, which makes me wonder how things were for Terry.

He tossed and turned, playing things out in his mind. Aside from their team freak out, the way Doctor Martin reacted in their meeting and the fear Rita showed worried him. Aside from Doc Krippner, they knew more than everyone except Jack Scanlon and Lorenzo. Crowley didn't know shit.

He drifted off into an uneasy sleep, waking to the sound of raised voices from the other room.

"You were so busy showboating that you forgot about the rest of the team," Wesley said. "Your stupid fucking stunt sent the rest of us into a place that made everything real. Do you have any idea what that was like?"

"Who are you calling stupid?" John shot back.

"I don't see any other stupid mother fuckers around here."

Shit's about to get real, Jordan thought. He threw back the covers and rolled out of bed.

"Do you hear what you sound like?" John said in a mincing voice. "You guys are a bunch of pussies!"

Jordan hustled out of his room in time to see Wesley punch John in the chest, knocking him back over a chair, onto the coffee table, smashing it.

"How does it feel to have your ass whooped by a pussy!" Wesley yelled, red-faced. He started toward John again until Jordan got between them, facing Wesley. Carl came from his room and helped John up, blocking him from getting to Wesley.

"Chill out," Jordan said. "We're supposed to be a team, remember?"

"C'mon pussy boy," John taunted, beckoning with his fingers. "You want some more of me? Come and get it!"

"Shut up," Carl said holding a struggling John back.

Wesley's eyes grew wide with rage. Jordan wondered if he could keep the big guy back, then the door to the room opened.

Crowley came in followed by two guards. "Little difference of opinion here?"

The fire in Wesley's eyes dimmed and he backed away from Jordan. "You might say that."

Jordan turned around to see John standing back from Carl. "It's nothing," he said. "Just blowing off a little steam, that's all."

Crowley looked at the smashed table, then at John and Wesley and smirked. "I'd hate to see what happened if you boys wanted to blow off a lot of steam."

No one said anything.

Crowley shook his head. "I've got something good to share with you that should improve your mood. Get dressed and I'll show you."

Twenty minutes later, Crowley ushered them into a private hospital room in another part of the complex where they found red-haired Corporal Friedman sleeping. Jordan noticed by the contours under the blanket that he had an arm and leg missing from one side of his already thin frame. Friedman's eyes fluttered open in mild surprise.

"Shit, you guys *are* real," he said, reaching out to John, who tentatively took his hand. "My dream angels," he continued. "I can't thank you guys enough for saving my bacon."

John looked around at everyone quizzically and shrugged.

"When's the last time you had a nightmare?" Crowley asked.

Friedman's smile radiated happiness and his eyes welled with tears. "Not since you put me on that dream thingamajig. I still can't believe it. Were you guys really in my nightmare with me?"

Everyone nodded, but no one spoke.

"It's a miracle." Friedman raised the stumps of his missing arm and leg beneath the blanket. "This was bad enough, but the endless nightmares, depression, guilt and anger, not to mention the lack of sleep made my life a living hell. Thanks to you guys I can finally sleep all night without getting doped up and I feel like a giant weight was lifted off of me."

"I hope it lasts," Carl said.

"Something deep inside of me changed," Friedman said.

John brightened more with each word Friedman said. His eyes found Wesley's and the corner of his mouth turned up in a smirk. Though Friedman's words vindicated him, Jordan worried that it might make him more reckless.

"It's like you guys pulled the last piece of invisible shrapnel out of me by forcing me to face what scared me the most." He looked up at John with gratitude. "I can't explain it or make any sense out of it. All I can say is that it's a feeling that tells me deep in my heart that the nightmares and the rest of the crap that goes with them are gone and won't be back." He let go of John's hand and wiped tears from his face, then pointed to his missing limbs. "Now I can get on with my rehab. The docs promised me some new hi-tech prosthetics. I can't wait to try them!"

CHAPTER SIXTY ONE

"We're running at around eighty percent capacity," Crowley said, leading Rita, Lorenzo, Jack, and Cheryl through a doorway to one of the outer domes of the complex that opened into the hospital where doctors, nurses, and orderlies busied themselves with patients, many of them amputees in wheelchairs and on gurneys. He led them past a nurse's station, down a long hallway to a series of curving hallways to the main building until they stood under the arch with backlit metal letters that said:

IMMERSIVE COMBAT

Crowley crossed his arms and looked from Rita to Cheryl, who looked stone-faced. "I know you folks have reservations about how our first PTSD dream exercise went, but I want to stress that Corporal Friedman has been healed of virtually all of his symptoms…"

"Except his missing limbs." Jack gave him a tight smile and wiggled his eyebrows.

Touché! Rita thought, struggling to keep from giggling. She glanced over at Cheryl who remained expressionless.

Crowley went on undaunted. "I'm confident that we'll work through the issues we encountered and push ahead. Look what we did with Corporal Friedman and imagine how much good we can do for all the others suffering from similar symptoms."

He opened the door to the inner domed room lined with rows of dreaming cradles so everyone could peer in. "I can't wait to see this ward full!" After a moment he let the door close and led the group over to the arch that said:

CYBERNETIC LIMB FACILITY

"In answer to your comment about missing limbs," he said to Jack. "Wait 'til you see this!" He rubbed his hands together.

The door opened to a darkened room punctuated by flashes of light that reminded Rita of fireflies, only these were too bright. The sounds of pneumatic hisses, whirs, clicks, and what sounded like whispers came from the darkness. Rita imagined a menagerie of small insects and animals scurrying about in some kind of high-tech electronic jungle. Crowley paused, obviously enjoying the moment.

"With workers like these," he said with an expansive grin, "there's no need for lights, air conditioning, coffee breaks, maternity leave, disgruntled workers, or anything like that."

"The ultimate in dehumanization," Cheryl muttered.

Crowley shook his head and tapped a panel by the door, brightly lighting the large dome. Several assembly lines rolled along with robotic arms performing precision tasks. The tiny flashes Rita saw came from micro welders. Conveyor belts provided a steady stream of raw materials. Robotic arms, legs, joints and other assemblies came off the ends of individual assembly lines and placed on racks.

"As I mentioned before, we have plans to tie in the command and control functions of the cybernetic limbs into the command and control functions of the microprocessor in Jack and Cheryl's dreaming hood."

He winked at Cheryl, closed the door and ushered them over to the arch that said:

CYBERNETIC ORGAN FACILITY

When he flicked on the lights the assembly lines looked similar to the previous ones, but moved at a much slower crawl. Its stations had diverse elements complemented by large Plexiglas holding tanks fed by colored tubes that fed down from ceiling pipes and conduits.

Livers, hearts, lungs, eyeballs, and other organs floated in these tanks in different colored fluids. Though she had seen many things in her career as a nurse, the sight of these made Rita's stomach queasy.

"It looks like Frankenstein's playroom," Lorenzo said.

Jack chuckled at this and Cheryl remained straight-faced.

Crowley motioned them in, leading them to a tank full of floating eyeballs with long red stringy nerve bundles that hung down like the tentacles of a Man-of-war jellyfish. On close inspection the eyeballs themselves looked like an amalgam of human tissue, glass, plastic, and metal.

Lorenzo leaned in and examined it from different angles. "Looks like a prop from Blade Runner."

Cheryl followed his lead, her face a study of concentration.

Crowley pursed his lips and nodded. "We've combined stem cell therapy and soft tissue growth to augment and replace functionality that was compromised from injury."

Jack whistled. "It takes the concept of human machine interface to a whole 'nother level."

Where the finished prosthetic limbs were stored on racks, these organs were stacked in individual storage tanks fed by hoses and multicolored wire bundles.

Instead of going back out the door they came in, Crowley led them through the facility to another door on the far side. The sign over it said:

CYBERNETIC RESEARCH AND DEVELOPMENT

It opened to a long windowed passage that reminded Rita of the observation hall of a car wash. She could barely hear pneumatic hisses, whirs, and clicks on the other side of the glass.

"Jesus, if I didn't know better," Lorenzo said under his breath, "I'd think we were getting a tour of a slaughter house."

"We just started bringing in test subjects this week," Crowley said. "So far, everything is working perfectly. It's all automated, but we have teams of physicians monitoring every aspect of the process."

What looked like a huge operating theater bustled with activity. Robotic arms severed useless limbs with spinning, blood spattering scalpel saws while other robots attached human machine extensions, followed by testing sequences. On another part of what Rita thought of as the killing floor, sophisticated mechanisms plucked out damaged organs, reinstalling cybernetic replacements into the bloody sockets left behind.

Each work station glowed with scanners, MRI devices, numeric displays, monitoring probes and robotic instrumentation displaying vital signs. In the foreground a computer controlled robotic surgeon implanted one of Jack's microprocessor chips into the base of a patient's skull. His eyes grew wide when he saw it. "Is that..."

Crowley smiled. "You bet!"

"I had no idea that you planned to take it in this direction," Jack muttered.

"No doubt he has lots of other surprises in store for us," Cheryl said.

"Watch this." Crowley pointed. "That was just one specialized mode of implementation.

The click and whir of relays and motors signaled a table with an unconscious man on it drawn by locked hydraulic arms into a large unit. Once inside, green, red, and blue laser grids mapped and scanned the patient, especially around his head. Screens outside the unit performed calculations reflected in colored brain scans and vital sign readouts.

A hiss came followed by white smoke billowing from the chambers. An observation camera showed a bird's eye view of a large computerized square of steel that matched the table descend onto the patient, sealing itself with a magnetic clack followed by a pneumatic hiss. The tops of the unit flashed with displays, then the entire assembly rolled back out of the scanning device and rotated so the patient faced the floor.

A small opening in the back of the unit exposed the base of his skull to his shoulders, then an apparatus descended from the ceiling and a laser sliced open his neck. Small white puffs of smoke indicated where cuts were made.

The laser scalpel completed the first incision and made two more cuts at the top and bottom of the first cut. With insect-like clicks, and hisses, two sets of robotic fingers extended from the sides of the neck opening and peeled back flaps of skin, locking them down like window shutters, exposing the spine. Another robotic hand with fingertips like dentist drills lowered onto the man's exposed spine.

Its fingers moved through a series of manipulations as it drilled into different points on the vertebrae. When the hand pulled away, another one moved Jack's microprocessor into position and pressed it down onto the drilled vertebrae where a laser danced through rapid microsurgeries that fused nerves and veins to chip leads and ports.

When the operation was complete, the fingers pulled and pressed the skin flaps into place and the laser scalpel retraced its original path, cauterizing the wound in puffs of smoke.

"The ultimate in dehumanization," Cheryl said again. "So much for caring hands or human contact."

Rita felt overwhelmed by the bloodshed. She had participated in many surgeries and procedures, but never anything on this large of a scale - on assembly lines no less. Her mouth felt dry and her stomach knotted, but she didn't say anything for fear of vomiting. Sure, people were being healed, but she had to agree with Cheryl. The entire operation struck her as dehumanizing.

"I think I've seen enough," Cheryl said.

Amen, Rita thought. Get me out of here!

Crowley held up a finger. "One more stop on the tour. I promise it will be more sedate -- literally."

Cheryl glanced over at Rita. The look on her face said that they shared the same thoughts and feelings.

Crowley brought them back out to a curved hallway that led to the arch titled:

DREAMSLEEP

This doorway brought them into another domed room lined with rows of occupied coffin-like Plexiglas enclosures similar to the one that held Hodge. Each had tubing and wires running into monitoring consoles. Nurses and orderlies moved down the aisles checking on patients and tapping notes on the console keyboards.

"None of this would be possible without the groundbreaking work you have done." Crowley looked directly at Cheryl, then to the others.

"All of these poor lost souls you see in this ward are floating blissfully in an environment created by you instead of suffering. Whether brain damaged like Hodge, or psychologically damaged, they can find happiness and relief from their suffering -- because of you. Every dream sleeper here will be evaluated on a case by case basis to see if they are candidates for chip implantation."

"What happens if they don't get the chip and don't come out of their comas?" Lorenzo said.

Crowley held up a finger. "They'll get the best treatment we can give them and if they are beyond any hope of coming back to the real world, it's a simple, painless process to transition them into the Euthanasia Room where nature can take its course without any suffering."

CHAPTER SIXTY TWO

The hot flash of a mortar explosion knocked Jordan to the ground, making his ears ring, then everything went fuzzy. Shit, not again, he thought.

"Over here!" John called out.

Through the haze, Jordan saw him waving from a foxhole. Another explosion sent Jordan sprinting toward the ditch where John crouched. His eyes looked wild and his mouth turned up in a half-crazed grin.

Carl and Wesley hunkered down beside him with Corporal Friedman. "We're going to get blown up right here in this foxhole," Friedman cried.

John grabbed him by the arm and ran along the foxhole, half dragging him.

"That crazy fuck!" Wesley said.

Jordan threw up his hands and bolted after John, zig-zagging through explosions toward a cratered road.

"That's it!" Friedman blubbered pointing at an exposed mine.

"Fuck it!" John grabbed his hand and pulled.

"Nooo!" Friedman shrieked.

John slammed into him and the two tumbled forward onto the mine which exploded in a thunderous flash.

Jordan came to hearing anguished moans amidst a cloud of acrid smoke. Someone's twisted arm sat in front of his face, its fingers quivering. The smoke cleared and he saw John writhing on the ground wailing and realized that the arm belonged to him. He had lost it and a leg from one side of his body, replicating Friedman's wounds exactly.

Another long, anguished moan brought Jordan up out of sleep.

The moan continued as if he were still dreaming, then it diminished to a whimper. John?

Jordan hopped out of bed, hurrying to John's room where muted wails came from the semi-darkness. Wesley and Carl arrived at the door the same time he did, their sleepy faces reflecting confusion. Jordan pushed open the door and saw John moaning and writhing on the bed the same way he had in the dream, as if he had actually lost his limbs.

Wesley rushed over and shook him. "Wake up, John, you're having a nightmare!"

John's eyes popped open showing no recognition, then a sharp intake of breath brought his eyes into focus. "Holy shit," he half-whispered.

"You okay?" Jordan asked.

John sat up talking more to himself than the others. "It's so weird. Like I became Friedman and lived his dream. The worst part was that I forgot I was dreaming, so I thought it was really happening!"

No one said anything for a long uncomfortable moment, then Wesley said, "Now you know how it feels."

"Sucks, doesn't it," Carl added.

John looked from Wesley to Carl to Jordan and grinned sheepishly.

"I had the same dream," Jordan said, "At the same time you did."

Carl and Wesley looked at each other, stunned. Their faces went white.

"You too, huh?" Jordan said, stating the obvious.

"That's right," Carl said breathlessly. "Just now. Same time as you guys."

Wesley nodded.

"We need to talk to Doc Krippner about this." Jordan looked around the room, then leaned in motioning the others into a huddle, whispering, "In private." He stepped back, speaking normal. "I haven't said anything because I didn't want to freak you guys out, but I've been having nightmares every night since Friedman's dream."

"Me too," Carl said.

"Me three," Wesley added.

"I've been going through it too," John said, "but I've been into it like the first time we did it. It's never been a nightmare to me. It's more like reliving an instant replay. This is the first time I got lost and forgot I was dreaming." He shook his head.

"The weirdest part is that you of all people got lost in a dream that became real to *you*, and you weren't even hooked up to Pandora!" Carl said.

"Mister Kamikaze himself," Wesley said. "You're such a bad ass that you don't need any dream hood to get lost. You can do it all by yourself without any help from Pandora."

They all laughed nervously.

"Sorry I was such a dick you guys," John said to Wesley. "I can see why you nailed me. I deserved it."

Wesley patted him on the shoulder. "No worries. Let's put it behind us."

John nodded and shook hands with him. "Deal."

"We've all been spinning too hard if you ask me," Carl said. "I've been doing a pretty good job of keeping it in, but I have to admit, I feel like I'm pissed off all the time. You guys too?"

Everyone nodded.

Jordan glanced at the digital clock beside John's bed and saw **3:15**. "It's the witching hour," he said, feeling a little spooked by that fact that it actually was. "Why don't you guys try to get back to sleep? I think our nightmares are played out for the night. We'll talk to the doc in the morning."

Seven hours later Seal Team 0 sat around a circular table in a smaller conference room with Stan Krippner.

"Before we get started," Stan said, "If you don't mind me asking, why do you want to keep this from Crowley?"

Jordan looked from Carl to Wesley, to John and thought about the cameras in their room. He felt like he could trust Doc Krippner, but couldn't trust anything else. He looked over at the flat screen on the wall, zeroing in on its red power light and camera. Especially rooms like this one. "We'd rather not say right now."

Stan held up a hand. "Fair enough. I respect your privacy, but it's important that you let me know everything that's happening with you guys -- for your own good. I'm on your side. Everything you say to me is in confidence, but at some point I will have to share this with Crowley. He'll find out anyway. He always does. More important than that we can't be withholding information that has a big impact on the project. Not only is it dangerous, but Crowley's the one making bigger decisions and those are driven by the information he has, so the more he knows the better decisions he can make."

Jordan nodded. "Fair enough. Mostly, we don't want him trying to sweet talk and manipulate us. We need someone to listen to what we have to say without trying to sell us on anything."

"That's what I'm here for," Stan said.

Jordan took a deep breath and let it out, then sat back, relaxing a little. The others followed suit. "You and I have talked about this before," he said. "Do you remember that weird dream sharing thing I had with Terry when he freaked out?"

"Sure."

Jordan glanced around at his teammates. "It's happening to all of us every night since we rescued Corporal Friedman from his nightmare."

Stan frowned. "All of you? Every night since?"

Everyone nodded.

Stan held up both hands. "Hold on a minute. I need to call in the others. Let's go find a bigger room. We'll keep Crowley out of it until we figure a few things out, but the rest of our scientific staff needs to hear every bit of this. Their input might be critical in understanding what's happening here. You guys okay with that?"

CHAPTER SIXTY THREE

Rita awoke remembering traces of a dream where John, Seal Team Zero's resident hotshot threw himself on a mine, losing an arm and a leg in the process. She felt "icky" after yesterday's tour, so she took a long hot shower before bed, but felt like some residue stuck with her, so she showered again in the morning, but the feeling lingered.

Sure, there's healing going on, she told herself, but the way they were going about it feels wrong. Dehumanizing, Cheryl called it. She felt uneasy enough about it on her own, but Cheryl's reaction chilled her more.

Lorenzo popped his head into the bathroom. "I just got a call from Stan. He want us to meet him in the conference room by his office right away. There are some new developments with the boys that he's anxious to discuss."

Ten minutes later she and Lorenzo walked into the conference room where they found Stan at the head of the table with Jack and Cheryl on his left and the boys lined up on his right.

"Where's Crowley," Lorenzo said, easing into the chair beside Cheryl. "Shouldn't he be here?"

"Not at this point," Stan said. "We need to put our heads together and come up with a consensus before we talk to him."

Good call, Rita thought. Things felt less pressured without Crowley.

"Thank you for coming on such short notice." Stan's gaze stayed on Rita a moment, then went to Jordan. "Some of you had recurring nightmares from Terry's first shared dream. Now every member of the team has been reliving Corporal Friedman's nightmare every night since they rescued him."

"And Corporal Friedman," Cheryl asked. "Still symptom free?"

"Psychologically," Stan said. "He continues to be as pure as the driven snow in terms of his trauma and his positive attitude is carrying him into his prosthetic surgeries. It's not him I'm worried about. I'm concerned with the welfare of his rescuers." He held his hand out. "Jordan, can you summarize what's happening."

"We all relived Friedman's dream at the same time," Jordan said.

"How do you know it was the same time?" Lorenzo asked.

Jordan looked to his teammates for acknowledgement. "Because it was the witching hour."

Rita cringed at the mention of witches and a flurry of horrific images flashed through her mind.

"What kind of woo woo shit is that?" Scanlon said.

"Woo woo or not, we all woke up at the same time and heard John moaning. When we woke him I looked at the clock. It was three-fifteen in the morning. What they call the witching hour. Look it up if you don't believe me." He shrugged. "Coincidence? I don't know. Woo woo? All I know is that's when it happened."

Jordan nodded toward John. "Why don't you tell them?"

John sat up and rubbed his chin. "It was weird. Like it wasn't me, but it was me. Like I became Friedman and lived his dream. The worst part was that I forgot I was dreaming after the explosion, so I thought it was really happening!"

Lorenzo looked puzzled. "Let me get this straight. You didn't get lost in the Pandora dream, you got lost in your own dream after when you were sleeping normally without any computer intervention?"

"We all had the same dream," Jordan said. "Not the one we had on the computer, but the same dream John had that maimed and wounded him, making him forget it was a dream."

"Corporal Friedman's original nightmare," Lorenzo said, "before we created the scenario from it."

Cheryl pushed her glasses up on her nose. "It would appear that your shared dream gave you some kind of group PTSD."

Rita thought about the dream she half-remembered from the night before and felt a chill, but kept her mouth shut.

"I find it odd that Corporal Friedman is symptom free," Cheryl continued, "and all of you on the team are displaying *his* symptoms like some kind of psychic transference has taken place, making his trauma yours." She massaged her temples. "I'm not sure what to make of that." She looked to Stan.

"This is outside the realm of straight science," he said, "so the lines are blurred between psychology and technology. I won't go as far as saying it's woo woo, but there might be something to the fact that it happened at the witching hour as Jordan called it."

Jack nodded. "I agree, but we have no precedent for what's happening here."

"DreamLand!" Cheryl muttered, then louder. "If that wasn't a precedent, then I don't know what is."

Stan held up a hand. "I agree that what happened there is worth considering, but we need to stick to the specifics of this particular situation and not muddy the waters with information that doesn't directly influence what's happening in the present." He nodded to Cheryl. "But your comments are noted and worth looking into in a later analysis."

"So what can we do about this transference phenomenon as Cheryl called it?" Jack said.

Stan leaned forward, resting his chin on his hand. "Needless to say, the shared dream phenomenon is fascinating. The fact that it's intruding into normal sleep like a shared PTSD symptom is an unfortunate side effect that I think lies at the heart of it. In one respect this symptom represents the wound we've been after."

"I'm not sure I follow," Carl said, frowning.

"Let me explain something," Stan said. "A bit of anthropology if you will. Aside from being masters of navigating altered states, shamans are considered masters of energy on physical, mental, and spiritual levels. When a shaman does a healing, he takes the bad energy from his patient and moves it or clears it. Disposing of it is probably the best analogy. He does this by any combination of channeling it into the earth, wiping or fanning it away with feathers or leaves using the element of air, cleansing it with water, or purifying it with fire. This includes smudges, tobacco, sage, essential oils, and numerous other plants and essences."

"So we took the energy from Corporal Friedman," Jordan said, "but we didn't do anything with it, so we're stuck with it."

"Like a big hot potato," John said.

Stan grinned. "I can't tell you how many therapists I have come across that were successful taking away the traumas of their patients. The problem was that they were not aware that they had taken the energy on themselves and had no clue about the concept of disposing of it, so they carried it until it built up to a point where they found themselves caught in their own personal PTSD."

"We have that same situation here," Rita said. "Shared dream, shared PTSD. The whole team is holding Corporal Friedman's hot potato."

"That's how I see it," Stan said. "I have some ideas, but I'm not sure yet of how to approach it. I don't want to go to Crowley with a problem. I want to go to him with the solution. I'm open to any ideas." He inclined his head toward the team. "That goes for you guys, too. If anything comes to mind, don't be afraid to speak up. Something you think of as insignificant might be important."

"I've been thinking." Jack put his hand on Cheryl's arm and leaned in closer to her, lowering his voice. "I'll be curious to hear what you think about this."

"I'm all ears," she said, patting his hand.

"Terry's nightmares showed the first instance of this transference as we're calling it. As you remember, he was quite emotional about the whole thing. That might be a critical factor. We're dealing with an emotional wound here. Compare the emotional intensity of what happened to him in a realistic dream where he was in no danger of being physically harmed and the amplified effect of the very real trauma from Corporal Friedman's nightmare. How much more emotionally traumatized can you be from the real experience of getting your arm and leg blown off and losing everyone around you?"

"There does appear to be a definite emotional correlation," Stan said.

"It seems like the strength of the emotion amplifies what appears to be an echoing effect." Cheryl nodded to the boys. "What I characterize as a kind of psychological recidivism that affected everyone on the team."

Jack patted her arm. "I'd like to propose attenuating the gain on the magnetoresonators on the dream hood and dialing back their signal strength."

"I can see where it might dampen the intensity of the dream," Cheryl said.

Lorenzo held up a finger. "I can also decrease the video gain which might make the experience more manageable."

"Good thought," Jack said. "We dialed in the modified dream wear hood on Hodge for maximum performance because he was suffering so much and we wanted to overwhelm whatever trauma he was experiencing, but we're not looking to overwhelm anybody here, we're simply looking for some interaction."

"Based on what we know so far, I think that's a good approach," Stan said. "And I think it's something Crowley will approve of."

Jack shrugged and gave a toothy grin. "That's great. I hope he approves it, but whether he does or not doesn't matter to me. I could give a rat's ass what he thinks. I'm going to give this a shot. You with me Lorenzo?"

Lorenzo nodded. "That goes without saying."

Stan held out a hand to the boys. "What about you guys? Are you willing to give it another shot after these changes?"

They all looked to each other, exchanging glances, then John spoke up, shaking his head no. "This is getting to be too much for me. I think I'm going to bag the whole program, make like a sheep herder and get the flock out of here."

The group's expressions ran the gamut of surprise, disappointment, and shock.

John frowned and smacked his palms on the table and stood, looking at each person in turn. "Not!"

It took a moment before it registered, then everyone laughed, which relieved the tension some, but looking at the other members of his team, Rita thought that John's threat might be closer to the truth than anyone cared to admit.

CHAPTER SIXTY FOUR

"Before we do anything, we need to do a wipe," Crowley said from behind the console of his command and control center. The wall of screens sequenced through different areas of the complex showing bustling activity. Jordan and the other members of Seal Team 0 sat across from him alongside Stan Krippner.

"What do you mean a wipe?" Wesley said.

"I want you guys to have a clean slate before we proceed with any of these changes," Crowley said.

John sat up. "Lorenzo's ecstasy dream?"

Crowley nodded. "It cancelled out the stress last time?"

"Got rid of our nightmares too," Jordan said.

"I'm wondering if it might not be more prudent to do the wipe after Jack and Lorenzo make their adjustments," Stan said.

Crowley held up a hand and shook his head. "No. I want the boys to go in clean."

"We could get the same results with lower signal strengths," Stan said. "We won't know unless we try it."

Crowley continued shaking his head no. "The intensity of Corporal Friedman's trauma had a bigger effect on the boys than Terry's dream generated nightmare. I think full strength is in order. We don't want any traces of Corporal Friedman's trauma influencing our results going forward and I don't want any of our crack rescue team losing sleep with other people's nightmares. I'd rather have them implanted with memories of a blissful dream if they still experience the echoing effect in their natural sleep."

"Good plan!" John grinned and leaned forward in his chair, looking sideways at his teammates. "Let's get it on. I don't want to get lost in any more bad dreams. Once was enough for me!"

The following morning they went to the Dream Lab where they found Jack, Lorenzo, Cheryl, and Rita waiting. Scanlon's deep-set eyes seemed extra focused. "I would have preferred making my adjustments before doing this again," he said when they took their seats. Cheryl Martin came in, her pale blue eyes unreadable behind her horn-rimmed glasses, her hair in its usual bun. "Go ahead and get comfortable." She went down the line helping each one on with their hoods, followed by Jack who did a final check before going back to the control room.

"Okay guys," Lorenzo said through the headset. "Here we go. Five, four, three, two…"

Like before, Jordan felt heavy at the count of one and fell into the void between dark and light until he heard and felt the white noise followed by the image of waves that brightened with the rising music and other sounds that intermingled into the multilayered lullaby that made the pent up tension he felt inside wash away with every crash of the waves.

His heart lightened and his emotions rose with the music and flowing imagery until he vibrated with exquisite feelings that peaked in a crescendo of running water, waves, chants, digeridoos, flutes, and strings that sent him sailing into an exquisite tapestry of thought, feeling, and emotion.

Jordan opened his eyes after what could have been years, months, or milliseconds feeling refreshed. Sitting up, he looked to his left and saw Carl and Wesley awakening while John remained immobile in his dream cradle, lost in REM.

It struck him as odd that Carl and Wesley awakened the same time as he did while John kept dreaming. What kind of stunt was he pulling now? Jordan crossed his arms, waiting.

Wesley and Carl turned their attention to John, whose eyes continued their mad dance. Something's wrong, Jordan thought. This is going on too long.

The door at the end of the room flew open confirming his fears when Jack and Cheryl rushed in followed by Rita and Lorenzo who pulled John's limp body upright while Jack and Cheryl removed the dreaming hood.

John's eyes fluttered open when the hood came off. He shook his head. "Huh?" His eyes came into focus. "Wussup? What the fu…" he mumbled.

"Are you okay?" Rita asked.

He seemed to recognize her and the others for the first time and brightened. His pupils looked extra large. "Couldn't be better!"

Rita and Cheryl exchanged alarmed looks.

"What happened?" Rita asked.

John looked at her, puzzled, then at Jack and Lorenzo, who eased him back in the chair, then to Cheryl, Carl, and Wesley in turn as if counting them off. When his gaze came to Jordan, he said, "Sorry. I guess I kind of dozed off."

CHAPTER SIXTY FIVE

"I think we need to shut the whole project down," Cheryl said, "until we know exactly what's going on."

Stan, Jack, and Lorenzo were all taken aback by her comment, but Rita felt the same way Cheryl did, only not as extreme. They had decided to meet in the conference room next to the Dream Lab without Crowley or the team so they could discuss their concerns without interference from Crowley, and they didn't want to alarm the boys.

"Crowley's not going to let that happen," Jack said. "He's approaching full capacity in the hospital and he's jacked up over the PTSD mitigation we achieved with Corporal Friedman, who is still symptom free, not to mention the success he's having with his automated prosthetic replacement facilities."

"That's all well and good," Rita said. "I'm all for healing the wounded, but not at the expense of others who are healthy to begin with."

Cheryl, Jack, and Lorenzo nodded in agreement.

"Instead of overreacting and jumping ahead to a drastic course of action," Stan said, making calming gestures. "We need to focus on the specifics of what happened in this last test."

Lorenzo leaned forward. "With all due respect, Stan, I agree that we don't want to jump ahead, but I want to stress that what comes across as overreacting, comes from our experience with DreamLand." He pointed to Jack, Cheryl, and Rita. "We're the only survivors. In spite of what you or anyone else may think about our delusions or supposed shared hallucinations, we are the only ones with first hand experience of the surrealistic hell it became."

Stan nodded. "Not having been there, I can't address that fairly, but regardless of what did happen, it resulted in the deaths of six people and severely damaged the seventh. Real or imagined, I have no doubt that it was real to you, so I do take that into consideration. Aside from that, you folks are the experts on this technology, and real or imagined, anybody that doesn't pay attention to what you have to say is a fool. I know what I saw just now, but it's you I want to hear from."

"Fair enough," Jack said. "Everything was identical to our last test, including the length of it. I would have preferred trying the lower signal strengths like you suggested. It would have been a safer approach, especially in light of the anomalies we've seen."

"Ditto," Lorenzo added. "What puzzles me is the way John continued dreaming after we terminated the sequence."

"Even after we initiated the shutdown protocol," Jack said, "the sensors in his hood remained active, as if the shutdown command was never acknowledged."

Lorenzo rubbed his chin. "The video sequence continued too, but not for the other three team members. Only for John."

"Can you imagine how this could have turned out if we had been connected to Morpheus instead of Pandora?" Cheryl said.

"Everything worked as it should have, except the telemetry on John's feed," Lorenzo said.

Jack's bushy eyebrows exaggerated his frown. "It didn't terminate until we removed the hood. If I didn't know better, I'd say he figured out some way to override it."

"That's not possible, is it?" Rita asked.

Cheryl shook her head. "Not under normal circumstances, but..."

"I think we can rule that out," Stan said. "Did you see the way he reacted when he came out of it? He didn't strike me as someone who was in control."

"He was lost in the dream," Rita said, "the same way the rest of the team got lost in Corporal Friedman's scenario, only this was an exceedingly pleasant dream."

"There's something to that," Stan said. "I also find it interesting that this is the first time John was lost in a computer dream, yet he got lost in his natural dream."

"Regardless," Cheryl said, "He's been the most aggressive and appears to be developing a propensity to lose himself in his dreams whether they came from Pandora, or somewhere inside him and there doesn't seem to be any rational explanation."

"Agreed," Jack said. "If it was a hardware failure it doesn't make any sense and I'd lay money that there's no way we can replicate it."

"It's a slippery slope," Lorenzo said. "Who's really directing things?"

"Where does technology end and psychology begin?" Rita said.

"It's a chicken or egg situation, isn't it?" Stan said. "We have lots of questions, but no answers. We need to keep a close eye on the boys to see if their nightmares remain in remission and watch to see if any other unintended side effects appear."

"Even though I know it's a waste of time," Jack said. "I'll recheck the hardware to see if there is any possibility of failure there."

"I'm going to keep some smelling salts handy, just in case something like this happens again," Rita said.

"And I'll do a thorough analysis of the video sequence to see if anything shows up there," Lorenzo added.

"I'll run some tests on John's dream hood," Cheryl said, "and we'll replace it with a new one for good measure to eliminate any possibility of problems."

Stan nodded slowly. "Thank you all for your valued input and willingness to try and solve this. If the situation remains stable, Crowley's going to want to push ahead. If that happens, at least we'll be working with reduced signal levels going forward, which I hope will also diminish any dangers."

"I wouldn't hold my breath," Cheryl said.

CHAPTER SIXTY SIX

As an added incentive, Crowley sent Seal Team 0 on another field trip to spend time with the Mexican girls who gave them anything they wanted, any way they wanted. That in combination with the clearing from Lorenzo's ecstasy dream left everybody upbeat, positive, and giddy. The nightmares and tension they experienced now felt like traces of half-forgotten bad memories.

"Did the girls give you everything you asked for?" Crowley said, winking from behind the console of his command and control center where Jordan, Carl, Wesley, and John sat across from him.

"They were awesome," John said. "Almost as good as Lorenzo's ecstasy."

Crowley looked puzzled. "*Almost* as good?"

John gave a single nod. "Don't get me wrong. I love that exotic poontang, and I am very appreciative of you getting it for us, but there's something about that happy place that Lorenzo made. It's a full on experience that hits all of your senses and more."

"A full body orgasm," Jordan added.

"What about the rest of you guys?" Crowley said. "Do you feel the same way?"

Carl and Wesley nodded. Jordan couldn't have felt better, but something about all the fun and pleasure bothered him. If it's too good to be true, he thought.

Crowley whistled low. "I didn't realize that it felt *that* good." He shook his head. "A happy dream over nooky. Who would have thought?"

"No shit," Wesley said. "I find it hard to believe myself. I never in a million years thought I would ever hear something like that coming from a pussy hound like Striker."

They all laughed, especially Crowley.

"I want you guys to know that I want nothing but the best for you and your health and safety is my number one concern."

There's the ass kiss, Jordan thought. Here it comes.

"While you guys were romancing your *señoritas,* we did an investigation into the anomalies we've seen and we couldn't find anything wrong with the hardware or the software. We're not sure what happened, but we have no proof of anything. Having said that..."

"What kind of battle dream do you want us to go into now?" Wesley said.

Crowley gave a slight grin. "The word's out about what you did for Corporal Friedman and I'm here to tell you that everybody is really excited about it up to the highest levels. The powers that be are anxious to validate what they're calling Friedman's miraculous psychological healing with another one to prove that it's real and not a fluke."

Jordan looked to Wesley and the others, who all leaned in. He knew this was coming. It was part of the reason he had trepidation about where all the fun and games were leading.

"Even though we didn't find anything in our hardware and software checks," Crowley continued, "we replaced all the hardware. On top of that, Jack Scanlon and Doctor Martin reduced the signal strength on the DreamWear hood by more than half and Lorenzo did a similar attenuation of the signal strength on his video feed."

"So you want us to try again," Carl said.

Crowley leaned back, putting his fingers together. "I'm getting a lot of pressure from the brass, not only to move the project forward, but we have a very special vet with severe nightmares who would benefit from a dream team rescue."

"What's so special about this guy?" Wesley asked.

Crowley tapped his iPad until the picture of a no nonsense looking man with sandy hair, an angular face, and piercing blue eyes filled the central screen. "Nick Stevens is a Navy SEAL who was one of the most lethal snipers in U.S. military history with over 175 confirmed kills. He served two tours in Iraq, two in Afghanistan, and was awarded several commendations for heroism and meritorious service in combat. He also received two Silver Stars, five Bronze Stars, one Navy and Marine Corps Commendation Medal, two Navy and Marine Corps Achievement Medals and numerous other unit and personal awards until he lost an eye and an arm from a grenade that killed his spotter."

"He looks like a pretty tough customer," John said.

Crowley nodded. "One of the toughest we've ever seen."

Jordan leaned forward and looked to his teammates. "What do you think, guys?"

John crossed his arms and smiled. "You know where I stand."

Carl held out his hands. "Shit, we've come this far. I think we owe it to ourselves to give it another shot."

Wesley nodded, agreeing.

Jordan sat back in his chair. "All in!"

Like they had for Corporal Friedman, Lorenzo ran them through his gaming version of the scenario as a rehearsal to give them another advantage so they would know what to do and what to expect.

"Though this is scheduled to be a game at some point," Lorenzo said, after they reached their mission objective, this first time out you guys are on a rescue mission. Even though you'll be in a shared dream world, I think you know it will be more than real for Stevens."

"Unless we can convince him otherwise," Carl said.

"And shit's gonna hurt if anybody gets whacked over there," Wesley said. "So we need to pay attention."

After a solid night's sleep and another briefing, the members of Seal Team 0 settled back in their dream cradles.

"I need to do a sensor array calibration," Jack said through their headsets, "then Cheryl can run through a telemetry check. Once we're satisfied that everything is functional, Rita will verify everyone's vital signs and we'll turn it over to Lorenzo."

After a few minutes of muffled chatter with Crowley in the background, Jack's voice came through the headsets again. "Lorenzo, you're cleared to initiate the sequence."

"Okay," Lorenzo said. "We are initiating in five, four, three, two, one…"

Jordan felt the now familiar perception of growing heavy at the count of one, then the sensation of falling into the void, shifting from dark to white before coming into awareness with his M4 on a street in a war ravaged Middle Eastern town that he recognized from Lorenzo's game. Wesley, Carl, and John flanked him.

He felt the weight of the gun, the breeze against his skin, and the faint smell of smoke, which made him hyper-alert. It's still only a dream, he reminded himself. Stan Krippner's guidance echoed through his mind. Try to find a higher awareness to navigate a reality that follows a more flexible set of rules.

"Let's do it," Wesley said, jolting him out of his reverie.

Jordan nodded and together they sprinted toward a battle scarred building while bombs and sporadic gunfire echoed in the distance. When they reached the darkened doorway Jordan pressed himself against the wall beside Wesley while Carl and John did the same on the other side. Once in position, Jordan motioned with his head and ran through the door, gun at the ready, his teammates coming in after him.

They found themselves at the bottom of a narrow darkened flight of stairs leading up. Jordan let his eyes adjust to the semi-darkness, then crept forward, moving up the stairs, the rest of his team following close behind. The top of the stairs led to a long hallway.

Together they moved down it checking each abandoned room for surprises until they came to a door at the end of the hall where they heard the muffled sounds of distant battle coming from its other side. Easing it open they saw Nick Stevens lying in a prone position, rifle at the ready, peering through its scope. His spotter crouched low beside him.

Jordan eased the door open and Nick's spotter spun on them, aiming his sidearm.

"Hold off!" Jordan said, raising his hands. "We're on your side."

"What the fuck are you doing here?" The spotter asked, keeping his gun trained on Jordan. "No one's supposed to know we're here."

"You can put the gun down," Jordan said. "I have three other men with me, so don't be surprised. We're Seal Team Zero and we're here to rescue you."

"Rescue us? From what?"

Jordan made a lowering gesture with his hand. "We're coming out with our hands up. Keep your cool, we don't have a lot of time." He looked back at Wesley, Carl, and John. "Follow my lead guys." He stepped out onto the roof with his hands up.

Stevens looked back from his prone position and rolled over to sit up straight against the wall. "You can put the gun down, Butch. They're not the enemy and they have their hands up." He gave Jordan a curt nod. "What's all this about a rescue?"

"You guys are about to get hit with a grenade," Wesley said. "We're here to change that."

Nick's expression went from suspicion to alarm. "How do you know we're going to get hit with a grenade? You some kind of fortune teller or something?"

Jordan and his team squatted down, huddling in close to Nick and Butch. "We're here to change things," Jordan said. "Any second now…"

A grenade came over the wall near Butch and bounced, spinning to a stop beside him and everything slipped into slow motion. His eyes widened and he looked at Jordan in disbelief before rolling over on top of it.

"Shit," Wesley said.

Recognizing what was happening, Jordan grabbed Stevens by the shoulder. "Help me John!"

John plowed into Jordan and the struggling Stevens with an awkward tackle, knocking them both onto Butch who screamed.

"Pile on if you have any balls," John yelled back.

Jordan felt Wesley and Carl plop on top of him at the exact moment a deafening explosion and blinding flash enveloped them.

Instead of waking up or feeling pain Jordan had the sensation of falling through an endless tunnel of geometric colors and patterns that expanded and contracted, making him feel both finite and infinite, as if he existed in a dynamic eternity outside of time. Feelings of fear, powerlessness, victimization, and guilt shot through him in concert with his mesmerizing visuals.

In what could have been months or milliseconds he flew into another bright light that rocked him to the core of his being and in the next moment he was blinking his eyes open in the test lab.

CHAPTER SIXTY SEVEN

"Holy shit!" Wesley sat up and looked over at Jordan, who had the same look of surprise. Carl popped up beside Wesley, equally awake and aware. John stayed back in his dream cradle, eyes darting back and forth.

"Shit!" Lorenzo said under his breath. Everyone hustled out of the observation room. By the time Rita got to the test lab, Jack Scanlon had John's hood off and Lorenzo was shaking him. She reached into the pocket of her lab coat for the smelling salts and was about to crack one when John's eyes fluttered open.

"Huh?" He turned his head from side to side and his eyes came into focus. "What the fu…" he mumbled, as if seeing everyone for the first time. His pupils looked extra large, then a sheepish look stole over him. "Sorry, I was just messing with you."

Rita forced herself to breathe deep to calm her racing heart. "Bullshit!" She said. "Something's going on with you."

"Slow down," Crowley said, elbowing his way to the front. "We'll get Stan and another doctor to take a look at him. In the mean time we need to get the team into a conference room for a debriefing while it's still all fresh."

Crowley led everyone to the conference room where Stan Krippner waited.

"Before we get started," John said, dropping into his usual spot. "I want to say I'm sorry for pulling that stupid stunt. I didn't mean to freak everybody out. I was just messing with you. I thought it might lighten things up a little instead of being so serious all the time." He lowered his head like a guilty little boy, shaking it. "My bad!" He looked up. "This last rescue ended a lot differently than I expected, and I'm not ashamed to say that I did wish I could have stayed there." He looked at Carl, Wesley, and Jordan. "Did you guys go through what I went through?"

"Geometry?" Carl said.

The others nodded.

"We had a five second blackout at the end of the sequence," Lorenzo said, but everything kept going, only there was no audio or video, only a white screen that blacked out when you woke up."

"Makes sense," Jordan said. "Everything unfolded like the game you ran us through -- until the end. Things happened fast when we got to Stevens. Before we could explain to him why we were there the grenade came over the wall and in that short few seconds before it went off I had a realization that I can't explain. More of a feeling, but bigger, like an impulse. I'm sure this sounds weird, but it hit me like a flash of higher knowing or something. I had no time to think, so I grabbed Stevens and with John's help we all jumped onto the grenade with his spotter Butch."

"Carl and Wesley jumped right in after us," John said, grinning broadly and slapping Carl on the back. Crowley's grin widened to match John's.

Jordan gave him a thumbs up. "In that instant I knew John would get it. Even though he pissed us off, that's what he did with Corporal Friedman." Jordan's eyes took on a far off look before coming back into focus. "He *died* with Friedman and I'm pretty sure that's how Friedman was cured of his nightmare. I realized all of that in that moment, which is why I did what I did."

"Shit!" Carl said, leaning forward. "You mean every rescue mission that we go on is a suicide mission?"

"Of sorts," John leaned back with a self-satisfied grin.

"What you guys did had a profound effect on Stevens," Stan said, barely able to contain himself. "He had one of the most powerful emotional outbursts I've ever seen. I didn't want to leave him, but I needed to hear what you guys had to report. I left two nurses to watch over him. I'll check in on him as soon as we're finished here, but right now I'm curious about the blackout Lorenzo described. What happened to you guys?"

"Excuse me ladies." John held up his hands in surrender. "No disrespect intended here, but the only way I can describe what we went through is a big cosmic vagina." He held his hands wider.

Stan Krippner's eyes looked like they were going to jump out of his head.

"Instead of waking up or feeling any pain," John went on, "I fell through an endless tunnel of complicated geometric colors and patterns that expanded and contracted, making me feel super crushed in one moment and flying apart in the next as if I was everywhere and nowhere at the same time until I flew into a bright light that shook me in a way I've never been shaken before until I woke up to you." He looked over at Carl, Wesley, and Jordan. "Sound right to you guys?"

They nodded and their eyes all glazed over as if some part of them was reliving the experience.

"Cosmic vagina?" Crowley said.

"It's not as far off or as far out as you might think," Stan said.

"Do tell." Cheryl took her glasses off and leaned back, polishing them.

Yes do, Rita thought.

"What John described," Stan said with authority, "is our first experience coming into this world. The original PTSD that we bear passing from the safety of our mother's womb to be born into this world."

Cheryl frowned. "Birth trauma?"

Stan's hands danced as if on their own accord. "Stanislav Grof, a friend and colleague of mine mapped out what he calls the perinatal matrices which divide the birth process into four stages. The First is the intrauterine existence, characterized by positive feelings of floating, warmth, connectedness, and having all your needs met. The second matrix begins when the chemistry in the womb changes and overwhelming contractions push against the fetus and interrupt its nourishment." He made a pushing gesture with both hands. "This engenders feelings of intense fear, powerlessness, victimization, and often guilt. Because the cervix is not yet dilated, there is no way out, adding a sense of hopelessness. Once the cervix dilates enough to allow movement through the birth canal, the Third Matrix elements of struggle, aggression, giving and receiving pain, and sexual charge begin. Finally, the birth is completed and the infant reconnects with the mother, leading to a positive state like the first, but qualitatively different."

No one said anything. They all appeared to be digesting what Stan said.

"That seems like a good description of what we went through," Jordan said, "don't you think, guys?"

"Nailed it for me," Wesley said.

"Me too!" Carl added.

"Bang on!" John said.

"Our two deepest fears are fear of entrapment and fear of abandonment, which both come from this original primal trauma."

Lorenzo rubbed his chin. "There's nothing like that in any of the programming, so this must have come from Stevens. It was his fear, powerlessness, victimization, and guilt we were rescuing him from, right?"

Stan looked a little shocked and spoke in a lower voice. "Not only did you all experience his dream as programmed, but it appears as if you experienced his death along with him. I'm anxious to see how he's doing. It might help us make sense out of all this."

The room went quiet until Jack Scanlon spoke up. "So I guess it's safe to say that all the adjustments that Lorenzo and I did turning everything down, didn't make a didley-squat bit of difference in the dream."

"It might have made them better!" John wisecracked.

CHAPTER SIXTY EIGHT

A grenade came over the wall and bounced, spinning to a stop and everything slipped into slow motion.

"Shit," Wesley said.

Jordan grabbed Stevens by the shoulder and John plowed into them, knocking them onto the spotter Butch who screamed.

"Pile on if you have any balls," John yelled.

Jordan felt Wesley and Carl plop on top of them as a deafening explosion enveloped everything, then Jordan fell through the tunnel of expanding and contracting geometry of colors and patterns, making him feel both finite and infinite at the same time. Fear, powerlessness, victimization, and guilt shot through him in concert with the visuals until he woke up sweat soaked, his heart thumping in his chest like a fist.

He looked at his clock. **3:15**. No shit, he thought.

He heard someone cry out from another room and hustled out of bed to find everyone on Seal Team Zero sharing the same dream or nightmare, depending on who you asked.

Fully awake, they sat in their lounge comparing notes. John was captivated with the "cosmic vagina" and felt drawn to it while Wesley was in awe of it, suspended between fascination and fear, while Carl was both awestruck and terrified.

Jordan felt like all of those things spun around inside him, shifting with each passing moment. "That's the second night in a row," he said.

"No shit." Carl rubbed his eyes with balled fists. "I've had enough of this shit!"

Jordan nodded. "I half-expected it after that first go-round with Stevens. It was the most emotionally intense experience I can ever remember having. After two nights of it back to back, it's time to run this by Doc Krippner."

"I know what's going to happen," John said, barely able to control his smirk.

"What?" Wesley asked.

"Crowley's going to send us back to Lorenzo's ecstasy dream!"

One of Carl's eyebrows shot up. "You sure you're not going to run off to la la land when we do it?"

John's smirk grew into a full blown smile.

"Don't fuck around on us with this," Wesley said. "You scared the shit out of everybody when you did it last time. There's too much weird shit going on to be playing games."

"I realize that," John said, holding up a hand. "I promise I won't pull any shit like that anymore."

Soon after waking and eating, Crowley came for a visit. "How's my dream team?"

"Other than our nightmares we're doing okay," Jordan said.

Crowley perched himself on the arm of an easy chair. "We'll talk about that in a minute. Right now I have some great news!"

"Give it up," Carl said.

Crowley rubbed his hands together. "You guys performed another miracle." He paused, then, "Nick Stevens is cured!"

"Cured?" Wesley said. "Like Friedman?"

"He's calming down and becoming less emotional with each passing day. He hardly believes you guys are real and wants to meet you to prove to himself that you are. More importantly, he's anxious to thank you for what you did. As soon as you're ready, I'll take you to him."

Ten minutes later Crowley led them through a series of circular hallways and an elevator ride to a private room somewhere in the bustling hospital complex where they found Nick Stevens propped up in his hospital bed. Stan Krippner stood beside him.

A no nonsense looking man with sandy hair, one-armed Nick Stevens had an angular face, one piercing blue eye, and a missing eye marked by an empty red socket. One side of his split face was maimed while the other looked perfect and chiseled.

"Holy shit, you guys *are* real," he cried in a trembling voice when they entered his room, then he burst into tears. "Sorry, that's still happening," he said between sobs, "but it's less every time." He grabbed a tissue from a box on his nightstand, wiped his eye and blew his nose.

"There's no need to apologize," Stan said in a fatherly tone. "That stuff has been stuck inside you for a long time and it makes you better with each release."

Stevens nodded and blew his nose again.

"If you don't mind," Stan continued, "Can you tell the guys what you were just telling me?"

Stevens finished wiping his nose and tossed the tissue in the trash. He drew in a long, shaky breath and looked at Jordan, Wesley, Carl, and John, studying each one in turn. "I still can't believe you guys are real," he said in a half-whisper.

"Yeah, we're real." John jerked his thumb toward Wesley. "Except for Wesley. We're still not sure about him."

Wesley flipped him the bird and everyone laughed.

"Let's hear it," Carl said.

"I went through four tours with my spotter Butch." His voice trembled. "Two tours in Iraq and two in Afghanistan. He was more than family to me. We were a top notch team just like you guys, except there were only two of us. Losing him was worse than losing my eye and my arm and I would give them up in a heartbeat to get him back."

He looked at each of them one at a time to make his point. "Then you guys came along!" He gestured with his one arm. "And you threw me onto that grenade, not only with him, but the rest of you too! I couldn't believe what an insane thing you were doing." He stopped and his one eye took on a distant look, then, "Now I know what it's like. I went there with him."

"There?" Crowley said.

"With Butch." He swung his arm, pointing at Jordan and the others. "And these guys were with us. They took us there." His one eye glazed over and his voice rose. "I went through every negative emotion possible, fear, helplessness, guilt, not to mention awe while I spun through complicated geometry that changed colors and patterns along with my feelings. The whole thing moved in and out like I was everywhere and nowhere all at the same time."

His eye came back into focus and he looked at everyone as if seeing them for the first time. "Here's the kicker!" He held up a finger. "I came out of it bawling like a baby and didn't think I'd ever stop until I cried myself into exhaustion and had my first peaceful sleep since the grenade."

"For eighteen hours straight," Stan said.

"I was groggy when I came out of it, but I felt like a ton of bricks was lifted off me. Off my heart! Sure, I have a missing eye and arm," he said wiggling the stump on his damaged side, "but after going through that wormhole, or whatever you want to call it, I feel like I was reborn. I feel right with my emotions. Balanced is the best way I can describe it. Don't get me wrong, I'll always feel a piece of me missing with Butch gone, but now I feel like I have him inside me - always. It's like surviving all that fear, guilt, and other bullshit was sucked out by that psychedelic tunnel."

Jordan thought about their shared experience and the recurring nightmares he and the others now had, but he kept his mouth shut and was glad Wesley, Carl, and John did the same.

"I can't tell you how I know this," Nick said, "but the fear, guilt, and nightmares are gone." He nodded to Jordan and the others. "And they're not coming back! I can't thank you guys enough for what you did. I'll forever be in your debt. If there's ever anything I can do for any of you, just say the word." He saluted them with his one good arm.

Jordan felt compelled to salute him back and the others followed suit.

"You would have done the same thing," Wesley said.

"But I didn't. *You* guys did!" Stevens inclined his head toward Crowley. "Now that my head is getting clear, Uncle Sam over here has some A number one brand new super hi-tech computerized prosthetics that they're fitting me for. I can't wait to test them out!"

His face lit up with a broad grin that somehow included the damaged side of his face and he laid back on his propped up bed.

Crowley saluted him. "Thank you for the debriefing, soldier. We're happy you're on the road to recovery."

A doctor and two nurses pushed their way into the room. "If you'll excuse us gentlemen, we have to give mister Stevens a checkup and change the dressing on his wounds."

"Okay team," Crowley said. "Let's give Nick a break here."

Nick Stevens waved and continued smiling. "I hope you guys come back and visit," he said. "I feel like we're connected, like spiritual brothers or something."

"Don't worry about that," Carl said. "We'll be keeping a close eye on you!"

They exited the room leaving Nick Stevens behind, laughing.

CHAPTER SIXTY NINE

Rita watched Jordan's eyes pop open first, followed in quick succession by Wesley and Carl. They all sat up with dreamy expressions while John's eyes remained closed, darting back and forth in REM.

"That doesn't look good," Cheryl said with an edge in her voice.

"I have everything turned down to minimal levels," Lorenzo said.

"Same here," Jack added.

"He's not coming out of it." Cheryl's voice rose an octave. "And I'm not about to sit around waiting!" She pushed back from her chair and rushed into the dream lab followed by Jack and Lorenzo. Stan followed with Crowley close behind. Rita went in last.

Jack and Cheryl shook John, who remained unresponsive.

"Enough of this!" Rita pushed herself between them and reached into her pocket, grabbing a smelling salt packet. She crushed it and jammed under his nose.

His eyes shot open and he sat up coughing.

"What the fu…" He looked around dazed.

"Are you all right?" Cheryl said.

"Yeah, sure." He shook his head. "I was having a great time until you guys ruined it."

"You didn't come out of it when we stopped the sequence," Lorenzo said.

"Sorry, I was blissed out and didn't want to come back."

"You scared the hell out of us," Rita said.

"Don't you think you're overreacting a…"

"Bullshit!" Rita said, surprising herself.

"We were shaking you pretty good," Lorenzo said.

Crowley made calming gestures. "I'm sure it's nothing serious,"

"Don't be too sure," Stan said. With Jack's help he pulled off John's dream hood and helped him out of his dream cradle. "You're getting a complete physical, MRI, PET, X-rays, the whole enchilada. We're not taking any chances and we're not testing any more dream scenarios until we get to the bottom of this."

Rita breathed a shaky sigh and glanced over at Crowley who had a sour look on his face. Stan guided John out of the room while Jack and Cheryl helped the rest of the team out of their cradles and hoods.

"How do the rest of you feel?" Rita asked.

"Great," Carl said. "I could have stayed longer. For what it's worth, I don't feel uptight anymore and I'm willing to bet that my nightmares are gone."

"Same here," Wesley said. "I can't explain how I know, but I feel it." Jordan nodded in agreement.

"It really feels good." Carl's eyes took on a faraway look and he had a wistful smile. "And it feels so good afterward. Kind of a glow."

"That's what I'm worried about," Cheryl said.

"You're worried that they feel good?" Crowley said.

Jack Scanlon inclined his head toward Jordan, Wesley, and Carl. "Let's take this offline and give the guys a break. They're feeling good and rested, so let's not bore them with our psychobabble."

Jordan looked to Crowley for permission and Crowley nodded, giving it.

"Thanks for all your great work," Crowley said as they filed out. "You can pride yourselves in having made all the difference in the world to a hero like Nick Stevens."

Once the door clicked shut, Lorenzo said, "Let's go find a conference room."

Crowley led them to a main conference room and took his seat at the end of the table with Lorenzo and Rita to his right and Jack and Cheryl on his left.

"Now what's this all about?" Crowley said, addressing Cheryl. "The guys are all feeling great!"

"No matter what you may think about what happened in DreamLand," Cheryl said. "Mass hallucination or whatever you want to call it, it had a way of trapping you. We've already seen it happen once and we don't care to go through it again."

"Hold on a minute." Crowley held up a hand, stopping her. "For one thing, this is Pandora, not Morpheus, a totally different platform built from the ground up."

Cheryl crossed her arms. "With no connection to Morpheus?"

"None."

"What about the building infrastructure?" Jack said. "We requested a separate and isolated system."

"We did that," Crowley said, but we utilized the existing infrastructure for the hospital, labs, prosthetic assembly lines and the rest of it which saved us billions."

"Wait a minute," Rita said. "We're on the same network?"

Crowley sighed. "Everything here is connected to everything else and the wires and fiber optics were already in place. It would have been foolish to put in new wire and fiber."

"What about that backup?" Lorenzo asked."

Crowley shook his head. "I assure you, Pandora is isolated from everything else on its own self contained network like we agreed and that backup is not connected."

"Is it powered off?" Jack said.

"It's disconnected," Crowley said with finality. "Under heavy guard. No one's going to get near it. What are you worried about?"

Rita's chest tightened when Crowley didn't acknowledge that the backup had been powered down. "I have a bad feeling about this," she said. "Morpheus or not, and like it or not, it looks to me like John is being sucked in.

"Addicted is a better term," Cheryl added.

"Before we go jumping to conclusions," Crowley said, holding up a finger. "Let's see what the doctors have to say, huh? And we want Stan's input before we do anything more. Fair enough?"

"For now," Rita said. "But for the record, I don't trust this thing at all. You can justify, you can push ahead, and you can rave on about what a great job our boys are doing for our wounded vets, but you're a fool if you don't pay attention to what we're trying to tell you. You're the only person in this room who hasn't had first hand experience with what can happen when things get out of control."

Crowley put his hands together in prayer like fashion and rocked back and forth. "Understood."

CHAPTER SEVENTY

Jordan awoke feeling clear and rested, making him wonder if Lorenzo's ecstasy dream had some kind of cumulative effect. Aside from feeling energized, he wanted to get back in to another battle dream in spite of the nightmares that he knew would follow. Not only did the excitement of their dream rescues boost his feelings of power and control, but the nightmares that everyone took on could be erased and they were healing damaged veterans, which as far as he could see had no down side. All they needed to do was clear out the bad energy they took on, like taking a shower after a workout.

He wondered about the way John got stuck coming out of the happy place, but John had a tendency to overindulge in practically everything, which was one of the qualities that made him such a great asset to Seal Team Zero. He had been gone for two days now undergoing endless physical and psychological examinations to determine what if anything was wrong with him.

He heard Wesley and Carl talking in the other room, so he rolled out of bed to join them. As soon as he plopped into an easy chair, Crowley filled the big screen on the wall.

"How's my dream team doing this morning?"

"We'll let you know once we wake up," Wesley said.

"What's the latest?" Carl said. "I'm getting tired of sitting on my ass."

"That's why I'm contacting you now," Crowley said smiling. "We're meeting with the staff in the main Z-Level conference room in an hour."

"Will John be there?" Jordan asked.

The screen blinked off before he finished asking.

"Guess we'll find out when we get there," Wesley said.

An hour later, Jordan followed Wesley and Carl into the conference room where Crowley, Doc Krippner, Lorenzo, Rita, Jack, and Cheryl waited. Rita acknowledged him with a smile and a nod.

"Where's John?" Wesley asked. "Is he okay?"

"He's fine," Crowley said. "Fit as a fiddle as far as we can tell."

"Then why isn't he here?" Carl said.

"We're running more tests on him just to be sure," Crowley said. "We decided to keep him under observation for a few more days just to be safe."

"We've also done another exhaustive series of hardware and software diagnostics," Jack added, "and just as we expected, everything checks out."

"Same here," Lorenzo said. "I've been through every video sequence we have numerous times. It all comes up clean."

"So what's holding things up?" Wesley said.

"We are," Crowley said. "There's nothing wrong with the system, so we're concentrating on John. If there is a problem, it has to be with him, but that doesn't appear to be the case. Our medical team performed every test they could think of, but we can't find anything that even hints at any problems."

Carl shifted in his chair and pointed to Jordan and Wesley. "So let's get back to work. We're raring to go and we're getting stir crazy."

"Even though everything is coming up clean," Doc Krippner said, looking directly at Jordan. "We're still concerned about you guys taking on the nightmares of these victims."

"No problem," Jordan said. "Lorenzo's crack dream will handle it."

Crowley blinked like he'd been hit at the word crack and Rita and Cheryl exchanged worried glances, then Rita said, "We're concerned that Lorenzo's *crack* dream might be working a little too good."

"We're worried about the possibility of you guys getting hooked on it," Cheryl added.

Carl waved her off. "Only John's acting weird and that's nothing out of the ordinary."

"If he wasn't acting weird, *then* I'd be worried," Wesley said.

Jordan found himself laughing along with the others with the exception of Rita and Cheryl, neither of whom laughed.

"That's why we're giving him a break," Crowley said, taking advantage of the mood shift. "He's the only one who showed any reaction that might be considered detrimental, so naturally we're concerned, but his oversleeping as the doctors are now calling it pales in comparison to the great healing work you guys have done." He brightened and his voice rose. "Corporal Friedman and Nick Stevens have both been nightmare free for some time now. As a matter of fact, Stevens is getting fitted with new prototype cybernetic prosthetics even as we speak. With the exception of John's issue, the project has made extraordinary progress and the brass are quite impressed."

"It doesn't sound like they're going to find anything wrong with John," Wesley said. "What's going to happen if they don't?"

"As part of our investigation we thought we might run additional test sequences on you three to see if anything unusual shows up."

Wesley looked troubled. "You're not worried about us?"

"Of course we're worried about you!" Crowley said. "That's why the project is on hold. Having said that, none of you have showed any signs of this phenomenon except John and he's coming up clean on every test we've given him. Our medical team thinks it's simply a matter of slowed waking on his part. A delayed reaction. More of a temporary side-effect than anything else. They liken it to the way we drift in and out of sleep in the morning, not quite awake, but not quite dreaming either."

"Stuck between the worlds," Jack said.

Doc Krippner held up a finger. "It's called the hypnogogic state, but I have to say, I'm not in agreement with their assessment. I'm not so sure it's that simple."

"Cheryl and I agree with Stan," Rita said.

"Same with Lorenzo and I," Jack said.

Lorenzo nodded. "True dat!"

A flash of anger swept over Crowley's face. His expression changed when he saw Jordan watching. Waving off Cheryl and the others, he put his attention on the team. "You guys are the benchmark, so with your consent, I'd like to run you through a few scenarios without John to see if they affect you in any lasting way. If they go well, and he's still deemed fit for duty by our medical team, we'll bring him back in." He glanced at Rita and Cheryl. "And if we see any signs of trouble, we'll stop." He jerked his thumb back over his shoulder. "Needless to say there are a lot of damaged soldiers out there who could use your help."

He leaned back and put his hands behind his head, waiting for a response.

Carl and Wesley sat at the edge of their chairs. Jordan could tell from their body language that they couldn't wait to get back into a dream. He had to admit that part of him was ready to jump in, which gave him pause. "I think we need a little time to talk it over," he said.

Wesley and Carl turned to him with bewildered expressions, as if to say, 'What are you nuts?'

"Fair enough," Crowley said. "It'll give us more time to study John."

Wesley and Carl nodded quickly.

"That's great," Crowley said. "We don't want to delay too long. The brass are pressuring me for more conclusive results."

CHAPTER SEVENTY ONE

The moment the door clicked shut behind Jordan and his teammates, Crowley pointed at Cheryl and Rita saying, "I don't appreciate your references to Lorenzo's healing dream as crack and I won't have you undermining this project with your hysterical fears from DreamLand…"

Rita jumped when Lorenzo slapped the table, saying, "Bullshit!" She rarely saw him expressing anger. Crowley and the others looked equally surprised.

"For one thing," Lorenzo said, "It's the boys who are calling it crack. That's something you need to pay attention to." He jabbed his finger at Crowley, then at the door. "They have been under its influence, not you, and truth be told, the fact that they're calling it crack implies addiction, which is what we're worried about."

"Yes, I know." Crowley shook his head and spoke in a monotone. "You're worried about the monsters and the boogiemen from DreamLand. The only problem is that all we have is the word of you four, and truth be told, what you've told us is too fantastic to be taken seriously, except as a shared hallucination. The evidence we have regarding the safety of our dream team is based on hard scientific evidence. Furthermore this is Pandora, an independent platform…"

"But you admit using existing infrastructure," Jack said, matter-of-factly.

"Yes, there's a hardware connection," Crowley said in a mincing voice, "but it's without power and inactive."

"So you say," Jack said. "So tell me, when are you going to try Lorenzo's brainwash - er I mean, what should I call it? Vacation dream?

When are you going to experience it for yourself? We can hook you up right now," Jack said raising his eyebrows with a mischievous grin.

Crowley let out a long, exasperated sigh. "We're getting off track here. Let's stick with the issues and pay attention to what hard science and technology are telling us, not a bunch of fear based, nonsensical woo woo about witches, rats, monsters, and gangsters."

Rita half-expected Stan to bring some stability to the discussion, but to her mild surprise, he sat there lost in thought.

"Listen," Jack said as if lecturing a class room full of students. "I'm as scientific as the next guy. In fact more so. I'm a fucking hardware engineer." He patted Cheryl on the back. "Along with Cheryl here, Rita and Lorenzo too for that matter, we've done cutting edge research into electronically altering brain waves, and I'm the first to admit that what we've witnessed stretches the limits of credibility, and if I hadn't seen and experienced it directly myself along with my colleagues, I'd find it too fantastic to believe." He pointed to his eyes with two fingers. "But I know what I saw and I know what I experienced, which threw my so-called scientific mind a curve ball that's forced me to look at things in an entirely different light."

Stan leaned forward and put his chin on his hand, giving Jack his full attention.

Crowley lowered his head and leaned back. "I'm all ears."

Jack rested his hand on Cheryl's. "What Cheryl and I have discovered is that the brain works like a radio. We create specific frequencies through synaptic modulation and neurotransmitters driven by neural microprocessors, making computer generated dreams utilizing the same concept that radio and television have traditionally worked with. The magic happens when these tuners vibrate at the same resonant frequencies as the transmitters, and voila!" He threw his hands up. "We have audio and video in real time with no perceivable difference in time and place." He paused and looked around at the others as if letting his words sink in. Stan Krippner gave tiny nods.

"I understand how it works," Crowley said.

Jack held up a finger. "Do you? You weren't there when things went haywire at DreamLand which makes your grasp of what we're facing limited." He lowered his voice. "What did happen was so fantastic, I can understand why you can't accept it."

Crowley frowned. "What are you saying?"

"You clearly understand the technical aspects of what I'm postulating," Jack said. "Now I'd like you to open your mind a little. Have you ever wondered what really happens when you listen to recorded music or watch a video? What if you were listening to or watching something that was more than a duplication of that particular energy of that time and place?"

Crowley's frown deepened. "I'm not sure I follow."

"What if by creating the same set of resonant energetic vibrations, you were going beyond mere duplication and tuning in to the actual event, opening up an energetic portal to that specific time and place?"

"An opening to another dimension," Stan said.

Crowley shook his head. "You're talking science fiction. You actually believe that you've created portals to other dimensions? That's ludicrous!"

"You wouldn't think so if you went through what we went through," Cheryl said.

Rita found herself nodding along with Jack and Lorenzo. As crazy as it sounded it would explain DreamLand.

"I'm sorry, but I just don't buy it," Crowley said, still shaking his head. "It's too far-fetched."

"And computer generated dreams aren't?" Lorenzo said.

"Don't be so quick to write off explanations for what we don't understand," Stan said with authority. "We're dealing with the subconscious and the collective consciousness which are just as much of a mystery today as they've always been. It's the place where science fails and perception blurs. Barring any references to DreamLand and what may or may not be happening here, the fact remains that what we have been doing in the short time I've been involved has been nothing short of miraculous, so Jack's speculations are worthy of consideration."

"Thanks for the back up, Doc," Jack said.

Stan gave an affirmative nod. "There are schools of thought centered around what some call the Akashic records which are believed to be compendium of thoughts, events, and emotions encoded in the astral plane. There are numerous anecdotal accounts of it, but no scientific evidence. It's not a new concept. Akasha is Sanskrit for aether or atmosphere characterized as a life force referred to as tablets of the astral light that record the past and future of human thought and action. It's been likened it to a cosmic memory bank that registers all the desires and earth experiences of our planet."

"Sounds like a bunch of new age mumbo jumbo," Crowley said.

"That may be so," Stan said, unruffled, "but the idea is prehistoric. Shamans in indigenous cultures the world over don't compartmentalize and waste time trying to figure things out by the western scientific method of divide and conquer. Their perception of what we consider to be reality is far more comprehensive. In their world view sleeping, waking, dreaming, visions, and for that matter any state of consciousness are all part of the same continuum, and each one carries just as much weight and requires the same amount of attention as the others."

Jack Scanlon's bushy eyebrows raised and a broad grin spread over his face. He leaned back in his chair waving his fingers singing, "Row, row, row your boat, gently down the stream. Merrily, merrily, merrily, merrily, life is but a dream."

"I hate to say it," Rita added, "but in this case we're looking at nightmares."

Cheryl nodded emphatically.

CHAPTER SEVENTY TWO

Jordan woke up feeling clear headed and impatient to get into one of Lorenzo's battle dreams. As soon as he joined the others in their lounge, Crowley popped up on the wall screen. The thought of him watching and waiting every morning irked Jordan, but he knew it was best to keep his mouth shut.

After a private briefing in a smaller conference room that felt like an ass kissing from Crowley about what a great service they were doing for their country, and the amazing healing they were providing for untreatable PTSD victims, Crowley laid out the details of how he wanted to proceed. The more he talked, the more impatient Jordan felt to get back into a battle dream.

"In order to take advantage of our present situation," Crowley said from his usual spot at the head of the table, "I've come up with a short, accelerated program that has the potential to leap frog us ahead."

"What about John?" Carl said. "I don't like the idea of doing any dream battles without him."

"Yeah, what he said." Wesley jabbed his thumb toward Carl.

"He'll be back soon," Crowley said. "In the mean time we have a unique opportunity to work in parallel with the testing he's undergoing. We want to do a couple of shorter sequences with you three to gather more data. If John gets a clean bill of health, which is what we are seeing so far, we'll bring him back into the program with you guys."

"What do you mean by a short accelerated program?" Jordan asked. He was more than ready to go, but part of him still felt apprehensive.

Crowley smiled. "We want to skip the preliminary gaming part of the process. As you have discovered, battles are not neat and predictable like games. You guys have gained invaluable experience in how things can unfold in surprising ways, so part of this test is to send you in without warning to gauge your reactions under fire the way it happens in the real world."

"Shorter means faster and more intense," Wesley said, voicing what Jordan was thinking.

Crowley gave a short nod.

"No matter what you do," Carl said, "we're going to end up taking on the nightmare of whatever you throw at us."

Crowley's nodding increased.

"Seeing as we know that," Wesley added, "How about giving us the crack dream right after the battle dream so we can sleep in peace tonight. If there's one thing we do know for sure, when we save a vet, we end up with his nightmares, and the crack dream is the only thing that seems to cure it."

Crowley's face pinched into a scowl and his voice took on an edge. "I know you guys have a sense of humor about this, which is a good thing, but I don't appreciate you calling our healing sequence crack. I like to think of it as a refresh, or better still a wipe." He looked at each team member, one at a time, driving his point home. "As a matter of fact we are giving it the official designation of tabula rasa."

Wesley smirked. "Tabula rasta? I like the sound of that!"

Crowley shook his head. "Tabula *rasa*. It's Latin that translates into smoothed or erased tablet. Ancient philosophers argued that babies are born with minds that are blank slates. Later, psychologists took up the case until a figurative sense of the term emerged, referring to something that exists in its original state that has yet to be altered by outside forces, and yes, rasta man, that is what we plan to do. Give you a short intense experience followed by the tabula rasa sequence. If that goes according to our predictions we'll follow up with another double sequence. If that goes according to plan, we'll consider easing John back into the mix."

Carl leaned forward, a frown creasing his face. "What is it that you are planning on throwing us into that we can't rehearse as a game?"

"We have someone who was shot down in a helicopter by a rocket who would greatly benefit from your help."

Jordan felt a chill pass through him. Part of him felt an impulse to get into the dream, while his thinking self quivered in indecision. He shook it off and looked to Wesley and Carl, who both looked to him with questioning expressions. He found himself nodding in spite of his inner conflict.

"Then let's quit talking about it." Wesley pumped his fist in the air, "and let's get it on!"

Twenty minutes later Crowley led them into the Dream Lab where they found Lorenzo, Jack, Rita, and Cheryl waiting with dreaming hoods at the ready. Rita looked tight-lipped, as if she were there against her will, but compared to Cheryl who had a deer caught in the headlights look, she seemed calm. Their strained expressions added to Jordan's uneasiness which was compounded by the fact that Stan Krippner was nowhere to be seen. "Isn't Doc Krippner joining us?"

"He's following up with John," Crowley said, "But he'll get all of the video and telemetry from your session, so you don't have to worry."

"I'd feel much better with him here," Jordan said.

"Me too!" Wesley said.

Carl nodded with him.

"This will be over quick enough," Crowley said, "and we want to make sure John is safe, so I think it's only right that Stan focus on him for the moment."

Rita and Cheryl exchanged dark looks which told Jordan that they disagreed with the direction things were taking.

Cheryl and Jack moved down the line helping them on with their dream hoods in silence. Once his was secure, Jordan's conflict quickened and he realized he was shaking.

"Breathe deep," Rita's comforting voice said in his ear after she and the others left the lab. "Your vitals are rising. Remember, it's only a dream."

Her words calmed him, but something about how she said 'it's only a dream' had the opposite effect, so he forced himself to breathe slower when Lorenzo began counting down.

"Five, four, three, two, one…"

Jordan grew heavy and fell into the shifting void of darkness and light until a thumping sound accompanied the beat of the flashes.

Everything vibrated with flashes of sight and sound, coming first through his feet, then up through the rest of his body until his surroundings came into focus in the back of a transport helicopter. He first saw the wide-eyed expressions of Wesley and Carl. He made it a point to wink and grin at them, which seemed to lessen their fear.

He took a quick look around the close quarters of the thumping copter, recognizing the red crosses on the gear that signified medical supplies.

"What are you doing here?" an annoyed medic with a Red Cross armband and captain's bars on his collar yelled over the noise. His nametag said MORASH.

A beeping alarm and flashing red lights filled the cabin, punctuated by a "Shit!" from the pilot. Jordan looked out the open door and spotted an intense bright glow followed by a trail of smoke heading straight for them. The combination of the alarm and missile sighting triggered the same impulse that prompted him to throw himself on the grenade when they rescued Nick Stevens.

"It won't make any sense to you," he said, motioning Wesley and Carl in closer. "But we're here to get shot down with you and help you through your nightmare."

"How the fuck do you..."

"We're with you in your nightmare to rescue you from it. A rocket's going to hit any second now." Jordan wanted to look again, but didn't dare.

Morash's expression went from suspicion to alarm. Jordan grabbed Carl and Wesley, yanking them in close with him and Morash, making it a point to look Morash straight in the eyes as the bright searing flash and concussion of sight, sound, and feeling ripped through everything.

Jordan screamed. He had never felt such intense pain as he did when his world erupted into a disorienting spin of flashing lights, flames, and whining explosions that spun crazily in every direction, shot through with an agonizing white hot flame that slammed them into the ground.

In the midst of his seemingly endless terror and suffering he dropped into a bottomless tunnel of expanding and contracting geometric colors and patterns that shot him into another bright light that morphed into extreme pleasure, soothing every molecule of his being like a cold compress on a fevered brow.

White noise turned into the sound of waves on a beach, followed by a dim image that brightened along with rising music and other sounds that intermingled into the multilayered otherworldly lullaby that he had come to love.

His heart lightened and his emotions expanded with the music and imagery, then his whole body vibrated with an exquisite depth of feeling that peaked in a crescendo of running water, waves, tribal chants, digeridoos, flutes, and strings.

Wave after wave of ecstasy overwhelmed him, sending him into an exquisite tapestry of thought, feeling, and emotion until time and place lost all meaning and the only thing he knew for sure was bliss. Nothing else mattered. He had found his way home and he didn't want to leave.

CHAPTER SEVENTY THREE

None of the dreamers opened their eyes when Lorenzo terminated the sequence, which spurred Rita into panicked action. She bolted from the observation room into the Dream Lab followed by Cheryl, Jack, Lorenzo, and Crowley. She went to Jordan first and shook him while grabbing smelling salts from her lab coat. Just as she was about to crack the packet, his eyes flickered open and came into focus, then he smiled broadly.

"I've gone to heaven and I'm being blessed by an angel," he said, gazing into her eyes.

"Shake the others awake," Rita said, feeling her face flush. "I've got smelling salts if you need them."

Jack shook Wesley who awakened after a couple of shakes and Cheryl shook Carl a little too rough, causing his eyes to shoot open.

"Hey, what the fu -- what the fuck's going on?" He said. "Jesus, back off doc!" He held up his hands. "You're gonna shake me to pieces."

Cheryl stepped back wiping tears from her eyes. "Sorry," she whispered. "You scared the shit out of us."

Wesley looked from Rita to Jack to Cheryl. "We didn't mean to freak you out, but that was one intense dream and it didn't end easily. In fact it hurt like hell. After all that pain that seemed to last forever, I wanted to stay in the crack, er..." He shot a glance at Crowley. "I mean the tabula rasta dream."

"Tabula *rasa*," Crowley corrected him. "How do you guys feel?"

"Awesome," Carl said. "Like I can take on the world."

Jordan did an internal check. His thoughts felt precise, his emotions rock solid, and his body energized, with an edge. In spite of the pain and terror he had been through, he wanted to go back. "I don't think I've ever felt better."

"I'm willing to bet that we won't have any nightmares tonight," Wesley said. "I can tell by how I feel."

Crowley's smile went all the way up to his eyes. "Excellent!"

Rita and the others helped the team off with their hoods and escorted them to the conference room. Rita put her hands in her pockets so no one could see them shaking and breathed in extra deep to calm herself. Seeing Stan Krippner come in behind them had a calming effect. Once every one settled in, Crowley started the discussion.

"I know what we saw on our monitoring equipment, but what I am really interested in is how you guys feel and what your subjective experiences have to tell us. Who wants to go first?"

"Now I know what John feels like," Carl volunteered. "I feel great. That was a rough experience, but I think it's safe to say that I feel better from it. Even though it scared the shit out of me in the beginning, it was worth it by the end."

Crowley rubbed his chin. Leaning forward, he said, "Would it be safe to say that you're willing to do it again?"

"I don't know about Jordan or Wesley, but I'm raring to go! I feel like I know more now, like it sharpened me."

"But you didn't come out of the dream when we stopped it," Cheryl said, reflecting Rita's concerns. "Doesn't that bother you?"

Carl waved his hand, dismissing the question. "If you ask me, we could have stayed in the cra - the tabula wipe zone a little longer. Getting shot down by a rocket in a helicopter was the most terrifying and painful experience I've ever had. I thought it would never end, so I think we all needed the extra time to get rebalanced."

Cheryl still looked rattled and Jack and Lorenzo looked skeptical, while Crowley's open expression contrasted everyone else's, especially Stan Krippner, who looked the most concerned.

"I can't argue with how good I feel afterward," Wesley said, "but part of me feels like cannon fodder. We went through the meat grinder. It dawned on me that so far, we haven't done anything except take on suicide missions. We normally go into these nightmares and use our tactical skills to complete our objectives, which it looks like in the end can only be won by committing suicide along with our targets." He shook his head. "Shit, this last one didn't take any tactical skills at all, except a death wish."

Stan nodded and Rita sensed that he wasn't buying it. She couldn't wait to hear what he thought, but he seemed to be in observation mode, not just of the dream team, but of everybody in the room, especially Crowley.

"But it wasn't a waste," Crowley said making his point by holding up a finger. "All of your missions have resulted in healing, and I have no doubt that you did the same this time.

"My sense is that we have been dealing with a hot potato," Jordan said. "We go storming into these horrific situations and after going through them with the victims, we take away their nightmares and end up holding the bag until we neutralize their negative effects by wiping our brains. I agree with Wesley. I have a strong sense that we won't have any nightmares, and yes, we do seem to heal these guys, and yes, I don't think I've ever felt better in my entire life, but a lot of it puzzles me."

Stan Krippner leaned forward, putting all of his attention on Jordan. "Can you elaborate on what it is that bothers you?"

Though his question was direct, Rita sensed skepticism and a touch of irony in his tone.

Jordan sighed, crossed his arms and sat back. "As I understand it, dreams are a reflection of our inner and to some degree outer life, and from what I learned from you, doc, they also reflect our shadow, whether we like it or not." He looked to Stan and the others for confirmation.

"Go on," Stan said.

"Funny thing about mirror reflections," Jordan added. "If you look at signs or anything else written in a mirror, it's all backwards."

"I'm not sure where you're going with this," Crowley said, "but..."

Stan held up a hand stopping him and nodded to Jordan. "Please, continue."

"I feel like two different people, like a cartoon character with a little devil on one shoulder and an angel on the other telling me two different things. If I look at myself in this regular waking world, everything's normal," he said with a sweep of his hand, "but when I'm in those dream worlds, it all seems upside down and backwards. We do everything we can to stay alive in the regular world, but we have to commit suicide to do any good over there. When I had that first impulse that I learned from John, it hit me like some kind of higher knowing. It's hard to put into words, but that feeling seems to have taken root as a driving force."

"I know what you're saying," Wesley said.

Carl nodded.

"So part of me is afraid to go back, and another part of me can't wait. I'm starting to feel like the proverbial moth to the flame. I can't deny the power of its attraction, but I have to destroy myself in the dream to soothe it."

Wesley looked at Crowley and smiled. "Lorenzo's Tabouli rasta dream added on the end of the battle makes it easier."

"Yeah," Carl said. "With all the shit we went through this last time, it's like beating your head against the wall."

"How so?" Lorenzo asked.

"It feels so good when you stop."

CHAPTER SEVENTY FOUR

Jordan lay awake thinking about his moth to the flame comment. He wasn't worried about nightmares. He wouldn't have any. Instead of the usual emotional chaos he had come to expect after a battle dream, he felt invigorated with a little bit of an edge, and it was the edge that worried him.

The same impulse that drove him to the thrills and adrenaline of his dream suicides also drove him toward the bliss of Lorenzo's crack dream. It soothed his entire being like a cool drink of water to someone dying of thirst.

He always felt apprehensive going into the battle dreams, and in spite of the pain and suffering he experienced, he always felt a strong sense of gratification, especially when he saw the healing results.

He rode the edge through the polarities of pleasure and pain which enhanced each other like a swinging pendulum. After his hellish experiences in the battles, especially this last one, the drive inside him sought the blissful peace of Lorenzo's escape. The pull of it felt so strong, and it felt so good, that he feared getting trapped in it.

He drifted off to sleep with these thoughts and sank into a deep, dreamless slumber that energized him more. When he awoke the following morning his desire to engage in a battle dream had grown into a longing that filled him with a dull ache in his heart. He felt clear, sharp, purposeful, and driven to go into a dream battle to save someone as if it were his only reason for being.

He heard the others and went to the lounge where he found Carl and Wesley looking wide-eyed and alert.

"I don't know about you guys," Wesley said from an easy chair, "but I'm ready to go! If they don't have a dream scheduled for us, I'm going to ask for one. I feel really on top of my game."

Carl stretched out on the couch with his hands behind his head. "I feel like I'm some kind of superman who can't do anything wrong."

"In your dreams," Wesley said. "In real life, it's a different story."

Carl threw a pillow at him. "Fuck you," he said giggling.

Wesley looked at Jordan deadpan and they joined Carl's giggling fit. Jordan dropped into another chair and the door to their lounge opened.

John came in and crossed his arms, saying, "What the fuck? They take me out for a couple of days and look at you losers. Fucking off the first chance you get!"

"John!" Carl said, sitting up.

"Welcome back, bro," Wesley said turning to face him.

"Dude," Jordan said, "We know whose really been fucking off."

John's mouth turned up in a lopsided grin. He seemed to move jerky like a puppet when he sat next to Carl on the couch.

"How the hell are you?" Wesley asked. "Did they give you an anal probe like you wanted?"

John grinned wider and flipped him off. Now that Jordan saw him up close, in spite of the mirth in his eyes, something bubbled below the surface. His smile faded and his eyes darted back and forth like little trapped animals. The subtle change in his mannerisms made Jordan uneasy.

"Seriously though," Carl said. "Did they find anything wrong? Are you okay?"

John leaned back and stretched out his legs. "Couldn't be better."

Wesley stood and gave John a high five. "That's great to hear. I miss that little shit, Terry, but it really hasn't been the same without your crazy ass in the mix."

"Thanks Bro!" John fist bumped Carl and Jordan while Wesley fell back into his chair. "I'm sorry to spoil your fantasy, but I didn't get an anal probe. They did everything but. I feel like a fucking pincushion. They took blood, MRIs, X-Rays, ultrasound, psych tests, you name it." He shook his head. "Maybe an anal probe would have been better. You know, get it all over with at once."

"And they didn't find anything," Jordan said.

"Nada."

"So I wonder how that's going to affect things after yesterday," Carl said.

John's eyes widened. "I heard about that shit. I can't believe you guys went on without me and to top it off, you guys got stuck in the happy place too. What's up with that?"

Wesley muttered, "Crack city."

"I hear ya," John said. "I'm jonesing to get back into a battle dream and all I've been thinking about is that crack dream. Shit, instead of nightmares, I've been dreaming about it like it's calling me and it seems like the longer I'm away from it, the more impatient I am to get back to it. It's driving me a little bug fuck."

John's enthusiasm jolted Jordan with the thought that what he thought of as his edge had two sides like the proverbial double-edged sword. His body, feelings, and emotions wanted to plunge into the dream world, especially with the feel good relief that Lorenzo's wipe dream gave them, but his mind and instincts resisted, as if protecting a core of fear centered in his heart.

"I'm curious to see what they'll have to say," Carl said. "Sure we got a little stuck yesterday like John did, but he just got the full on psych and physical exams."

"Except the anal probe." Wesley said.

John shot him another middle finger.

"And he came out clean," Carl said. "Nothing wrong, so there's no physical danger to us."

"Which means it's all in our heads," Wesley said.

Jordan studied them. "Is it?"

"What's that supposed to mean?" John said, looking disturbed.

"Well, they didn't give you an anal probe," Wesley joked, "so it could be up your ass."

Everyone laughed, especially John. When it subsided they sat in silence, each lost in their own thoughts. Jordan flip-flopped between fear and impulse, one moment surrendering to abandonment and the rush of feeling and emotion that the contrasting battle and relief dreams brought. He smiled to himself when he thought about what Carl said. The battle dreams were like beating your head against the wall and the crack dream felt so good when you stopped.

The wall screen came to life and Crowley's face filled it. "It's great to see the dream team together again. We've had a few challenges, but

I have to tell you, you guys are becoming underground heroes in the defense community."

"So let's get going," John said. "Time's a wasting. I'm ready to rock and roll."

Crowley smiled and waved. "Not so fast. That's the right attitude and I couldn't agree with you more, especially with all the good you've done, but the rest of the support team has concerns that need to be addressed."

"Even after I passed all their tests?" John said.

Crowley nodded. "I wanted to talk this over with you guys in private, but they've convinced me otherwise and refuse to go any further without hashing out the issues."

John looked a little hurt. "I don't understand. I passed all their tests."

"I'm with you," Crowley said, "but they are the ones who invented this technology, so I think their concerns deserve to be heard, don't you?"

John lowered his head, muttering, "I guess so."

CHAPTER SEVENTY FIVE

After all the deaths and traumas Rita had witnessed, her heart still sank at the sight of the one-armed, scarred and legless torso of Captain Morash in a hospital bed surrounded by monitors that beeped and flashed. She looked back over her shoulder at Cheryl, who had a pained expression of her own. Jack Scanlon and Lorenzo, stood close behind her, just inside the door.

She heard Crowley coming down the hall outside with Jordan and his team and put a finger to her lips, quieting them when they pushed their way into the room. Lorenzo, Cheryl, and Jack backed out, making room for Crowley and the team, who all stared at Captain Morash in silence.

After a couple of minutes, Rita sought out Crowley's attention and motioned toward the door with her head. He put a hand on Carl's shoulder and ushered him and the rest of the team out. Once outside, everyone with the exception of Stan Krippner moved down the hall away from the room. Rita followed them staying close to Lorenzo. When they reached the end of the hall, the questions came.

"That was depressing," Wesley said. "What good did we do for that poor bastard?"

"It seems like a waste," Carl said.

"He's fucked," John said under his breath.

Crowley beckoned with his finger. "I'm going to show you, but while we're walking, I want you guys to realize how much suffering you've eliminated. Prior to your intervention, Captain Morash couldn't sleep without heavy sedation and even then he moaned all the time. Now, thanks to your efforts, his medication has been reduced and he's sleeping soundly, something he hasn't been capable of since his injury."

Crowley led them through curved hallways and elevators to another part of the complex, closer to the Dream Lab.

"Even though he only has one arm, the rest of him is intact and we expect to have him fully functional in a matter of months."

"Fully functional?" Carl asked. "How can he be fully functional with one arm?"

"With a little help from his friends," Crowley stopped and gestured to Cheryl and Jack who had been walking behind them.

"With friends like us, who needs enemies?" Jack muttered.

"I don't get it," Wesley said.

"You will in a minute." Crowley guided them down another hallway that ended at a double door. The sign above it said:

FIRING RANGE

Faint popping sounds came from behind it.

Crowley led them into a windowed observation booth with a dozen seats in two tiers looking out onto a firing range where a lone figure wearing ear protectors stood, rifle at the ready. He turned and stood at attention with the rifle on his shoulder.

Five large flat screens lined the wall above the window. One showed a close-up of a target. The one beside it had a moving targeting display that calculated mathematical trajectories, displaying projective geometry and vector calculations in red and blue overlaid on everyone in the observation booth. The third screen had the same images in eerie green that Rita recognized as night vision and the fourth had identical images highlighted in the fuzzy reds, yellows, blues, and greens of thermal images. The fifth showed vital signs, including skin temperature, heart rate, blood pressure, respiration, brain chemistry, hormone levels, and more.

"Holy shit," Lorenzo said, taking it all in.

Crowley smiled. "You ain't seen nothing yet." He tapped an intercom on the wall and his muffled voice echoed from the PA in the firing range along with his voice in the booth. "Are you ready to show them how it's done, Sergeant Stevens?"

Stevens snapped off a smart salute with his prosthetic arm. "Yes sir."

"On my mark," Crowley said, "Three, two, one."

Stevens spun around in one graceful motion and shouldered his rifle, popping off six fast rounds. The close-up target on the first monitor showed one slightly enlarged hole for all six rounds at dead center of the bullseye, precisely calculated at one hundred yards down range while the targeting screen flashed red with the coordinates locked on to overlaid vectored geometric images. It all happened so fast that Rita scarcely believed what she saw.

"Bad ass!" John said.

Crowley applauded and the others looked on, stunned. Silence filled the booth until Jack Scanlon broke it, saying, "That's really impressive, but can he cook?"

The absurdity of his question caused everyone to break out in nervous laughter.

We can always count on you for comic relief when we need it Jack, Rita thought.

"Come on and let's say hi to him." Crowley gestured toward a door that opened to the firing range. "I want you to see first hand the difference you made in this man's life."

The group left the booth and went out to the range. Their feet made a muted echo as they walked and the smell of spent gun powder hung in the air. Nick Stevens set his rifle down on a table, slipped off his ear protectors, and turned to face them once more saluting with a shiny cybernetic prosthetic right arm that puffed with the whispered hiss of robotics when he moved it.

Rita studied him, unsure of what to say. A no nonsense man with sandy hair, one perfect, chiseled side of Nick Stevens' angular face had a piercing blue eye. The other side looked scarred and empty, with the exception of a twinkling cybernetic eye that sparkled with its own jeweled intelligence, giving him a perpetually startled look on that side of his face. He looked like some kind of hi-tech armored super hero - - and acted like one too!

"At ease sergeant," Crowley said. "Top notch performance, Nick. Thank you. Please, speak freely."

"I can't tell you how happy I am to be of service," Nick said, "and I'm at a loss for words to express the gratitude that I have for you all." He bowed to Jordan and his team. "You gave me my life and my purpose back." He moved through the group shaking each person's hand.

Nick extended his robotic right hand, covering Rita's hand with his good left one when he shook hers. The artificial one had a grip that felt light and strong and its rubberized covering felt weirdly human, but devoid of warmth.

Up close Nick's cybernetic eye looked natural, but it increased Rita's discomfort as she imagined it targeting and analyzing every part of her onscreen in the observation booth. It had a tiny colored sparkle that shifted and refocused, changing colors and the size of the pupil in rapid-fire adjustments.

"I can never repay you for the gift you've given me," he said in hushed tones, "but I can promise to fight for freedom. God bless America!" He cried, with a tremor in his voice. A tear trickled down from his good eye.

"Based on Doctor Martin's work in synaptic modulation and neurotransmitters, coupled with Mr. Scanlon's breakthrough in neural microprocessor design, combined with the efforts of Seal Team 0, Sergeant Nick Stevens is not only fully functional, but his performance exceeds anything we've ever seen. Sergeant Stevens is history in the making," Crowley said, beaming. "His digital eye and arm are under the precise command and control functions of the microprocessor implant that you developed, and as you saw on the observation room monitors, they can be wirelessly monitored and manipulated from virtually any computer. The hardware implanted in his brain's motor cortex has integrated GPS, RFID and other functions so we can easily locate, monitor, and if needed, we can treat him if he has any complications or medical emergencies. You just saw a demonstration of auto response mode."

"Remote control?" Jordan asked.

"Sort of," Crowley said. "When Nick's physiological monitors trigger a pre-set threshold, the automatic targeting system activates. His new eye and arm are precisely synchronized by a high speed feedback loop -- we're talking microseconds here. At this point in alert mode, the only decision Nick has to make is whether to pull the trigger or not."

"I don't even need a spotter," Nick said. "I have it right here with me." He pointed at his head with his prosthetic arm. "Inside me at all times. A direct connection." He lowered his head and tapped his chest. "And I have Butch with me here always."

"Thanks for that bad ass demo!" John said.

Nick patted him on the back and fist bumped the rest of Seal Team 0. "I'll never forget as long as I live that you guys gave me my life back. I'll always be in your debt. If there's anything I can do for you, just say the word." He snapped to attention and saluted.

"Thank you, Nick," Crowley said, returning his salute. "Now that you are all up to speed," he said to the group, "and have seen the good you have done with your own eyes, we have an appointment with Doctor Krippner." He extended his hand toward the door.

Jordan and his teammates all saluted Nick and led the group out of the firing range, with Crowley in the lead and Rita and Lorenzo taking up the rear.

A few minutes later they filed into a Z Level conference room where they found Stan Krippner waiting. Once everyone settled into their usual spot, Crowley started the discussion. "I want to take a moment to acknowledge what a phenomenal job all of you have done." He pointed at each person around the table in succession. "Every one of you! You are not only giving people back their lives, but you're making history and blazing a trail for greater things to come."

With the exception of Jordan, the two sides of the table had opposite reactions. Jordan's team looked pumped up as if inflated with each word of praise, which Rita understood. They had gone through the pain of battle and death in the dreaming scenarios and they had cured PTSD vets in the process. No small feat.

On the researcher's side of the table, Cheryl looked stone-faced, while Jack and Lorenzo exchanged dark glances. Rita knew what they were thinking and felt surprised that the liberal, war hating Jack Scanlon kept his mouth shut about what amounted to a cyborg sniper. She didn't think Stan Krippner would be thrilled about it either and had a sneaking suspicion that his absence from the chilling demo they had witnessed was a subtle form of protest.

CHAPTER SEVENTY SIX

Jordan reveled in the sense of accomplishment he felt with his teammates from Crowley's praise, but couldn't help noticing the sour expressions of the support team, especially Doctor Martin. The difference in the reactions from the two sides of the table made him uneasy. There had to be something that they weren't telling him. He had to admit, the healing he and the others brought to the wounded vets in their "suicide missions" filled him with an expansive sense of good will and compassion. Nick Stevens said they had given him his life back and they had the potential to do that for a lot more if they could work out the kinks.

He felt driven to plunge into another battle dream for the thrill it would bring as well as the healing and joyful reward that Lorenzo's magical healing dream would bring at the end of it. Hopefully they could move forward with it. He didn't think he could wait.

"Here are the issues we need to resolve before we can move ahead," Crowley said, gesturing to Jordan and the others. "We've established that the members of our dream team can go into the nightmares of our veterans and effectively remove the trauma in what amounts to a rescue operation, but in the process they take on the nightmares as their own. The only way we know how to mitigate this is to put them through the tabula rasa sequence."

"Which appears to work a little too good," Cheryl said. "They're not coming out of it when the signals are terminated. They're getting stuck and I'm not afraid to say that it scares the hell out of me!"

"That makes two of us," Rita added, looking to Jack and Lorenzo, who nodded in unison.

"All of us," Lorenzo said.

Other than a slight nod, Stan Krippner showed little reaction.

John leaned forward, pointing as he spoke. "I think you guys are paying way too much attention to something that's not such a big deal. Sure, I didn't wake up fast enough for you, but I got poked, probed, and scanned with everything but a rectal probe and came out clean. Did you ever stop to think that it might just be a kind of sleep hang over? That's what the other doctors are saying." He made a sweeping gesture. "I'm sure everyone here knows how hard it can be to get out of bed sometimes, especially when you've been dreaming."

"I wish it were that simple," Stan said, "but there are too many variables."

"He's right," Rita said. "If it were simply a matter of a 'sleep hang over' as you call it, then why did I need smelling salts to bring you out of it?"

"You overreacted too soon," John said. "I needed a little more time, that's all. I think there's something entirely different going on here and as far as I can tell, the only way to find out for sure is to give it a shot."

"What is it that you think is entirely different?" Stan asked.

"I've given this a lot of thought." John pointed to Jordan, Carl, and Wesley. "We're the ones going through this. None of you know what it's like, except from what we tell you. We've all been trying to learn as we go, and the more experience we get, the more we know. What I think so far is that the more intense the battle dream is, the more time we need in Lorenzo's healing dream. In other words, the more the suffering, the more healing time is needed."

I hadn't thought about it that way, Jordan thought, remembering how good it felt this last time. It was a possibility. "Yeah," he said. "I did feel like I was burning forever when that rocket hit us in that copter nightmare. The time in Lorenzo's dream definitely killed the pain."

"You don't think it's addicting?" Cheryl asked.

"No more than oversleeping," John retorted.

"What worries me are the addictive qualities that are part and parcel of these programs," Stan said. "I'm afraid that you guys are showing signs of addiction."

Stan's words made Jordan give pause. He closed his eyes, remembering the overwhelming comfort of Lorenzo's dream and how it soothed his entire being like a cool drink of water.

"Listen," John said, cutting in on his thoughts. "Right now everything is speculation. I want to push for another shot at it, then then we'll know for sure." He looked to Carl and Wesley, who both nodded emphatically.

No one from the support side of the table responded.

"Look if there's a problem," John continued, "you can just pull the plug, right?" He nodded to Rita. "You can even hit us with the smelling salts if you're worried."

Cheryl crossed her arms and leaned back shaking her head while Lorenzo and Jack looked down, deep in thought. Rita looked to Stan Krippner, but Crowley spoke.

"That's not a bad approach."

"I advise against it until we know more," Stan said.

Cheryl sat up straight, nodding and Jack, Lorenzo, and Rita followed suit.

"There's a lot to be said for keeping a finger on the 'kill switch'," Crowley said. "We can cut them off and have someone standing by in the dreaming lab with smelling salts at the ready. At the first sign of anything that looks problematic in any way, shape, or form, we can halt the sequence and apply the smelling salts."

"I'm not comfortable with it," Cheryl said. "You have no idea..."

Crowley held up a hand, cutting her off. "Hold on a minute. As John said, they are the ones who are actually going through it. I think it's their call. What do you guys think?"

Carl and Wesley nodded without hesitation and Jordan found himself automatically following.

"Let's get it on," John said. "Time's a wasting."

"Right now?" Rita said.

"What are we waiting for?" John countered. "We have the safety covered. Now is as good a time as ever."

"I think that settles it," Crowley said.

"Not so fast, hotshot," Jack said. "We need time to fine tune and recheck the hardware and software." He pointed to Cheryl, Lorenzo, and Rita. "We want to do all we can to minimize any danger."

John's eyes blazed. "Do you think we're some kind of..."

"Thanks!" Jordan said louder. "We appreciate you watching out for us, then a little softer, "Chill John, it's not going anywhere."

"Tomorrow morning at ten," Crowley said.

"For the record," Doc Krippner said, "I don't condone this course of action and advise against it."

"That makes five of us," Jack said.

"Point taken," Crowley said. "Nonetheless, tomorrow morning at ten we'll have everything ready with every conceivable precaution in place so we can find out what we can do to safely resolve any issues that we might be facing."

CHAPTER SEVENTY SEVEN

Rita seemed to float to her feet without using her hands to see signs marking two separate paths into the woods, THE PIED PIPER and HANSEL AND GRETEL. From far away she heard a children's chorus singing.

"The witch is coming for you,

The witch is coming for you,

She'll nibble your fingers and snack on your toes,

And fatten you up for stew."

She shook her head and her world swam into focus until she found herself in the ICU studying video readouts over the coffin-like enclosure that held Hodge.

Stop day dreaming, she chided herself.

Hundreds of wires came from Hodge and the window around his frail, balding head, while fiber optics on his hood and gloves flashed, and colored fluids flowed through the tubing at his wrists.

His eyes shot open startling her and the depth of his imploring gaze captured her attention like a snake mesmerizing a rodent. His mouth opened and closed. When she leaned in closer he reached out, grabbing her wrist.

The touch of his hand sent her hurtling through a maelstrom of darkness into frigid water. She held her breath as bubbles of emerald phosphorescence boiled around her. Far above on the glittering silver surface the sky grew hazy. She flailed, struggling to reverse her descent.

The bubbles changed direction and she pulled herself up toward the hazy light where dusky spots swirled among sparkling bubbles. As she neared the surface, the dark spots whirled closer.

She gulped when her head broke the surface. Sweet, delicious, fresh air.

Something wet and hairy brushed her cheek. Looking up, she saw rats tumbling off a jagged cliff, floating on swells, scratching at her. One clawed at her hair. Another scrambled onto her head and a furry head surfaced in front of her, snapping at her face until the dark chaos whirled in the opposite direction, dropping her back into the ICU where Hodge still grasped her wrist.

His empty gaze showed no intelligence until the music and imagery rose to a cacophony of running water, waves, chants, digeridoos, flutes, and strings.

Hodge's eyes grew bigger and his mouth opened wider. From somewhere far away she heard the children's chorus whisper-singing.

"The witch is coming for you,

The witch is coming for you,

She'll nibble your fingers and snack on your toes,

And fatten you up for stew."

"Rats!" Hodge yelled.

Startled, she pulled free from his grasp and stumbled back. Hodge sat up looking like a monstrous hi-tech vampire.

"It's not that they're coming," he gasped. "They're *waiting!*"

The song from the children's chorus tinkled through her mind like wind chimes, but the words had changed.

"The witches are waiting for you,

The witches are waiting for you,

They'll nibble your spirit and snack on your soul,

And swallow you up out of view."

Hodge put his hands to his mouth and his eyes bulged. "With Emily!" He screamed like a little girl. "Chazz and Ollie too! Run as far away as you can. You think you stopped them by shutting down Morpheus, but you didn't. They're waiting." His breath came in spurts. "Denise. Eddie. Morgan. Emily."

Rita turned and ran straight into Chazz Daggett. Tall and emaciated with a shaved head, he wore his black tee-shirt, leather jacket and hobnailed boots. His pale blue eyes glinted green. He grabbed her by the throat, pulling her face close to his.

"We're waiting," he croaked, violating her with the foulest smelling effluvium she had ever known, then he pressed his garbage mouth to hers and jammed his cold, slimy tongue between her lips.

Rita jolted awake, slick with cold sweat and the shakes. Lorenzo slept soundly beside her. She drew in long sobbing breaths and wiped the sweat from her face with the sheet.

CHAPTER SEVENTY EIGHT

Jordan awoke hearing the whispered traces of a children's chorus tinkling through his mind like whispered wind chimes. Something about witches waiting for him and eating his soul. Where did that come from?

He sat up, shaking it off and took stock of himself. He felt strong and bristling with energy. Deep down he could barely stand to wait any longer to go into the dream, like his desire had grown overnight. He thought about the thrill he would experience and smiled, thinking about where it would end up. Its attraction seemed to draw him forward, putting a tiny seed of fear into the midst of his passion.

Remembering Doc Krippner's admonition, he resolved himself to find a higher awareness in the dream so he could navigate a reality with a more flexible set of rules. Repeating it to himself gave him confidence, and in spite of the pull, he felt he had the will power to override any seduction Lorenzo's dream might have.

Paying attention was the key.

He felt added confidence when he went into the dream lab later that morning with the rest of the team when Crowley said, "All the safeguards are in place."

Rita, Lorenzo, Cheryl and Jack stood by. Rita looked a little ashen and Cheryl definitely looked unhappy.

"Rita and Doctor Martin will be standing by right here in the room with you," Crowley said.

Rita brandished a handful of smelling salts. "With your wake up call at the ready."

Jack jabbed his thumb at Lorenzo. "And we'll be back in the control room with our fingers on the kill switch."

"So you'll be safe," Crowley said, "and the data we collect will go a long way toward finding solutions to the problems that are slowing down getting more healing for our wounded troops."

John climbed into his dream cradle and slipped his hood on. "What are we waiting for? You bitches cheated on me with your last dream and had all the fun without me. I'm not going to forget that. I intend to make up for it now. Let's rock and roll!"

Jordan found himself grinning along with Carl and Wesley. "Don't mind him," he said to Rita and Cheryl. "He had a deprived child hood."

"More like a depraved child hood," Wesley said.

"What's this *had* shit," Carl chimed in. "He's still in it!"

John answered with his middle finger and the whole room laughed. Even Cheryl giggled.

"All right," Crowley said, saluting the team.

"We have your back," Lorenzo said, following Crowley and Jack out.

A few moments later Lorenzo's voice came through. "Okay troops, on my mark. Five, four, three, two, one…"

Jordan grew heavy and fell into the void, shifting between dark and light, repeating, "This is only a dream and in it I'm trying to find a higher awareness to navigate a reality that follows a more flexible set of rules."

He came into awareness walking up a mountain path alongside Carl, Wesley, and John, who quickened his step to catch up to four men on the path in front of them. Jordan looked around and saw mountains in every direction. Birds chirped and a gentle breeze stirred the trees and bushes dotting the landscape.

He took it all in, mentally repeating his mantra, assessing the situation. With John back everything felt better. Right somehow. Its perfection made him feel almost superhuman and anxious to discover what form an attack would take. He wanted to go right into the middle of it. Where death would normally lie in the waking world, he thought of as the portal to the bliss of Lorenzo's dream.

The peacefulness of the setting had the opposite effect of putting him on alert. He slid his finger alongside the trigger guard and felt it twitch.

"Listen guys," John said, catching up to the four men ahead of them.

"What the fu…" one of them said.

"We don't have time to explain," John said, "but you're about to get ambushed and we're here to usher you through it." He pointed back at Jordan, Carl, and Wesley.

"Usher us through it?" Another soldier said. "What does that mean? Where did you guys come from?"

A deafening explosion knocked them to the ground, blinding Jordan. His eyes, nose, and throat all burned in the ear ringing aftermath. All he could see through the thick white smoke were snatches of flailing arms and legs, then guttural Arabic sounding cries came from everywhere through the din.

Jordan rolled onto his knees, M4 at the ready. A breeze gusted, clearing away a cloud of smoke and he saw them coming, so he opened fire on an advancing horde of robed mountain tribesmen, dropping the first few he saw.

He screamed when white hot needles of pain shot through his hand, arm, cheek, and legs where bullets pierced him, then a second explosion ripped through his upper torso, causing his world to erupt into a chaotic, disorienting spin that left him staring up at the sky helpless, wishing with all his heart that he were dead.

After excruciating moments of all-encompassing pain, a group of bearded men wearing patterned head coverings circled him like wolves. Their faces were covered like old time bandits, showing nothing but hard, narrowed eyes. The biggest, most sinister looking of them kicked Jordan in the side and jabbed into his entrails with his rifle, all the while glaring at him with cold, dark, eyes that lit up with each thrust.

Jordan felt such great pain everywhere that none of these assaults registered. Only the hate-filled, heartless glare of his tormentor cut through him when the tribesman pressed the barrel of the rifle to Jordan's forehead and held it there for another small eternity.

Jordan imagined him smiling beneath his face covering when he saw the flash of glee glinting in those dark eyes when he pulled the trigger. That hateful image followed him into a tunnel of fluctuating geometric colors and patterns that shot him into the bright light of extreme pleasure that instantly soothed every molecule of his being.

White noise turned into the sound of waves and a dim image of them brightened with rising music and the other sounds of the multilayered lullaby he loved so much. His breathing came lighter and his pain and terror diminished with every crash of the waves.

His heart lightened and his emotions rose, then his whole being vibrated with exquisite feeling that peaked in a crescendo of running water, waves, chants, and exotic music mixed in a divine cosmic symphony.

Wave after wave of blissful ecstasy sent him into exquisite tapestries of thought, feeling, and emotion that had no words, then time and place lost all meaning until the only thing he knew was bliss. He had a transitory flash that he had the strength to override getting stuck here by paying attention, but everything felt so good after so much pain that nothing else mattered except the depths of the timeless moment he presently enjoyed.

CHAPTER SEVENTY NINE

Spurred to action by the non-responsiveness of the dreamers after Lorenzo shut down the sequence, Rita and Cheryl popped smelling salts under the noses of the members of Seal Team 0, shaking them awake and slipping off their dream hoods. When Rita went to Jordan it took a few seconds for his eyes to come into focus after he jerked awake. "Jeez," he said under his breath. "I forgot everything." He looked up into Rita's eyes, awestruck. "And I didn't care."

"Oh my God," Cheryl said. "Come on! Come on!"

Rita glimpsed back and saw Wesley and Carl, sitting up without their hoods looking dazed. Cheryl leaned over John shaking him hard.

"God no!" Cheryl said, looking back over her shoulder holding a limp John. "He's not coming out of it! Jack! Get on the horn! We need an EMT stat!"

Rita's heart jumped into her throat and her stomach clenched. She ran to Cheryl and helped her lay John back, then put her face near his. He breathed slow and deep which eased her alarm a little. She took his wrist, feeling for a pulse and counted off in her head. Normal.

His expressionless face didn't move, except for his eyes, which flitted back and forth beneath his eyelids.

"His pulse and respiration are normal," Rita said. "It's almost like he's sleepwalking, without the walking. Lorenzo, call Stan."

The door to the Dream Lab opened and Jack Scanlon rushed in followed by two stretcher bearing EMTs and a doctor. Jordan, Carl, and Wesley watched with stunned expressions as the doctor took

John's blood pressure, checked his vital signs, and looked into his dancing eyes with a flashlight.

"What do you think?" Rita asked.

The doctor shrugged and slipped the flashlight back into his pocket. "I've never seen anything like it. Other than being nonresponsive, his vitals are rock solid. We need to get him into an ICU. How about the rest of you guys?" The doctor said to Jordan and the others. "Feeling okay?"

"Yeah, we're okay," Jordan said. "A little fuzzy, but we're okay."

"Keep a close eye on them," the doctor said to Rita and Cheryl. "If you see the slightest sign of anything amiss, call us right away."

"Got it," Cheryl said.

The EMTs hoisted John onto the stretcher and carried him out, leaving Rita, Cheryl, Jack and Lorenzo with the rest of the team.

"Let's get out of here," Lorenzo said, taking charge. He looked to the team. "You sure you guys are okay?"

"There's nothing wrong with us," Wesley said, looking from Carl to Jordan. "As a matter of fact, I couldn't feel any better, but I'm scared shit about what happened to John. Is he going to be okay?"

"We don't know anything," Lorenzo said, motioning them forward, "except that he's breathing normally and his vital functions are where they should be. We'll let you know as soon as we know anything of substance. In the mean time let's get you back to your quarters so we can keep an eye on you and you can get your bearings. Once we check in with Doc Krippner and Crowley, I'm sure we'll have a full debriefing."

"We should have listened to Doc Krippner," Jordan said.

Rita, Lorenzo, and Cheryl escorted them back to their quarters. Aside from being shocked from their experience, they seemed to be functioning normally and showed no signs of slipping off, which calmed Rita, but beneath it all she worried about John. Memories of DreamLand and Chazz Daggett's inexplicable coma frittered at the edge of her awareness, bordering on panic, but she pushed them back, forcing herself to focus on the present. Where the fuck was Crowley? The son-of-a-bitch disappeared the moment the shit hit the fan.

As if in answer to her question, Crowley's face popped up on the big screen in the team lounge when they walked in. Before anyone could speak, he said, "I need all the support staff in the main Z-Level conference room right away."

"What about us?" Jordan said.

"I need to talk to the support staff first."

"I'm not leaving them alone," Cheryl said in a shrill voice.

"Don't worry about that," Crowley said, making calming gestures. "I've sent a doctor to keep an eye on them. After we talk to you and they have had a little time to decompress, we'll debrief them."

"Where's Doctor Krippner?" Lorenzo said.

"Here with me. We're waiting for you."

The door to the lounge opened and a white coated doctor with a short military hair cut followed by an attractive red haired nurse came in.

"We'll take over from here," he said. "Don't worry, we'll keep an eye on them."

"Are you going to be okay?" Rita said to Jordan.

He waved her off. "Don't worry about us. John's the one you need to worry about."

Lorenzo and Cheryl headed for the door. Rita followed and glanced back at Jordan as the door closed behind her. His eyes found hers and he nodded, conveying his confidence. Rita wished that she was worthy of it, but she felt hopelessly lost.

"I'm going to kill that bastard," Cheryl muttered, rushing down the corridor ahead of Rita and Lorenzo.

Rita let her rant, hoping she would blow off steam before the meeting. She felt the same fear and anger, but knew it wouldn't help any. They needed to be as clear as possible.

Rita felt the tension in the conference room where they found Crowley waiting, red-faced. A reserved Stan Krippner sat beside him showing no emotion.

"What the hell happened in there?" Crowley said as they hurried into the room, then in an accusing tone, said, "I thought you had safeguards in place."

"You son-of-a-bitch," Cheryl growled, then louder, "You didn't listen to a God-damned thing any of us said. Don't you dare point your finger and pin this screw up of yours on us!" She jabbed a finger at him like an angry, scolding mother, accenting each shrill word with a jab. "You just pushed ahead, even after Doctor Krippner advised against it!"

Stan acknowledged her with a subtle nod.

Cheryl stood and put her hands on her hips. "What do you have to say for yourself?"

Crowley looked at her through narrowed eyes and sighed. "Listen," he said quietly. "I understand your anger, but it's not going to solve anything and to set the record straight." His voice rose, tinged with his own anger. "No matter what decisions I make, good or bad, I don't have to answer to you." He scowled and jabbed a finger at Cheryl, exploding with, "I'm the one in charge here, so shut your ignorant pie hole and sit down!"

The open-mouthed shock on Cheryl's face hit Rita like a gut punch. Before Cheryl could respond, Jack yanked her down into her seat and jumped up from his own in one motion. "You better watch your mouth and show a little respect when you're talking to my partner," he said through clenched teeth. "She's the most dedicated researcher I've ever had the pleasure of working with, you miserable piece of shit, and unlike you, she has integrity!" He shook his fist. "I've had enough of your shit. You keep flapping your jaws and disrespecting her with that big mouth of yours and you're going to be drinking milk shakes through a mouthful of broken teeth."

Now Crowley looked shocked and his face reddened even more, but his voice came low and measured. "Take your best shot."

Jack lunged across the conference room table swinging, just missing Crowley's jaw before Stan caught him by the seat of his pants and dragged him back with the help of Lorenzo who held the thrashing Jack in a bear hug while Stan moved between him and Crowley, who had backed away from the table.

"Chill out," Lorenzo said quietly. "None of this is going to do John any good."

Jack quit struggling at Lorenzo's words.

Stan turned to Crowley making downward calming gestures with both hands, then he turned back to Jack. "Lorenzo's right," he said evenly. "If anyone should be pissed off it's me. My recommendation was ignored and we're seeing the consequences, but what we all need to understand right now is that who's right or wrong has no relevance to this discussion."

He looked at each of them, meeting their eyes, ending with Crowley to drive his point home. The room went quiet.

"I'm okay," Jack muttered.

Lorenzo let him go and he dropped back into his chair. Cheryl put her hand over his and graced him with an adoring look of gratitude that Jack didn't seem to notice while glaring at Crowley.

"I'm asking everyone to put aside your anger and personal biases," Stan continued with the voice of reason. "Even though it may be justified, it serves no purpose and only distracts us from the only thing that has any importance here, the health and safety of John, and after him the rest of the team who I fear may be in more subtle, but equally, if not more threatening danger."

CHAPTER EIGHTY

"We want to go see John," Wesley demanded.

"We have orders to keep you here under observation," the doctor said. "For your own safety." The cute, willowy nurse stood beside him nodding.

"No disrespect intended," Wesley said, "but I don't give a shit about your orders. I don't give a shit about anything but my bro, and he's in trouble, so I'm going to be with him." He rose to his full height and pushed out his chest. "And nobody's going to stop me!"

The doctor looked to Jordan as if asking for help, but Jordan stood and joined Wesley, followed by Carl.

The doctor stepped back. "I'd better check…"

Jordan waved him off. "There's nothing to check. Call Crowley and tell him whatever you want, but we're going to be with John, so you can either take us there…"

"Or were going tear this whole fucking place apart," Carl said, finishing the sentence, "and then we'll find our way there anyway, so lead on or get out of the way."

"That's unnecessary," the doctor said. "Call Mister Crowley," he said to the nurse as he led them out the door. "Tell him that the natives are starting to revolt, so I took them to see their friend."

Jordan glanced at Carl as they exited and he winked. Carl's smirk disappeared when the doctor looked back at them, shaking his head.

He led them through a maze of corridors and elevators to a ward on the other side of the complex where they found John stretched out on a bed in a private room with an IV and wires coming out of him, and a wall of blinking electronics and displays stacked alongside him.

Jordan went to the head of the bed and stood beside him, studying his resting form. Wesley went on the other side and Carl stood by his feet.

The lights are on, but nobody's home, Jordan thought. For the first time since they met, wiry, fast moving, fast talking John looked deathly still. A dreamy smile filled his otherwise expressionless face. Though immobile, his wild mop of curly blond hair seemed to buzz like the live end of a downed power line. His breathing came slow and steady and all of his vital signs looked normal.

Jordan looked up and saw his own concern reflected in the somber expressions of Carl and Wesley.

"Jeez, I thought he'd never shut up," Wesley said, "but leave it to him to do even that in the extreme."

Carl chuckled. "He wouldn't be Striker if he didn't."

Jordan found himself suppressing his own chuckle. "He might have finally shut up for the first time in his life, but I'm wondering if he can hear us. We've all heard stories and seen movies where people in a coma can hear everything going on around them."

Carl nodded. "Sure! He could be listening to everything we're saying. We have no way of knowing."

Wesley bent down close to John's ear and said a little too loud, "Hey fucktard! Wake the fuck up and quit jerking off in there. You got to be the center of attention like you always wanted. Now you can quit fucking off wherever you are and come back to the team. As much of an asshole as you can be sometimes, you're *our* asshole. Our bro who's a part of us, so come on, wake the fuck up. Your team needs you."

"And misses you," Carl added.

John's placid expression showed no reaction and his vital signs remained steady and unruffled. Jordan shrugged. "Though he's not showing it, it doesn't mean he's not hearing it and we can't give up on him. I think we should keep talking to him. It might make a difference. You never know."

Carl cleared his throat. "Listen, Striker," he said in a conspiratorial voice. "If I were you and had to come back to put up with Wesley's ugly ass, I wouldn't want to come back either, but if you're a real man, you'll come back and take your place with us where you belong, instead of throwing me and Jordan in front of the bus to babysit that big, dumb, son-of-a-bitch all by ourselves."

Jordan looked up at Wesley, who smiled at Carl's jibes.

"We can't do it alone," Carl said a little softer. "We need you to help keep him on a leash. We need you on the team. Not only are you one of the best point men a team could ever want, you're a big part of who we are. There's no Seal Team Zero without you."

Wesley nodded to Carl and gave him a thumbs up. Jordan did the same, then Carl and Wesley both looked to him, expectation in their eyes.

"Striker!" Jordan said with an air of authority, "Knowing you, you *are* on point right now somewhere, which we appreciate." Speaking louder he said, "Now we need you to come back with your report. Striker, report for duty! We're in this together, buddy. You, me, Renegade, and Sureshot, and yes, Sureshot is right. You're a big part of who we are and there is no Seal Team Zero without you. I'm asking you." He clasped his hands together and bowed his head. "I'm begging you. Please come back to us. We're your bros. Your family."

Jordan looked up and saw Wesley and Carl with heads bowed. John remained unchanged.

"I don't know what else we can do," he said. "I don't feel comfortable sitting around with my thumb up my ass not doing anything to help John."

"WWSD," Wesley said.

"What the hell does that mean?" Carl asked.

Jordan felt something shift inside him. "What would Striker do?"

Wesley smiled.

"That's a no - brainer," Carl said. "He'd already be storming the fort, charging in full kamikaze, coming to get us."

Jordan felt his own smile. "Exactly."

CHAPTER EIGHTY ONE

Rita sat in silence with the others digesting Stan Krippner's ominous warning about John and the rest of the team.

Crowley's pensive expression flipped to surprise when the door to the conference room opened and Seal Team Zero marched in, led by Jordan.

"We're not ready for you yet," Crowley said, sounding indignant.

Jordan and the others took their seats, ignoring him.

Crowley bristled. "Did you hear what I just..."

"Before we do anything else," Jordan said, talking over him, "we need to go back into that dream *right* now and bring John back."

Crowley waved his hands and shook his head no. "Hold on! I'm the one who gives orders around here, not you."

"You're not the one going into the dreams, *we* are, and if we can do it with all your wounded vets and commit suicide and relive their nightmares, then we can go to the happy crack dream and bring John back!"

Jordan's eyes blazed with conviction and the expressions on Wesley and Carl's faces left no doubt that he spoke for all of them. Rita had never seen him angry like this.

"I couldn't agree with you more," Stan said, taking over the discussion. "I'd feel the same way if I was you, but everything's not as black and white as you see it." He sighed. "Unfortunately, it's more complicated than you realize."

The fire in Jordan's eyes diminished.

"What do you mean more complicated?" Wesley said.

"There's been something else going on that I have disagreed with from the start, but my concerns were ignored."

Jordan, Wesley, and Carl leaned in together, giving Stan their full attention.

"To say it succinctly, Stan continued, "we're dealing with addiction here, specifically, yours."

"Whoa, whoa, wait a minute," Wesley said. "You're saying we're junkies?"

"Though Mister Crowley disliked you calling Lorenzo's healing dream the crack dream, you weren't far off the mark."

"How can we be junkies?" Carl said. "We haven't done any drugs."

Stan gestured to Jack, Cheryl, Lorenzo, and Rita. "Your support team pioneered the methodology to help their colleague Hodge Michaels, a man who lives in dream sleep."

"Just like John is now," Jordan said.

"Perhaps, but that doesn't mean that it has to be a permanent state." He rested his hand on Cheryl's shoulder in a fatherly gesture. "Would you do us the honor of explaining how your process works?"

Cheryl stood "We never intended for this technology to be used by you. Mister Crowley pushed us to add some of its features to your programming. We were against it and warned him of its addictive possibilities, but like Stan's warnings, I was overridden." She turned her nose up at Crowley. "It's a method that releases neurochemicals to the brain's pleasure centers. We did it to relieve Hodge's suffering. For you, Crowley twisted it into a reward system of sounds, tones, and targeted subliminal messages designed to motivate you to play more. Unfortunately it became his idea of rest and recuperation for you." She looked down and shook her head. "It's one thing if you're in untreatable chronic pain. In that case opiates like Morphine or Oxycodone are secondary to the urgency for pain relief, but none of us on the development team, including Stan, approved of this approach with you. We all said that rewarding war games was wrong." She sat down. "You can thank Mister Crowley for that."

"All we wanted was to give your neurological reward system a little tweak similar to what people get from eating chocolate," Crowley said.

"You know," Jack said. "Like the cheese the rat gets at the end of the maze."

"No," Lorenzo said. "More like the cocaine it gets for picking the right dish after they flash the light."

"Enough," Crowley said.

"So we're hooked on the crack dream?" Wesley said.

"And the battle dreams act like the flashing light to set us up for the reward at the end of it," Jordan said.

"It's a friggin' yo-yo," Carl added. "That shit hurts in the dreams." He hit himself in the chest. "And you feel it, but when you get to the happy place at the end you don't care any more because the pain goes away like magic."

Wesley added. "And without the happy meal at the end we take on the nightmares from those poor guys."

"Needless to say, no one's going into any more dreams, John or not," Stan said, "which poses a new challenge. I'm reasonably sure that the longer you stay away from the dreams, the greater your desire will be to go back into them. Traumas are buried in non-verbal memories stored in different parts of the brain than chronological memories. They can be hazy images, smells, body aches, nightmares, or urges to do things that harm you, like your suicide dreams. They can also be situations, colors, or sounds that trigger emotional responses that are out of proportion with the situation."

Jordan sighed. "We've seen lots of that."

Stan nodded affirmatively. "PTSD is a vicious cycle of this. During trauma," he continued, looking directly at Rita and Cheryl, "your nervous system goes into hyper-drive, releasing stress hormones like cortisol that prepare you for action. If you can't run or fight, you head for other defenses like freezing in place so you might not be seen, or playing dead. Later, when you re-experience any of these images, smells or thoughts, your nervous system thinks its back in the original trauma, so it fires off cortisol again, putting you back into hyper-drive. That's PTSD and it's tied in to the pleasure pain pathways of your brains."

"Talk about burning the candle at both ends," Wesley muttered.

"More like a time bomb," Carl said, dropping his head.

"What if I said, thanks for telling me how you made us junkies?" Wesley said. "And that I want to beat the ticking junkie clock before I'm jonesing too much for a fix." He held his hand out to Jordan and Carl. "We need to go back in as a team right now *before* the craving gets out of control, and get John out of there, wherever *there* is. As a team."

Crowley leaned forward, "Maybe…"

Stan crossed his arms. "Out of the question and not up for discussion."

Jordan, Wesley, and Carl looked down and their shoulders slumped.

"But we may have other options," Stan said.

They all looked up, expectant and Cheryl, Jack, and Lorenzo sat up straight.

"I'm thinking outside the box here," he said absently, then held up a finger. "Then again maybe not!"

"Go ahead," Rita said, feeling her emotions rising.

"What our dream team has been doing going into the traumas of these veterans is what is called soul retrieval in shamanism." He nodded toward the boys. "Although their methods are a little crazy, even suicidal, our dream team has learned how to change the perception of traumatized vets, in essence freeing them." Stan's eyes sparkled. "That's the key. Trauma isn't defined by the experience itself, but on how you perceive it. That's the healing mechanism you guys have been using."

Crowley frowned. "I'm not sure I follow."

Stan's eyebrows rose. "Don't you?" He looked around at everyone, expecting a response. When no one did he said, "Perception is everything."

"Meaning?" Crowley said, still looking puzzled.

"That I might have a solution to our dilemma, but I need to do some research first."

CHAPTER EIGHTY TWO

Jordan, Wesley, and Carl visited John every day for the next week, spending time talking to him as if he were fully present. Each of them took up regular spots around him, Jordan at the head of the bed and Wesley across from him with Carl by his feet. Nothing changed in John's appearance, except that his wild mop of curly blond hair seemed to lose its luster and his expression looked more flaccid, as if some part of him had unmoored and was drifting out to sea.

Today his breathing continued, slow, steady, and shallow, and his vital signs weakened with each passing day. He remained deathly still and looked to be at peace with a dreamy smile.

Jordan missed his fast moving, fast talking presence and saw his own discomfort in the wild and confused expressions of his teammates. Wesley fidgeted, his eyes darting back and forth like he was cornered, and Carl rocked back and forth like an autistic kid about to literally jump out of his skin. Jordan couldn't look at either of them for very long as their barely contained energy stirred up his own frenzy, so he focused on John's serene expression, hoping to find some peace there.

Since their last expedition that held John and very nearly kept all of them, they grew more distraught with each passing day. No one spoke of it, but their nightmares crept back in, stronger with each passing night, bringing insomnia and long periods of zoning out in what Jordan imagined Doc Krippner would call waking catatonia or something like that.

"I'm sick of this shit!" Wesley yelled, punching the wall.

Jordan looked up from his reverie. Wesley's eyes bugged out. Jordan trembled inside and barely contained his own urge to lash out. A heavy set, dark-haired nurse rushed in, but Carl shooed her off, saying, "This has nothing to do with you, so get out of here and mind your own business or we will give you something to worry about."

She looked as if she had been slapped. "I understand your frustration," she sputtered, "but you can at least show some respect for..."

"Are you deaf?" Carl growled. "What part of fuck off do you not understand?"

She looked from Carl to Wesley and then to Jordan who gestured with his head for her to leave. She backed out and disappeared without another word.

"We're all getting a little psycho here," Jordan said. "We need to reign it in."

Wesley jabbed his finger at John. "Look at him! He's turning into a fucking turnip and we're standing here with our thumbs up our asses like a bunch of pussies." He looked from Jordan to Carl, eyes blazing. "You can bet your sweet asses that if it was one of us stuck there, Striker wouldn't hesitate to come in after us in full on kamikaze mode."

Carl added a nod to his rocking. "I don't give a shit," he muttered, then he stopped mid-rock, clenching his fists, shaking. His mouth opened and closed.

Jordan's heart raced, fearing that Carl was having a seizure until tears streamed down his cheeks and his words came in an emotional torrent.

"I can't live in hell being tortured like this any more. I'm ready to kill myself. This is the most fucked up thing I've ever been through. I can't tell you how badly I want to go into the crack dream and I don't care if I ever come back. Anything's better than this shit!" He waved his arms around, "And the fucking nightmares and lost sleep, and all the other kookiness gets worse every day and nobody's doing shit about it. And there's poor fucking John. I want to go in and get him more than I want to go there and get rid of this craziness. It's like throwing gas on a fire." He put his hands on his head and pulled his hair. "It's tearing me apart."

"We're moths to the flame," Wesley said under his breath. His eyes had a haunted, faraway look.

"Easy Carl," Jordan said. "Wesley and I feel the same way. We're in this together." He nodded to John and looked up, meeting Wesley's eyes. "One of us goes in we all go in."

"And if we don't come back?" Wesley said.

"Then we don't come back," Jordan said, surprised at the ease with which the words came out.

Carl pushed his chest out. "I say we demand that they send us on a rescue mission to bring John back."

Wesley leaned against the wall and crossed his arms. "What if they tell us to fuck off? You know they will."

"Then we make a show of force," Carl said, making a fist.

"They'll just lock us up," Wesley said. "We don't have the firepower or anything else to get them to send us."

"Oh yes we do," Jordan said.

"What?" Wesley said.

"Ourselves."

Carl shook his head. "I don't get it."

"I say we go in and demand to be put into that dream to rescue Striker, and if they say no, we go on a hunger strike."

"A hunger strike?" Carl said. "Really?"

"You said it yourself," Jordan answered. "Anything's better than this shit!"

Wesley held out his hands. "So what are we waiting for?"

Carl let out a high-pitched cackle and pointed at Jordan. "Nothing!"

CHAPTER EIGHTY THREE

Rita and Cheryl hovered over Hodge examining him in the ICU. His brow furrowed, his expressions changed and he moaned and mumbled while his eyes darted beneath closed eyelids.

Everything appeared normal until his eyes opened, startling her. Her knees buckled and she nearly blacked out as his imploring gaze pierced her and his mouth opened. When she leaned in he reached out, grabbing her wrist, sending her hurtling through darkness, plunging into frigid water and she relived it all again, the whirlpool, the drowning, the rats, and then the roiling water sucked her under into blackness, dropping her back into the ICU where Hodge still grasped her wrist.

The song from the children's chorus tinkled through her mind like wind chimes.

"The witches are waiting for you,

The witches are waiting for you,

They'll nibble your spirit and snack on your soul,

And swallow you up out of view."

"Listen," Hodge whispered. "Morpheus knows all about Pandora. He plans to *rape* her and make her his slave."

The way Hodge emphasized the word rape made Rita black out. She came to looking into the pale blue eyes of Chazz Daggett glaring at her from under lowered brows. He grabbed her by the throat, pulling her face close to his. "Know something, Rita-the-*Señorita*?" He licked his lips and wiggled his tongue. "Your ass is as pretty as your eyes, and now you're mine." He pressed his mouth to hers and jammed his rancid tongue between her lips while pulling his pants down. A stiletto glinted in his hand and in a few swift strokes her clothes lay in shreds, then he slammed her up against the coffin, forcing her legs open, brutally thrusting his hips forward, violating her in a blaze of pain until a hand caught her.

"You're okay," Lorenzo said softly. "You're safe here with me."

Her scream came as a whisper, then her breath came sharp, followed by wracking sobs.

"It's okay, babe." Lorenzo cradled her to his chest and rocked her. "I'm here. You're safe with me."

She pressed her head close and forced her own shaky breaths to match his.

After awhile, he said, "Chazz again?"

She nodded. "Worse than ever. I think there's more to it than a simple nightmare. Ever since John went to la la land, everything's gone into a dark, negative spiral."

"I think seeing him like that stirred up memories of Chazz for you. I know they have for me."

"I feel so helpless. Like a victim, and I hate it."

"You're no victim. I'm the one who feels like a victim because I have to watch you suffer and I can't do anything to help." He held her closer. "I'll go anywhere in the dark with you and for you, and if I could take those nightmares from you I'd do it in a heartbeat."

"I know that, honey." She kissed his chest.

"One thing's for sure," he said, stroking her hair. "Things are starting to break loose around here. Crowley's disappeared since John went under. It's time for us to have a heart to heart with Stan."

Later that morning, Lorenzo guided Rita into Stan Krippner's office where they found Cheryl sitting with him. She looked pale and her hair was in disarray, like she had just rolled out of bed. Her glasses looked a little cockeyed and the expression on her face looked guilty.

"Sorry to interrupt," Lorenzo said. "I didn't know you were here Cheryl. We can come back later."

Cheryl looked to Stan, who nodded.

"It's all right," Stan said. "I think you need to hear this too. Please, come in and have a seat."

"Hear what?" Rita said as they sat.

Cheryl took a deep breath and let out a long sigh. "I just awoke from the worst nightmare I've ever had. It was almost too real." She shook her head and looked Rita in the eye. "Rita and I were working on Hodge when his eyes opened and he grabbed my wrist. The next thing I knew we were spinning in a hellish whirlpool of rats and that inane nursery rhyme about the witches was playing in the background, then Hodge said the most puzzling thing."

"Morpheus knows all about Pandora and he plans to rape her and make her his slave," Rita said.

Cheryl's face went white and her mouth and eyes opened wide. She put her face in her hands and her shoulders shook as she cried, whispering in a quivering voice, "That's when Chazz raped me."

The room went quiet until a knock on the door broke the silence.

CHAPTER EIGHTY FOUR

Jordan stuck his head in the door and saw Rita, Lorenzo, and Cheryl sitting around Doc Krippner's desk. Cheryl was hunched over and looked like she had been crying.

"Sorry," Jordan said. "I didn't mean to interrupt you. I didn't realize you'd all be here, but I'm glad you are. Me and the guys need to talk with you. Right away."

Stan looked to Rita, Lorenzo, and Cheryl who all nodded. Cheryl dabbed at her eyes with a tissue. Rita looked a little out of it too. Shell shocked, Jordan thought.

"It's too crowded in here," Stan said. "Let's go find a conference room."

They found one a few doors down from his office.

"Where's Jack?" Wesley said, pointing to an empty chair.

"He'll be along in a minute," Cheryl said.

"What about Crowley?" Wesley continued. "Where the hell did he disappear to? He's our best ass kissing buddy when everything looks good, but as soon as the shit hits the fan, he's outta here like a hooker from a vice raid." He jerked his thumb over his shoulder. "John's wasting away and we're all going nuts. Why hasn't anything been done?" His voice went up in volume. "Where the fuck is Crowley?"

Jack Scanlon came in and pulled up a chair. "I hope you didn't start the party without me." He winked at Wesley, who smirked in spite of himself.

"When it became clear that John had drifted into a coma," Stan said. "Crowley was called to Washington. I haven't heard anything from him since. He did leave instructions to do anything possible to resolve the issue."

Carl's eyes lit up. "So you're in charge?"

"In a manner of speaking. I have some latitude."

"We've come to a decision." Carl angled his head toward Wesley and Jordan and his words gushed out. "I don't have to tell you how crazy it makes us to see John wasting away while nobody does anything." He took a deep breath and continued. "And I can't tell you how badly we want to go into the crack dream. We don't care if we never come back. We're sick of the nightmares and lost sleep and it gets worse every day. We want to go in and get John back more than we want to get lost in the crack dream and hopefully when we do that we can get rid of this craziness." He circled his finger beside his head.

"And if we don't come back, then we don't come back," Wesley said.

"I don't think that's the right solution," Stan said. "It could make things worse."

"Sorry for the disrespect," Wesley said, "but if you don't send us in, we're going on a hunger strike."

Jordan nodded with Carl.

Stan shook his head and a wry smile creased his lips. "I admire your commitment gentlemen, but I think I have a better solution." He glanced over at Rita and Cheryl. "Especially in light of recent events."

"Striker getting stuck?" Carl asked tentatively.

"Of course that," Stan said, "but on top of that, Rita and Cheryl have been battling nightmares of their own all along and they've gotten worse since John went under. Now they've had the same nightmare."

"No shit!" Wesley said under his breath.

Stan shook his head. "It's what I call cosmic irony. We're supposed to be curing PTSD, but both the researchers and the test subjects have it for seemingly different reasons and both are connected to computer generated dreams." He gestured to Jordan's side of the table. "You can add addiction to those symptoms evidenced by our enthusiastic friends here which adds another layer to this techno-psychological nightmare we've created. If things weren't so grim I'd find them amusing."

He held out his left hand to Rita's side of the table. "On the one hand we have the original creators, who are terrified of Pandora and refuse to go into any of its dreaming scenarios in spite of the fact that their symptoms have intensified." He held out his right hand. "On the other hand we have Seal Team Zero who want nothing more than to go into those dreams at the risk of never coming back, even willing to die if they have to."

"Damned if we do and damned if we don't," Jack said.

Lorenzo frowned and rubbed his temples. "We have opposite reactions and different dynamics, but we're facing the same root cause."

"Back to the root!" Stan made his point with his finger. "I think the solution may be further back, outside the box that technology has put us in. Back to the primordial roots of our psyche."

"How the hell are we going to do that?" Wesley asked.

"By going back to the real root - more accurately by going back to the vine."

Rita and Cheryl flinched together.

"Ayahuasca?" Rita said wide-eyed.

Wesley leaned forward. "What?"

"Ay - yah - wha - sca," Stan said, slowly sounding it out. "A mixture of two plants. The Ayahuasca vine used in the brew that carries its name is classified as Banisteriopsis Caapi, also known as The Vine of Death, The Vine of the Soul, Caapi, Yajé, and other names. Though it contains trace amounts of Dimethyltryptamine, more commonly known as DMT, the Ayahuasca vine is not the primary psychoactive component. Another plant the natives call Chacruna, classified as Psychotria Viridis, contains the DMT. Taken orally by itself, the stomach's monoamine oxidase enzymes digest the DMT before it can cross the blood brain barrier. Adding Ayahuasca to the Chacruna leaves provides an MAO inhibitor that makes the DMT orally active, producing profound and startling experiences." Stan's eyes widened.

Jack Scanlon's did too.

"Anthropologists, psychiatrists, and other metal health professionals have been drawn to it for numerous reasons, among them a reputation for providing telepathic powers. A psychoactive alkaloid in it was named telepathine, which is now known to be the alkaloid harmine. Amazonian shamans call Ayahuasca the Mother of all the plants."

"Tell them how it makes you sick," Cheryl said.

"In the Amazon it's referred to as *la purga*, the purge. It's credited with purging toxins and sickness on physical, psychological, and spiritual levels. Many experts think it is well worth a few hours of discomfort to alleviate deep seated traumas like your own. Many an addict and alcoholic have been cured by it. One life long alcoholic we worked with stopped drinking after one session."

"That sounds pretty intense," Wesley said.

"Like the nightmares everyone is having," Stan said. "The way I see it, we're facing a man-made techno-psychological rat's nest of nightmares. Technology has its benefits, but in the end it is consumptive and unnatural while Ayahuasca is Mother Nature herself, a natural, nurturing, but often harsh healer."

"I don't know." Carl shrugged. "I saw it on some TV shows and it looked like everyone who drank it had a good time at a hippie drug party with dancing girls, gurus, and music."

Stan scowled and his voice took on an edge. "That's pure Hollywood bullshit, and it couldn't be any further from the truth!"

"I'm ready for the E-Ticket," Jack said. "I'll take Ma Nature over technology any day!" He wiggled his eyebrows. "Will I see colors?"

"You and Lorenzo would be welcome to participate. In fact I think it would be a good thing, but it's the rest of you," he said pointing, "that I would urge to give this ancient medicine a try. At this point I don't see any other options. It can be a physically uncomfortable experience, but it's safe as long as you follow the guidelines. We're in an extreme situation here. No matter what your fear or trepidation, the only way to overcome PTSD is to face that fear and that is what Ayahuasca can do. A night of puking and shitting is a small price to pay for healing."

Jordan looked at Wesley and Carl, who both seemed hypnotized by what Stan said. "I'm in!" He said, raising his hand.

"Ditto on that," Wesley said.

Carl nodded and Jack Scanlon raised his hand, smiling. He didn't seem to have any fear at all.

"I'm in if Rita's in," Lorenzo said, putting his arm around her.

Rita nodded and all eyes went to Cheryl, who was looking down. When she raised her head and saw everyone looking at her, she gave a tiny nod.

"All for one and one for all." Jack raised his fist.

"We're in it together," Carl said, "but what about you, doc? Don't you feel a little left out?"

"Why should I feel left out?"

Wesley looked surprised. "You're going to drink it too?"

"I wouldn't have it any other way," Stan said. "In fact I insist on it.

I would never ask anyone to do something that I wouldn't do myself"

Jack leaned forward, eyebrows raised. "How soon?"

"Because of the way the MAO inhibitor interacts with serotonin levels, we need to do a special diet for about a week to make ourselves more or less chemically pure, which involves staying away from pork, lard, oily foods, salt, pepper, chilies, dairy products, pickled, fermented foods, alcohol, sugar, desserts, pastries, yeast products, citrus and acid foods, fermented foods like soy, tofu, miso, coffee, tea, stimulants, cold or iced drinks, and especially tranquilizers, anti-depressants, and drugs of any kind."

"That's a lot of shit to remember," Wesley said.

"I'll supervise our diets," Stan said. "The most important and dangerous thing to pay attention to are the drugs, especially anti-depressants."

Jordan looked at the others with a cold sense of dread in the pit of his stomach, not at the prospect of drinking Ayahuasca, but at the prospect of having to wait so long to do it. He didn't know if he could last that long without going totally bonkers.

CHAPTER EIGHTY FIVE

Stan Krippner took everyone on a Mini Bus under the cover of darkness to somewhere in the mountains a couple of hours away. Rita had no idea of where they were, only that they were in the mountains from the upward, twisting, turning road, and the sea of twinkling lights from some small town off in the distance. Everyone had been instructed to pack for a couple of days and to bring loose fitting clothing. Rita felt an odd sense of security when she saw the rattles, shaman's drum, and colorful embroidery from the wall of Stan's office with the gear until she saw a stack of red, two gallon plastic paint buckets. Her stomach did flip-flopped thinking about what they were for.

Eventually they turned down a long paved driveway that snaked between tall trees that ended in a circular driveway in front of a large two story Spanish style adobe house in the middle of a clearing. The air felt cool and refreshing when they stepped out of the Mini Bus. Rita looked up at the clear, star speckled sky. The pale light of the new moon made the mass of starlight all the more spectacular.

"Fucking beautiful, ain't it," Jack said, sounding reverent.

Inside, Stan led them upstairs where he assigned everyone their own bedrooms, giving Rita and Lorenzo the spacious master bedroom. "Get settled in," he said, "then meet me downstairs in the kitchen. We'll have a little snack and I'll give you the lay of the land and a rundown of the program."

Ten minutes later everyone sat around a large round wooden table off the kitchen where Stan had put out a tureen of soup and a bowl of salad, all made from ingredients that were part of the diet. During the ride there the members of Seal Team Zero had been quiet and withdrawn. Now they fidgeted and nibbled at the food. They all looked pale and distracted and their eyes darted back and forth like cats watching a ping pong game.

Stan drained the last of his soup from a cup and set it down, saying, "José our shaman will get in from Peru tomorrow and we'll have our ceremony tomorrow night."

"Where's it gonna be?" Jack said.

"There's a big yurt out back built on a platform that has everything we need. The kitchen is stocked with food, so help yourselves, but don't eat anything after three tomorrow. I'd like everyone to spend time in nature and decompress before tomorrow night. There are plenty of trails and wooded areas to explore. While you're on your nature walk try to be as conscious as possible of everything in nature as you can. Do your best to acknowledge individual trees, plants, and animals, even bushes and blades of grass if you can pay attention that long, and honor them for the intelligence that they represent." He held up a finger emphasizing his last words. "Pay close attention for any signs from any animals you might come across."

Stan pointed at Jordan, Wesley, and Carl, who all looked at each other with baffled expressions. "Especially you guys! I know how tough it's been. We're almost to the finish line. You three should take an extra long hike to burn off some of that nervous energy. Believe it or not, it'll help."

"What time should we show up at the yurt tomorrow night?" Jordan asked.

"Six o'clock," Stan said. "We'll do a little check in and meet Don José then."

"And what time will it end?" Scanlon said.

"In the wee hours of the morning, most likely a few hours before sunrise."

"All righty, then!" Jack slapped the table with his hands. "That's all I need to hear. If you're done with me for now, I'm ready to toddle off to bed and get some shut eye." He looked around at the others and pushed back from the table. Everyone else followed his lead.

The following morning, after an Ayahuasca compatible breakfast, Stan went to pick up Don José at the airport while Jordan, Carl, and

Wesley went off hiking together. Jack and Cheryl went their own ways and Rita and Lorenzo sauntered down a trail toward the back of the property holding hands, staying close.

The winding trail took them up and down through small hills covered with oak, conifers, manzanita, and other bushes until they came to a pond in a small clearing where a gentle breeze whispered through the reeds.

"Nothing stays with me for long with this diet," Lorenzo said when they stood at the pond's edge. He gave her hand a gentle squeeze. "If you'll excuse me, I'm going to go water a tree. I'll be right back."

Alone by the pond, Rita took everything in, following Stan's suggestion of acknowledging nature. Birds chirped, insects hummed, and dragonflies skimmed across the water. She spent a few moments, singling out and acknowledging each sound, and glanced around at each tree and bush, silently saying Hello, and even thanking the breeze.

A low frequency buzz shot in from behind her, startling her until she recognized it as a hummingbird, right behind her head. She remained rock still and it darted to the side of her head, so close that either the wind from its wings or its wingtips tickled her ear before it darted once more, hovering directly in front of her, its beak practically touching the spot between her eyes. She barely breathed for fear of breaking the magic.

She felt strangely honored and touched by its attention and her heart swelled in gratitude, silently honoring it and giving thanks. The hummingbird stayed for what seemed an unnaturally long time as if acknowledging her thanks, then as quickly as it appeared it darted off. Stopping a few feet in front of her, it looked back, shifting its position, showing off the beautiful radiance of its iridescence as if insuring that she got its message which felt like expansive emotion more than anything she could articulate, then it shot off across the pond, disappearing into the woods.

"Holy shit," Lorenzo said in a low voice.

"You saw that?" Rita said, turning to see him a few yards away.

"That was amazing!" He said. "I've never seen anything like that. I saw it go to you, so I stopped so I wouldn't scare it off."

"Thank you," she said, taking his hand when he came closer.

"Wait until Doc Krippner hears about this." He pulled her close and hugged her.

"Let's wait before we tell him," she said softly. "I want to keep it personal and treasure if for awhile."

"Fair enough," he said. "I can understand why." He hugged her a little tighter. "I won't say a word to anyone, but I have to admit, I'm jealous."

Rita drew back, looked into his eyes, and he gave her a lopsided grin. She hugged him tight again, pressing her head to his chest, then she pulled him along, continuing their walk.

They spent the rest of their hike mostly in silence as if preserving the spell the hummingbird left them with. Its uncanniness left Rita feeling like part of her lived in another world.

They met the others later in the afternoon for a last meal at the round table by the kitchen. Most of them ate quietly except for Jack Scanlon, who jabbered like a little kid going to Disneyland. His bushy eyebrows bounced up and down as he spoke. "I've heard about this shit. If it's anything close to the acid we used to get in the late sixties and early seventies, you guys are in for the time of your life!"

"Aren't you worried about shitting and puking?" Carl said.

Jack gave him a dismissive wave. "Those are just bodily functions. I did a lot worse to myself back in my drinking days. Besides, more often than not you feel better after puking, so I say bring it!"

Carl shook his head and looked to Wesley and Jordan, who both shrugged. "What about the dark scary stuff that might come up?"

Jack smiled his best and biggest Cheshire cat grin. "Didn't you ever go into haunted houses or scare the shit out of yourself as a kid on roller coasters? You worry warts are too scared about the wrong stuff. If what I've read is right, we're all about to get to go on one of the best E-Ticket rides that life has to offer." His eyebrows shot up again. "I can't wait!"

"Aren't you in the least bit scared?" Cheryl said.

Jack drained the soup from his cup. "I admit, I have a little trepidation, but I have way more fascination." He stood. "As a matter of fact, I'm going to get into my sweats, powder my nose, and get ready for the shindig."

"What about you guys?" Lorenzo said, nodding to Jordan, Carl, and Wesley after Jack left.

"I'm the opposite of Happy Jack," Jordan said with a little grin. "I have a little fascination and a lot of trepidation, but after some of the crazy shit we've been through I'm ready for anything, including suicide. Anything to get out of my head. I'm really going bugfuck." He pointed to his head and then at Wesley and Carl. "We all are!"

"What about you guys?" Wesley said.

Cheryl hugged herself. "Terrified."

"I don't know," Lorenzo said. "I'm somewhere between you and Jack on the fascination, trepidation scale. Maybe a hair closer to Jack."

"I'm leaning more on the trepidation side with you guys," Rita said, "although I have to say that I am optimistic." She sought out Jordan's eyes saying, "I have a lot of faith in Doc Krippner. There's a lot more to him than we realize."

Jordan nodded. "And I have a feeling we're about to see more of that tonight."

CHAPTER EIGHTY SIX

Jordan sat in a circle inside the yurt with the others in subdued candle light. Beautifully colored tapestries and large multicolored embroideries with intricate mandala-like geometric patterns covered the inside walls. The painting on each beam holding up the roof was a unique work of art in itself. Deer antlers, rattles, painted drums, and other shamanic artifacts hung strategically throughout.

Stan sat at the head of the circle in a low slung folding lawn chair dressed all in white with elaborate red, blue, and green embroidery on the front of his pull over shirt. An altar was laid out in front of Don José's central spot to his left consisting of a heavy colorful woven textile the size of a welcome mat. Neatly arranged on top of it were the largest black feathers Jordan had ever seen, rattles, quartz, and other minerals and crystals, a Tibetan singing bowl, chimes, a couple of cards with saints on them and other religious artifacts. Around it sat colored bottles of what looked like essential oils and a taller bottle of yellow water with a long gold foil covered neck and a colorful flower covered label that said *Agua De Florida*.

Lying beside the altar was a bundled palm leaf rattle Stan called a *chacapa* and in front of it sat the most formidable object of all, a liter sized bottle of what looked like crankcase oil. The sight of it made Jordan's stomach clench. Beside it sat an elegant silver and inlaid gold metal shot glass.

Jack Scanlon sat beside Don José's spot supported by an angled wooden back rest that held him upright. A sleeping bag covered his stretched out legs. Circling clockwise from there on other back rests sat Cheryl, Rita, Lorenzo, Wesley, and Carl, some with their legs stretched out and others sitting cross-legged. Jordan felt doubly blessed to be sitting next to Stan and across from Rita. Everyone had a red bucket in front of them and paper towels.

Stan sat up straight and cleared his throat. "Don José will be with us shortly. In the mean time I want to review a few things and answer any last questions you might have."

"What's it going to feel like at first?" Wesley said. "What can we expect?"

"Ayahuasca is unpredictable," Stan answered, "which is one of the things I like about it. I don't know if there are any statistics, but it has no effect for something like one in every one hundred people, so that's one possibility."

Jack leaned forward. "So I might not see any colors?"

Stan grinned. "That's possible, but somehow I think that out of everyone here, you're not going to have any problem with that."

Jack's eyebrows raised, opening his biggest self-satisfied grin yet. He crossed his arms and leaned back.

"What about vomiting and shitting?" Cheryl said in a hushed voice.

"Don't be overly concerned with that," Stan said, waving his hands. "Just go with it if it happens. Believe it or not, it can be a very rewarding experience. That's what your bucket is there for. You may not vomit at all, but no matter how it affects you, hold it down as long as you can, and if you have it coming out the back end, as no doubt some of you will, we have someone stationed outside to assist you. Your equilibrium can be seriously impaired and walking can be challenging if not impossible, so only go out for that if you have to, otherwise don't break the circle. Don't suddenly decide to take a nature walk or admire the moon and stars. Don José will make this a protected circle. It's important to keep its integrity and the energy of this time honored tradition contained in this safe and sacred space where you can be vulnerable with no danger from the outside world."

"What if we get caught in a nightmare?" Rita asked.

Stan held his hand close to his stomach and raised it slowly. "Breathe deep through any rough spots. No matter what you think, your experience is temporary. If you find yourself particularly challenged, call for help and either Don José or I will come to you. In the end, it's all about the energy and finding a balance with it, no matter how precarious and mercurial it may seem. Don't fight it. That will only send you deeper into the darkness. Though it can be a hellish experience, it is ultimately beneficial. Ayahuasca has the special quality of seeking out and amplifying your deepest fears."

Jordan shuddered.

"Open yourself and surrender to it," Stan continued, "but not totally. It's more like a give and take. A dance."

"The good, the bad, and the ugly," Jack said.

"Depending on the individual." Stan held his hands out and alternately raised and lowered them pantomiming a scale. "I think of it as dancing between the agony and the ecstasy, the goal being to keep your balance neutral, regardless of what you might be going through."

Everyone stayed quiet until Lorenzo spoke up. "I'm not sure how to put this, because I have no doubt that we all have our own versions of the heebie-jeebies." He nodded toward Jack, eliciting nervous giggles from the others. "Including our cosmic storm trooper over there, but can you describe the best mindset to have?"

"Think of it as asking questions," Stan said. "Another way of putting it is to set your intention for what you hope to discover, but be prepared for an entirely different answer in ways you may have never suspected. You might even get answers to questions you didn't realize you had. It's one of the wonderful mysteries that *La Madre* can reveal."

The group fell quiet again, taking in what Stan said. When no more questions came, he stood and lit a sweet, exotic smelling piece of wood until it glowed orange. "This is *Palo Santo* from the Amazon," he said, "which means holy wood." The flame went out and fragrant black smoke curled from its end. He went around the circle fanning smoke over everyone one at a time with a large black feather.

Don José, a short, husky, dark-haired, brown skinned man wearing a white robe with intricate patterns similar to Stan's and a pillbox style hat came in and bowed to the group. "*Buenas Noches y bendiciones,*" he said.

Stan returned his greeting and stood. "Allow me to introduce my *buen amigo y hermano de la selva*, Don José. He speaks very little English, but he's a top notch *Ayahuasquero*. He may not be a master of English, but he is a master of the human heart and spirit."

"*Mucho Gusto,*" Jack Scanlon said.

Don José smiled and nodded.

"*Encantada,*" Rita added.

He bowed low to her and came up with a crooked smile and a mischievous twinkle in his eye.

"*Encantado tambien*," Lorenzo said.

Don José's smile broadened. He chuckled and saluted Lorenzo, then gave a nod toward Rita and gave Lorenzo a thumbs up, which made everyone laugh.

Stepping over to his spot beside Stan, he looked to Cheryl, then the rest of the non-Spanish speaking members of the group, connecting with each one in turn by making eye contact, ending with Jordan who he looked at, or better looked *into* for a little longer than the rest.

Jordan gazed back into his dark brown eyes seeing infinite depth, but behind all that he saw and felt childlike glee. Don José gave him another crooked smile and a pat on the shoulder that made Jordan feel special, like they shared some conspiratorial secret.

"Don José is going to open the ceremony with a prayer for help, protection, and a blessing," Stan said after he settled in.

Don José picked up the bottle of Florida water, took off the cap and put the bottle to his lips, whistling a strange tune into its top, then he sipped from it and held his hand out, palm up, blowing out a floral scented spray in each of the four directions followed by a prayer in a low, impassioned voice.

"*Ayahuasca, Ayahuasca, mamacuna shamacuna kyariri.*
Ayahuasca, Ayahuasca, mumacuna shamacuna kyariri
Cura cura cuerpecito, limpia limpia espiritu."

His voice shifted higher, taking on a slight pleading tone.

"*Chacrunita, Chacrunita, Chacrunita, curandera,*
Pintar Pintar las visiones con las colores de la tierra."

With this he blew out a breathy *whew* sound, then he sat and picked up the bottle of Ayahuasca, tilting it back and forth shaking it. He cracked the cap, holding the bottle close to his lips like he had with the Florida water and whispered, blew, and whistled a similar strange tune into it. With Stan's help he filled the silver and gold shot glass, blew and prayed over that, and nodded to Jack Scanlon, who crawled from his spot and kneeled before Don José, taking the proffered glass.

Holding it up, he said, "Salud!" He downed it, holding the cup straight upright and tapping it a few times before setting it down. When he crawled back to his seat, Stan picked up the glass and wiped the dark brown, viscous Ayahuasca from it.

Jordan caught his first whiff of it and wrinkled his nose, thinking that it smelled like vomit itself. At first he had felt special and lucky to be sitting next to Stan, but Don José was working his way clockwise around the circle, which meant that Jordan had to watch Cheryl, Rita, Lorenzo, Wesley, and Carl drink before he did, which increased his trepidation.

Cheryl gagged twice trying to get it down and gagged a few more times getting back to her seat. Rita grimaced, pinching her face in revulsion and gagging once. Lorenzo drank his stoically, making only a slight grimace. Carl and Wesley both looked Jordan in the eye and nodded before gagging and belching their doses down and shaking their heads after they drank. By the time Jordan's turn came, he felt chilled and his palms were slick with sweat.

He crawled over and kneeled in front of Don José, who poured the shot glass full, sang and blew over it and handed it to him, looking him in the eye, nodding encouragement. Jordan caught a whiff of it and stifled a gag, then took a deep breath and looked to Stan who winked.

Thicker than a milk shake, he tipped it fully upright, letting the bitter sludge pour down his throat, gagging when he felt a few chunks. It caught in his throat as if his body refused to accept it and he had a moment of panic where he thought he might puke it up. It remained stuck for a long moment, permeating his taste buds until he forced it down.

The vile, crankcase oil tasting concoction hit his stomach like a bitter rock and sat there burning. He went back to his spot and sipped water to wash the nasty taste from his mouth, but it persisted the same way he imagined used motor oil would. Looking over, he glimpsed Don José and Stan taking their doses, but it made him want to puke, so he closed his eyes and sat as still as possible, feeling the burn penetrating his stomach along with a rising sense of nausea. Keeping his eyes closed seemed to contain it some.

After a few uncomfortable minutes he opened his eyes and saw that they had extinguished the candle, putting the yurt in semi-darkness. He glimpsed the shadowy forms of the others and closed his eyes again to wait. After a period of near silence, Don José sang softly, sometimes whistling, sometimes whispering. With each passing moment Jordan felt his body and mind grow heavy, as if someone had laid a wet blanket over him. The burning in his stomach intensified until it felt like he had a knife in his stomach and his body grew hot, causing him to sweat, but his hands and feet felt ice cold.

He opened his eyes and closed them again, sensing no difference between the two, so he kept them closed, battling his queasiness, using all of his will power to keep the lid on the simmering pot of his stomach. Behind his eyelids he saw the beginnings of chiaroscuro spider webbed patterns and movement that seemed to have a life of their own -- and they felt alien.

Forcing himself to breathe in slow and deep, the low level fireworks felt like half hidden shadow monsters creeping toward him, filling him with dread.

Don José broke into a full throated song about *Ayahuasca Mama Cuna* that triggered deep guttural purges from the group. Jordan's stomach retched like a meat hook had sunken into it, then he vomited harder than he could ever remember, sending him spinning off into dizzy, overwhelming, explosions of bright indescribable colors, patterns, thoughts, and emotions that came too fast and too numerous to make any sense of.

CHAPTER EIGHTY SEVEN

After drinking his dose, Jack Scanlon settled back into his spot and amused himself watching the others choke down theirs, feeling a little sorry for them as he watched them struggle. His shot felt warm in his stomach with a bitter aftertaste, but he thought it tasted more like molasses than anything else.

When the brew's effects started, he felt energized while passing through shadowy realms, like he had been plugged into some kind of cosmic high voltage power supply and when Don José sang louder and the others started puking, their purges seemed to empower him, giving him permission to fly further. Other than a continuing warmth, his stomach felt stable.

When Jordan let loose a deep throaty purge it triggered something that looked like someone had flipped a switch, turning Jordan into a human roman candle, spewing bright balls of energy with colors and hues Jack never could have imagined. They billowed out, enveloping him in dynamic unfolding geometric progressions that Jack understood as a demonstration of blossoming macroscopic and microscopic life, genetic expression, and the expansion of consciousness in the molecular, human, planetary, and galactic realms. Shit, he thought as he flew through masses of unearthly colors. This is way better than any acid or mushroom trip I ever had.

His body rocked as wave after wave of ecstatic visions washed over him and then something he could only comprehend as another presence took over his body, making him sway to and fro. Recognizing it as a snake he surrendered to it, and with that recognition, he became a tiny bug that was eaten by a bigger bug, and after that a bigger bug which continued through infinite successions of being swallowed until he passed through what he thought of as a cosmic luge of shifting colors that became a passage through a snake, once more demonstrating the progressive cycles and unfolding of life in multiple dimensions of consciousness. Throughout it all, he heard rattles, flutes, and Don José singing melodies and words that sounded both alien and unintelligible.

Somewhere in the midst of it all he heard Stan say, "Ayahuasca is the river and the songs and chants Don José is singing are *icaros* and *marirs* that are the boats that transport you along that cosmic river to other dimensions."

He liked the sound of that and took it as permission to fly as fast and as far as possible until something came over him the way the snake had, only this felt far more powerful and grounding until he sensed the spirit of Buddha, and then he *became* Buddha. He didn't have to go anywhere, he could reach it all from here.

Embracing compassion, he expanded outward until he passed into a comforting violet haze that pulled him along until he recognized the presence of John, the kid in the coma, then he sensed him in other inexplicable ways, but he couldn't see him.

Jack felt a twinge of guilt. He was having such a good time that he forgot about the kid, which was the reason they were there in the first place.

"Tell them not to come," John's voice whispered from everywhere. "Once they're here, there's no turning back and even if they could, they won't want to."

This last "to" echoed through Jack's mind, repeating itself until he realized that it was coming from Cheryl, who whimpered at his side. He shook his head. Not only had he forgotten about her beside him, he had forgotten that he was even in the same room with everyone else. Once he realized this he heard purges, cries, and laughter, and above all that the voice of Don José on his right, sweetly singing his strange sounding songs.

Jack's compassion returned and he found himself smiling at its power. Buddha power, he thought, clenching his fists. He would expand it out again, only this time he would direct it to Cheryl, who needed help. The thought of helping her escape her suffering made him feel powerful, omniscient, and a channel from a higher source. He had the power to help her and the thought of it made his smile stretch out hard across his face.

Shit, he thought, if any damage comes to me from this, it's going to require special surgery for my face muscles. They hurt from smiling so much.

CHAPTER EIGHTY EIGHT

Once she started purging, darkness swept in, enveloping Cheryl like the wings of a giant bat, swallowing her into chaos. She heaved deep and violently, spewing vile slithering snakes of different colors she had never seen before into her bucket. Horrified, she watched them squirming while snot ran from her nose and tears flooded her eyes.

She sat up to escape the sight of it and the nasty, sour, bitter stink of her vomit. While wiping her nose and mouth with a paper towel, she looked to the side and saw Jack smiling like the village idiot. His demented smile drove her deeper into chaos, so she closed her eyes.

Whatever song Don José was singing sounded alien and satanic. Opening her eyes again, she saw smiling Jack's head turn into a giant snake that opened a massive mouth and lunged for her, swallowing her into the darkness of a hell ruled over by a grinning, demonic looking nude Jack slapping a cat-o-nine tails across his palm.

"Shame on you, spreading your legs like a Goddamn chimpanzee. Where's your self respect?" He grinned. "Don't get me wrong, a lack of self-respect isn't necessarily bad." He swung the cat-o-nine tails and the barbs whistled through the air, inches from her face, then he rolled his bony hips, causing a horse-sized, purple-knobbed appendage to wave back and forth. Bright emerald green flashed in his eyes.

"Momma," she said. "Momma!"

She tried to escape and found herself in the arms of a badly burned Eddie Driscoll, who laughed. "Not yet, Cheryl, Jack isn't finished."

They came like a movie montage, sometimes alone, sometimes

together. Eddie turned into the crass, disgusting Chazz Daggett, then his father Ollie with the bullet hole between his eyes, then Denise, shattered like a broken doll, and Emily, who turned into a giant rat that swallowed a pleading Morgan. The last to come was Hodge with his damaged head. "I'm so sorry, Cheryl," he said. "It's all my fault."

"What's your fault?" she whispered.

"They're going to rape you."

"Who?"

A winged demon appeared wearing a black and white coat with a horn and an ivory box of the same colors.

"Morpheus is going to rape Pandora."

Before she could fathom what he said, she was at the mercy of Eddie Driscoll, Chazz, and Ollie Daggett, who slithered over her like the snakes squirming in her vomit, penetrating her every opening in a brutal act of rape until something inside her shifted and she shouted "I've had enough of this shit and I'm not going to take it anymore!"

Darkness and light flickered and fluttered and Don José's singing came louder until she rose up out of the depths on blissful waves of *Aqua de Florida* that washed out the foul, fetid garbage she had been submerged in. The floral scented breeze passed over her like the wind from the wing of a large bird, lifting her higher. She passed through a violet haze and heard John whisper from nowhere in particular, "Tell them not to come. There's no turning back, and even if they could, they won't want to."

She burst into the most sublime celestial beauty she could barely conceive of. What she thought of as crystal castles shone so bright and beautiful she found them too painful to experience until she vomited again, making her spirit feel lighter as if her body was too slow and had too much mass that kept her from vibrating fast enough to maintain the higher level of energy needed to exist in that transcendent heavenly realm of beauty that she could find no word to express, only tears, equal parts joy and pure unadulterated awe.

It continued for what felt like too long and not long enough as she didn't want it to ever end, and yet she didn't think she could take such intense beauty for any longer.

When it faded, she opened her eyes to a smiling Don José standing over her shaking his bundled palm leaf rattle and blowing sweet smelling Florida water over her.

CHAPTER EIGHTY NINE

Rita's experience started in an explosion of bright otherworldly colors and patterns that quickly plunged into darkness when she heard Cheryl desperately crying, "Mama!" The angst, sorrow, and hopelessness of her cries prompted a massive, rat-filled purge from Rita that horrified her more than she thought possible. Hordes of rats scrabbled from the bottomless depths of her bucket, rocketing her into the nightmare that was DreamLand as they dropped over the bucket's edge and scrambled up her arms and legs, heading for her face.

Hodge's ravaged visage swam into view. He winked blood from his all but closed eye. "My rats are friendly."

"Liar!" Emily Fulbright shrieked from somewhere.

A foul odor permeated the air and Emily appeared. Her mouth stretched into a hairy snout, her ears grew long and pointy, and her eyes blurred into shiny black marbles that glinted an eerie green.

"This isn't fair," Hodge muttered. "I created lovable rats."

The giant Emily rat opened its maw and swallowed Rita, hurtling her through a maelstrom of darkness into frigid water, swirling into a whirlpool. Bubbles of emerald phosphorescence boiled around her. Her lungs felt like balloons stretched to the breaking point. She struggled to reverse her descent, kicking and clawing up toward a distant hazy light where dusky spots swirled among sparkling bubbles.

Something wet and hairy brushed her cheek and rats tumbled off a jagged cliff, floating on the swells, scratching at her clothing, clawing at her hair, and scrambling onto her head. She let out a muted scream and grabbed its cold, slippery tail. A furry head snapped at her face, eyes glinting green.

A faint, shimmering sound prickled the nape of her neck and a haunting melody stirred long forgotten feelings. She couldn't remember the name of the song or where she heard it. The profundity of the melody intensified, then her heart leaped at the sight of the tall, handsome, blond Pied Piper in Hamelin town square wearing skin tight forest green cloth and matching suede boots. A long scarlet feather highlighted the silver band of his pointed hat.

Somewhere in the back of her thoughts she realized she had something important to do.

As the Piper played, the rodents followed, snapping, biting, and scratching in a wild scramble to be first in line.

"I'm so done with this shit," she said between gritted teeth. "Fuck off!"

The music stopped and she heard a low growl beside her. A gigantic black jaguar leaped into the scene and gobbled up all the rats before Morgan Jackson appeared, wearing a red flannel shirt, sitting against a rock by the water's edge. His face looked discolored and bloated and his lips and eyelids were gone. She saw frenzied movement beneath his shirt where rats had eaten into his stomach and for the briefest moment his eyes glittered green, then the spectral image flickered and faded like the picture on a suddenly darkened television.

"Prettier the girl, the livelier the worm," a raven squawked from the darkness. She heard writhing sounds and shrill squeals coming from an open black and white ivory box. The squawking bird spread its wings and scuttled back and forth on a window sill.

"Aaaaah, here's a nice fat one." A picture perfect beautiful blonde pulled out what looked like a squirming foot long pink snake as thick as a broomstick. Its tail wriggled from the bottom of her closed fist, slapping against her arm.

Rita gagged when she saw a tiny human head at its top with long stringy hair and a girl's face twisted in horror. Faint shrieks streamed from its quivering mouth. "Help me! Help me!"

With a laugh, the blonde tossed the abomination to the shiny-eyed raven that snatched it from the air and flew to a fence post where it tilted its head and devoured the screaming morsel in one gulp.

The blonde beauty smiled at Rita. "You'll be the liveliest worm in the box."

Rita heard guttural sounds and an enormous mound of naked, pale-gray flesh, topped by a patch of carrot colored hair wobbled in, laboring to inhale through tiny nostrils and exhaling with a whistling sound. Thick, puffy lips and two rows of teeth marked its gaping mouth.

"Albert," Rita gasped.

Through bulging slits in the oleaginous flesh, tiny glazed eyes pleaded for help as the creature groaned and lurched forward on toeless feet, grunting and squealing like a baby pig. Stumps that had once been fingers wiggled from between thick rolls of fat.

"Gotcha!" An icy hand grabbed Rita's shoulder, sending a bolt of terror through her. Fear flashed to anger and Rita balled her fist, firing a left hook. She purged again and Chazz Daggett staggered out of the shadows, scrawny arms sticking from the sleeves of his blood spattered leather jacket. Oozing red sores peppered his sweat-soaked head and a bright red spot appeared on his cheek, forming a blister that broke, leaving a circle of raw flesh that turned pink and disappeared. Another blister appeared on his nose.

His huge bony head wobbled back and forth, barely supported by his reed-like neck and reddish-purple blood congealed around the gaping hole between his eyes. A toothless grimace contorted his pallid face and then he was on top of her, forcing her legs apart.

Looking into his dead eyes she felt she could read his thoughts. Eddie Driscoll's face flitted by, horribly burnt and ravaged, then Chazz's father Ollie with the bullet hole between his eyes, and Denise, shattered and bloody like a broken doll while Chazz fucked her hard, slamming into her with a brutality she didn't think possible.

"It's not really Chazz who's raping you," Hodge said from somewhere. "It's Morpheus, and it's not you he's raping, it's Pandora." His damaged head floated into view. "I'm so sorry," he said. "It's all my fault."

"I don't understand," she managed.

A phantasmic winged demon with a horn wearing a black and white coat flickered and disappeared and somewhere in the enveloping darkness a throbbing red light double pulsed to the rhythm of a heartbeat.

"That, my dear," Jack Scanlon's voice said matter-of-factly, "is the Tell-Tale Heart."

Rita had a moment of confusion before her anger returned, stronger than before. Her knee shot up catching Chazz solidly between the legs, then she clutched the silver angel at her neck and surrendered.

Darkness and light fluttered and Don José's singing came to her until she rose up on waves of *Aqua de Florida* that dissolved Chazz and the rest of the darkness. An intoxicating flower scented breeze passed over her, becoming the flapping wings of a large bird that lifted her through a violet haze.

John whispered, "Tell them not to come."

Feeling an urgency to share the message, she opened her heart and her eyes and looked at Jordan across from her. Don José played a sweet mandolin sounding instrument that made Jordan explode into the most sublime, exquisite, celestial hummingbird she could have ever imagined. Words fell short of describing the depths of its beauty and the levels and layers it pierced within her heart and soul while each stringed note he played elicited sprays of flowers and butterflies.

She heard Don José singing *picafloracita* in a sweet adoring voice and heard the buzz from earlier in the day as the hummingbird rose into the air in a blaze of vibrating colors, wings buzzing, head darting in and out as if sipping from a flower, and then it shot straight into her heart in an explosion of high frequency pastel colors that could only be heaven.

Rising higher, she felt the flapping wings of a larger bird, but this was no bird. With unbounded joy bursting from her heart, she realized that these were the wings of an angel.

Mesmerized, she looked deep into the eyes of the most beautiful woman she had ever seen and felt safely enveloped by a loving feminine spirit that obliterated the boundaries of her wildest imaginings. She gave herself fully to it and knew instantly that this angel was *Santa Teresa De Avila*, who spoke without words.

Rita felt her presence as an intimate part of herself as her spirit became one with Teresa's. Not only did Rita merge, she surrendered to being fully possessed by Teresa, and in that sublime and ecstatic rapture, she possessed Teresa with equal fervor, embracing the sweet essence of femininity with undying love. No matter how much of herself she gave away, she couldn't seem to give enough to equal Teresa's love. Never before had she felt such an overpowering love entwine and become such an integral part of her. Teresa's loving presence filled her, profoundly merging their spirits to the core of Rita's being, deep, intimate, and all encompassing.

For an infinite time outside of time Rita's legs and body twitched, rocked, and convulsed in pure bliss, in the throes of an ecstasy that she understood to be the true meaning of rapture and she never wanted it to end.

CHAPTER NINETY

Wanting to set a good example, Lorenzo downed the thick, nasty contents of the shot glass, suppressing a gag. It hit his stomach like a hot rock and sat there burning more with each passing moment. Back at his seat, he sipped water to try and wash the taste from his mouth and the heat from his stomach, but it persisted.

When they extinguished the candle he looked around at the shadowy forms of the others. After a period of near silence, Don José sang softly, sometimes whistling, sometimes whispering. Lorenzo teetered on the edge of nausea feeling himself grow heavy while gauzy sprays and patterns filled his mind until Don José broke into a louder song about *Ayahuasca Mama Cuna* that triggered purges from most of the group.

He managed to hold his in as colors, patterns, and explosions that made Fourth of July fireworks pale in comparison followed by memories and emotions that shot back and forth between past and present. In the midst of it he felt profoundly amazed that he was sensing himself fully present, aware, and engaged in the past as if reliving it, while being fully aware of himself in the yurt with the others in the same present moment with the same immediacy.

Don José's cosmic sounds and music took him through a succession of experiences and places that defied logic, eliciting strange, otherworldly perceptions. He opened his eyes from time to time, looking up at the head of the circle where Don José sat. He could make out the forms of the others, and saw Stan's shadowy form sitting upright, but Don José's spot looked like a nonexistent void where he should have been. Where is José? He wondered, and in that moment felt him everywhere throughout the room, as if his awareness existed both everywhere and nowhere.

It all felt blissful and expansive until he heard Rita muttering and gasping beside him, changing everything from light to dark. He knew her nightmare by heart from hearing it so many times that he envisioned what she saw, stirring his rage.

The Pied Piper marched through Hamelin town square playing his flute dressed in skin tight forest green cloth and matching suede boots. Rita followed, overrun by hordes of rats that snapped, bit, and scratched in a wild scramble to be first in line.

"I'm so done with this shit," she said between gritted teeth. "Fuck off!"

Her rage brought a low growl from deep inside him, startling him with its timbre and depth. Two huge yellow eyes and the shadowed form of a massive jaguar's head rose in front of him, opening its massive jaws and leaping forward, swallowing him.

In the next moment everything looked sharper, with better clarity than he imagined possible. He heard noises and felt his ears moving forward. Every sound inside the yurt came with greater volume and his smell became acute and magnified, making him realize that the jaguar hadn't swallowed him.

He had become it.

Acting on instinct, he leaped into Rita's visions and devoured rats by the mouthful with his oversized jaws.

"This isn't fair," Hodge said. "I created lovable rats."

When the witches came, he faltered and his heart went out to poor Eddie Driscoll and his untimely end in DreamLand. Lorenzo almost vomited reliving the grisly horror in the battered pod that held stringy bits of ragged flesh hanging from charred rib bones and pieces of gray gristle clinging to the joints of a skewed skeleton. The scorched San Diego Padres cap contrasted with the chalky white bone of Eddie's skull. His grimacing rictus, with its double row of gleaming teeth seemed to mock him.

He went from feeling all-powerful to helpless when he heard Rita call Chazz's name. Her purge sent him spinning deeper into his own tortured memories of Chazz Daggett wobbling into their lab, his huge head bobbing above his shoulders like a spectral balloon, lumbering closer, arms outstretched, fingers twitching, the shriveled eagle tattoos on the back of each hand flailing like withered bats. Careening around the end of a console, his boot tangled in a clump of wire and he stumbled forward, knocking over a chair. Lorenzo turned away from Chazz to reach for Rita's hand.

Putting his head closer to her, he said, "Rita, are you awake? Talk to me." Sensing the depths of her darkness he called out. "Rita needs a little help here."

In the nightmare visions of his memory, bony hands clawed at his collar and clamped around his neck. Chazz yanked him up, spun him like a doll and slammed him into the wall, clutching his throat.

"Dah!"

"Run, baby, run," Lorenzo croaked, punching ineffectively at Chazz's head. "Save yourself."

Rita scrambled to her feet and bolted for the door, stopping short when she saw a screwdriver.

Lorenzo's eyes bulged as Chazz pressed his windpipe shut with skeletal thumbs. He tugged at the rigid fingers, wheezing for breath until his knees buckled, his eyes rolled up into his head and his hands fell to his sides.

"Bastard." Rita plunged the screwdriver through Chazz's skinny neck. He stiffened, a wet gurgling sound bubbled up, and his tongue shot from his gaping mouth in a rasping scream. Eyes glittering green, he fell backward, crashing to the floor and then it all faded.

Through his own highly altered perception, Lorenzo watched fascinated as Don José shook his *chacapa* palm leaf rattle and blew Florida water over Rita in surreal rainbow golden sparkles that held a light of their own.

When he heard the mandolin like sweetness of the instrument Stan called a *charango* he saw Rita with her hands in prayer, clutching the silver angel he had given to her. Feeling his heart burst open to her sweetness, the light, intoxicating flower scents washed over him, becoming so bright he had to look away, but he felt the power of the waves of love washing away the fetid darkness.

CHAPTER NINETY ONE

Carl didn't think he'd ever stop puking. He felt queasy after downing the shot glass full of what tasted like rancid battery acid and used every ounce of his will to keep it down. He tried to keep his mind off of his stomach by focusing on Don José honoring the spirits of the forest with his prayers, songs, and whispers until the physical effects of the Ayahuasca washed over him, announcing itself with visions of millions of spiders of all sizes.

Don José's first loud song brought waves of purging that squeezed everything out of every orifice he had. Tears rolled from his eyes, snot ran from his nose, and an unexpected shart squirted out his ass, soiling his pants. Sweat soaked him.

Somehow in a blur of confusion someone took him out, cleaned him up, and brought him back to his spot. Most if not all of the group were moaning, vomiting, laughing, crying, babbling, and talking to themselves. Beside him, Wesley made growling noises like a lion straight out of the jungle.

Listening, he wondered, who the fuck were Chazz and Albert, and why was someone crying for their mother? Jesus, this is what it's like to be in a loony bin. His heart raced, followed by the thought that this was one of those secret government MKUltra projects he had read about and he was their guinea pig. The experiment was a failure and he would never be normal again. As if in agreement to his conclusion, the cacophony of the group rose, fueling his terror.

He *was* in a loony bin - and he wasn't getting out!

Madness pulled at him from every direction like he had become a million different crazy people taking turns possessing him one after the other in rapid succession until he forgot who he was, where he was, and what he was supposed to be doing.

A straight jacket held his arms tight as he bounced off the walls of a padded cell until he realized that the only way he would ever get out was to die, so he did, escaping into oblivion.

He came back into awareness seeing the pudgy red tear-streaked face of Terry, who sobbed. "I'm scared shit. I don't know if I can handle this. It's too real."

All of the dream battles they had fought floated up overwhelming him and sucking him down into successive events that played out in fast forward, feeling like they were never ending.

A horde of black uniformed enemy spilled out of the fortress and charged him, guns blazing. Multiple points of white hot pain pierced him.

Corporal Friedman's mouth moved and his head shook "No," but the rest of him remained frozen.

"Fuck it!" John grabbed him and pulled hard.

"Nooo!" Friedman shrieked in an unsettling high-pitched scream.

John slammed into him and they tumbled onto a mine that exploded in a bright thunderous flash that ripped through everything. Carl had never felt such intense pain when his world erupted into a mad, disorienting spin of flashing lights, flames, and whining explosions that spun crazily in every direction, shot through with an agonizing white hot flame that slammed them into the ground, followed by white noise.

The sound of waves crashing on a beach drew him in, followed by a dim image that brightened with rising music and other sounds that intermingled into the alien sounding lullaby. He started to lose himself in it when John's voice stopped him.

"Get the fuck out of here," he growled. "You might think it feels good, but it's like flypaper," then louder, "get the fuck out of here and don't come back. Forget about me. I'm not coming back. It's a trap!"

Feeling hurt and displaced, Carl drifted through a hazy zone feeling like he left the heaviness of his body behind and flew in his energetic spirit that he imagined was his astral body.

Terry's directionless voice came from far off crying, then his wide-eyed face appeared, ashen with terror. "Momma!" he cried through his sobs. "Mommy!"

"Momma!" Rita cried out from Carl's right, jolting him into opening his eyes and pushing himself back up to sitting straight.

"Momma!" Cheryl cried even louder from across the room.

Her anguish tore at his heart and he felt the impulse to lose himself in her suffering until Stan's voice came from nowhere saying, "It's not yours."

He balled his fists and rubbed at his eyes, riveted by the flurry of activity around Cheryl. Like the opening curtain of a show, Stan and Don José stood aside and a fluttering around Cheryl turned into a gigantic condor with a ten foot wing span that rose up from her and floated across the room, diving into him.

He sensed mottled feathers enveloping him and soaring down through the depths of his being, capturing the nightmarish fragments that haunted him, dumping them at the bottom of its plunge like a dive bomber dropping its payload.

The condor rose and fell over and over again, releasing more with each dive, bringing clarity in stages that lifted him higher with each pass while bringing him closer to an ineffable, exquisite realm that struck him as nonrational, multidimensional, and total nonsense on one level, while making total sense in another that he could not express.

He swayed like being rocked in a cradle, feeling himself swept backward and forward in time, space, and strange dimensions, sometimes inhabited by even stranger beings, feeling that he was learning volumes in an abstract and symbolic language that spoke in dynamic holograms that he had heard a man named Terence McKenna describe as "self-transforming machine elves".

This continued indefinitely until he felt himself drifting into the peaceful delight of Don José's songs, flutes, whistling and the strumming of a sweet sounding mandolin-like instrument someone called a *charango*.

CHAPTER NINETY TWO

Wesley looked Jordan in the eye and nodded before gagging his dose down and shaking his head. He kept sipping water and belching, feeling like the horrid taste would never leave. His heaviness grew for a long time after Don José started singing, and just when he thought nothing would happen, a rush of incomprehensible colors and patterns slammed into him, unsettling his stomach even more while soaking his torso with sweat and making his hands and feet ice cold. He felt on the verge of upchucking and wanted to with all his heart, but nothing came up, as if the brew wanted him to suffer without relief.

"I'm scared shit," Terry, whined from somewhere. "It's too real."

Wesley sensed Terry rather than seeing him. His words and panicked tone struck at Wesley's heart, making it impossible to move. He heard a multitude of voices and willed himself to run, but his whole being felt sluggish, weighted, and rooted to his spot, spurring panic that drove him into his deepest fears. Every dreaming battle he had been in flashed through his mind along with the sensation of falling into a shifting void, punctuated by a rising thumping sound that went to the beat of the flashes.

Everything pulsed and vibrated with flashes of sight and sound, first through his feet, then up through the rest of his body until his surroundings came into focus in the back of the helicopter. A beeping alarm and flashing lights filled the cabin and Wesley spotted an orange white glow followed by a trail of smoke heading straight for him.

A bright flash signaled a concussion of flashing lights, flames, and whining explosions that spun in every direction, shot through with an agonizing searing white flame that slammed him into the ground.

He tried to escape his fiery hell by seeking out the white noise that turned into waves crashing on a beach, followed by a dim brightening image that rose with rising music and other sounds that intermingled into the complicated lullaby he had come to love until John's voice dissolved it.

"Get the fuck out of here, Wesley," he urged. "It's not the safe space you think it is. Forget about me. I'm not coming back. It's a trap!"

In the next instant he was on the ground in excruciating pain, staring at his arm three feet away from his body, his right leg blown off, and his left leg gone from the knee, hanging by a single glistening tendon. He blacked out, coming to on a gurney, caught in the oddest perception of being tied securely to it watching himself being wheeled from outside of it all, both being in and watching a movie about himself.

The sign above the door said:

CYBERNETIC LIMB FACILITY

It opened to a darkened room punctuated by tiny flashes of light like supernaturally bright fireflies. Pneumatic hisses, whirs, clicks and whispers came from the darkness like insects and animals scurrying through a bizarre high-tech electronic jungle.

Assembly lines rolled along with robotic arms performing precision tasks punctuated by flashes from micro welders. Conveyor belts provided a steady stream of robotic arms, legs, and joints.

He continued rolling through another doorway marked:

CYBERNETIC ORGAN FACILITY

Livers, hearts, lungs, and other organs floated in tanks of colored fluids. One tank of floating eyeballs had long red stringy nerve bundles hanging down like jellyfish tentacles. The eyeballs looked like a combination of human tissue, glass, plastic, and metal.

He passed under a third door with the sign:

CYBERNETIC RESEARCH AND DEVELOPMENT

He struggled against his restraints as he wheeled into a huge operating theater where robotic arms severed his remaining limbs and stumps with spinning, blood spattering saws while other robots attached prosthetic extensions. Sophisticated mechanisms plucked out his damaged organs, reinstalling cybernetic replacements into the bloody sockets left behind.

He screamed with all of his heart and soul.

When he thought it couldn't get any worse, the click and whir of relays and motors signaled his gurney being drawn by locked hydraulic arms into a large unit where green, red, and blue laser grids mapped and scanned his head.

A hiss followed white smoke billowing from the chambers and a metallic computerized square the size of a table descended on him, sealing with a magnetic clack and a pneumatic hiss. The entire assembly rotated so he faced the floor and he went numb from the head down.

A robotic apparatus descended from the ceiling and a laser sliced open his neck. Small white puffs of smoke indicated where cuts were made. The laser scalpel completed an incision and made two more cuts at the top and bottom of the first cut. With insect-like clicks, whirs, and hisses, two sets of robotic fingers extended from the sides of his neck opening. With dull claws they peeled back flaps of skin and locked them down like window shutters. Another robotic hand with fingertips like dentist drills lowered onto Wesley's exposed spine.

Its fingers moved through precise manipulations drilling into different points on the vertebrae. When the robot pulled away, another one moved a microprocessor into position and pressed it down onto the drilled vertebrae where a laser danced through microsurgeries fusing nerves and veins to chip leads and ports.

When the operation was finished, robotic fingers pulled and pressed the skin flaps into place and the laser retraced its original path, cauterizing the wound in puffs of smoke.

At the peak of his angst, he heard Don José singing a song about *otorongo*, eliciting a low growl from deep inside him, startling him with its power. He opened his eyes and saw two huge yellow eyes and the shadowed form of an enormous jaguar rise in front of him, opening its massive jaws and leaping on top of him, gobbling him up into inky darkness.

The piercing sound of a flute came to him in that moment, prompting an unexpected and welcome purge that ripped into his guts and in the next moment everything looked sharper than he thought possible. Every noise made his ears move forward, every sound came with greater volume, and his smell magnified.

As quickly as they came, his hellish visions left like the aftermath of a downpour leaving him feeling clean, clear, energized, and on the end of that, wonderfully colored visions and patterns rolled in like a diffused psychedelic rainbow carrying him through the last part of his journey as if floating on clouds down the honeyed river of Don José's songs, flutes, and the sweet notes of his *charango*.

CHAPTER NINETY THREE

While hurtling through a cornucopia of bizarre sights, sounds, emotions, and sensations, Stan Krippner's guidance echoed through Jordan's mind, reminding him that perception is everything and he was trying to find a higher awareness to navigate a reality that followed a more flexible set of rules.

Feeling like he had topped the high point of a roller coaster and now plummeted downward with his heart in his throat, Jordan's falling sensation dropped him into white noise that grew into the sound of waves crashing on a beach, followed by images that brightened with rising music into the complicated otherworldly lullaby until John's raging voice shocked him.

"Get the fuck out of here!" It echoed.

"You're here," Jordan said, feeling puzzled at his anger. "Don't worry, buddy. We're coming for you."

"No you're not!" John ordered. "Get the fuck away from me as fast as you can. There's no way out."

Jordan blinked and saw Terry's wide-eyed expression, ashen with terror. "I'm scared shit," he whined. "I can't handle this. It's too real."

His panicked tone struck at Jordan, making it impossible to move. He heard voices and willed himself to run, but he felt weighted when a horde of black uniformed enemy charged him, guns blazing, then the hot flash of a mortar explosion knocked him to the ground. His ears rang, everything went fuzzy and a chaotic moving sideshow of lightning fast sights, sounds, smells, and feelings overwhelmed him.

"Momma!" Terry cried. "Mommy!"

A bomb exploded showering him with dirt and bullets pinged above him. Jordan looked up over the foxhole. The endless expanse of the battlefield made him feel lost. Staying low, he zig-zagged through explosions toward a cratered road, flinching when a mortar exploded, nearly knocking him off his feet. Someone slammed into him, wrapping him in a bear hug that tumbled them onto a mine that exploded in a thunderous flash that spun him into a cloud of acrid smelling smoke. Feeling the ground shaking beneath him, a Humvee blew up, taking him with it.

A grenade came over a wall, spinning to a stop beside him and everything slipped into slow motion as bodies plopped on top of him followed by a deafening explosion and flash.

A beeping alarm and flashing lights filled the cabin, punctuated by a "Shit!" from the pilot. Jordan spotted an orange white glow followed by a trail of smoke heading for him. The accompanying concussion of sight, sound, and feeling ripped through everything.

He walked up a mountain path to catch up to four men when an explosion knocked them to the ground, blinding him. Through the thick white smoke he saw flailing arms and legs, then guttural cries came from everywhere. Jordan rolled onto his knees, M4 at the ready and a breeze gusted, clearing away smoke.

He screamed when searing needles of pain shot through his hand, arm, cheek, and legs where bullets pierced him, then a second explosion ripped through his upper torso, causing his world to erupt into a spin that left him staring up at the sky, alive, helpless, and wishing he were dead.

Bearded men wearing head coverings that showed nothing but hard, narrowed eyes circled him like hungry wolves. The biggest, most sinister of them kicked Jordan in the side and jabbed into his entrails with his rifle, glaring at him with cold, dark, eyes that lit up with each stab.

The hate-filled, heartless glare cut to Jordan's core when the tribesman pressed the barrel of his rifle to Jordan's forehead. Jordan imagined him smiling beneath his face covering when he saw the flash of glee glinting in those dark eyes when he pulled the trigger.

The sound of gunfire faded to popping sounds that put Jordan into the observation booth looking out onto a firing range where Nick Stevens stood at attention with a rifle on his shoulder.

Five large flat screens lined the wall above the window. One showed a close-up of a target. The one beside it had a roving targeting display that calculated mathematical geometry and vector calculations in red and blue overlaid on everyone in the observation booth.

Crowley smiled. "You ain't seen nothing yet." He tapped the intercom. His muffled voice echoed from the PA in the firing range along with his voice in the booth. "You ready to show them how it's done, Sergeant Stevens?"

"Yes sir," Stevens said, snapping off a salute with his cybernetic arm.

"On my mark," Crowley said, "Three, two, one."

In one graceful motion, Stevens shouldered his rifle and popped off six fast rounds into Jordan. The close-up target on the first monitor showed one enlarged hole dead center in Jordan's heart. He dropped to the floor, numb.

He puzzled over why he wasn't dead until he heard Rita struggling and her predicament became his. Forcing open his eyes, he sat up with crossed legs and peered into the darkness enveloping Rita, wanting with all his heart to help her.

Rats poured out of her bucket, scrambling up her arms and legs. A scrawny woman's mouth stretched into a hairy snout, her ears grew long and pointy, and her eyes blurred into shiny black marbles that glinted green. The giant rat opened its maw and swallowed Rita then the Pied Piper played, and rats snapped, bit, and scratched in a wild scramble until a black jaguar gobbled them up.

A squawking crow spread its wings and raced back and forth on a window sill. Rita gagged when Jordan saw a human head at the end of a huge pink worm and a girl's face twisted in horror, then a mound of naked, pale-gray flesh, topped by a patch of carrot colored hair wobbled in.

"Albert," Rita gasped, purging again.

Someone or something he understood to be Chazz Daggett staggered out of the shadows, scrawny arms sticking from the sleeves of a blood spattered leather jacket. His huge bony head wobbled back and forth, then he was on top of her, forcing her legs apart, turning into a winged demon with a horn in a black and white coat.

"It's not Chazz who's raping her," a voice said. "It's Morpheus raping Pandora."

Somewhere in the enveloping darkness a throbbing red light double pulsed to the rhythm of a heartbeat.

Jordan opened his heart and every part of him that he could, directing his energy toward Rita when she clutched something at her neck.

Darkness and light flickered and Don José's singing empowered him while he surrendered, feeling Rita's eyes on him.

When Don José played the sweet sounding *charango*, Jordan's crossed legs bounced up and down like fluttering wings and his body and head jerked forward like a hummingbird feeding on a flower. He couldn't remember ever moving in this jerky way and it would have terrified him if it didn't feel so exquisite.

He exploded into a sublime celestial hummingbird and rose into the air in a blaze of vibrating colors that moved faster and faster until he left his body and shot straight into her heart, losing himself in an explosion of high frequency pastel colored heavenly visions.

In the midst of his rapture, Rita floated up like an angel, or better still, embraced by an angel with huge gossamer wings until its brilliance faded from her and from himself as well, gently dropping him into playful colored visions and patterns that carrying him through the last part of his journey on the river of Don José's music, leaving him feeling clean, clear, and invigorated.

When the energy of the circle diminished, Don José formally closed it with a prayer. Stan lit a candle and Don José made the rounds, checking up on everyone. When he came to Jordan, he squatted down in front of him, and with a huge grin, said in Spanish accented English, "The mother *loves* you."

CHAPTER NINETY FOUR

Rita sat in the yurt with the others in the same spot she had the night before, with Lorenzo to her left followed by Carl, Wesley, and Jordan, who sat across from her. Cheryl sat to her right, followed by Jack and Don José, with Stan completing the circle. Most of them spoke in hushed tones while Stan murmured conversation with Don José in Spanish.

After four hours of sleep, she felt worn out, like she hadn't slept at all, yet she felt hyper-aware. With the passing of the night her feelings of certainty about her experiences had faded and she began to doubt the validity of what happened, but her heart felt open, clear, and expanded. She hoped she was finally free of her nightmares.

Thought and emotion wrestled inside of her, flip-flopping between the certainty of her heart and the doubt of her mind and she didn't know what to believe, so she put her faith in her heart, and clung to the hope she harbored there.

She looked around at the others one at a time, wondering what they thought and felt, ending with Lorenzo, whose dilated pupils radiated love. As if reading her thoughts, he smiled and put his arm around her, and they both leaned back as one.

Stan nodded to Don José and sat up straight, ringing a chime that quieted the group. "Where going to do an integration session," Stan said. "This part isn't usually done in indigenous traditions, but westerners have found it useful to share their experiences for more insight both into themselves and others. Please talk as openly about your experiences as you are comfortable with, but say as much or as little as you feel. There's no pressure. What you choose to share or not is up to you. Along with that, if you are so inclined, please share what you may have seen or felt from the others. It's often helpful to them in integrating their own experiences. Sound good?"

Everyone nodded.

"But before we do," Stan continued, "Don José has asked me to thank each and every one of you for being brave and participating in a very powerful session."

Don José leaned in to Stan and said something in Spanish, to which Stan nodded. "He also wants me to tell you that this was one of the most powerful sessions he's ever led. He had to work extra hard to keep the container fortified and keep the dark forces at bay."

Don José nodded as Stan spoke as if he were the one talking.

"He says he is quite worn out and is very aware of the fact that more darkness was present here in a more concentrated manner than in any other sessions he's ever led, so much so that he felt it as a distinctive dark presence."

Don José put his hands together in prayer like fashion and slowly bowed his head.

"And finally," Stan went on, "He urges everyone to continue the diet for at least as long as we were on it before the session and a little longer if possible to allow the effects of the Ayahuasca to continue working on your body, mind, and spirit in the coming days, weeks, and months."

"*Muchas gracias, Maestro*," Lorenzo said.

"*Tambien*," Rita added.

Everyone applauded and Don José put his hands together and bowed his head again. Stan grinned and patted him on the back, then he held up a rattle. "This is the talking stick. Whoever has it does the talking and the rest of us listen. Anyone want to be first to share their experience?"

Everyone looked around at each other, eyes questioning.

"Don't feel like you have to speak either," Stan said.

Jack Scanlon shrugged. "Shit, I don't care." He brushed back his thinning hair and grinned a broad smile that went all the way up to his bushy eyebrows, then he took the rattle from Stan. "First off," he said, nodding to Don José, "It tasted like shit, but that's some grade A, top notch, A number one," he raised his finger, "*numero uno good* shit you got there!"

The group laughed. That's Jack for you, Rita thought, breaking the ice for everyone else.

"Seriously though, Doc. This shit outshines everything I've ever tried, and believe me, I tried a lot. It makes the best Acid look like preschool." He shook his head. "Every time someone blew chunks it felt like they made me stronger." He pointed at Jordan and smiled. "And when Mister Nothing over there let loose it launched me into the best light show *ever,* then I turned into a bug that got eaten by a snake, then everything was eating everything and I was in the middle of it all, eating and being eaten." Jack's eyes lit up. "It was divine!"

He held his hand out to Don José. "And the don's singing and music with the *charango* thing and the flutes. I became Buddha or Buddha became me. We were the same thing." He shook his head. "It was all of that and more, then I heard our lost trooper John. He said, 'Tell them not to come. There's no turning back.'"

Cheryl whimpered beside him, Rita gasped, and Jordan, Carl, and Wesley's eyes all widened in unison like they had been hit with a wave.

"I was having such a good time," Jack continued, "that I forgot about John, then I heard poor Cheryl beside me." He put his hand on her back and rubbed. His bushy eyebrows dropped and his voice trembled on the verge of tears. He wiped his eyes with his sleeve. "Poor kid was going through hell, so I thought if Buddha was here, I was gonna share him, so I sent him out to her."

He pursed his lips and sighed. "The last thing I can say is that I had the time of my life." He rubbed his cheeks with both hands. "My only complaint is that my face muscles hurt from so much smiling." He handed the rattle to Cheryl.

Holding it close with both hands, Cheryl looked down for a long moment as if praying, then she looked up, eyes resolute. "That was a horrible experience, but after going through all that hell, I'm hoping that my nightmares are gone. I have no way of knowing for sure, but I feel like I worked through them if that makes any sense."

Stan nodded encouragement.

She drew in a long shaky breath. "I've had recurring dreams of sexual abuse and rape since DreamLand self destructed. I won't go into the horrid details, but last night I went through all of them when Jack turned into a giant snake that swallowed me into a hellish darkness. I vomited harder than I ever have in my entire life. It felt like all of my organs might come out, and it was disgusting!"

She shuddered at the memory. "Vile slithering snakes of different colors came out of me, tears poured from my eyes and mucus ran from my nose. Now I know why they call it *la purga*. I didn't think it was ever going to end and everything sounded alien and satanic." She clutched the rattle closer to her chin as if protecting herself. "It was all about rape and some insanity about Morpheus raping Pandora."

She bowed to Don José. "And then Don José rescued me with his sweet music and flower smells that came to me like the breeze from a huge bird's wings, washing out the putrid, rotting stink." Her eyes took on a faraway look. "It lifted me out of the abyss, through a violet haze where I also heard John saying, tell them not to come. There was no turning back."

She closed her eyes a moment, then opened them wide. "Then I flew up into the most sublime celestial beauty imaginable." She looked around at everyone. "Even that falls short of describing the depths of its awe and beauty."

She drew in a deep breath and let out a long sigh before handing the rattle to Rita.

Rita held it in both hands. "My experience was a lot like Cheryl's," she began. "I think it was connected to hers in some way. I started out exploding into bright colors and patterns until I heard her crying, 'Mama!', which sent me purging right into my DreamLand nightmares, except I didn't see snakes." She shook herself. "Rats came out of my bucket and everywhere else for that matter, then I saw Hodge and Emily Fulbright, only she was a giant rat with black eyes that glinted green, then like Cheryl's snake from Jack, it swallowed me into my worst nightmares from DreamLand until I got pissed off and thought, I'm done with this shit, so I told them to fuck off! When I said that, a beautiful black jaguar leaped into the scene and gobbled up the rats."

"Holy shit," Lorenzo muttered.

"Then I was back in my witch nightmare," Rita continued, taking note of Lorenzo's comment. "They wanted to turn me into a worm and poor little Albert Moffitt..." She drew in a breath. "He looked like a horrible mutilated little monster, then Chazz came. By this time I had enough of his shit too, so I stood up for myself, thinking, I'm done being a victim." She lowered her voice. "And then there was rape. Hodge said it was Morpheus raping Pandora, whatever that meant. Chazz and Ollie Daggett and Eddie Driscoll were part of it. I felt overwhelmed again until my anger came back stronger, so I fought harder and held my angel." She held it out with one hand. "Then I surrendered to it and Don José's singing came to me on waves of flowers that turned into the flapping of the wings of a large bird that lifted me through a violet haze where I heard John too, saying, 'Tell them not to come.', so I opened my heart and eyes and looked at Jordan across from me and in that moment Don José played his *charango* which made Jordan turn into an exquisite hummingbird."

Jordan's eyes opened wide at this and seemed to widen more with each word she uttered.

"The depths of its beauty and the layers it pierced inside me expanded me more and more. Each note Don José played brought sprays of flowers and butterflies, then Jordan rose in a blaze of vibrating colors, wings buzzing, his head darting in and out like he was sipping from a flower, just like a hummingbird Lorenzo and I encountered on our walk, then he shot into my heart in an explosion of heavenly, high frequency pastel colored visions."

Jordan's mouth dropped, matching his wide eyes.

Rita sighed at the memory. "I rose higher on what I thought of as the flapping of a larger bird until I realized that it wasn't a bird, but the wings of an angel. The most beautiful woman I have ever seen. A loving feminine spirit who I understood was *Santa Teresa De Avila*, who spoke in my mind without words." She shook her head. "Like Jack with his Buddha, I became Teresa or Teresa became me, or we were both the same thing. For what seemed an infinite time outside of time my legs and body rocked and convulsed in a pure bliss that I never wanted to end."

She looked around at the others, noting their stunned expressions and realized that her words were falling short of any description she could put into words, so she shrugged and handed the rattle to Lorenzo, who put his hand over hers and gave it a squeeze before taking the rattle, his eyes still shining wide with love.

Shaking the rattle, he nodded to Jack. "I have to agree, that was some of the nastiest shit I ever drank, and I struggled to keep it down, especially when everyone else was purging theirs." He held up the rattle. "But I did it! After passing through colors, patterns, and explosions that made any fireworks I've ever seen pale in comparison, my memories and emotions shot back and forth between past and present." He lowered his head a moment, then looked up. "I was fully present, aware, and engaged in the past like I was reliving it in the present while being fully aware of myself here in that same present moment with the same immediacy." He shook the rattle at Don José, emphasizing each word. *"Hermano, su música es el sonido de Dios!"*

Don José answered with a wide smile and a twinkle in his eye. He put his hands together and bowed low to Lorenzo. *"Gracias hermano."*

Lorenzo bowed back. "The Don's *música* sent me through amazing, bizarre, alien vistas of sight and sound. At one point I looked over at him and saw a void where he should have been, then I felt him everywhere and nowhere until I heard Rita struggling."

He glanced at her and his eyes looked wet. Rita felt her own heart touched and stifled a sob.

Lorenzo's voice took on a tiny tremor. "My heart went out to her and I found myself in her nightmares with her. Rats were everywhere until I heard her say, 'I'm so done with this shit. Fuck off!'

"A growl came from inside me and I saw big yellow eyes and a massive jaguar's head that swallowed me in darkness, then I *was* the jaguar, leaping into Rita's nightmare, gobbling up rats, then I went into my own nightmare memories from DreamLand." He looked to Jack and Cheryl, who nodded recognition, then to Rita. His gaze lingered on her before continuing.

"When I fell into my own black memories, I called out for help for Rita as I felt like my own rising darkness kept me from helping her. Stan and Don José came over and Don José shook his *chacapa* palm leaf rattle and blew Florida water over Rita in rainbow golden sparkles that had their own light, then his sublime *charango* made my heart explode into her sweetness." He choked up at this and wiped tears from his eyes with his sleeve. The sincerity of it made Rita's own tears flow.

Lorenzo gave her a crooked smile and put his arm around her. "The light and the beautiful flower smells washed over us and became so bright I had to look away, but I still felt the waves of love washing away the darkness that's been with us for so long, and I have to believe it's gone for good." He kissed Rita on the cheek and handed the rattle to Carl.

CHAPTER NINETY FIVE

Jordan felt stunned by what Rita said and how closely it tied in with his own experience, making his present waking moments in the here and now feel more dream like in many ways than the dreams themselves.

Carl shook the rattle once. "I didn't think I'd ever stop puking. At first I saw millions of spiders of all sizes." He gave a sheepish grin and looked down. "Then I shit my pants." He looked up again. "Thank you to whoever helped change them and my skivvies. I don't think I could have done that myself. When I came back from that, everyone was moaning, puking, laughing, crying, and babbling. Home boy over here," he said, punching Wesley lightly on the shoulder, "kept making growling noises like a lion or, I think now a jaguar, then I heard Rita and Cheryl talking and crying about Chazz and Albert, and I heard them both crying 'Mama!' over and over again, which made me think I was in a funny farm as part of some secret government MKUltra project. I even saw and heard from Terry." He shook his head at the memory.

"Seeing him made me go back through every dream battle we fought in fast forward, and it felt like they would never end until I talked to John." He fell silent, then took a deep breath and let it out slowly.

"I heard waves crashing on a beach that pulled me into the crack dream. I wanted so bad to totally lose myself in it until John told me to get the fuck out of there. He said it might feel good, but it was a trap like flypaper and that I should forget about him, but that's never going to happen!" He shook the rattle hard.

"The girls were still crying for Mama, which I'm not ashamed to say, tore at my heart until I saw a flurry of activity around Cheryl from Stan and Don José. I kind of heard and saw fluttering around Cheryl that turned into a huge condor." He held his arms wide, demonstrating. "It flew up from her, floated across the room, and dove into me, dumping all my horrors out at the bottom of its plunge through me like a dive bomber dropping its payload over and over again. I felt more clarity with each dive and it lifted me higher and higher into a magical place that was multidimensional and total nonsense on one level while making total sense on another."

He shrugged. "I can't put it into words, but I felt like I was being rocked in a cradle, back and forth through time, space, and strange places with even stranger beings, like I was learning volumes in an abstract and symbolic language that a man named Terence McKenna described as self-transforming machine elves. After I don't know how long, I drifted back into the peaceful delight of Don José's songs, flutes, whistling, and the sweet sounding notes of his *charango*, where I spent the rest of the night in bliss." He shook the rattle again and handed it to Wesley.

"I heard Terry and John too!" Wesley said, holding the rattle high. "It seemed like it took a long time for anything to happen, then it hit me like a ton of bricks in a rush of colors and patterns that made me want to hurl. I was soaked with sweat and my hands and feet felt ice cold. All I wanted to do was upchuck, but nothing would come up. It felt like the Ayahuasca spirit wanted me to suffer by holding me in that place forever. That's when I heard Terry say he was scared shit and didn't think he could handle it because it was too real." Wesley's eyes glazed over and he rubbed his chin.

"The best way I can say it is that Terry's panic became mine and just like Carl, it pushed me into every dreaming battle we had, ending with that horrible copter crash and in the most excruciating part of it, I felt John. I can't explain it, but he was there with me. More than seeing him, he was part in me and I was part in him, but even that doesn't describe it." He threw his hands up in surrender.

"Anyway, seeing him reminded of the crack dream, so I tried to connect with him by finding and following the white noise that turns into waves so I could escape into it." A troubled expression crossed his face. "That's when John yelled at me to get the fuck out of there because it was a trap. He said to forget about him. He wasn't coming back."

Wesley glanced sideways at Carl and shook the rattle hard at him. "But that's never going to happen!" He paused, then, "The next thing you know I'm on a gurney, my right leg totally gone, and my left leg gone from the knee. It was weird watching myself being wheeled into the Cybernetic Limb Facility, like watching a movie about myself, but I was in it too! Robot assembly lines rolled along with prosthetic arms, legs, and joints, then I was in the Cybernetic Organ Facility where I saw livers, hearts, lungs, eyeballs, and other organs floating in tanks." He looked around at everyone as if searching for reactions. All eyes remained on him.

"Finally, I went into an operating room where robots cut off my limbs and stumps with blood spattering saws, then other robots attached prosthetics, plucked out my organs, and put cybernetic replacements into the bloody sockets. Just when I thought it couldn't get any worse, I was taken into a machine that scanned me with laser grids around my head, then some kind of computerized square came down over me and spun me around until I was facing the floor." His eyes grew wide at the memory and he spoke faster as if wanting to get through it.

"The next thing you know lasers and robots were drilling into my spine and planting a microprocessor into my neck. I'm telling you," he said, shaking his head. "It was a macabre, hi-tech torture chamber. When it couldn't get any worse, I felt a deep growl inside me." He jerked his thumb toward Lorenzo.

"I opened my eyes and saw a Jurassic ass jaguar with giant yellow eyes pounce from Lorenzo and jump on top of me, swallowing me. Right then, a shrill note from Don José's flute launched my long overdue purge and I was the jaguar. Everything looked, felt, and smelled sharper and my torture chamber and all the suffering disappeared, leaving me feeling clear and energized. I floated in beautiful colored visions and patterns that came from Don José's songs, flutes, and most of all the sweet notes from his *charango*." Wesley shook the rattle three times to make his point and handed it to Jordan, who sat cross-legged beside him.

"After all kinds of crazy sights, sounds, and feelings I felt like I went over the top of a roller coaster," Jordan said, "and dropped into the crack dream, and like Carl and Wesley, I heard Terry and felt John in the same way Wesley described." He sighed. "Terry's panic set me off into all of our battle dreams mushed together where I kept getting blown up and killed over and over again. The last one was the guy with the rag head glaring at me with his cold, dark, eyes before shooting me in the head." Jordan shook himself to banish the memory.

"The next thing you know I was on the shooting range. Nick Stevens shot me in the heart six times, but I wasn't dead. What caught my attention was Rita struggling and all the noise and activity around her. I wanted to help, so I reached out with..." He paused, at a loss for words. "Doesn't matter," he said, waving it off. "I reached out and was swallowed in a nightmare with the Pied Piper, giant rat people and swarms of rats until a jaguar came and ate them, then I saw witches, a nasty raven, and worms with people's faces."

CHAPTER NINETY SIX

The more Jordan spoke, the more paralyzed Rita felt with each layer of detail.

"Then there was this huge mound of naked, pale-gray flesh," Jordan continued, "topped by a patch of orange hair with puffy lips. Rita called it Albert and puked again for the umpteenth time. After that a Chazz monster came with a big wobbling bony head and scrawny arms sticking out of a bloody leather jacket trying to rape her when a voice said, 'It's not Chazz who's raping her. It's Morpheus raping Pandora.'" Jordan's eyes took on a faraway look. "I don't know what it meant, but I saw a red light flashing like a heartbeat."

He looked directly at Rita, eyes imploring. "I couldn't bear to see that happen to you, so my heart opened when you grabbed the angel on your neck and Don José played his *charango*." Jordan pointed to his knees and bounced them up and down. "My legs started flapping on their own like super fast fluttering wings and my body and head jerked in and out." He brightened. "Like a hummingbird feeding on a flower, then I flew into the air in a blaze of vibrating colors that moved faster and faster until I shot straight into you, losing myself in an explosion of pastel colored heavenly visions." A beatific grin filled his face. He shook his head and pointed at Rita.

"You floated up like an angel, or an angel with huge silvery shining wings held you."

Any doubt Rita had about the validity of her experience dissolved, opening her heart with a wave of joy that made her tremble. Lorenzo held her closer.

"It was beautiful," Jordan said in a wistful voice. "I don't have any idea how long it went on for. I was awestruck in every sense of the word until I drifted into playful visions and patterns that carried me through the last part of my journey on Don José's music, leaving me clear and buzzing with energy."

He put his hands together and bowed to Don José. "And the best part of it was the end when Don José came to me and said, "The mother *loves* you.""

He handed the rattle to Stan who set it down and looked around at the group, then he began clapping. Everyone joined him, including Don José, who beamed.

Stan held his hands out when the clapping ended. "I've seen more than my share of strange things working with this medicine, but never anything to this extent! Like José, I want to commend you all for your bravery. What I've seen here more than in any other session that I've participated in -- we're talking twenty five years worth here, is the joining of everyone in a group mind." He nodded to each person in the group one at a time to emphasize his point.

"Though the concept is questioned by the scientific community, the boundaries we've been pushing with the Pandora Project and what we experienced here follows a model postulated by Rupert Sheldrake, a parapsychology researcher. He called it morphic resonance. It posits that memory is inherent in nature and that natural systems like termite colonies, pigeons, plants, and other biological systems inherit a collective memory from all previous things of their kind."

Lorenzo nodded and held his arms out wide. "Another way of saying that everything is connected."

Stan smiled. "Precisely. Sheldrake proposed that it's responsible for telepathy-type interconnections between organisms, which we appeared to have experienced here. His advocacy of the idea encompassed paranormal subjects like precognition and telepathy as well as unconventional explanations of standard subjects in biology like development, inheritance, and memory. What that means in our present context working with *La Madre* is that while we were all working on ourselves in our own journeys, the energy of the entire group was available to each of us."

Stan's explanation made sense to Rita and helped her comprehend what happened, though she still struggled to understand it all.

Stan nodded at each of them in turn again to drive his point home.

"I think that has paramount importance here as José and I agree that there was another mysterious dark element at work here, so it's imperative that we proceed with caution. There are too many unknowns."

The group fell silent until Wesley spoke up. "Now that we've done this and connected here, what are we going to do about John?"

"I need time to assimilate things myself," Stan said. "You may or may not have noticed, but the strongest connection between everyone here was John. It's the one thing that everyone had in common." Stan directed his attention to Jordan. "Everyone said that they heard or felt him warning them off because it was a trap, and he wasn't coming back. Did he warn you, Jordan?" His eyebrows raised. "You didn't mention it."

Jordan nodded. "I didn't put much stock in it. If you know John like we do," he said pointing to Carl and Wesley, "it would be just like him to dare us, because he knows there's a good chance we'd do it."

"Ain't that the truth," Wesley said. "Classic Striker."

"Not only that," Carl added, "but you can bet your ass that if the shoe was on the other foot, he'd be the first one to jump in and save us without giving any thought to himself."

Jordan and Wesley nodded their agreement.

"I think that should be our first order of business when we get back," Wesley said. "We're all joined together in our morphogenetic field and we should make our move while it's still fresh. It makes us stronger than before."

Stan held up his hand and shook his head. "I appreciate your enthusiasm."

"And your bravery," Cheryl said.

"But I can't allow it," Stan said. "It's too dangerous and there are too many variables that we don't understand. I don't want to risk losing anyone else. At this juncture, I need a little time to sort through the whole situation."

"Not to mention all of the rape warnings," Cheryl said. "That concerns me."

CHAPTER NINETY SEVEN

J ordan watched Jack, Rita, and Lorenzo nod, acknowledging Cheryl's concerns. Glancing sideways, he saw Wesley sitting with his arms crossed and Carl beside him, immobile. Neither of them wanted to hold off, and neither did he. John was fading and Jordan was afraid he would slip away forever if something wasn't done. Soon.

"I know we're leaving this afternoon," he said. "Would it be all right to take another nature walk before we go? We've spent so much time cooped up and we all have so much to sort through, I think it would do us all a lot of good."

Stan beamed. "An excellent suggestion! I suggest you all do that, keeping mindful of everything in nature, doing your best to acknowledge trees, plants, and animals, while considering their part in their unique morphogenetic fields and in the bigger one that encompasses us all." He made a wide sweeping circle with both hands. "We'll leave after sunset."

After a leisurely lunch where everyone shared their experiences with each other more, Jordan signaled Wesley and Carl to follow him out to a trail head at the edge of the property. "I know what you guys are thinking," he said under his breath, "but keep your mouths shut until we're further away, just in case."

Wesley stuck his hands in his pockets and he and Carl looked around a little too casually.

"Knock it off and act normal," Jordan said. "You look like you're up to something. We're probably okay here, but I want to be sure."

They both nodded, looking guilty.

Once they passed over a couple of hills they found a circle of moss and lichen covered boulders overlooking a gurgling creek where Jordan invited them to sit. "Thanks for indulging me," he said. "I don't want to have any doubts about our privacy."

"No shit." Carl looked around. "Especially after that sneaky spy shit in our room from Crowley."

"Speaking of which," Wesley said. "Where the fuck did *he* go? That weasel dick mother fucker conveniently disappeared when John got stuck and he hasn't done a fucking thing to help. He just bailed!"

"No kidding," Carl said.

"Listen," Jordan said. "I've been giving this a lot of thought and I have a plan coming together in my head. You know all that stuff Doc Krippner said about morphogenetic fields and how we are all connected, including Rita, Lorenzo, Jack and Cheryl?"

Wesley and Carl nodded.

"We're at our strongest now and I still think that if we're going to do something to save John, we need to do it now, while it's still fresh. I have it mostly figured out, except for one glitch that I'm not sure how to get around."

"Spill it," Wesley said.

"It's going to take team work," Jordan said in a conspiratorial tone, "but that's what we're best at. I'll need one of you barricaded in John's room with him and a dream hood, one of you in the control room manning the console, and me in the dream lab with another hood."

"Sounds simple enough," Wesley said. "So what's the glitch?"

"We have to figure out how to get a password."

Carl put his hand to his mouth and shook with suppressed laughter.

"What's so funny?" Wesley said.

Carl looked to him, then to Jordan, his eyes dancing with mischievous glee. "You remember when we first came and Lorenzo showed us how everything worked at his console and you accused me of trying to kiss him?"

"Yeah," Wesley said tentatively.

Carl's eyebrows jumped up and down. "Guess what I got?"

"No shit?" Jordan said.

He nodded and Jordan fist bumped him and Wesley, then they fist bumped each other.

"I guess that puts you at the console," Jordan said. "Can you remember how he called up the dream sequence?"

"Easy peasy," Carl said, smirking.

"As soon as we get back?" Wesley said.

Jordan shook his head. "Right now I'm tapped out. I need to get some sleep before we do this, so I'm at my best. In fact we should all get some rest and go on our mission in the middle of the night at O-dark-thirty when everyone else is asleep. No doubt they'll figure out what we're up to, but by the time they do I'll be on my way to John. You guys down with that?"

Wesley clenched his fist. "Bet your ass."

"Ditto on that," Carl said, patting him on the back.

Wesley studied Jordan. "You sure you want to do this? You don't have to. I'll go instead."

"I will too," Carl said. "In a heartbeat."

They both looked at Jordan, pleading. He smiled and shook his head. "I appreciate that, but I've thought this through and I'm the best man for the job. We all know that in the end, it doesn't matter who goes. As Doc Krippner says, we're all connected." He made a circling motion between them with his finger. "But from a tactical perspective, it makes the most sense to have Wesley in John's room, 'cuz he's the biggest and will do the best job of blocking the door and keeping the storm troopers out, and you Carl, are Mr. Password, which puts you in the driver's seat, and me?" He shrugged. "I'm the only one left."

"And if John was here," Carl said. "You can bet your ass he'd be the first one in."

"Are you shitting me?" Wesley said. "He'd be there and back already."

Jordan patted them both on the shoulders. "Damned straight. Now listen, we can't trust anything near any electricity. It can all be bugged, have cameras or whatever, so we need to keep our mouths shut, and we don't want to say or give any hint to Doc Krippner or the rest of them about what we're up to. They'll know soon enough." He stood. "Let's be good little boys and go to bed as soon as we get back and do our best to get right to sleep. I'll set an alarm for three-fifteen."

"The witching hour," Wesley said, giving a ghoulish laugh.

Jordan smiled and shrugged. "Seems right somehow. Anyway, we'll get up in the dark and keep the lights out, so we won't be spotted easily, and by the time anyone responds, I'll be in."

Everyone stayed quiet on the ride back, all of them worn out and lost in their individual thoughts. Most of them dozed, or struggled not to nod off. When the Mini Bus dropped them off everyone went straight to bed including Carl, Wesley, and Jordan, who fell asleep in minutes.

When the soft beeping chime on his cell phone woke him flashing **3:15** in blue, Jordan felt like he had just closed his eyes and opened them, but he had slept for more than six hours. He sat up, taking a moment to get his bearings, and realized that he felt clear headed. He put his clothes on in the dark and shielding the flashlight on his cell phone with his cupped hand, he went and woke Carl and Wesley.

Twenty minutes later, he and Carl sat beside each other at two consoles in the darkened DreamLab control room, the only source of light coming from the dimmed monitors of the work stations they sat at. Wesley's face popped up on the monitor in front of Jordan. On screen beside him, John was propped up in a sitting position, a dreaming hood fitted over his head.

"The door's blocked and we're locked and loaded here," Wesley said in a low voice. "The hood is activated and we're dialed in."

"Remember," Jordan said through a headset, "if this works, yank that hood off as soon as he comes out of it."

"You got it."

Jordan patted Carl on the back. "Carl's going to do the same thing for me here."

"Good luck," Wesley said. "Our thoughts and our spirits and whatever other kind of mojo we have are with you."

"Thanks." Jordan's stomach, feet and hands all felt cold. He took off the headset, and resting a hand on Carl's shoulder, looked him in the eye. "I'll be right back."

"I'll be waiting for you right here in the driver's seat," Carl said, patting Jordan's hand.

Jordan took a deep breath and let it out slow, then made his way to the Dream Lab where he found his usual spot. Settling into the dream cradle, he slipped the hood over his head, feeling his panic rise when he secured it, so he kept breathing deep. No turning back now. John needed him. Closing his eyes, he gave Carl a thumbs up.

A flurry of thoughts assaulted him as he plummeted into the white noise, his last being a feeling that he was so clear, that it all felt stronger the way alcohol might affect someone who drank for the first time. The sound of crashing waves washed over him, followed by the brightening image and rising music that intermingled into the blissful multilayered lullaby.

His heart lightened and his emotions expanded with the music and imagery, then he shook with a crescendo of running water and waves that blended with chants, digeridoos, flutes, and stringed instruments sending him sailing into the exquisite tapestry of thought, feeling, and emotion that touched him so deeply.

He sensed John far off in the middle of a violet haze, and the more he went toward him, the more Jordan felt its intensifying pleasure wearing him down. The closer he got to the center, the more he realized that he could only enter into it with total surrender.

Vowing to keep his resolve for John's sake, he let himself be drawn straight into the extreme bliss until it swallowed him to the point that he forgot all about John and no longer cared about himself or anything else.

CHAPTER NINETY EIGHT

A phone rang from somewhere and someone pounded on the door startling Rita out of the soundest sleep she had in a long time. Lorenzo stumbled out of bed and answered the phone, then she heard him talking to someone at the door in hushed tones, then he was back, flipping on the lights.

Rita shielded her eyes at the harsh brightness, glimpsing him, hair tousled, eyes wide.

"Jordan's trapped in the crack dream with John," he said, pulling on his jeans. "We need to get to the Dream Lab right away." He stopped and looked at her, muttering. "I'm afraid we're too late."

Rita threw back the covers and pulled on her clothes.

Minutes later they joined Jack and Cheryl beside Carl who sat at Lorenzo's work station looking frightened and embarrassed. "It's like it has a mind of its own," he said in a whiney voice. He jabbed at the keyboard and clicked the mouse. "It won't shut off!"

"Move aside." Lorenzo pushed him out of the seat. "Where's Doc Krippner?"

"On his way," Jack said.

"We need to get that dream hood off of him," Cheryl said.

Rita pointed to the monitor beside Lorenzo's where Wesley's wide-eyed pale face loomed beside John, who was propped up, a dreaming hood fitted over his head.

"Shit," Lorenzo said under his breath. "At this point I don't think it's going to make any difference. He's too far gone." He shook his head. "They *both* have hoods on. We'd better wait and see what Stan says."

Stan came in and peered into the cradle room where Jordan rested immobile, then he did a quick scan of the consoles, pausing to study the image of Wesley and John.

"What can we do?" Cheryl said in a shaky voice.

"I'm so sorry," Carl said, barely audible. "We should have listened to you, but..."

"It's a little too late for that," Stan said.

Everyone started talking at once in a buzz of questions and suggestions until Stan held up a hand saying, "Stop!"

They looked at each other with stunned expressions.

"I need everyone to shut up so I can think straight." He rubbed his temples, deep in thought for what felt like a small eternity, then he looked up, his face a study of resolve. "We're dealing with something outside of any rational, western scientific, divide and conquer mentality. No rules or logic apply here, which leads me to all I have left." He stopped, letting the question hang before saying, "My heart."

His words, the resigned expression on his face, and the conviction in his voice hit Rita's own heart, while the others reacted as if they'd been hit by something palpable.

"I need you to shut off the lights in the Dream Lab and put it in darkness, then I want all of you to join me by putting the energy of your hearts and minds together in silence, focused on me with all the attention you can muster to support what I'm going to do."

Everyone nodded solemnly. Stan put his hands together as if praying and bowed, then he reached in his pocket and pulled out a small bottle of Ayahuasca. He opened it, whispered prayers into it, and blew into it three times before downing it, then he disappeared into the darkened Dream Lab.

CHAPTER NINETY NINE

Nothing.
Movement created a wave of white that collapsed back into the black of nothing, beginning a slow, rising cycle of being and not being that rose to the beat of invisible wings that lifted him at a gradual accelerating rate. His body and head jerked forward like a hummingbird, shaking him into consciousness when he remembered John, sensing his presence, as if his wing beats bounced back at him like radar.

He reached out with all of his being and the wingbeats and the light diminished as if John sucked all of their energy away, pulling Jordan back into the abyss. He had no sense of time or being until the waves returned, slower and weaker, taking longer to build until he eventually rose in a blaze of vibrating colors that swallowed him in high energy pastel colored heavenly bliss.

In the glow of its aftermath, he came to in darkness, feeling the dream hood on his head, making his heart jump. "Hey!" He yelled, pulling it off of his head. "What happened to the lights?"

He sat up when the lights flicked on and saw Doc Krippner blinking awake in the dream cradle beside him. It struck him as odd that Stan wasn't wearing a dream hood.

The door to the lab opened and an exuberant, Carl, Rita, Jack, Cheryl, and Lorenzo rushed in, buzzing with excitement.

"We did it!" Carl said between sobs.

Jordan's heartbeat quickened. "John?"

"Come and see," Rita said, eyes glistening.

Stan rose slowly from his dream cradle and together they went in to the control room where they saw Wesley and John on the monitor with their arms over each other's shoulders, smiling and teary-eyed, then everything in the entire building blinked out, enveloping them in blackness before every screen and display in every part of the complex flickered into what looked like shimmering stardust sparkling across an ebony background, then a torrent of music filled the air.

A green fluorescent dot pulsed in the center of every screen, accompanied by the sizzle of musical stingers and the booming thunder of timpanis. The fanfare soared to a crescendo and the dot quivered while rocketing forward from the void, expanding into a multicolored geometric configuration that shifted and changed dimension, growing to man-sized proportions.

Cymbals crashed and children's voices filled the room, singing an upbeat version of the old tune, "Mister Sandman." The pattern morphed into a tall, thin computer generated figure with shoulder length white hair, feathered cap, and a hooded cloak of midnight blue. Gold neon eyes sparkled from behind a black mask that concealed the upper portion of his lined face. "Welcome to DreamLand," he said in a soft purr. After a low, sweeping bow, he added, "I am your host, the Sandman."

Smiling, the Sandman beckoned with long slender fingers. "Follow me, to the land of dreams." With the flourish of a master magician, he produced a red satin sack from the folds of his cloak. Reaching in, he removed a handful of shimmering light and tossed it overhead.

Colored sparks rained down, blurring his image and a computer drafted circular building with mirrored windows came into focus, surrounded by trees, flowering shrubs and fountains spouting pastel water. The Sandman reappeared, romping across an expanse of plush green lawn. He leaped onto a wide path and pranced toward the building, stopping at the entrance.

"Step up and see the wonders inside.

Your eyes won't believe our incredible ride."

Spreading his arms and billowing his mantle, the Sandman vanished in a cloud of luminescent green smoke. The building loomed closer, as if the viewer were being drawn into it and the mirrored facade dissolved, leaving only a rotating skeletal framework that stepped through a series of cad renderings and three-dimensional drawings showing a maze of corridors, rooms, and entranceways arraying outward from a central control center.

Another puff of emerald smoke and the Sandman appeared beside a series of holographic archways. He pointed to one containing figures of elves, wizards, and witches. "Storybook Kingdom," he said.

"Have some fun and have a scare.

The dream machine will put you there."

Above a second arch, a baseball player swung a bat, a football player made a diving catch and a basketball player slam-dunked a ball. "Sports Land." The Sandman waved an arm, in a sweeping gesture.

"Pitch to Babe Ruth.

Make a slam-dunk.

Sink a hoop.

Score a goal and win the game.

Feel the glory, live the fame."

Leaping high, he performed a triple back flip, landing by a third arch, on which toothy dinosaurs prowled. George Washington crossed the Delaware and a World War Two Navy fighter ace stood beside his Grumman Hellcat, chest swelled with pride.

"In HistoryLand the past is now.

The dream machine will show you how."

A spectrum of colors flashed, punctuated by sharp stabs of music from the brass section. As the archways blurred and faded, a deep off screen voice said, "The Sandman is waiting to put *you* in that special dream. More great dreams are on the way, including the exciting new SpaceWorld where you'll pilot a rocket to the moon, journey to Mars, or be lost in an uncharted universe. Don't miss it."

The Sandman reappeared on the path in front of the mirrored DreamLand building. Smiling, he turned and with a dramatic flourish of his cape, vanished. The building shimmered and expanded outward, atomizing into stardust.

"Shit," Carl whispered. "We opened Pandora's Box."

"It might be Pandora's Box," Jack said, "but Morpheus came out."

ABOUT THE AUTHOR

Matthew J. Pallamary's works have been translated into Spanish, Portuguese, Italian, Norwegian, French, and German. His historical novel of first contact between shamans and Jesuits in 18th century South America, titled, *Land Without Evil* received rave reviews along with a San Diego Book Award for mainstream fiction. It was also adapted into a full-length stage and sky show, co-written with Agent Red, directed by Agent Red, and performed by Sky Candy, an Austin Texas aerial group. The making of the show was the subject of a PBS series, Arts in Context episode, which garnered an EMMY nomination.

His nonfiction book, *The Infinity Zone: A Transcendent Approach to Peak Performance* is a collaboration with professional tennis coach Paul Mayberry that offers a fascinating exploration of the phenomenon that occurs at the nexus of perfect form and motion. *The Infinity Zone* took 1st place in the International Book Awards, New Age category and was a finalist in the San Diego Book Awards.

His first book, a short story collection titled *The Small Dark Room Of The Soul* was mentioned in The Year's Best Horror and Fantasy and received praise from Ray Bradbury.

His second collection, *A Short Walk to the Other Side* was an Award Winning Finalist in the International Book Awards, an Award Winning Finalist in the USA Best Book Awards, and an Award Winning Finalist in the San Diego Book Awards.

DreamLand a novel about computer generated dreaming, written with legendary DJ Ken Reeth won first place in the Independent e-Book Award in the Horror/Thriller category and was an Award Winning Finalist in the San Diego Book Awards.

It's sequel, **n0thing** is titled after the main character, who in the real world is his nephew, an international Counter-Strike gaming champion. After winning what amounts to the Super Bowl of gaming, n0thing and his winning teammates, are recruited as a literal "dream team" whose mission is to go into the nightmares of battle scarred veterans and rescue them from their traumatic memories while becoming ambassadors for a gaming platform that exceeds virtual reality with an experience that pushes the boundaries of reality itself.

Eye of the Predator was an Award Winning Finalist in the Visionary Fiction category of the International Book Awards. **Eye of the Predator** is a supernatural thriller about a zoologist who discovers that he can go into the minds of animals.

CyberChrist was an Award Winning Finalist in the Thriller/Adventure category of the International Book Awards. **CyberChrist** is the story of a prize winning journalist who receives an email from a man who claims to have discovered immortality by turning off the aging gene in a 15 year old boy with an aging disorder. The forwarded email becomes the basis for an online church built around the boy, calling him CyberChrist.

Phantastic Fiction - A Shamanic Approach to Story took first place in the International Book Awards Writing/Publishing category. **Phantastic Fiction** is Matt's guide to dramatic writing that grew out of his popular Phantastic Fiction Workshop.

Night Whispers was an Award Winning Finalist in the Horror category of the International Book Awards. Set in the Boston neighborhood of Dorchester, **Night Whispers** is the story of Nick Powers, who loses consciousness after crashing in a stolen car and comes to hearing whispering voices in his mind. When he sees a homeless man arguing with himself, Nick realizes that the whispers in his head are the other side of the argument.

His memoir **Spirit Matters** detailing his journeys to Peru, working with shamanic plant medicines took first place in the San Diego Book Awards Spiritual Book Category, and was an Award-Winning Finalist in the autobiography/memoir category of the National Best Book Awards. **Spirit Matters** is also available as an audio book.

Matt has also produced and directed *The Santa Barbara Writers Conference Scrapbook* documentary film and co-wrote the book of the same title in collaboration with Y. Armando Nieto, and conference founder Mary Conrad.

His work has appeared in Oui, New Dimensions, The Iconoclast, Starbright, Infinity, Passport, The Short Story Digest, Redcat, The San Diego Writer's Monthly, Connotations, Phantasm, Essentially You, The Haven Journal, The Montecito Journal, and many others. His fiction has been featured in The San Diego Union Tribune which he has also reviewed books for, and his work has been heard on KPBS-FM in San Diego, KUCI FM in Irvine, television Channel Three in Santa Barbara, and The Susan Cameron Block Show in Vancouver. He has been a guest on the following nationally syndicated talk shows; Paul Rodriguez, In The Light with Michelle Whitedove, Susun Weed, Medicine Woman, Inner Journey with Greg Friedman, and Environmental Directions Radio series. Matt has appeared on the following television shows; Bridging Heaven and Earth, Elyssa's Raw and Wild Food Show, Things That Matter, Literary Gumbo, Indie Authors TV, and ECONEWS. He has also been a frequent guest on numerous podcasts, among them, The Psychedelic Salon, Black Light in the Attic, Third Eye Drops, C-Realm, and others.

Matt received the Man of the Year Award from San Diego Writer's Monthly Magazine and has taught a fiction workshop at the Southern California Writers' Conference in San Diego, Palm Springs, and Los Angeles, and at the Santa Barbara Writers' Conference for twenty five years. He has lectured at the Greater Los Angeles Writer's Conference, the Getting It Write conference in Oregon, the Saddleback Writers' Conference, the Rio Grande Writers' Seminar, the National Council of Teachers of English, The San Diego Writer's and Editor's Guild, The San Diego Book Publicists, The Pacific Institute for Professional Writing, The 805 Writers Conference, and he has been a panelist at the World Fantasy Convention, Con-Dor, and Coppercon. He is presently Editor in Chief of Mystic Ink Publishing.

He has been teaching at the Santa Barbara Writers Conference, the Southern California Writers Conference, and many other venues for the past twenty five years and frequently visits the mountains, deserts, and jungles of North, Central, and South America pursuing his studies of shamanism.

WWW.MATTPALLAMARY.COM

BOOKS BY MATTHEW J. PALLAMARY

THE SMALL DARK ROOM OF THE SOUL

LAND WITHOUT EVIL

SPIRIT MATTERS

DREAMLAND (WITH KEN REETH)

THE INFINITY ZONE (WITH PAUL MAYBERRY)

A SHORT WALK TO THE OTHER SIDE

CYBERCHRIST

EYE OF THE PREDATOR

PHANTASTIC FICTION

NIGHT WHISPERS

THE SANTA BARABARA WRITERS CONFERENCE SCRAPBOOK
(WITH MARY CONRAD & Y. ARMANDO NIETO)

www.ingramcontent.com/pod-product-compliance
Lightning Source LLC
Chambersburg PA
CBHW070352260626
47161CB00001B/117